Richard Zimler was born in New York but has lived in Portugal for the last 24 years. His novels have been translated into 23 languages and have appeared on bestseller lists in many different countries. Four of his novels have been nominated for the International IMPAC Dublin Literary Award, and he has won literary prizes in America, France, Portugal and the UK. His website is www.zimler.com.

Also by Richard Zimler

Unholy Ghosts
The Last Kabbalist of Lisbon
The Angelic Darkness
Hunting Midnight
Guardian of the Dawn
The Search for Sana
The Seventh Gate
The Warsaw Anagrams
Strawberry Fields Forever

The Night
Watchman

Richard Zimler

corsair

Constable & Robinson Ltd.
55–56 Russell Square
London WC1B 4HP
www.constablerobinson.com

First published in the UK by Corsair,
an imprint of Constable & Robinson Ltd., 2014

A copy of the British Library Cataloguing in
Publication Data is available from the British Library

ISBN: 978-1-4721-0930-9 (B-format paperback)
ISBN: 978-1-4721-1351-1 (A-format paperback)
ISBN: 978-1-47211-127-2 (ebook)

Printed and bound in the UK

1 3 5 7 9 10 8 6 4 2

'It is by no means certain that our individual personality is the single inhabitant of these our corporeal frames ... We all do things both awake and asleep which surprise us. Perhaps we have co-tenants in this house we live in.'

Oliver Wendell Holmes

'Once believed to be a rare and dramatic aberration, Dissociative Identity Disorder is actually a highly evolved survival mechanism acquired by some individuals as they cope with severe and prolonged trauma, abuse, and fear.'

Deborah Bray Haddock,
The Dissociative Identity Disorder Sourcebook

Dedication and Acknowledgements

For Alexandre Quintanilha and my readers in the UK, Australia, South Africa and New Zealand.

I am extremely grateful to the officers of the Judiciary Police in Portugal who spoke to me at length about their work, answering all my many questions with great patience: José Braz, Verissimo Santos Milhazes and José Carlos Nunes. Any mistakes in police procedure contained in this book are purely my own.

I want to express my heartfelt thanks to Alexandre Quintanilha, Cynthia Cannell, Jordi Roca, Peggy Hageman and Isabel Silva for reading the manuscript of this novel and giving me their invaluable comments. As always, I'm very grateful for the support of all the good people at Constable & Robinson, especially Sarah Castleton, James Gurbutt, Andreas Campomar, Sam Evans and the late Nick Robinson. I owe a great debt in particular to Nick for all the kindness and generosity he showed me over the past decade. He will be sorely missed.

A special hug for Chris Boreggio and Jo Coldwell.

'Maybe our second chances are the only ghosts who ever appear to us.'

Henrique Monroe

Chapter 1

As I scanned my notes at my desk, the murder suspect sitting across from me told me that he and his wife had never had children but that he had pictured his son every night in bed for the last month.

'I don't get it – what son?' I asked.

'My imaginary one. We do things together all the time.'

His watchful eyes seemed to be yearning for my trust. While weighing my options, I blew on my steaming tea. 'All right, so how old is this imaginary kid of yours?' I asked as I jotted down the date in my notebook: *Friday 6 July 2012, 10.17 a.m.*

'He's seven,' the suspect replied. 'At least, he usually is. It can depend on what I'm daydreaming about.' He bit his lip and looked up at the ceiling, as if needing a moment to script more of his story.

'Come on, we both deserve better than you making up some crazy fantasy for me,' I told him, and I pointed towards the stack of files sitting on the chair behind my desk. 'I have at least twenty cases competing for my time, so if you're just pretending to—'

'Don't you ever dream about what might have been?' he cut in desperately. He took a rushed sip of his water. I realized he was running on nervous energy. His name was Manuel Moura. He was thirty-two years old but he looked years younger – more like a college student. He was a high school chemistry teacher.

'So you're serious about this made-up kid?' I asked.

'I've never been more serious about anything in my life.'

'Does he have a name?' I asked, and I felt the small, mild, tentative loss of balance we sometimes feel when we take a step forward into someone else's story.

'Miguel.'

'And what's he look like?'

'He has silky black hair cut in bangs, and big green eyes – an alert, intelligent face.' He smiled broadly at the beauty he'd created. 'A bright kid, outgoing. And brave – really brave.'

Moura had light brown hair, combed neatly to the side, and his wire-rimmed glasses made him look shy and secretive – a bit like Harry Potter. Since I regarded poisoning his wife as anything but courageous, I said, 'It sounds like you're trying to tell me – without actually saying it – that Miguel takes after his mother.'

Moura held up his hands as if surrendering – regrettably – to the truth of what I'd surmised, then took off his glasses and wiped his eyes. He looked more adult without them – more honest, too.

He surveyed my office, left, right, then left again, craning his neck out in a way that would have seemed comical under other circumstances. 'No photos of your family on your desk, no paintings – it's kind of cold in here,' he said. 'Don't you want anything personal in your office?'

He'd happened on one of my continuing sources of discomfort at work. 'Police policy,' I told him. 'No diversions for you, and none for me either.'

'The detectives on TV always give their offices lots of personality,' he pointed out.

'A number of things happen on television that don't happen around here.'

'And they nearly always get their cases over in forty-eight hours.'

'Let me guess, you watch *CSI*,' I replied in a weary tone;

this wasn't the first time I'd been compared unfavourably to fictional investigators.

'Yeah, but I only like the version that's set in Las Vegas.'

'The thing is, police dramas are all scripted to keep you on the edge of your seat, and this . . .' – here, I circled my hand in the air to indicate my office and, more generally, the dimension in which it existed – '. . . this, Mr Moura, happens to be what most people would call real life. People around here are only rarely entertaining and, between you and me, some of them could be considered pretty incompetent. Just so you know, it took a whole week to get your wife's tests for toxic substances back from the lab. And that was with me pushing hard.'

'But you knew I was responsible as soon as you got the report?' he asked in a hopeful tone.

He seemed anxious to think better of me, which struck me as both loopy and endearing. 'Chemistry teacher, cyanide poisoning – connecting the dots didn't require a higher degree in logic,' I told him.

He gazed down as though he were having second thoughts about opening up to me. To win back his trust, I leaned towards him and whispered conspiratorially, 'I've been known to defy the rules on occasion.' I turned around the coffee mug where I keep my pens so he could read its big, blue-lettered message: **I ♥ BLACK CANYON**. 'My wife had it made for me,' I told him. 'She runs a ceramics gallery.'

He smiled with gratified surprise – probably just like his imaginary son – and asked, 'Where's Black Canyon?'

'In America – in southwest Colorado.'

'I thought I heard a slight accent!' he announced proudly.

'I was born near there.'

'It must be really far away – I mean, not just geographically.'

'It's a different world.'

'I bet.' He gazed down, considering his options. By the time he looked back up, he was once again eager to tell me about what most mattered to him – but in his own

3

idiosyncratic way. 'My son is really lovable,' he told me. 'Everybody takes to him.'

I took a quick gulp of my tea and wrote *Suspect's Fantasy Life* in my notebook; whether indicative of insight or lunacy, this was just the kind of thing I liked to get down on paper. I had stacks of photocopied notes from my interrogations at our apartment, though what I intended to do with them was still a mystery.

'Who's everybody?' I asked.

'Other teachers, neighbours ... Wherever we go, everybody can see he's special.'

Moura went on to tell me that picturing his make-believe son was the only way he could get to sleep at night. As he spoke, he knitted his hands together. It seemed as though he needed to keep himself under tight control.

Nodding to himself, anxious to convince both of us of the rightness of what he was about to say, he told me that his wife sent their lives spiralling off towards disaster when she began an affair with the philosophy teacher at his school. 'She behaved like a real whore!' he said angrily.

I mumbled to myself: *Good authors, too, who once knew better words . . .*

'What was that?' he asked.

'Song lyrics in English pop out of me sometimes – it's a nervous habit,' I explained.

'No problem. You know the worst part?' he asked, sneering. 'The guy she had an affair with is a total asshole!'

'But she obviously didn't think so,' I said challengingly. 'And it seems to me she had the right to think whatever she wanted.'

'Maybe so,' he admitted.

'Maybe or yes?' I insisted; suspects who hurt women tended to make me forget my tactics for maintaining their trust.

'You're right,' Moura agreed, but I could see it was only to get me off his back.

'Look, I'll tell you something I was forced to learn real

4

young,' I said. 'Men who regard their wives and girlfriends as property are responsible for far more than their fair share of the unhappiness in our world.'

'Yeah, I can believe that,' he conceded. 'So how long have you been a policeman?'

'Seventeen years.'

'You must have seen some pretty bad things in your time.'

I thought of saying, *Cruelty never goes out of style*, but it sounded too glib – too much like Philip Marlowe or one of the other fictional detectives whose cases I imagined myself solving when I was a kid. 'So what do you and Miguel do together while you're trying to find dreamland?' I asked instead.

'Mostly we go to the beach in Caparica. I take his hand and we run down to the edge of the ocean. He likes to stand still and watch the sand by his feet slide away – it makes him feel like he's skating. It makes him laugh. Me, too!'

Moura explained that he also took his son to the Feira da Ladra, the sprawling flea market behind the Pantheon, because the boy was wild about old farming tools and cooking gadgets – just like his dad, of course. In front of the tiger enclosure at the Lisbon Zoo, Miguel told his father that he wanted to be ferocious and fearless, and to have razor-sharp teeth. He wanted to run through the Himalayan forest. 'And I don't want anyone to be able to catch me!' he added, as if it were an absolute necessity.

I underlined that hope twice, because it seemed to be Moura's way of saying that he'd been worried for a long time that his wife and friends might catch up with *him* and figure out that he wasn't such a boyish, sweet-natured guy after all.

At this point in his zoo fantasy, Moura picked up Miguel, hugged him with all the relief of finally having found a trustworthy companion and told him that he, too, had always wanted to be big and powerful, but that he'd never dared tell anyone before.

5

Holding my gaze, asking for my understanding with the shadowed depth of his eyes, Moura confessed that it was a great comfort to tell his son that he never thought he was strong enough. 'Ever since I was ten or eleven, that's what I've wanted to tell someone. Though I was only ever able to confess it to Miguel. I couldn't trust anyone else.'

Tears caught in his lashes, and I was convinced that this was what he'd most wanted to tell me since the moment we'd met. A week ago, I'd come to his flat to question him about his wife's death, and he must have spotted something in my face that gave him hope that I'd be sympathetic. And by now he must have also realized that this might be his last chance to explain something important about himself to another person.

'Now you've confessed your secret to me, as well,' I pointed out.

'Because my life is over,' he said, wiping his eyes. 'So it doesn't much matter. I'll probably be . . . I don't know, fifty, before I get out of prison. Maybe even older.'

He waited for me to contradict him with a more optimistic assessment. When I didn't, he gazed off into what he thought his future might look like. His jaw throbbed; he was steeling himself for a long battle.

The phone rang next door. Through the glass window separating my office from the room where two of my inspectors have their desks, I saw the new officer on my team, Lucinda Pires, take the call.

Moura took a deep, calming breath and said, 'I really thought Miguel had changed everything. It was stupid for me to believe he could make things different, I guess.'

His despairing tone touched me and, with a jolt, I realized that he had used his fantasies about a son not just to put himself to sleep, but also to try to prevent himself from committing murder. He'd wanted to do the right thing. He'd fought and failed.

I wanted to help him – to make his stay in prison more bearable. 'It wasn't stupid,' I told him. 'But maybe . . . maybe you needed to hide even deeper in your fantasies – and to stay there until you were sure you could talk with your wife without hurting her. They might be able to still help you in some way – to get through all this, I mean.'

Hearing the solidarity in my voice, he turned towards the wall and began to sob. His desolation caught me off guard, and I sensed Gabriel creeping up behind me, which was odd, because I wasn't in any danger. At least, that was what I then thought.

'Listen, Mr Moura,' I said softly, hoping to bring him back to me, 'do you think that your fantasy son will age along with you? I mean, twenty years from now, when you get out of prison, will Miguel be nearing thirty or still only seven?'

He rubbed his eyes and took a deep, calming breath. 'I'd prefer he stay a little kid,' he replied. 'Though I'm not sure it matters that much any more.'

Knowing we'd both appreciate a safe subject for a few minutes, I got him talking about his teaching. As he told me about his difficulties with kids cheating in exams, I sensed Gabriel withdrawing. A feeling of lightness eased through me. And then he was gone, leaving a hollowness behind in exactly the shape of my curiosity about him.

As Moura and I spoke, I understood from his laboured search for the right words that he hadn't had anyone to reveal his heart to for a long time. Maybe he never had.

When I reached the ins and outs of the murder itself, Moura told me he'd synthesized cyanide because it was a poison that was quick and sure. 'I didn't want my wife to suffer unnecessarily,' he told me. 'And it didn't matter that it would show up on your tests.' He shrugged as if to say that foiling our efforts was never the point.

'Still, you could have tried to get away afterwards,' I said.

'I thought of flying to Brazil. But seeing my wife dead, looking at her face . . . I found something in its stillness, its forced silence – something about the two of us and our destiny. About how things started and how they'd turned out. And what being married meant. I understood then that there was no point in fleeing.'

His words made me uneasy. Maybe because he'd understood something important about his marriage too late. 'Is cyanide hard to cook up?' I asked, a bit disappointed in myself for retreating from a conversation that might have been more meaningful.

'*É canja,*' he replied, flapping his hand. *A piece of cake.*

He fought a smile. He clearly thought it wouldn't look so good if he showed too much pride in his abilities. He was a strange guy – one minute in despair, the next seemingly ready for a starring role on his own TV drama. On a hunch, I asked, 'Are you on any medication?'

'An antidepressant,' he replied. 'My doctor thought it would help. I used to think about suicide pretty much all the time. Though now I'm here at police headquarters and about to go to prison. I'm not sure I would call that progress.'

He laughed mirthlessly – the laugh of a man who hasn't ended up anywhere near where he'd always expected to be. I drank my tea. I was tired of talking to suspects who'd ruined every chance for happiness they had once had. And who betrayed their loved ones. Their destructive impulses exhausted me.

When Moura put his glasses back on, I realized he preferred looking younger than he was; it was his camouflage. Maybe he was even a lot more dangerous than I imagined. It was possible that he'd even invented his fantasy son to win me to his side – that he'd sensed from the moment we'd first met that he could trick me with that particular strategy.

Since 1994, when I joined the Judicial Police, at least two sociopaths have fooled me completely. Both sat right where Moura was sitting. Number One was a young bank teller with a winning smile who lived with his parents in Almada. He'd been a spellbinding storyteller. We ended up talking mostly about his collection of rare coins. I was sure he was innocent until sniffer dogs led us to the bodies of his father and mother under the paving stones of his patio. Number

Two was a pretty nurse who worked at the Santa Cruz Hospital in Estoril. She could laugh, weep and flare into self-righteous anger on command: Meryl Streep dubbed into Portuguese. I thought she was the victim of a hateful conspiracy, but it turned out that she had killed at least nine patients with morphine injections.

One certainty police work has taught me is that, if you think you can't be fooled, you're wrong.

Moura went on to tell me that he'd poured his cyanide powder into the spicy tomato sauce he'd made for dinner one evening. 'My wife liked really hot food,' he explained.

A knock came on my door. Moura gasped as though he'd heard a bomb go off.

'It's okay, nothing's wrong,' I told him.

Inspector Pires poked her head in. She'd joined the Judiciary Police only a week earlier. 'Sorry, sir,' she said. 'There's been a murder.'

'Where?'

'In São Bento. On the Rua do Vale.'

It was my week to be on call, which meant I was given all the major crimes reported by the Public Security Police, the PSP. Their officers were nearly always the first on the scene because all emergency calls to 112 were directed their way.

'Okay, Pires, get the techs from Forensics over to the Rua do Vale ASAP. I'll get there as soon as I can.'

'Right, sir,' Pires agreed, but in a tone of warning, she added, 'the PSP says that the victim was wealthy and well-connected, with lots of friends in the government.'

I came out to talk to her, closing the door behind me. 'I know you're just trying to protect me, Inspector, but a cadaver isn't likely to phone any of his big-shot buddies to complain that I took a few extra minutes with a suspect. Don't let the PSP spook you.'

'Yes, sir. Sorry, sir.'

I'd spoken gently, but she looked as if she might burst into tears, so I took her shoulder. 'I didn't mean to sound harsh.

This suspect has put me off-balance. One thing you can do for me is call Dr Zydowicz. I want him on this case.'

Zydowicz was the chief medical inspector. He'd just returned to work after two months on sick leave. We weren't required to have a medical expert on hand, but I preferred having one around for high-profile cases.

I slipped back into my office to finish up with Moura. He was finishing his glass of water when I stepped in. A few minutes later, we'd reached an agreement on the exact wording of his statement. Once he'd added his tiny, careful signature, he handed me back my pen and said in a hopeful tone, 'I don't think I'm really such a bad person.'

I considered what to tell him; I wanted to be honest but hurting him seemed pointless. 'Sometimes people get so lost that they can't find their way back to themselves. I think that's maybe what happened to you. Though you should keep in mind that nobody who ends up being interrogated in my office ever thinks of himself as a bad person.'

I was tempted to say more, but he'd wrecked his quiet little life in a way that could never be repaired, and that seemed to earn him the right to hold on to an illusion or two. Still, he sensed that I had more on my mind. 'Go ahead, I can take it,' he told me.

I looked at him hard to make sure he meant it. He nodded decisively.

'I'm sorry to have to say this, but do you really think your fantasy son will believe you're a good dad when he finds out you poisoned his mom?'

'I thought of that, too,' he acknowledged, sitting up straight. He seemed gratified that our minds worked alike. 'That's why I've made it so he'll never find out.'

'You're never going to think of him again?' I asked sceptically.

Passing over my question, he said in a grateful voice, 'You're a nice guy. And you listen well – thanks. I'm lucky I got to speak to you last.'

'Don't worry, you'll have plenty of people to talk to in prison. And more than a few of them will be thrilled to have a friend who's an expert chemist. You might even—'

Reaching up to his chest, he swallowed a sharp intake of breath, then coughed.

'What's wrong?' I asked.

He gazed down and took a fish-out-of-water gulp of air. 'I didn't want to have to tell my kid,' he said in a choking voice. 'Or anyone else.' He leaned over my desk, his hands gripping its edge, his knuckles white.

'What did you do?' I demanded, jumping up.

He closed his eyes. His grip slackened. 'Don't bother calling an ambulance.'

'*Merda!*' I hollered.

As I rushed to him, his head fell forward and hit the surface of my desk with a thud. His right hand shot out at the same time and sent my **I ♥ BLACK CANYON** mug and all my pens flying. His eyes were open but not seeing anything in our world. A rivulet of blood trickled out of his nose.

Inspector Pires came rushing in from next door. I shouted for her to call an ambulance. 'And tell the medics to bring an antidote for cyanide!'

I found a faint but steady pulse in Moura's wrist. Lifting him up out of his chair, I eased him down to the floor, positioning him on his back so his heart wouldn't have to work so hard. I noticed a tiny square of foil glimmering by one of the legs of my desk.

'Don't you do this to me!' I told him, but a few seconds later his chest stopped rising. Sensing that this was a test around which my own right to be alive was turning, I knelt beside him and pressed down hard over his sternum, then tilted his head back and gave him two of my breaths.

Chapter 2

After the medics confirmed what I already knew, I lost my breakfast in the toilet. Washing my face with hot water at the sink, staring into the mirror at the shocked fragility in my eyes, I rewrote my conversation with Moura over and over, giving him all the reassurances he needed to keep from taking his own life.

The sensation of breathing life into him still coated my lips, like a salty crust. Was it guilt that tugged me back to my childhood? Maybe it was simply that any man looking long enough into his own lost face will eventually find the boy dwelling inside him who first realized he would commit many wrongs over his lifetime.

I locked myself in a stall because I wanted to be alone with the ten-year-old that I'd been. In there – in my memory – the crescent moon shone lantern-bright over our Colorado home. Gusts of frigid wind were bending the barren branches of our apple trees, and I could hear the broken-bone crunch of Dad's feet tramping across the ice towards the porch, where I'd concealed my six-year-old brother Ernie behind a stack of firewood.

'Hey, look what I've got here!'

Dad grabbed Ernie and flung him into a snow bank by the stairs leading up to our front door, then waved to me. 'Get on over here, Hank!'

When I reached him, he took my arm and hugged me to him. He trembled. At first I thought he might be crying, but as he held me away, he showed me a mocking smile. 'You know what, son,' he told me, 'I'm going to do to Ernie what the Colorado winter does to our apple trees!'

He pushed me hard, and I fell next to my brother. As I looked up, Dad took a clear plastic bag out of his back pocket . . .

From inside my stall, I phoned my brother. He heard the panic in my voice right away.

'What's wrong?' he asked.

'Trouble at work.'

'But you're okay?'

'Yeah, fine,' I told him. 'Is everything okay with you? I suddenly got worried about you.'

'Everything's fine. The roses are gorgeous right now. Oh, and you should see the—'

'You don't think Dad could find us after all these years?' I cut in.

'Jesus, Hank, where'd that come from?'

'Just answer the question!'

'You know it's impossible. Even if he's still alive, which I doubt, he doesn't speak a word of Portuguese. And neither of us is in the phonebook. If he could've found us, he would have. We've been here more than twenty-five years now.'

It often infuriated me how Ernie could be so sure we were safe from our father and so insecure about nearly everything else, but for the moment it was what I needed to hear. 'Remember how he said the worst things real softly?' I said. 'To show us how at peace he was with himself and God.'

Ernie drew an alarmed breath. 'You haven't told Ana or someone else about what happened to him, have you?' he asked, thinking he'd figured out more of what was wrong with me. 'The police back home might still think he didn't just disappear – that we did something we didn't do.'

'I haven't said a thing. Don't get so upset.'

'Tell me what's happened,' he said in a gentler voice.

13

Given Ernie's history with pills, I didn't dare mention Moura's suicide, so I said, 'A suspect got killed here at headquarters.'

In the slow-passing silence between us, I realized I'd expected Ernie to die on that December day when Dad found him under our porch. Sometimes, when my brother and I didn't speak for a few days, it even seemed to me as though Dad *had* suffocated him, then or at some other time, and that all of my adult life has been a dream.

'Stay away from the blood,' my brother told me now. 'And look both ways before you cross the street.'

His last advice was our childhood code that meant: be careful at all times. When I agreed, the time came to hang up, but I couldn't; I was stopped by all that I didn't dare say but needed to. Most of all, I wanted to tell Ernie that if Dad showed up, I'd kill him – and not only that, but that I'd trained as a cop to be sure that I'd stay calm enough to put a bullet right between his eyes and dispose of his body without anyone finding out.

Pires had picked up all the pens that had scattered across my floor by the time I got back to my office. After thanking her, I went to Director Crespo's office to explain what had happened with Moura. His impatient, get-on-with-it look disoriented me so badly that I forgot the word for CPR in Portuguese and I had to say it in English. I hated the way I sounded far away and helpless – as if I'd fallen off the edge of the world.

'Where did he keep the cyanide?' Crespo asked me when I'd finished my story.

I held up the square of aluminium foil I'd found. 'In this. He dropped it on the floor.'

'Careful with that!' he said, thrusting up his hand. 'It may still have poison on it.'

While folding the foil in four, I told him I'd ask Forensics to dispose of it. I tucked it in my shirt pocket for safekeeping.

Crespo took a stick of gum from his pack – he'd been trying to give up cigarettes for more than four years, ever since the new legislation against smoking indoors had come into effect. 'Look, Monroe,' he said in the overly patient tone he adopted when he was trying not to show how annoyed he was with me, 'there was nothing you could do. Just write up your report and get on with your day.' He came around his desk and patted my shoulder. 'The guy was a nutcase – a total loser. Just forget about him.'

My anger, quick and demanding, made me lean away from him. 'I don't see what made him a loser,' I said.

While chewing greedily on his gum, Crespo sized me up, wondering how honest he could be with me. 'We all know life sucks half the time, Monroe, but we keep fighting. The losers give up. It's as simple as that.'

I knew that giving up wasn't simple at all, but I was afraid I'd shout something rude if I started to argue with him. I told myself that Crespo wasn't worth the effort to make him understand how many years of despair you needed to suffer in order to find the courage to walk to the end of your life and jump off.

In a conciliatory tone, he said, 'Look, you aren't going to win any medals by taking these things personally. Go have a shot of brandy at the Açoriana after you get the paperwork out of the way. You're white as a sheet.'

'I don't drink, sir.'

'Christ, Monroe, a shot of brandy isn't drinking, it's coping!'

I scrubbed my hands and typed up my report. By then, it was almost 11 a.m. Ana would be at her gallery. Liliana, her assistant, answered. When my wife took the line, I told her about Moura. 'I really fucked up,' I concluded. 'I didn't need to be so clever.'

'Listen, Hank, if he hid the cyanide, it meant that he decided he was going to take his own life long before he started talking to you.'

15

She spoke in that no-nonsense voice of hers that's usually my road out of hell, but not this time. 'I . . . I identified with him,' I stammered, and I explained how he'd invented a son to oblige himself do the right thing.

'Look, he told you he was lucky that you were the one who questioned him,' she said. 'So stop blaming yourself.'

Comforting words, but death was still lodged in the pulsing at the back of my head and in the fatal numbness of my hands; the blood and skin remember what the mind forgets.

A Valium might have helped but I tried to avoid taking any medication in the morning. I couldn't put off going to the Rua do Vale, so I promised Ana I'd do my best to make it home early and grabbed my gun. I reached our parking lot before I realized I'd forgotten my bolo tie and dashed back for it; counting on a three-inch-tall silver bird to keep me safe was idiocy, but Ernie insisted on it.

When I reached our car, Pires was sitting behind the wheel, scanning the movie listings in the *Público*. Hearing me, she looked up. Her eyes were red and glassy. She'd already told me – choking up – that she'd never before watched anyone die..

We didn't speak. As she navigated through the noisy traffic, her hands gripped the steering wheel as though she'd just learned to drive. The accumulation of opening lines I wanted to try – but didn't – ended up making me jittery. 'So, is there anything of interest at the movies?' I finally asked.

'Someone told me a new Angelina Jolie movie just came out, but I couldn't find it.' In an urgent voice, she added, 'Listen, sir, I'm really sorry about what happened in there.'

'You didn't do anything wrong,' I told her.

'If you hadn't had to come out to talk to me, then it's possible that—'

'He'd have taken the cyanide anyway,' I interrupted, repeating what my wife had told me.

'Maybe.' She grimaced.

'Let's just get to the crime scene. Nothing we say can change what's happened.'

'Okay, sir.'

She seemed resigned to her dissatisfaction, but I must have needed more convincing; as we rumbled down the Calçada do Combro, I said, 'We all need to tell our story to someone, and once Moura did that, his life stopped making sense.'

Pires took a deep breath and held it. I had the feeling she needed to hold onto a last, unkind thought about herself.

'Everyone your age seems to think Angelina Jolie is the greatest,' I told her.

'And I take it you don't, sir,' she replied, clearly as glad as I was to welcome trivialities into our conversation.

'I watched *Lara Croft* with my wife and kids once. It was like a bad cartoon. She seems like a good person, but I thought she was absolutely terrible in the film.'

'Acting may not be one of her strong points,' Pires admitted.

I laughed. A reticent smile crept over her lips – her first since we'd started working together. I realized that Moura's death had probably changed the shape and scope of everything that would now happen between us.

'Do you want to hear what the PSP officer on the scene told me about the murder?' she asked.

'Good idea.'

She spoke quickly and decisively about the case without having to consult her notes. Impressive. But I was unable to catch most of what she said. When I closed my eyes to ease the throbbing at my temples, she stopped talking.

'I think you're going to have to start over,' I said. 'Sorry.'

She told me that the victim's name was Pedro Coutinho. He'd been shot in his living room. His body had been discovered about an hour and a quarter earlier by his housekeeper. His wife Susana and daughter Sandra had been on vacation in the Algarve, along with the family dog, a poodle named Nero. They'd closed up the house and left for Lisbon on being informed about the murder.

17

I watched Pires furtively as she spoke. She had a secretive profile. With her skullcap of black hair and rigid, upright posture, she looked like a flamenco dancer. If I'd have been younger, I'd have asked leading questions in the hopes of getting a glimpse at the mysteries inside her, but I was forty-two and sick of training new inspectors.

Pires went on to tell me that PSP officers on the scene had found Coutinho's address book in the bottom drawer of the desk in his library, and in it were the cell-phone numbers of a number of ministers. They'd also found an issue of *Ola!* on his night table with a showy story about his family's vacation in Goa last February. Apparently, he liked being photographed without a shirt, probably to show off his boxer's build.

Finishing up, Pires told me that the wife and daughter were expected back in Lisbon by mid-afternoon.

'How old was the victim?' I asked.

She wrinkled her nose. 'I forgot to ask that, sir,' she said. 'Sorry.'

'No problem. And how's Nero holding up?'

'The poodle?'

'Yeah.'

She looked at me as if I were mad.

'Sorry,' I said. 'My wife and kids tell me that I try to be amusing at inappropriate moments, but it's really just to keep myself afloat.'

I suspected that we wouldn't make any further attempts at humour, but a little while later she said, 'I wonder if Nero also goes bare-chested in gossip magazines.'

'We can hope that he feels confident enough to do so,' I retorted.

We laughed together – but a bit too wildly, as people do who were aware that the very bad day they were having is about to get worse.

My cell phone rang. It was Mesquita, the deputy head of the Judiciary Police for all of Portugal. 'All right, listen up,

Chief Inspector,' he told me. 'I hear you're on your way to the Rua do Vale. Is that right?'

'Yes, sir, we'll be there soon.'

'Good. Make sure you do everything by the book. And if anything is leaked to the press, I'll have you strung up by your balls. Understood?'

'Perfectly.'

'Good. And if you start getting pressured, tell whoever it is to fuck off and call me. I don't care if it's the prime minister. Got it?'

He hung up without waiting for my agreement. When I told Pires who had called and that she wasn't to discuss the case with anyone, she looked at me uneasily.

'I'm listening,' I told her.

'Do you think the victim might have some compromising information on people high up in the government?'

'I was just warned that the prime minister might ring, so you tell me, Inspector.'

We parked on the Travessa do Alcaide, about a hundred yards from our destination; I always liked a few minutes in the open air before seeing blood. As we walked towards the victim's home, an ancient wooden trolley shivered past us, with a knot of screaming kids leaning out the side, communing with the God of Danger they still had every right to worship at their age. Trash blew over the cobblestones and a radio blared out news about our never-ending economic crisis. Unemployment was up to 15 per cent, and more than half of those without jobs – 500,000 people – were receiving no government assistance. A recent nationwide poll revealed that 69 per cent of Portuguese college students intended to emigrate after graduating. And our miserable salaries – the lowest in Western Europe – had once again been deemed too high by Nobel-prizewinning economist Paul Krugman and a panel of international experts.

On passing a decaying apartment house with a big hole kicked in at the bottom of the door, two thick drops of liquid plopped onto my head. I prayed that one of Lisbon's bloated pigeons hadn't used me for target practice again. On looking up, I discovered festive red geraniums gazing down at me from their canary-yellow window box. It seemed encouraging – after all, some of us could still afford flowers and fresh paint. I dried my hair with the handkerchief that I always keep in my back pocket.

The wind smelled of heated pavements, olive oil and yeast. Loosening my bolo tie, I discovered my collar was soaked. 'All summer long I want rain and my kids want more sun,' I told Pires. 'Do you think we've hit ninety degrees yet, Inspector?'

'We passed a pharmacy a few blocks back and the flashing sign said eighty-one.'

'Only eighty-one? It feels much hotter.'

'Because there's no breeze at all.'

'If I were Raymond Chandler,' I told her, 'I think I'd tell you now that men and women do crazy, violent things on hot summer days without any wind. Especially when they lose their jobs and despise their leaders.'

'Sounds about right,' she said.

'Do you read mysteries, Inspector?' I asked.

'Yes, sir – mostly the classic American ones. Especially Dickson Carr.'

So she was a woman who enjoyed closed-door detective novels – which probably meant that she liked nothing better than beating the odds.

The crumbling sidewalk was only wide enough for one person at a time, so I had Pires walk ahead of me. She turned back now and again to make sure I hadn't lost my way or been taken advantage of by another leaky geranium. Her concern reminded me of how I'd always have one eye out for Ernie when we were little.

Pires walked with her hands joined behind her back, leaning slightly forward, as if bent by a heavy locket. It seemed to me that she might have been having continuing doubts about her responsibility for Moura's death.

'Listen, Pires,' I said, taking advantage of a break in the traffic to walk beside her, 'some of the older cops will wish you'd never joined the force. They may even make fun of you. Just ignore them if you can. The younger men will all come to accept you as a colleague if you hang tough. Come talk to me if you have any big troubles.'

'Yes, thank you, sir,' she said, but without enthusiasm.

From the urgent way she looked down the street, I could see I'd embarrassed her. Pity a man entering middle age with so little experience of women. 'Tell me,' I said, 'do you ever go to the beach at Caparica?'

She turned around to face me. 'Sir?'

'Moura, our chemistry teacher ... He used to take his imaginary kid there.'

'I've been to Caparica a few times.'

'Listen, Inspector, when it's just the two of us, how about calling me Henrique?'

'If ... if that's what you want,' she replied, though her anxious hesitation told me she was unlikely to abide by our agreement.

I gestured for her to start off again. 'So is Caparica nice?' I asked.

'It's beautiful,' she said, turning around momentarily, 'though there are too many people on weekends. You've never been?'

'No. Where I grew up, there were no beaches. The sound of waves still unnerves me. And all that sand ... Though my wife takes the kids out near Guincho sometimes. She likes her beaches wild. Like her men.'

That last comment was meant to win me another laugh, but my American delivery had been too dry. It happens all the time.

'Where did you grow up, sir?' Pires asked.

'Why do you want to know?'

'Because we'll be working together, sir.'

'Oh, for just a couple of years, Lucinda,' I told her. 'It is Lucinda, isn't it?'

'Luci,' she said.

'Well, Luci, in no time at all, you'll be free of me.'

She gazed off. Did I see disappointment?

'It has nothing to do with you,' I assured her. 'The director always substitutes my inspectors every two years. He doesn't want anyone working with me too long. I'm sure you've heard about it.'

Pires nodded, clearly embarrassed by what she'd been told behind my back.

The Rua do Vale turned out to be a slender, tired old street – wide enough for only one car at a time – leading up to the imposing columns of the Jesus church, which seemed far too majestic for so derelict a neighbourhood. Whoever built that sanctuary had wanted to remind residents that God was for-ever around the corner – even if He wasn't, of course.

The first house on our left – unpainted, and in a bad state of disrepair – was covered with scaffolding. About a hun-dred feet up the street, a small group of neighbours was already standing vigil outside the victim's front door: an elderly man in a soiled undershirt, all crooked angles and bones; and four women, the youngest holding a baby in a blue blanket.

Pires said, 'I'd still like to know where you grew up.'

'On a ranch in western Colorado,' I replied. 'Go to Google Maps and find Black Canyon of the Gunnison National Park and move your cursor about twenty miles to the left. Unfortunately, there's nothing at all for a tourist to do there except get stared at by a few hungry rattlesnakes and drunken shopkeepers.'

Despite my cynicism, her face brightened. 'I went to Rocky Mountain National Park four years ago. Filipe and I went camping in the American West for our honeymoon.'

I almost said, *I've been there, too*, but I didn't want to dis-cuss my homeland with her; the Portuguese generally resented having to give up their misconceptions about America. 'So you're married?' I asked.

'Yes. Filipe just got his doctorate in anthropology,' she said proudly.

'Kids?'

'Not yet. And you, Chief Inspector?'

'Two – Nathaniel and Jorge. When we're out of range, my wife and I call them Godzilla and King Kong. God knows what they call us.'

Luci laughed, which pleased me – and allowed me to imagine for a fleeting moment that the events of this morning would have no lingering effect on my work.

The neighbours were only fifty paces away now. They faced us with open, curious eyes; they'd guessed we were cops, though we weren't in uniform. As we reached our destination, the old man said gruffly, 'You the police?'

'That's right,' I answered.

He chewed over that information while eyeing me suspiciously. If my life had been the 1950s Western I sometimes wished it was, he'd have spat on the ground between us.

Number 24 Rua do Vale was a three-storey townhouse with pink paint flaking off the stucco. A youthful PSP officer was standing outside, reading one of those giveaway newspapers that invariably end up wafting and rolling across our desiccated streets – Lisbon's very own tumbleweed. As we shook hands, the young woman with the baby asked me if Pedro Coutinho was dead.

'I'm sorry, senhora, I'm not at liberty to discuss the case,' I replied.

'If he weren't dead, then what the hell would you be doing here!' the old man told me with a venomous frown.

'We'll be coming round the neighbourhood later today to ask you questions,' I said to him and the others, 'and I'll let you know a little of what I've found out at that time.'

The front door was armoured; six dead-bolts slid into the wall at the turn of a key. After I'd joined Luci in the foyer, she asked, 'Is your bolo tie from Colorado, sir?'

I realized with a jolt that I'd left it out.

'Yes, it's a Thunderbird. A Sioux friend gave it to me.'

'You had Indian friends?' Her voice swelled with little-girl enchantment.

'Just one – Nathan was his white-man's name. He was a *winkte*.'

'A *winkte*?'

'A clown who's also a wise man. They're crazy by profession. They dress up in strange clothing and do everything backwards. Up is down and in is out. And to them, normal is the oddest thing of all.'

More importantly in my case, they find what's lost, I might have added if I'd known Luci better. Instead, I said, 'We sometimes need everything turned inside out. *Winktes* are the only people resourceful enough to do that.'

She didn't laugh or smirk, which was a very good sign – and the one I must have wanted, or I wouldn't have brought the subject up.

We stepped into the foyer. The floor was dark parquet, and so polished that it reflected like glass. Two man-size Chinese vases painted with sinuous golden dragons guarded the door to the living room. Beside one of them was a droopy ficus plant in a big white pot and a red watering can filled to the brim.

As we put on our protective coats, gloves and slippers, Pires said, 'We had a great time in the Rocky Mountains. Except for the altitude. Filipe got disoriented while hiking at three thousand meters and we almost didn't locate him in time.'

'You have to keep hydrated at high altitude,' I told her, but I spoke absently; I'd already spotted the dead man sprawled on the plush white rug centring the living room.

I stepped inside. A grey sock had been stuffed in the victim's mouth and kept in place with a necktie wound twice around his head and knotted. It was cobalt blue with scarlet stripes, and it had been tied so tightly that his lips had been stretched far back, making his nose stick out grotesquely, like the proboscis of an insect. He was lying on his belly facing a faded yellow wall covered with museum-quality paintings, including a small one by Paula Rego of a prim-looking girl force-feeding a monkey. A fluffy green towel was tied around his waist, and his blue dress-shirt was unbuttoned. A blood-fringed bullet hole discoloured its back. He was short and stocky, with large, powerful hands. His grey hair was thick and closely cropped. He looked a bit like Pablo Picasso.

Five characters of Asian writing were scripted on the wall behind him, each letter about the size of my thumb: ディアーナ. They were a familiar shade of brown – the colour of dried blood. As I traced them with my eyes, a pounding headache started in my head, which meant that I might soon lose track of myself. To remain where I was – and who I was – I concentrated hard on the dead man.

What appeared to be pinkish yogurt had been smeared across his cheek and left ear; two empty Adagio packages – strawberry-flavoured – had been tossed on the carpet. I'd have guessed he was forty-five or fifty, but it was difficult to tell; death always made bodies appear wax-like to me – an illusion my mind conjures up as protection, I've been told by our police psychologist.

The victim's wrists were bound behind his back with thick, white nylon rope. A pool of blood had soaked into the carpeting.

Making sure to keep my eyes off the thick stain, I knelt beside him. I lifted his arm. From its level of grudging flexibility, I knew that rigor mortis had reached its peak a few hours earlier and was beginning to ease up. Under the towel I confirmed what my nose already suspected about how deep his final panic had been.

The tag on the necktie read Zara, a clothing store with shops at nearly every mall in Portugal. The price tag was still on: 19.95 euros. Keeping it on seemed a message sent to me by the killer about the cheapness of the victim's life.

I probed at the sock in his mouth with my pencil. It was

jammed in tight, which meant it would've made it nearly impossible for him to breathe or swallow. The tie had torn both corners of his mouth, which was crusted with blood. He wouldn't have been able to scream or even beg for his life.

Sure enough, the bluish-grey tinge to his lips meant he'd suffocated. As I put myself in his place, my balls contracted and my throat went dry, and when Luci touched my shoulder, I jumped. Astonishingly, my headache was gone, and I had the impression that I'd moved back a foot or more from the victim. I looked down into my hands. Gabriel hadn't written any message to me; instead, he'd drawn a stick figure surrounded by a circle of twelve dots, the Sioux sign for a threat that has you cornered.

Chapter 3

The murderer steers me through the house until I stand just where he wants, staring at the finality of his work. Kneeling, I search the dead man's misshapen face for the why of this death, listening hard for what he is unable to tell me. And although I'm aware that his blue-grey lips will never shape another word, the expectation of hearing a whisper of his final thoughts waits patiently inside me, hands folded in its lap, unwilling to walk away. Proof, I suppose, that I have never been able to accept the cold, one-sided deal that death makes with us.

A confession: when I tiptoe through my insomnia at night, I occasionally catch myself searching for shapes in Ernie's paintings that will prove to be coded messages from my mother. If she were still alive, I'd understand her better now – and be able to offer her more than my clowning. So perhaps it is my own wish for another chance that I always listen for when I am unable to sleep. Maybe our second chances are the only ghosts who ever appear to us.

The police officer who'd been in charge till my arrival introduced himself as Marcos Soutelo and asked if I wanted his briefing.

I've noticed over the years that PSP cops tend to begin their rundowns with an unusual detail, and the more startling the better. My theory was that the surreal atmosphere at the crime scene – the rigid, judgemental silence of the dead under all the commotion – made them need to be reassured that we shared the same notions about what was unusual and unexpected. And reassured, therefore, about what was normal. And yet in comparison to them, I felt fortunate; I'd had the advantage of learning when I was very young that there was no normal.

'The vic doesn't look fifty-nine years old, does he?' Soutelo began, and as though hoping to astonish me further, he added that Coutinho had been married to a former TAP stewardess twenty-two years his junior. 'Her name is Susana Soares,' he said, 'and judging from the photos in the library, she's a knockout!'

If Luci hadn't been next to me, I'd have felt compelled to reply with a remark establishing my manly credentials, such as, *Some guys have all the luck*, but, as it was, I was able to simply ask if the couple had had any kids. With his voice shifting into a more professional register, probably feeling mildly censured, Soutelo replied that they had one daughter, Sandra. She was fourteen years old and in the eighth grade at the Charles Lepierre French High School. He went on to tell me that the victim owned a construction company with offices in Paris and Lisbon, and that, in addition to this house and one in the Algarve, he kept a large apartment just across the Seine from the Eiffel Tower. He'd moved back to Lisbon from Paris four years earlier. His car, a 1967 Alfa Romeo spider, was parked in a private garage nearby. None of the neighbours who'd been questioned so far had heard a gunshot the day before. The housekeeper had discovered the body at ten o'clock this morning. Her name was Maria Grimault.

'I thought you'd want to talk to her right away,' Soutelo told me. 'She's waiting for you in the kitchen. Through that door,' he said, pointing.

While I fought the urge to stay where I was, and remain safely outside a case I didn't yet feel up to investigating, the most experienced of the techs, Eduardo Fonseca, started down the staircase at the back of the room, cradling his Nikon, his face poking fox-like out of his hood. He snapped

off two quick photographs – the flash spraying in our eyes –
with the glee of a kid testing a brand-new birthday present.
'Henrique Monroe, caught red-handed at the scene of the
crime!' he exclaimed.

Like most of the Portuguese, Fonseca pronounced *Monroe*
as *Monroy*. I forgave him that and his cringingly loud voice
because he was the sweetest man I knew.

He pumped my hand in both of his as he always did. After
introducing him to Luci, I told him, 'I'm guessing you've
already taken pictures of the body.'

'Yeah. Now I'm photographing anything that catches my
eye.' He tugged off his hood. Sweat had plastered thinning
bangs to his brow. He was looking more and more like a
chihuahua as he aged – tiny and sunken-eyed, with wrists
as slender and pale as celery. I wished he'd eat more. And
cut down on his smoking. Though he claimed that tar and
nicotine were the only things keeping him standing.

'Four things you need to know for now, Monroe,' he said
in a quick, businesslike voice. 'One – we found cigarette
butts in the ashtrays here in the living room and in the vic's
bedroom – four Marlboro Lights and two Gauloise Blondes
down here, one more Marlboro in the bedroom. No lipstick
stains on any of them. We've already collected them. Two –
there's a bloody footprint on Coutinho's shirt. Three—'

'Hold on,' I cut in. 'Is the footprint complete enough to
identify the shoe?'

'Yeah, and I've got it photographed. Three – I found some
slivers of plastic and what look like tiny bits of sponge on
the carpet here. I've got samples.'

'A silencer?' I asked.

'Yeah, a soda bottle with cut-up sponges would be my
guess. Four, we found—'

'Does that really work?' Luci interrupted.

'Yeah, but only for small-calibre firearms. Which is point
number four: we found the bullet casing – nine-calibre – and
the slug itself. Exited Coutinho's back and lodged in the wall
near the staircase. Bruno has them.' He read my mind and

29

cut off my next question. 'He's upstairs, hunting for more dinosaur tracks.'

'Bloody footprints,' I explained to Luci.

'Bruno is Bruno Vaz,' Fonseca added. 'A cassette player, so watch what you say.'

'I'm afraid you're going too fast for me,' Luci told him apologetically.

'He's PC,' Fonseca explained, meaning a member of the Portuguese Communist Party. 'If you talk about politics, he turns on the tape.' He circled his finger in a loop and began to snore.

'Has Sudoku taken a look at the body yet?' I asked.

Sudoku was our biomedical expert and a whiz at the Japanese number puzzles. His real name was João Ferreira.

'Sudoku is home with a cold, poor boy, but Bruno and I have everything under control.' Fonseca edged towards me and added in a whisper, 'The vic had a guest in his bed last night. And a hundred euros says she's responsible for this mess. Fifty more that she's from France and smokes Gauloise Blondes.'

'Sorry, Ana has cut off my betting allowance,' I told him. 'She doesn't like Godzilla and King Kong going hungry. Has Dr Zydowicz arrived yet?'

'Is he joining the festivities today? Christ, it's going to be the fucking United Nations around here!'

'Exactly. Did you take photos of the Asian writing on the wall?'

'*Absorutery*,' Fonseca replied, imitating a respectful Japanese bow.

I moaned at his bad taste, which only made him burst out laughing.

'When you've finished having so much fun,' I said, 'email me your key photos. Was the writing done in blood?'

'Yeah, and we've got a sample. It'll turn out to be the vic's, most likely.'

'How long has he been dead?'

30

'Eighteen to twenty-four hours – taking into account that it's a sauna in here and that he's decomposing at warp nine.'

When I asked if he'd recovered the victim's cell phone, he told me they'd looked in all the obvious places and hadn't spotted it. 'A hundred bucks says the murderer grabbed it,' he said to Luci.

'I get the feeling it would be a mistake to bet against you,' she told him.

'Smart girl you got here!' he told me, and he winked suggestively at her.

'Smart *inspector*,' I warned him, pleased to be able both to needle him and make a serious point.

'Oh, come on, Monroe, you know I meant no offence.' To Luci, he said, 'Sorry. It's just that you're new to the job and what . . . fourteen years old?'

She pointed her index finger up.

'Eighteen? Twenty?'

Fonseca's childlike enthusiasm made Luci grin. 'Twenty-seven,' she replied.

'Well, next to this grumpy old donkey,' he said, jabbing his thumb towards me, 'you look like a teenager . . . Oh, guess what I did, Monroe!' he added, and without waiting for my response, he exclaimed, 'I photographed every page in the vic's address book!'

'Why'd you do that?'

'The Case of the Missing Mercedes.'

It was a famous fuck-up. Back in 1984, a Portuguese ambassador was arrested for having crashed his car into a former business partner just outside the man's house in Benfica. The suspect's Mercedes was impounded, of course, so the photographer on the scene didn't bother taking shots of the dented and bloodstained fender, or much of anything else. At least, that's what he told his superiors, though everybody later suspected he'd been bribed. Unfortunately, the car went missing that very afternoon. With no Mercedes and no pictures, and some exchanges of cash at the Justice Ministry, the ambassador didn't even have to face trial. Now and again I still come across his fat, self-satisfied face in the *Público*, Ana's newspaper of choice. He's become a fervent Catholic in his old age and pontificates against adoption by same-sex couples and medically assisted procreation. Presumably, he'll bribe his way into heaven.

'Good work,' I told Fonseca. 'Where's the address book itself?'

'Waiting for you on the first floor – on the desk in the library. You know what else, Monroe? Coutinho was a four-minister man!'

I whistled to make him happy.

'He's got the cell phones for four ministers in his address book,' Fonseca explained to Luci, beaming. 'A new Lisbon record!' He wiped a big drop of perspiration from his chin with a bravado swipe. 'I have a hunch we'll find more goodies in his computer – maybe the numbers of his Swiss bank accounts! Anyone feel like a trip to Zurich?'

'Where'd you find his computer?' I asked.

'Also on the desk in his library. A MacBook Air. Sweet! We sent it off to Joaquim.'

Joaquim was the senior computer specialist in our technological office. 'So what's next for you?' I asked.

'Nicki and I have a date with the vic's bedroom.' He pressed his lips to the shutter of his camera. He was performing for Luci.

To take his spotlight off her, I said, 'Inspector Pires, see if you can turn up a cell phone in a bathroom or some other unlikely place. I'll be in the library.'

Despite Fonseca's having taken photos of every page, I wanted to have the address book in my possession before doing anything else, so I climbed up the stairs behind him, instructing him along the way not to discuss the murder with his wife or kids.

Happily, he'd already put the air conditioner on in the library. The walls were wood panelled, their shelves packed with books from floor to ceiling. Everything was in perfect order except for a French–Farsi dictionary shoved in horizontally on a bottom shelf near the desk.

At the front of the room was a locked, glass-fronted case containing antique editions of classical French authors such as Zola and Stendhal. Coutinho's CDs were there, too – mostly Piaf, Polnareff, Aznavour and other popular French singers from the 1960s and 1970s. His small classical music section was almost all Erik Satie and Claude Debussy.

The desk was a dark, ponderous antique, with lion's-paw feet. The address book sat next to a sleek black telephone. It was suede, and the exact same shade of green as the leaves of the junipers that used to grow on our ranch. Coutinho had neat, compact handwriting, though his capital S and G were ornamented with florid curlicues. Ana would have said that he probably startled those around him with occasional flourishes of exuberance.

I found the entries for the four ministers right away; they were written in the G section, under the heading *Governo*: José Pedro Aguiar Branco, National Defence; Miguel Macedo, Internal Administration; Paula Teixeira da Cruz, Justice; and Miguel Relvas, Parliamentary Affairs. Jumping around from A to Z, I also discovered the cell phone numbers for António Amorim, the chief executive officer of our biggest cork exporter; Mariza, the renowned *fado* singer; and Fernando Gomes, the former mayor of Porto. He also had the cell phones for several important contacts in France, including the Minister of Foreign Affairs.

On the wall above the desk was a framed magazine cover: the victim featured in *Exame*, standing in front of his red Alfa Romeo sports car, looking confident and gentlemanly – but with a twinkle of mischief in his eye, too, as if to show the reader that he wasn't yet too old to sneak out of the house at 2 a.m. and race his car down the Avenida da Liberdade at a hundred miles an hour – a favourite pastime for the failed Formula One drivers in our city. The flashy car on the cover seemed his way of letting us know he was a secret risk-taker. And unashamed of making huge profits in a bankrupt country.

The tagline on the magazine cover read: *Steering Clear of the Economic Crisis*. It was hard not to dislike him and the editors, especially because my pay had been cut by about twenty per cent over the last two years.

Below the cover were six framed watercolours of a small girl – naked and exuberant. They were executed with the broad, sweeping strokes of Oriental calligraphy. In the most striking, she was racing across a beach, her arms thrust out in front of her, as if she were chasing after her own potential for joy.

The victim's blue linen trousers were folded over the seat of an armchair in his bedroom. A fat leather wallet – stuffed with nearly four hundred euros in bills – was in the right front pocket. A gold Dunhill lighter and silver keychain with the Alfa Romeo insignia were in the left. On the night table was a half-full pack of Marlboro Lights and a jade-coloured, celadon ashtray. Coutinho – or someone in the family – clearly had an interest in China or Japan, which gave me the idea that the killer might very well have forced him to paint the Asian writing on the wall with his own blood.

Photos of the victim's wife and daughter crowded one corner of the desk. They were blonde and pretty and, in one particularly evocative shot, taken at the beach, both of them had the same bemused, impatient-with-the-photographer look. It must have been an old source of family irritation and amusement that Coutinho took too long to focus.

Back downstairs, I found Pires studying the paintings in the living room.

'Paula Rego is too famous for even an uneducated burglar to pass up,' she told me. She pointed to a drawing of the poet Fernando Pessoa reading a spread newspaper. 'And that one is by Julio Almeida, an up-and-coming artist who's getting a lot of press lately. It's got to be worth a few thousand euros at the very least.'

'Which means that if our man was a burglar, he was obviously after something he considered more valuable.'

'What do you think it might be?' she asked.

'Maybe business plans that hadn't yet been made public. Or bids on public projects. Listen, did you find a cell phone?'

'Nothing yet.'

I tested Coutinho's keys on the front door. The second one worked. We theorized that he'd heard noises while dressing and made his way downstairs to investigate. Judging from the height of the bullet hole in the wall, he'd been shot standing. Three knee-prints in the white rug indicated that he'd crawled towards the wall of paintings.

'He edged towards his killer to beg for his life,' I suggested, thinking of what I'd do in the same situation. 'Or maybe he hoped he still had enough strength left to lunge forward and tackle him.' As I voiced my speculations, the meat stench of the body hit me. We'd need to open every window in the house or . . . 'Luci, see if you can get the air conditioner going,' I said. I'd noticed it on entering the room and pointed above the antique map of Europe on a side wall. 'If not, we're going to have to wear masks.'

While she fiddled with the controls, I knelt next to the body, my hand over my mouth and nose. The bloody footprint stamped on the wing of the shirt indicated the pattern of the shoe sole: slender ribbing intersecting at a boomerang shape. Lifting up the fabric with the tip of my pen, I discovered a dark bruise above Coutinho's ribs. Just then, the hum of the air conditioner started up and the cool air brushed its fingertips at the back of my neck.

'You're a life-saver,' I told Luci as she stepped towards me. I gestured towards the body. 'Two assailants, I'd guess. One tied the rope around his wrists and stuffed the gag in his mouth while the other held the gun.'

'Or the murderer made him tie the gag on himself,' she observed, 'then tightened it and moved on to his wrists.' Gazing at the victim, she added in a solemn voice, 'Sensing

35

he wasn't going to make it, he lowered his head any way it fell and let death take him.'

'Maybe so, but I'd say it's more likely that the murderer kicked him hard to take the fight out of him.' I showed her the bruise on the side of his chest. 'Some people wake up every morning eager to hurt somebody, Luci. Unfortunately for us, they don't wear any special sign. They're the chemistry teacher who looks like Harry Potter and the carpenter who sings country music ballads while weeding his vegetable garden.'

I hadn't intended to mention my dad, but references to him occasionally popped out of me without warning.

While I was examining the surgical scars behind Coutinho's ears, David Zydowicz, the medical inspector, shuffled into the room. His droopy, heavily hooded eyes opened wide with pleasure when he spotted me, but they betrayed weariness as well. He'd aged a lot in the two months since his heart attack. I'd visited him twice in the hospital. His walk had become a fragile balancing act.

'Checking to see if he washed properly?' David asked in his Brazilian singsong. He was from São Paulo and Jewish. His father had survived Treblinka. David had had his Dad's prison-camp number tattooed on his own forearm in solidarity, which was the most moving testament to filial love I'd ever heard.

'He was a friend of Catherine Deneuve,' I told him – our slang for anyone who'd had a face-lift.

He shuffled closer. 'But not such a good friend,' he noted, flapping his bony hands. 'I could do better blindfolded.' Taking out his latex gloves, he said, 'Just after I left the hospital, I decided to get a few collagen shots myself.'

'But your wrinkles have always given you classic good looks,' I protested.

He snorted. 'I was talking about my ass, Henrique.' He patted his behind. 'My wife says it's become a balloon with all the air let out. Nothing to hold onto any longer.'

We shared a laugh meant to ease the oddness of his being

36

so diminished. He leaned over the body and sniffed. 'Four,' he said; he gave stenches a rating from one – barely noticeable – to ten, a rating he'd never given out because it was the stink of Hitler and his cronies rotting away in Gehenna, the Jewish hell. 'After I get a good look at him, I'll clean him up a bit.'

While David pressed on an ache in his lower back, I introduced him to Luci. Squinting, he focused a beam of masculine delight on her face. Even in his debilitated state, his libido was dancing a samba.

To come to her rescue again, I reached into my shirt pocket for Moura's foil. 'This may have a trace of cyanide on it,' I told him. 'How about disposing of it for me?'

He grabbed it in a tissue and tucked it in the pocket of his smock. 'Where'd you get cyanide, son?' he asked.

'From a suspect who killed himself this morning. It's been one hell of a day.'

'Sorry to hear it,' he said, patting my arm.

Turning to Luci, I said, 'Time for us to interview the housekeeper.'

Senhora Grimault was an elderly, sparrowish woman with her hair clasped in a tight grey bun and the big knobby hands of a peasant. Her earrings were golden hearts, and she smelled pleasantly of lavender perfume. When we stepped inside, she was pouring steaming milk into her coffee cup. She looked up at us with an eager, curious, intelligent face. I trusted her right away.

After we'd finished the introductions, I asked if she was French, and she told me she was from Braga, but that her husband was from Rouen. With hopeful eyes, she asked us to sample her homemade sponge cake, but my gut wasn't up to the challenge. Luci thanked her but also said no, citing her need to keep fit, but I insisted that she eat half a slice so as not to disappoint our host.

The kitchen was all stainless steel and white marble, except for the wall beneath the cupboards, which was ornamented with centuries-old Portuguese tiles forming blue and yellow geometric patterns. A village church had obviously been plundered.

Senhora Grimault asked me to fetch a plate for Luci from a high shelf, and for a few seconds I was fifteen again, and happy to be needed by Aunt Olivia around the house.

When we were all comfortably seated, I asked, 'So how long have you worked for the Coutinho family, senhora?'

'Nearly four years. Just after Dr Coutinho moved back to Portugal, he hired me.' She explained that he'd wanted a housekeeper who could speak French, then, tearing up, volunteered that Senhora Coutinho was sure to take her husband's death very hard. As for the daughter, she predicted a long period of silent suffering. When I asked why, she told me that Sandra and her father both tended to hide their emotions. She added that they were also both workaholics, reinforcing her point by telling me that Coutinho returned to Lisbon once or twice a week over the summer to supervise building sites. For the moment, I chose not to mention that infidelity might have been the real reason he came to the city so often.

Unfortunately, she had no idea who the visitor was who had smoked two Gauloise Blondes. 'Inspector,' she said, giving me a weighty look, 'you think the murderer was here last night and talked for a while with Dr Coutinho, don't you?'

'It's possible, senhora, but between you and me, I doubt it. Anyone as careful as the killer we're dealing with had to know the butts could be used as evidence. More likely they were left by a friend – and very possibly the last person to see your employer alive.'

Senhora Grimault told me she'd arrived at precisely four minutes past ten in the morning and let herself in with her key. She'd neither seen nor heard anything odd. She explained that during the family's summer vacation in the Algarve she came to the house twice a week to air it out, dust a bit and water the house plants. The garden itself had an automatic watering system. She'd brought along a sponge cake because she'd been told a few days earlier by

Susana – in a phone call – that Dr Coutinho would be back in Lisbon for a couple of days. He had a sweet tooth and she prided herself on her baking.

I'd been thinking that the front-door key might have been copied by the murderer, and though Senhora Grimault swore to me she'd never lent it out, she could not promise the same for the family.

'The kitchen looks spotless,' I pointed out. 'Did you find it that way?'

'Yes, when I arrived, there were no plates to wash – not even from breakfast. Dr Coutinho must have eaten out last night and not yet had his morning cereal.'

I found one Adagio strawberry yogurt in the refrigerator, along with some cheese and milk, and two lemons.

'Dr Coutinho could live on cheese and sweets,' Senhora Grimault volunteered.

'When did you first spot him this morning?' I asked.

'The moment I stepped into the living room.' She closed her eyes and reached out a hand – slowly, straining with the effort, as though approaching a flame. 'I touched his shoulder,' she whispered. 'I thought that he might still be alive, but . . .' She lowered her arm to the table with a morose finality. 'And then I called 112.'

'Did you leave the house at any time after coming in?'

'No. I sat in the foyer.'

'But there's no chair in the foyer,' I pointed out.

'I sat on the ground. I was feeling dizzy, and my first thought was to get outside for some air, but I didn't get that far.'

She was close to tears again, and I pressed her to take a few sips of coffee. When she was ready to talk again, I asked, 'When did you decide to water the plant in the foyer?'

She showed me an astonished look.

'You left your watering can there,' I explained.

'My goodness, I completely forgot!' In a slow, deliberate voice – reviewing her morning as it appeared in her memory – she said, 'After I called 112, I thought that if I went through my usual routine I might calm myself down. I mean, if I could pretend that nothing had happened for a few minutes. But after I got the watering can, I broke down again.' She let out a frustrated sigh. 'Inspector, this seems like a dream . . . like something absolutely impossible.'

'Given what happened, that might be a good thing,' I observed, but she shook her head as though she would have preferred to be stronger. To my next question, she told me that Coutinho bought nearly all his neckties at the Hermès shop on the Avenue George V in Paris. She told me he would never have shopped at Zara.

'Now I'm going to ask you something indelicate,' I warned her. 'Were you aware of any extramarital affairs that he may have been having?'

She drew in her head, hen-like, and said tautly, 'I wouldn't know anything about that.'

'Other lives may be at risk,' I emphasized. At the time, I didn't believe that, but I wanted to apply a bit of pressure.

When I nodded insistently, Senhora Grimault confessed in a reticent voice that on maybe a dozen occasions she'd noticed creases on Susana's side of the bed when Dr Coutinho was supposed to be on his own. Once, she'd also discovered a towel stained with an unfamiliar shade of lipstick. 'And no, I don't have any idea who the woman was,' she rushed to add. Continuing to sense the direction of my thoughts, she told me, 'Dr Coutinho and Susana are good people – respectful to each other. I can't believe someone would want to hurt him. He was kind and generous. And so good at nearly everything he did – so talented.'

'Talented?' I asked.

'Take a look at the watercolours in his library. And the one in Sandi's room.'

'The ones of the little girl?'

The pleasure of astonishing me lit her eyes. 'They were done when Sandi was little,' Senhora Grimault continued, 'but he still took out his brushes on occasion.' She executed

40

two quick strokes in the air and gave a little laugh. 'He painted like Zorro!'

'He seemed to have been particularly interested in Asian cultures.'

'More than interested, Inspector. Just after he got his engineering degree, he worked in Tokyo for two years. He could speak Japanese!' The old lady's eyes opened wide, as if to take in the grand dimension of all the adventures he must have had. Undone by her delight, she began to tear up badly. 'I'm so sorry,' she whispered.

Luci spoke for the first time. 'You're doing great,' she said, and she gave the senhora's hand a firm squeeze.

After some more kind words from Luci, Senhora Grimault went on to tell us that Coutinho had had two cell phones. I tried both numbers but automatic messages indicated they weren't in use. I asked Luci to find out if any calls had been made from them over the last twenty-four hours. 'And while you're at it, get me a list of all the calls the victim made and received over the last two weeks,' I added.

I'd saved the most important detail for last: 'This morning, senhora, did you have to turn the key several times in the lock or did it just click open?'

She considered that. 'I had to turn it several times. I remember, because twisting it around gave me the idea that no one was at home. Now I realize that Dr Coutinho must have locked himself in for some reason.'

'No, the killer re-locked the door on leaving,' I told her. 'Which was a mistake.'

'Why is that?'

'Because now we can be certain he had the key.'

'Not necessarily, sir,' Luci rushed to say. 'He could have taken it off Dr Coutinho.'

I reached into my pocket to retrieve the Alfa Romeo key-chain. I shook it in the air. 'He could have, but didn't. These were still in Coutinho's trousers.'

Chapter 4

After seeing Senhora Grimault to the door and warning her
not to discuss the case with anyone, I studied the paintings
in the living room. Coutinho had bought only figurative
work. My favourite was a Carlos Botelho drawing of pastel
houses – in pink, yellow and blue – tumbling towards the
Tagus River.

When I returned to the kitchen, Luci was rinsing her cake
plate at the sink. She told me she'd just learned that no calls
had been made from either of the victim's cell phones since
the time of his murder.

'By now, the killer has probably destroyed their SIM
cards,' I said.

'To prevent us from following his trail?'

'Yes. But I also have the feeling he called Coutinho at some
point and didn't want us to find out about it.'

'You think the victim knew his killer?'

'Luci, there's too much hatred here for it to be a botched
burglary or random attack. And that Japanese message he
probably made Coutinho write . . . It's possible that some
trouble he got into all those years ago in Japan has caught
up with him.'

We found David Zydowicz seated on a chair he'd pulled
up next to the body, shining his flashlight on Coutinho's
fingernails.

'Signs of only a very brief struggle,' he told me. 'Our man
here was shot, then kicked above the ribs while on his hands

and knees, and finally tied up.' Switching off his light, he told Luci, 'Get out your notepad, young lady, and I'll tell you your bedtime story.'

David observed Luci's swift gestures with affectionate eyes, as if she were a little kid performing a card trick for her granddad. And as if there were only two kingdoms: the old and the young. When she was ready, he removed his glasses as though to summon forth a deeper part of himself and began to speak in the voice of authority that first won me to him. 'The victim was hit with just one bullet in his gut, but I don't believe it punctured his stomach lining or any other major organ, though I'll only know for sure when I do the autopsy. In any case, he'd have taken at least half an hour to bleed out. Though as you know, Henrique, he didn't.'

'No, for better or for worse, he didn't get that chance.' To Luci's puzzled glance, I added, 'His lips have a bluish tint – not enough oxygen.'

David took off one of his gloves and grabbed a candy from his pocket. While he undid the yellow wrapper, I told him, 'Whoever did this enjoyed seeing his victim suffer.'

'I can't speak to his emotions, Henrique – that's more your field. But it's true that Coutinho would have been in a lot of pain.'

It felt like my chest and head were being crushed. That's how my brother – at the age of six – had described what being suffocated felt like.

'And he's been dead eighteen to twenty-four hours?' I asked.

'Closer to twenty-four.' David put his glasses back on.

'Okay, here's how I see it,' I began. 'After his shower, Coutinho came downstairs to investigate noises he'd heard.' I stepped over to the wall of paintings and formed a gun with my hand. 'The killer surprised him from here.' I pointed towards the bottom of the staircase and squeezed off a shot. 'Our victim fell to his knees and started crawling. The killer kicked him and stepped on his back in order to subdue him, and to compel him to extend his arms behind his back and put his wrists together. He tied them, then jammed an old sock in his mouth and gagged him.'

As David nodded his agreement, Fonseca came down the staircase with a cheeky smile on his face. 'Madame X was a brunette,' he announced happily. 'And she had long hair.'

'How long?' I asked.

He held his hands about two feet apart.

'Good to know,' I said, 'but I bet she'll cut most of it off as soon as she finds out Coutinho is dead. And maybe dye it too.'

'Why's that?' Luci asked.

'Women who have affairs with married men generally prefer keeping their identity a secret. And the last thing she'll want is to have her name associated with a murder.'

'But if she was hiding here when Coutinho was killed,' David said, 'she might feel compelled to come forward and say what she saw and heard.'

'Except that if she was here, then she's scared to death right now.'

Fonseca scoffed. 'You guys are so fucking naive! With a rich old guy like this, she was probably in on his murder! And if she was, you can forget about finding her in Lisbon. She's gone, gone, gone!'

I got out my phone and called Senhora Grimault, who confirmed that Susana Coutinho was a natural blonde – and that Sandra was as well. To try to locate the homemade silencer and the victim's discarded cell phones, I had Luci fetch a plastic garbage bag from the kitchen into which she could empty all the trash receptacles in the neighbourhood. A few seconds later, she came back into the room with Bruno Vaz, our lab tech with the Communist tape loop in his head. A determined and powerful sixty-year-old, with a shaved head, goldfish-big brown eyes and the swirling hand gestures of a charismatic orchestra director, Vaz had a unique style that made you expect marvels and maybe even a little sorcery now and again. And he was indeed great at his work. Unfortunately, all my efforts to win his friendship had been in vain; to go along with his visceral contempt for all things American, he seemed to hold me personally responsible for everything from the right-wing coup in Chile to the use of English as the world's lingua franca. It didn't help our relationship any that he'd been arrested by Portugal's secret police in 1970 for his Communist Party affiliation and tortured at Caxias Prison. Before the great wash of his feelings about me solidified into stern dislike, he'd confessed to me – his eyes lighting up with recaptured meaning – that his imprisonment made the whole rest of his life seem insignificant. It had clearly been his Golden Age. Life in Portugal in 2012 – with its failed banks, deserted shopping malls and idiotic TV soap operas – must have seemed pathetic by comparison.

Vaz told me he'd turned up a host of fingerprints on the refrigerator and cabinets.

'Any more dinosaur tracks?' I asked.

'No. Our man must have either taken off his sneakers or wiped them clean.'

'The pattern on the sole looked like Converse to me.'

'Yeah, or knockoffs. As soon as I've identified the model, I'll let you know.'

When he asked me if he could collect the victim's shirt and tie, I turned to David and he gave me the go-ahead. Using the cheery tone that had become my shield against Vaz's hostility, I told him, 'They're all yours. And his pants are in his bedroom.'

'Look, Monroe,' he snarled, 'I've been dealing with evidence since long before you arrived in Portugal. So if you don't trust me, then just tell me to my face.'

'I don't get it,' I said, stunned. 'What did I do now?'

'He means you shouldn't have asked my approval, Henrique,' David told me wearily.

Did Vaz dislike David for being Brazilian and Jewish? Perhaps all his political ideals had morphed into a mistrust of foreigners. Maybe that's all they'd ever been.

'Oh, I see,' I said, allowing myself an angry frown because it was on David's behalf. I searched then for some searing warning that would alter everything between Vaz and me, once and for all – I suddenly couldn't imagine spending another ten years dodging his insults – but came up with nothing. 'You know, Vaz, solving crimes may be the only thing you and I are really any good at,' I said instead, relying on the truth. 'So I suggest we get on with our work before the evidence loses its patience with us.'

Vaz squinted at me, and from experience I knew he was taking aim, so I rushed to add, 'Your job at the moment is simply to tell me what size sneakers he was wearing.'

'Forty-three, most likely,' he said grudgingly, 'though forty-four is still a possibility, depending on the model.'

To David, I said, 'Either of those sizes would be pretty large for a Portuguese man.'

'Yeah, except that young people today are bigger than their parents – better nutrition.'

'Listen, Monroe,' Vaz said, as if my conversation with David were wasting his time, 'what do you say I go through the victim's car before taking his clothes? Any objections?'

He seemed as anxious as I was to put some distance between us. Or was he trying to provoke me further with his frustrated tone? 'Do whatever you think best,' I told him.

'I'll give him a hand and take a few photos,' Fonseca told me. His wink meant he sensed that his colleague might need some calming down.

It only occurred to me when Fonseca turned away from me that Coutinho's fabulous wealth must have set Vaz off.

After the two Forensics specialists had left for the private garage where the victim parked his car, I told Luci that – while she was out hunting for the killer's silencer – she should also see if she could turn up any men's sneakers or a pair of gloves. At the sound of the front door closing behind her, I shivered with relief.

'Pretty young women make you nervous?' David asked.

46

'Yeah. And fans of Che Guevara. At least, today – that suspect who killed himself shook me up pretty badly. But listen, David, I'd like you to talk something out with me.'

He sat down and joined his hands together in his lap, childlike eagerness in his eyes; he was relieved to be back at work – and to be anywhere at all.

'The killer must have spotted his shoeprint on the shirt,' I began, 'but he didn't make any effort to wipe it off or smudge it. He knew he could toss away his sneakers in some garbage across town and that we probably wouldn't find them. But do you think that he might have also been worried that Coutinho would fight back if he tried to take off his shirt?'

'Dying people can sometimes find extraordinary reserves of strength. Still, if the killer had just waited a few minutes, he could have taken the shirt without any struggle.'

'Except that he probably didn't want to risk hanging around. Also, it could have proved harder than he thought to watch a man choke to death.'

'True.'

'And one last thing. If the girlfriend wasn't involved, she might have been hiding in the bedroom the whole time that Coutinho was fighting to stay alive. In that case, after the killer left, she must have slipped out through the front door. And probably re-locked it. Which would mean that the killer didn't have to have the key, like I'd first thought.'

'You'll have to find her to know for sure,' David observed.

'She might even have caught a glimpse of who killed her boyfriend,' I suggested.

'Or at least heard the man's voice.' David glanced down at the body, and I sensed he was thinking about his own near escape from death. At length, he said, 'Which would also mean she might have been able to save the poor slob's life – if she'd called 112.'

'She'd have been scared shitless with the killer still in the house.'

47

'But what about afterwards?' His troubled expression told me he wasn't willing to let her off the hook so easily.

He stood up and reached again for his aching back. 'She'll be desperate to keep her love affair a secret.' He placed his hand against my chest and gave a little push, as though to make me stand firm. 'Which means, my boy, that she's going to do everything she can to prevent you from finding her.'

Coutinho's dining area was on the ground floor. In the middle of the room was a rectangular mahogany table, large enough to seat twenty. At each end stood a massive, waist-high silver candlestick with sinuous arms and ornamented at the base with scrolled acanthus leaves. Were they from the same church as the kitchen tiles? I was beginning to think that Coutinho had bought an entire Portuguese village.

The door at the back led to the garden, where a thirty-foot-high feathery palm stood guard over a circular wooden deck. In the centre of the scruffy lawn to the side of the deck was a small fishpond, and at the water's edge stood a proud-looking bronze heron with a minnow raised high in its beak. Behind the lawn, summer had transformed the ancient bougainvillea climbing over the entire length of the back wall into a cascade of ruby petals. Around the base of its gnarled trunk spread a thick jumble of agapanthus spraying their effusive blue pompoms into the air.

I felt the quiet, invisible need for sunlight hiding under all that green. And with it, I sensed my own desire to hold onto the good life I had made for myself.

Gazing over the back wall, I noticed that one of the neighbouring houses was topped by a stained-glass skylight with two of its panes missing. Most of the tile roof had caved in as well.

On returning to the library, I studied the pictures of the victim's wife and kid. There was one of Coutinho with his arms around his daughter – nuzzling into her neck and tickling her; it softened my opinion of him. Sandi must have been eight or nine years old in the picture, and she was squirming with joyful delight.

In the largest photo, set in a gold frame, the girl's face was more adult and expressive. She was holding a schoolbook to the camera like a shield, and though she was eyeing the lens as though to appear threatening, she was also about to burst out laughing. Her mom rested her head on the girl's shoulder and was staring pensively at the lens, and intimately, as well – with the ease of showing one's true self that comes from great love, it seemed to me. My guess was that Coutinho had blown this one up because of what her devotion meant to him – and maybe, too, because it showed that Sandi was growing up.

Next door, in the master bedroom, a large painting of a powerful centaur – swiftly executed with Coutinho's slashing brushstrokes – hung above the bed. The centaur's sleek, vigorous body was black, and his human eyes – the blue of a medieval fresco – were keenly intelligent and strangely wary. *I am watching you*, the mythical creature seemed to be saying. Perhaps Coutinho had painted it as a warning to his wife.

I headed to the top floor of the house, where Sandra had her bedroom. The hallway was stiflingly hot and smelled of overheated dust.

The parquet floor of her room was a minefield of scattered books and CDs. Yet the bed had been made military-school perfect. I suspected that her parents had struck a bargain with her: if she straightened her bed every day, they'd forbid Senhora Grimault from setting foot inside. My wife and I had made a similar accord with our eldest son, Nati.

As I raised the blinds, the slanting light caught the parquet and climbed over the girl's yellow bedspread towards her matching pillows. The walls and ceiling had been painted black, which seemed a strange choice, but also perfectly in keeping with the poster of a teenage vampire prowling the wall above her desk. He was slavering blood and trying his best to appear sinister, but his film-star pose

49

and Hollywood-perfect hair made his effort seem pointless. A well-worn Persian rug patterned with blue and gold arabesques led from the bed to the dresser, which was a simple, utilitarian design. Above the dresser was a Mexican mirror, with masked Carnival figures – in highly worked silver – prancing around the frame.

Stuffed animals and dolls were propped on the girl's bed: fourteen stuffed bears, four cats, three Barbies, a Spider-Man action figure and a big-bellied panda with oversized blue eyes. Those gigantic eyes – and her father's fondness for Japanese culture – made me think the design had originated in a Japanese cartoon. I'd have wagered that her dad had bought it for her.

Beside the bed, seven pairs of colourful sneakers, from midnight blue through electric pink, hung on nails hammered into the wall. A lime-green pair with golden laces was my favourite. Sandra must have liked standing out. I admired her courage.

On a wooden shelf leading from her desk towards the back wall were about 200 CDs, most of them American and English rock. A small glass table below her window was reserved for photos of Nero. He was grey and bouncy-looking. His long pink tongue seemed always to be hanging out.

Sandra had a teenage vampire novel called *Queimada – Burnt* – on her night table, along with three CDs: *Day & Age* by The Killers, *Lungs* by Florence + the Machine and *Let England Shake*, by P J Harvey. I'd heard of Harvey but not the others. Sandra's alarm clock doubled as a CD player. It was 11.47 a.m.

Struck by the notion that something was missing, I turned in a circle. A dark stain on the belly of her stuffed bear's belly drew my attention. As I touched it, I sensed someone approaching me from behind. Before I could turn, a blow caught me at the back of my head.

I found myself looking down at my fists, unsure of where I was. My heart was racing and my lips were dry. I was sweating as though I'd made a dash for safety. My mouth tasted of tobacco.

My writing pad was on the floor near my feet. I was seated on Sandra's bed. Her alarm clock read 12.19. I'd lost just over half an hour.

Only a few moments earlier, I seemed to have taken hold of my brother's wrist to keep him from falling; we'd been standing on the roof of our home in Colorado.

Closing my eyes, I became certain that the house in my dream wasn't just in my memory but was a design *of* my memory. The roof and all the rooms below – my bedroom and closet, most of all – were where everything I'd ever experienced was stored. By going up to the roof and taking my brother with me, I was trying to locate events I'd long forgotten – hoping, it now seemed to me, to find moments from the past that would help me solve this case.

As I stood up, I caught sight of the ink on my left hand. Running across my palm and along my thumb was a message from Gabriel: *H: bad memories under girl's bed. Painting by Almeida in the wrong place. Sneak a peek at the French–Farsi dictionary. Why doesn't Sandi display any photos of herself?*

Under the last line, Gabriel had drawn crossed arrows, an indication that he wanted me again – and soon.

Chapter 5

I first received a message on the palm of my left hand when I was eight years old. It was written in blue ink, in crooked, ant-sized letters. I read it while seated on the floral-patterned couch on our wooden porch. The handwriting didn't look like my mom's or mine. The message said: *H – Your dad will want to test you and Ernie on Friday. So after school, take Ernie away from the house and don't return until after dark.*

Who could have written it? And how had it been scribbled on my hand without my being aware of it?

Figuring that the writing could get me into trouble with my father, I ran to the rusty faucet at the back of our house and scrubbed it off.

Bigger kids had told me stories of haunted houses by then, and while I was examining the residue of ink on my palm that night – shining my flashlight on it while sitting up under my bed sheet – I came to the conclusion that a ghost had gotten in touch with me. That notion didn't scare me; the message had been meant to keep me safe, I concluded, and the idea that someone from beyond the grave was watching me made me tingle in that way kids do when they're embarking on a big – and potentially dangerous – adventure. I started to call him the Spectre because Dad had given me his old comic book collection, and there were several featuring that ghostly superhero.

I don't know how I formed my ideas about the Spectre,

but I came to believe that he was an adult who'd lost his battle with a fatal illness a few years earlier. I decided that he'd been forty-seven years old at the time of his death and had grown up a few miles from our house, at an old abandoned shack I'd passed a hundred times, out on State Road 92.

When he was alive, the Spectre had had an understanding, world-weary face, long hair, and a jangly, tired kind of walk. He had never married or had children.

I decided that he had come back from the dead to help me.

Just before I got his first message, I'd been watching my father yell at Ernie for peeing on his favourite armchair while napping. My brother was four years old then, and Dad's shouting started him bawling. My heart was drumming because I knew that our father would grab him and shake him until he shut up, and my brother's body would go all limp, and his eyes would become dull, almost dead. Then the writing appeared on my hand, and I was no longer in the living room. I was seated outside. I felt split in half – as if I were in two places at once.

After I washed off the message, I found Ernie in the room we shared, under his covers, snoozing away on his belly.

The Spectre's suggestion made good sense to me, so, on Friday, right after I got home from school, I went to my parents' bedroom and told Mom I was taking Ernie to a friend's birthday party. She lowered the wings of her paperback novel and told me, 'Do whatever you think best, honey.'

Now, thirty-four years later, it struck me as odd that Mom would trust me to take Ernie out with me all afternoon and evening, since I was just eight years old. But at the time it seemed normal; my mother hardly ever got dressed by then. During the day, when Dad was at the sawmill, she took lots of naps, nesting tight in her blankets, or read a book, though once in a while, when I'd go into her room and sing for her, or dance around to make her laugh, she'd find the energy to slip on some jeans and a blouse, go down to the kitchen and bake me and Ernie a pie or go with us for a walk outside.

Occasionally, the three of us would pick flowers together. Mom told me once that wildflowers were the sun's way of getting to know the earth. I loved to hear her say amazing things like that in her Portuguese accent.

After she died, I discovered Mom's stash of medications in a box behind her old coats in her walk-in closet, and I realized that she'd been taking huge doses of Valium, and that Dad had been picking up the pills for her at Morton's Drugstore in Gunnison, because the name and address of that pharmacy were on the label. And I realized, too, that she must have known that I looked through her night-table drawer sometimes, or else she'd have kept the pills there.

Mom had stopped driving by then. Dad must've liked her better as a stay-at-home zombie.

The topmost layer of Mom's night-table drawer was her first-aid station. It contained Bayer children's aspirin, gauze pads, mercurochrome, Polysporin ointment and lots of other useful things. Under all that were splashy brochures for cruises around Europe and her books of poetry. And also a deck of cards with pictures on the back of Lisbon's landmarks, like the Belém Tower and Jerónimos Monastery.

After my brother and I moved to Portugal, I discovered her beat-up old copy of Pablo Neruda's *Twenty Love Poems* in a box that Ernie had packed, and I discovered that she had underlined these lines:

I will bring you happy flowers from the mountains, bluebells, dark hazels, and rustic baskets of kisses.
I want to do with you what spring does with the cherry trees.

Reading that verse in Mom's book, I turned to ice, because I remembered my dad telling me, 'I'm going to do to Ernie what the Colorado winter does to our apple trees,' and I realized more clearly than ever before that he'd had a gift for recognizing what was most beautiful in the world and destroying it.

At the very bottom of Mom's night-table drawer was a

brown envelope containing pictures of her parents and older sister, Olivia, who lived back home in Portugal. The one I liked best showed the two sisters at the beach at Caparica when Mom was twelve and Aunt Olivia nineteen. They're each holding up a ping-pong racket and grinning. I keep that picture in my wallet. I like having the two sisters with me wherever I go.

After Mom died, Dad used to take me and Ernie on trips all over Colorado and New Mexico. We saw a golden eagle nest in Rocky Mountain National Park and stayed the weekend at a motel in Santa Fe that had deer antlers over the reception desk. He even let us share his bed on most nights, Ernie on one side of him and me on the other, and he'd keep his hand atop my head all night, because I'd decided I couldn't sleep if he wasn't exactly where he was supposed to be.

Maybe everything I've done in my life has its origin in my father's complexity. And maybe every case I've investigated has been one more opportunity to solve the mystery forever staring at me with his suspicious brown eyes – which are also my eyes, for better or for worse. Do we all lead the lives we lead because we have to know why things happened the way they did, and if there had been any other way they could have combined together to produce something more gentle and meaningful and permanent?

I have two photos of my mother from 1980. I know I took them that summer, because Dad bought me a Canon camera at the end of the school year. Mom looks all used up in them, as if she'd been on an uphill climb for so long that she was too exhausted to go on, though she was only thirty-eight years old at the time – still young, though her eyes are bruised-looking and her hair is like old frayed rope.

I don't look at those photos of her too often. They're in my night-table drawer, right at the bottom, where no one else will ever see just how dead inside she'd become.

I have no idea where the negatives are. I couldn't find them when it came time to leave for Portugal. I hope the new owners of our Colorado ranch discovered where they were and threw them out; I don't like to think of my mom's negatives stuck in a place where she was so unhappy; death should free us, if nothing else.

On the Friday after receiving the Spectre's first message, I grabbed Ernie and led him down by the stream, a quarter of a mile from our house, to a meadow where my dad and I used to practise shooting. I grabbed a blanket, too, since even though it was late May, we were at six thousand seven hundred feet and temperatures fell below freezing at night. We lived a half-mile from our nearest neighbours, a couple in their eighties named Johnson. Both Mr and Mrs Johnson were deaf, I figured at the time. Now, I realize that they must not have wanted to get mixed up in what went on at our ranch.

Ernie had an ornery, little-kid energy that could drive you crazy, since if you didn't watch him closely he might start tugging the cord of a lamp out of the socket or turn over the garbage in the kitchen. I can see now that he was just naturally curious, but at the time his actions seemed aimed at getting both of us punished by Dad.

Ernie lived on the surface of his senses as a kid. In particular, he was tuned in to the calls of birds in the morning. And to their colours. Their singing and screeching would wake him up at dawn, and he'd slide out of bed in his pyjamas and stand at our window as if he were watching Santa Claus and his reindeer prepare for their Christmas Eve adventures. Ernie had dark brown hair cut real short and big watery green eyes that were always darting around, with the long lashes that a lot of Portuguese people have. And he had a scent that was all his own, and that I loved – like warm oatmeal.

'They look to me like tiny fern fronds.'

That's what Mom used to say about Ernie's eyelashes.

When Mom complimented Ernie's looks, maybe she was also saying that there was still something special and beautiful about herself, too, even though it had become nearly impossible to see. I hope that was part of what she meant. I hope it every day of my life.

Dad must have also sensed that Ernie wasn't like everyone else. And he had to have noticed that Ernie – even as a little kid – looked a lot like Mom and almost nothing like him.

I know I disappointed my mother. That's the hardest thing of all for me to admit.

Anyway, on that Friday afternoon when the Spectre first wrote to me, I led Ernie down to our stream. He started to kick up a fuss because I hadn't remembered to bring along any food. I diverted his attention by asking him to name the wildflowers all around us. At that time of year, our meadow was like a botanical garden, and all of those yellow, purple and scarlet blossoms seemed as eager as we were to warm up in the sun after our long winter. And to be recognized for who they were.

Indian Paintbrush was Ernie's favourite flower because it had tufted scarlet blossoms that seemed to tickle your fingers when you touched them. Mom once showed us how to dry flowers in between the pages of a book, and so we sometimes used to pick Paintbrush blossoms and slip them into the American College Dictionary that she bought me for my eighth birthday. She said that Ernie and I needed to learn English perfectly if we were going to be a success in America.

She always predicted that Ernie would become a scientist. He had that sort of unstoppable, wide-eyed curiosity about simple things. I thought so too.

After an hour of leading Ernie around, I wanted to sit down and rest, but he started to bawl every time I left him alone. It was like he was battery-operated, programmed to erupt into hot tears if I didn't hold his hand.

After the sun eased down over the edge of a faraway mountain, we spotted a wild turkey – a hen – nesting beneath a big scrub oak. Her chicks were all around her, and we listened to them making those scratchy, high-pitched

57

fiddle sounds they made when they wanted to let their mother know just where they were.

When we finally got home, I was so pooped I could hardly stand. It was just after nine p.m. Dad was passed out on the couch in our living room. He reeked of tequila and cigars, and he'd taken off his shirt and trousers, but was still in his underwear and Milwaukee Braves baseball cap. Bessie Smith was singing on our record player in that big scratchy voice of hers. It was an old seventy-eight with a purple label.

I went to our parents' room and told Mom that Ernie was starving. She and I tiptoed into the kitchen. She opened up a can of Heinz baked beans and heated the mixture on the range with a little bit of tomato paste and water. I stood Ernie on a chair, and while he and I watched the thick liquid bubble and hiss, I whispered to Mom about the turkey family we'd seen.

Ernie and I gorged ourselves in our closet. He dug into our bowl with a soupspoon that made it only halfway to his mouth before spilling a good part of its beans on the towel I'd wrapped around his neck.

Before bed, Mom said it was good we'd gone away in the afternoon because Dad had come home real angry, and so drunk that *hardly could he keep his stability to make pee.* That was when I became certain that the Spectre had given me good advice.

Dad went out with his workmates and drank too much on the last Friday of every month; it was payday. I didn't realize that when I was little. But the Spectre knew it. That's how he was able to warn me not to be home that afternoon. He was cleverer than I was. Maybe because he was an adult.

From then on, the Spectre used to write on my hand once a week or so, mostly warnings about when Dad was sure to be so drunk that he'd get a really bad hangover. Almost right away, the Spectre started taking Dad's tests for me, too. He became much better at finding Ernie than I was. He saved my brother from getting badly hurt on a few occasions when I'd never have located him in time.

That was how I came to realize that the Spectre was a lot more efficient than anyone normally was at finding clues. He was able to decide real quickly what was significant and meaningful in a room – what had been removed or added, for instance. Dad's tests trained him for that. They made him like a blind person who hears tiny, faraway sounds that other people can't.

When I was a kid, I figured the Spectre didn't feel the emotions that living people felt. And because of that, he could focus on finding Ernie and exclude everything else. But now I know that he gets panicked. In fact, I think he knows more fear than anybody I've ever met, even my brother.

Kids don't have the experience to know what is unusual or unique, and I assumed that everyone was like me and got messages on their hand or some other part of their body. Only when I told Mom about them did I realize that I was more fortunate than other people. She said that she never got messages, and that nobody she knew ever did. She said that I ought not to tell anyone about them. It would be our secret.

O nosso segredo, she said in Portuguese, with her hand resting on top of my head, as if she were blessing me, which made it seem as if she might still care about me in her own, mostly silent way. Although if I wanted to be mean, I'd say her own *useless* way. Because she didn't defend Ernie and me enough. I try not to think about that but I do.

When I was eleven, in September of 1981, we had a guest preacher from Denver – a theology professor named Thurmond – who told us in his sermon that angels didn't really exist. He said they were metaphors for how God watched over us. The old man's words stunned me with a kind of electric jolt, because I knew instantly that he didn't know what he was talking about.

That's when I stopped calling whoever left me messages 'the Spectre'. Instead, I started calling him by an angelic name, and I chose Gabriel, though I never meant that he was the biblical archangel; I would have had to have been a lot crazier than I was to think that a powerful angel from the Bible would come down from heaven to visit us at our ranch in rural Colorado and help me take Dad's tests. No, I figured that my Gabriel was just a minor sort of angel who had only a tiny bit of God's power – not enough to save our lives.

Gabriel always calls me H in his notes to me, so I started calling him G. Before I get a message from him, I always lose track of myself. I usually disappear for between ten minutes and an hour. I never know where I go.

The notes I receive are always printed – never written in script.

At some point (I must have been twelve or thirteen), I began to figure out that G took control of my body. Though for a long time I wasn't sure of that, because I never came back to myself knowing what had happened to me. I never asked Ernie to tell me what I'd been up to, because I didn't want him to know that I hadn't been there – in my body, I mean.

My temples usually throb when he wants to take me over. But if G comes really fast, in an emergency, I get no warning – his entry feels as though I've been walloped on the back of my head.

I've known for sure that G takes control of me ever since I asked one of my police colleagues to watch me when I examined the blood-soaked clothing of a restaurant owner who'd been stabbed to death. That was sixteen years ago.

Staring at really bad bloodstains makes me vanish, though I can sometimes hold G off if I'm determined enough.

My police colleague told me I'd rushed around crime scene as if the walls of the restaurant were about to collapse on us. The few words I'd spoken to him were in English. I'd also asked him for a cigarette, and I don't smoke.

Gabriel knows Portuguese, I'm pretty sure, but he refuses to write it. He runs around a crime scene like his mind has been set on fire. Maybe because there's a countdown always nearing zero in his world.

When I was fourteen, I vanished for more than a week on two occasions. I was drinking too much at the time. In fact, I spent most of seventh and eighth grade in a beer-soaked haze. After an all-night binge in Gallup one Friday night, I went to bed in March and woke up in April. Losing ten days scared me really badly.

I came back to myself with a tattoo on my arm. I tell people it's an American eagle, and that I had it done because I was feeling patriotic. But it's a Thunderbird. My Sioux friend Nathan told me once that a great and wise Thunderbird watched over me from the spirit world, and I guess G wanted me to remember that.

Gabriel went to school for me when I disappeared for ten days. My teachers told me later that I'd been real quiet in class – and that it was a welcome surprise.

When I returned to myself, his message in my hand read: *H – take care of your body or I won't let you have it!*

I no longer drink even wine or beer. It's too big a risk. I'd never be able to look at Ana or my kids the same way if they knew about Gabriel. Because they'd never look at *me* the same way. They'd think I might be crazy and dangerous. And Ana might never want to speak to again. But even if she managed to get over her anger at me – and her fear of what was always hiding inside me – I wouldn't want to ever give G a chance to speak to her and the kids. I wouldn't want him telling them what happened to Ernie and me when we were little. Because they probably wouldn't believe him. After all, they might not even believe *me*. And if they didn't believe us, I couldn't stay married. It would be impossible for me to trust Ana ever again.

By now, I understand that G comes to me when I feel threatened or when a person I love is in danger, though sometimes he doesn't take over when I would expect him to. I guess he knows when there's nothing he can do for me.

Gabriel doesn't always share all that he's thinking with me. He's canny. And though his suspicions aren't always right, he's helped me find evidence that has put some very evil people in prison.

I don't think that G lets affection or everyday considerations get in his way. I'm pretty sure, in fact, that he'd kill the murderers, rapists and child abusers I interrogate if he were certain he could get away with it – meaning, not get me in trouble. Maybe it's because I'm sure that he remembers a lot more about what happened to us in Colorado than I do. In fact, I think Dad is still alive wherever G lives. That can't be very good for his peace of mind. Though maybe he also gets a chance to see Dad dance a tango with Ernie in his arms from time to time. Or teach him the melody of a Patsy Cline song. I'd like to see those things myself – to be there for the good times. I'd like that a lot.

Just before I got married, I went to the Psychology Department Library at the University of Lisbon and consulted *The Diagnostic and Statistical Manual of Mental Disorders*. In it, I learned that identity isn't always fixed in individuals who've been terrorized as kids. They can develop one or more separate identities that are better able to cope with unbearable situations.

Two sentences in that book gave me my first-ever panic attack. I don't know exactly what they said because I never dared read them again, but they went something like this: *Those with Dissociative Identity Disorder tend to have at least one personality who believes that he or she is bad and deserves to be punished – even beaten, brutalized or killed. Often, that is what their childhood abusers have told them.*

After I read that, I couldn't get enough air, and when a sharp pain cut through my chest, I figured I was having a heart attack. I lay my head to the desk where I'd been reading and closed my eyes. I thought it would be a good thing if I died because it would save Ana from marrying someone as damaged as me.

When I felt strong enough to stand up, I walked to my car and sat inside it for a couple of hours. I realized I'd been fighting for survival since the day Ernie was born and had never stopped.

My biggest fear is that I might one day hurt my kids or Ana – hurt them in ways that can never be undone. That's why I asked my wife to learn to use a gun just after we were married. I know that sounds crazy to most people. It certainly did to her, and she refused to take any of the classes I'd signed her up for.

If I'm ever tempted to hurt Ana or the kids, I'll drive out past Évora on local road 256, to a grove of oaks and pines I've already picked out, and I'll put the barrel of my police pistol into my mouth and pull the trigger.

My second biggest fear is that I might lose my mind and not come back to myself – not ever. Which would mean I'd be dead even if I were alive, because everything that made me *me* would be gone.

I'd never see Ana, the kids or Ernie again.

After I read about myself in *The Diagnostic and Statistical Manual of Mental Disorders*, I vowed never to read another word about what was wrong with me. And never to speak about it with anyone. I hated knowing that the same capacities that saved me also tainted me in ways that doctors had classified.

I worry every day of my life that my boys have inherited bad genes from me.

People don't want to know what violent torment does to kids. They like living in a make-believe world and need to believe in happy endings. Even hospital officials who should intervene don't want to have to go through all the trouble of filling out forms and risk being threatened by an indignant parent.

When we went to the hospital after our first test, the doctor believed what Dad told him – that I was the one who'd hurt Ernie. Dad said that Ernie and I had been playing with a garden shears. 'Their roughhousing got out of hand,' he said.

When the physician looked to Mom for corroboration, she nodded. I could tell from the downward slant of her eyes that she was hoping he'd see she was lying, but he didn't. He looked down at me as if I were dirt. 'Watch yourself, young man!' he snarled, a finger of warning pointing at me. 'Because I swear on the Good Book that if this ever happens again, I'll make sure you wind up in a juvenile prison for a real long time!'

'You hear that, Hank!' Dad told me, as if he'd tried endless times to teach me to be kind to my little brother. 'Next time, there'll be nothing I can do to save you.'

My reading at the Psychology Library in Lisbon made me realize, too, that Gabriel probably wasn't an angel or even a ghost. Unless, of course, you define *angel* as a part of you that looks after all the other parts, and who guards everyone you love. And who has experienced such terrible things that he can never be entirely at ease, either in his world or ours.

Chapter 6

Every murder is a failure – to forgive, to understand, to find justice any other way. To find a doorway out.

So what particular failure lay soaking in the blood of Coutinho's carpet?

The most likely possibility was that one of his friends or acquaintances hadn't been able to convince him to give up his affair with his wife or girlfriend.

What told me most about the killer was the gag, which implied that he and I shared a particularly fear – of another man's voice. And what he might order us to do.

In the living room, I discovered that Gabriel had taken down all the paintings from the walls. David was still examining the victim. I asked him to make arrangements for the body to be taken away; Coutinho's wife and daughter would be arriving soon, and I didn't want them to see him lying in a pool of his own blood. Later, I realized it was a sign of how badly Moura's suicide had unnerved me that I didn't realize that Susana might have preferred to see her husband at their home rather than at the morgue.

H: bad memories under girl's bed. Painting by Almeida in the wrong place. Sneak a peek at the French–Farsi dictionary. Why doesn't Sandi display any photos of herself?

Reading Gabriel's message again made me realize that I'd expected to see pictures of Sandi in her bedroom because both my sons had dozens of photographs of themselves and their school friends tacked to their corkboards.

After moistening my handkerchief at the kitchen sink and rubbing the ink off my palm, I found Fonseca dusting for fingerprints on the handle of the door leading to the garden. 'Want another cigarette?' he asked hopefully, pleased to have a partner in crime.

'No, thanks,' I replied, wishing there was a way to prevent G from smoking – and from talking to my colleagues.

I stepped outside into the sun, because the heat soaking into me would help me re-enter my body. When I felt up to a conversation, I asked Fonseca to finish up and get back to the lab, so he could start testing the evidence he'd already collected. I also told him to seal off the library; that was where Coutinho had been just before his murder and I didn't want anyone going in there, not even Senhora Coutinho.

'But Vaz is already back at the lab,' he told me in a puzzled voice. 'He did tell you he was going, didn't he?'

Lying seemed my safest option. 'He whispered something to me while I was talking on the phone to headquarters, but I didn't pay much attention to what he was saying. I guess this murder has me a bit distracted.'

'It's all the blood. You know how you get when there's a lot.' Pulling away the transparent tape he'd pressed to the doorknob, he lifted off a jumble of fingerprints. 'I love my work!' he said, beaming.

When I didn't return his smile, he asked, 'Is it just this case that's got you so upset?'

I told him about Moura's suicide. In an off-key tenor, and with thick Portuguese accent, he sang, *'Mama said there'll be days like this.'*

'The Shirelles, 1961,' I told him.

'How the hell do you know so much about old American songs and forget so many conversations?' he asked.

'You're the star of Forensics, you figure it out!'

Fonseca's appreciative laughter made me feel a bit safer.

Luci joined us. 'No sneakers or gloves, and no homemade silencers,' she told me with a disappointed shrug. Grime blackened her cheek and she was sweating badly.

66

I suggested she take a break but she insisted on helping me hang the paintings back on the wall. Sure enough – just as G had implied in his message – the frame around the Almeida drawing was too small to have created the square of unbleached yellow paint on the wall behind it. A slightly larger work had been here. Had the Almeida been moved by the murderer to substitute a painting he'd stolen? We searched in vain around the room for the nail on which it might have hung.

G must have looked through the French–Farsi dictionary and spotted something he needed me to see, so we headed next to the library. On flipping through the book, I discovered a cubbyhole hollowed out between pages 302 and 457. Hidden snugly inside was a flash drive the size of a small lighter. I held it up for Luci. 'Coutinho must have been looking at some files when he heard noises downstairs,' I said. 'He took it out and put it back in its cubby hole, but he didn't want to take the time to carry a chair over to the shelves so he could slip the dictionary back into its spot on the top shelf.'

I stood on the chair so I could reach into the space on the top shelf where it had been kept, but I ended up only with dusty fingertips. I handed Luci Coutinho's keys. 'Lock the door from the inside and then open it again. Let's see how well sound carries in here.'

After about thirty seconds, the tumblers clicked around. Luci bounded up the stairs and smiled girlishly on re-entering the library. Her enthusiasm charmed me; I realized she probably even enjoyed looking through the trash cans. 'Well?' she asked eagerly.

'Coutinho would have heard the key turning in the lock,' I told her.

'So he probably assumed his lover had returned – that she'd forgotten something. Or maybe they'd planned for her to come back all along.'

'If not, he might have figured that his wife and daughter had come home unexpectedly.'

'And if he'd been looking at files,' she speculated, 'then the laptop might have still been on when he went downstairs to see who'd just arrived.'

'Luci, for the moment, I don't want you to mention to anyone that we've found the victim's flash drive,' I told her, eager for a chance to search its files before handing it over to Forensics. I put it in an evidence bag and stashed it in my coat pocket.

I called Joaquim, our computer wiz, and he confirmed that the MacBook Air's battery had run down to zero by the time it reached him. He agreed to take a look this weekend.

Back downstairs, I told Fonseca to dust the Almeida painting for fingerprints and then hang it back on the wall.

'You don't want me to bring it back to the lab?' he asked, surprised.

'Not yet. I may need it to jog Senhora Coutinho's memory.'

I then handed him Coutinho's French–Farsi dictionary and told him to bag it as evidence, explaining that I'd kept a flash drive I'd found in a cubbyhole cut in its pages. 'I'll be going through its contents over the weekend and give it to you on Monday,' I added.

Turning to Luci, I said, 'And now you and I need to search the daughter's room.'

'And then?' she asked.

'Then we'll question all of Coutinho's neighbours. After that, lunch.'

'Lunch? By then, it'll be dark!' she said, laughing.

Her eyes took on a handsome depth. She must have dreamt about detective work since she was a kid; I recognized the symptoms. And beating underneath that realization was another that was far more important for me: I worked more trustingly with a female inspector.

On reaching Sandi's room, I took the panda off her pillow and handed it to Luci. 'There's a stain that's probably blood. Give it to Fonseca when you see him.'

'But the daughter was in the Algarve when her father was killed. I can't see what—'

'Indulge me,' I interrupted. I dropped down on the bed. 'Now, tell me what you've heard about my methods.'

'Just that you sometimes get into a kind of frenzy, sir.'

'What else?' I smiled to put her at ease.

'The men say that you race around the crime scene. You don't usually say anything, but if you do, you can be pretty rude.'

'Anything more?'

She bit her lip. 'Go ahead,' I told her, 'I won't be offended.'

'That you . . . you kind of hear voices telling you what to do – what to look for.'

'No, Luci, that's not true. And I don't see the dead either.' *Though I wish I did*, I added to myself. 'Now please get out your notepad and take notes about what I do.'

Lowering my head between my legs, I snuck an upside-down peek under the bed. A nest of clothes sat in the middle of the floor. Kneeling, I pulled it out. A lump in the leg of a pair of jeans caught my attention – panties stained with blood. I dropped them on the night table for safekeeping.

In the pocket of the jeans was a small flashlight.

The wooden platform on which the mattress rested was too low to the ground for me to slide under, but by lying down, I managed to squeeze my head a little way in. My flashlight beam revealed something metallic and shiny taped under the bed, and then my head began to pound, and a familiar hand was pulling me away . . .

Luci was seated beside me on the grass of the garden, gazing over the back wall at the neighbour's house. My heart was racing, and yet the world was revolving slowly around me, as though I were at the centre of a turntable. It was a disorienting sensation that often came to me in the *after-time*, as I called it. I wiped away the ticklish sweat on my brow. Looking up, I discovered I was seated in the shade of the palm.

Luci saw me stir and began to speak, but I gestured for her to wait; my voice would take a minute or two to return.

I gripped my revolver, craving the compact, tight, hard-edged confidence it gave me. I lay back and closed my eyes. Tears came, but I didn't know why. Exhaustion has its own reasoning.

When I sat up, it was into the embrace of the sadness that sometimes awaited me after Gabriel's departure. It was heavy with all that could never now come to pass – most of all, my mother getting to know me as a man. Out of habit, I searched out the most beautiful thing in my vicinity – the ruby-red bougainvillea climbing over the back wall. Closing my eyes, I imagined it ageing, as if in a high-speed film, starting as a sun-charmed thread poking out of the moist winter soil, slithering into the air, jumping and twisting like a magic lasso, leaping over the hot dark stone, unfurling and twisting, shimmering with a desire for more life.

When I got to my feet, I downed one of the emergency tranquillizers I kept in my wallet and put my gun back in its holster. 'How long was I gone?' I asked.

She looked at her watch. 'Thirty-one minutes.'

I opened my left hand and read, *H – Ask Ernie about the knife. And don't let the dead make you forget the living!*

'Did I find a knife?' I asked Luci.

'Yes.' She held up an evidence bag. The blade was about five inches long. The handle was black. 'It was taped to the bottom of the girl's bed,' she added.

Apparently, Sandra had needed to be able to grab it in a hurry. Which meant that whoever was hurting her could enter her room whenever he or she wanted. Maybe the same man or woman who'd killed her father had been her tormentor.

Luci handed me the evidence bag. The blade looked to be made of stainless steel. Tilting it, a glittering reflection gazed back at me with the searching eye of the boy I'd been. He was stunned – but very pleased, as well – by how something so dangerous could fit so perfectly into his hand.

Chapter 7

Inside the second evidence bag that Luci handed me was a slender stick with a small wooden egg fitted on the end. 'What do you think it is, sir?' she asked.

'It's a honey dripper,' I replied in English, since I didn't know the translation, but I explained in Portuguese what it was for. 'Where did I find it?' I asked.

'It was tucked into a corner of the daughter's bed sheets.'

'Anything else?' I asked.

'In the bottom drawer of her desk, you also turned up three old bread rolls – black with mould and really smelly.' She held her nose for comic effect. 'You opened a window and hurled them out.'

'That's it?'

'It was all you *handed to me*, sir,' she said, emphasizing the difference of meaning.

'Did I take something for myself?' I asked, cringing inside, hoping that G had pilfered only a bit of chocolate; apparently, it was in short supply wherever he lived.

'You snatched something up from beneath the girl's mattress,' Luci answered. 'You slipped it in your left front pocket.'

We were still seated in the victim's garden, in the shade of the palm, and I emptied my pocket on the grass. A woman's ring tumbled out – a small round turquoise set in a silver band. It sat in my hand like a bad omen; it seemed to me that Sandra would only have hidden it if someone had threatened to take it from her – or had previously taken other valuables.

On my request, Luci brought me a glass of water. Thankfully, she made no attempt to question me as I gulped it down. I imagined she'd learned discretion very young, but perhaps that was simply the shape of my greatest wish at the moment. I asked if I'd told her anything about taking the ring.

'No, but when you put it in your pocket, you grinned at me, like it was a game.'

G had been testing her, hoping she'd react badly to his theft, eager to prove to me that I ought not to confide in her. To him, all adults were potential enemies.

'Did I speak to you at all?' I asked.

'When you were searching frantically through the girl's room and I asked if you needed help, you told me to *put a lid on it*. You said that in English, sir.'

'I'm sorry I was rude to you. And when did I write on my hand?'

'Later, in the garden, while you were smoking.' She knelt by me. 'May I speak freely sir?' she asked, and when I gave my agreement, she said, 'For how long have you had these . . . episodes?'

'Since I was a kid. Now read me your notes about exactly what I did.'

'I'd like to say something first.' She started to speak, then cut herself off and shook her head in self-reproach. She gazed off in search of the words she wanted, holding up her hand to prevent me from interrupting, which seemed a very mature gesture for so young a woman.

Waves of heat floated up from the deck, as though trying to keep me at the centre of a world of secrets. Strange ideas often came to me in the after-time, and I realized – with a sense of having been cheated – that I'd never be a young woman like Luci.

'Sir . . .' she said, to bring me back to her.

'Yes, what is it?'

'You know, you're nothing like the men said you were.' She smiled to let me know she was relieved.

'How so?'

'They made you sound difficult and . . . tainted. But you opened my eyes just now, to something I never thought about.'

'What was that, Luci?'

'How far I'd go to help people who needed me. People I'd never even met.'

Some moments of understanding seem to come from very far off, as if they have been journeying for years to reach us. One alighted inside me then: Luci was willing to look under my surface to what lay concealed below.

I started rubbing G's writing off my hand to keep her from noticing how deeply she'd touched me. 'And how far would you go?' I asked.

'I'd like to think I'd risk as much as you did just now.'

Relying on professional decorum to hide my mixed feelings about finally being understood by a colleague, I said, 'Thank you, Luci, but now I need to hear your notes.'

'Just one last thing, sir. I know about the disorder you have. My university degree is in psychology, and I—'

'Luci, stop! You've said a beautiful thing. It would be a shame to ruin it.' I spoke harshly in the hopes of avoiding a quarrel.

'But if you'll let me finish, then—'

'No, please don't, just read me your notes,' I cut in. 'And whatever you do, don't ever say anything about this to anyone. Or . . . or we could never work together again.'

Her hurt feelings gave a clipped preciseness to her voice as she told me about how I'd tossed CDs and books from the girl's shelves onto the floor, hurled away blankets and sheets and tugged off the mattress. In the master bedroom, I'd created a similar mess.

'And after you were done there,' she added, her voice gaining intensity, 'you rushed into the kitchen and snooped around in the cupboards and came up with a bar of

73

chocolate. Forgive me for saying so, sir, but you ate it like a starving dog.'

My face must have revealed some of the shame twisting my gut, because she said, 'No, you intended it to be comic. You were performing for me.' She laughed sweetly, pleased by having been able to recognize the disguised clowning of her boss – if that was what it had been.

'After the chocolate,' she continued, 'you poured yourself a glass of milk and took a sip,' she continued, 'but you didn't like it. You spat it into the sink.' She grimaced. 'It was that chalky-tasting, super-pasteurized stuff.'

'And then?'

She read from her notepad: 'You searched through the bathrooms and the library, and the small storeroom on the top floor. And after that, you asked Fonseca for a cigarette and went outside to the deck to smoke.' She looked up at me, and her face was lit with astonishment. 'I don't believe I've ever seen anyone enjoy smoking so much, sir. Also, you stared at me for a while with an expression that's hard to describe.'

'Distanced amusement,' I suggested; it was a look that G specialized in, I'd learned from those who'd taken offence at his behaviour in the past.

'That seems about right. And then you asked if I was new to the force. I told you I was, and you said, "Good luck, Luci." Which was odd. Because I hadn't told you my name and you claimed at first not to have any idea who I was.'

'I was testing you,' I told her; I seemed to owe her at least a small explanation.

'For what reason?'

'I think you said it yourself – to see how far you'd go to be of assistance.'

She considered that possibility. 'Maybe that's right, sir. Because after you finished writing on your hand, you added, "We're grateful to you," and I asked you who *we* was, and you said, "Hank and I." Then, you took two last puffs on your cigarette and stubbed it out. And you asked if I liked Lisbon.'

'What did you say?'

'That I did. And I asked you the same thing. You smiled. A beautiful smile, sir. And you said, "It was hard to be here at first, Luci – very hard. But I've grown to like it – maybe even love it. Because Hank does."' And then your eyes rolled back in your head and you leaned over, like . . . like a puppet that no longer has any fingers holding up its head and arms. You stayed that way for a few seconds, and then you slowly raised yourself up. And you were you again.' Tilting her head, she added, 'Are you really all right, sir?'

'Yes, fine. You did very well, Luci, but now we need to get back to work. And remember to keep all this to yourself. It's very important.'

I took a few minutes off to straighten up the bedrooms upstairs, then helped Luci hunt around the living room and kitchen for any additional clues the killer might have left behind. While we worked, she gazed at me from time to time, anxious for an affirmation of the solidarity we'd achieved. It made me wary. Still, I nodded towards her whenever I noticed her staring, and that small acknowledgement seemed to be enough for her.

The other inspector on my team, Manuel Quintela, soon arrived, and I led him outside to question Coutinho's neighbours. Manuel was a lanky young man, hardworking and bright, but unable to keep his youthful eagerness out of his expressive hands and voice, which often irritated his colleagues, since nearly all cops – at least, in my experience – liked to regard themselves as world-weary pros. He took the top half of the street; Luci and I covered the bottom. We soon discovered that the artist who'd sketched the portrait of Fernando Pessoa hanging in Coutinho's living room – Julio Almeida – lived just down the block with his wife, Carlota. After I'd explained what had happened to their neighbour, Almeida told me that Coutinho had recognized him at a nearby café about six months before and come to his house a few weeks later for tea, and that he'd asked to see some recent drawings. He'd ended up buying the small portrait of Pessoa. Almeida had no idea where it had hung in the victim's home. Coutinho had told him that he felt most himself when painting with Japanese brushes. He'd added that he wanted to have Almeida and his wife over for dinner, but he'd never called. Before I left, Carlota mentioned that the building under construction near the bottom end of the street – covered with scaffolding – had been abandoned for more than a decade.

Over the next two hours, we discovered that none of Coutinho's neighbours on the Rua do Vale had heard a gunshot or seen anyone leaving or entering his house over the last two days. It was nearly four o'clock by then, and the Valium and heat had made me feel as though I were trudging across miles of sand dunes. I told Luci she had forty-five minutes to get a bite to eat and asked Quintela to return to headquarters, write up our preliminary report about the murder, and get it over to the Prosecutor's Office. I also told him to call Coutinho's office and get a list of all his employees' names in Lisbon and their phone numbers.

As soon as they'd left, I headed off without a destination in mind, craving a few minutes of purposelessness. I ended up sitting on a bench in front of the National Assembly, under a mammoth tree – was it a beech? – that must have sprouted almost a hundred years earlier, into the city of horse carriages and sailing ships that Fernando Pessoa must have known in the 1920s. Could the intersections of our lives be predicted? Would what I learned about Coutinho's murder today give shade to someone fifty years from now, or create more suffering?

I leaned back on my worm-eaten green bench and took off my shoes and socks. My only neighbour – lying on another of the benches – was a homeless man, bearded and shirtless, with filthy, swollen, doughy hands, like potatoes just pulled from the soil. He was snoozing with his head on an overstuffed Lufthansa bag. I played my high-speed game with him, living out his life, from newborn to death, in just a few seconds.

When I turned my phone back on, two SMSs lit up, the first from my wife: *Drink!* she wrote, since I became dehydrated when I was upset and often ended up with a sore throat. The other was from Ernie: *Dreamed of you last night.*

Eased by their concern, I closed my eyes to better feel the breeze playing over my hair and shoulders. The Valium had left me nearly weightless by then, and as I listened to the cars zooming past, Ernie gazed down at me from high up in a cottonwood tree, grinning because he had reached the topmost branch before me. I gave him the thumbs-up sign until fear leapt inside my chest. 'You might fall!' I shouted. 'Don't move!'

As though he hadn't heard me, he waved, and, through an alchemy beyond the laws of waking reality, the back and forth movement of his hand became the ringing of my cell phone. It was Fonseca. He told me that Susana and Sandra Coutinho had arrived at their home, and that he'd already obtained a full set of their fingerprints.

Chapter 8

Susana Coutinho stood in the kitchen, leaning back against the refrigerator, barefoot, holding a glass of whisky with ice up to her temple. A nearly full bottle of Glenlivet was sitting on the table by the last quarter of Senhora Grimault's sponge cake. I introduced Luci and myself, but when I reached out my hand, but she made no move to shake it.

'Tell me where your aspirin is and I'll get you some,' I said.

'Thanks, I just took three,' she replied in a hoarse voice. She smiled good-naturedly – a very generous gesture under the circumstances – then stepped to the back window and gazed out while standing on her tiptoes. She was blonde and tan – the colour of cinnamon. 'Just checking on our dog,' she told me. 'We only stopped once for him on the car ride up. Poor thing got frantic.'

She wore three golden bangles around her left ankle and a fourth – encrusted with red and yellow gemstones – on her right; India must have been in fashion among the Portuguese jet-set. A grass stain by the back pocket of her shorts convinced me that she'd grabbed the clothes she'd last worn before driving up to Lisbon. When she turned back to me, it was with a pained expression. 'I'm sorry, but if my headache gets any worse, I'm going to have to lie down.'

Her eyes were silver-green, and they had that lost, weary, impoverished look I nearly always saw in the wives and husbands of murder victims. Either she hadn't been involved in Coutinho's death, or she was a standout actress.

She grabbed a pack of Marlboro Lights from a small leather bag dangling from the back of one of the kitchen chairs and lit a cigarette with abrupt gestures. Her cheeks hollowed out dangerously when she drew in on the smoke. After giving her my condolences, I asked where her daughter was.

'Last I heard, she was upstairs in her room,' she replied, with a caustic indifference that seemed to imply they'd quarrelled. She swept her uncombed hair off her neck with an irritated hand. Her fingernails were long and scarlet.

Anxious to get the worst question out of the way first, I asked where she had spent the day before. Annoyance twisted her lips, which were cracked and dry, and naked-looking, as though needing lipstick. 'You don't have any idea who killed my husband, do you?' she asked, targeting me with a peeved squint.

And just like that, all the goodwill I'd felt from her was gone.

'We've collected a great deal of evidence,' I said, choosing my words cautiously, so as not to set her off, 'but as of yet, we haven't any firm leads.'

She seemed to take my precise tone as an indication that I was withholding information. 'My husband was friends with the Minister of Justice!' she warned me. '*Very* good friends!'

I kept the harsh replies I thought of to myself, since I saw no point in quarrelling. Also, there was a slim possibility that she meant she could get me extra troops if I needed them, though I had no way of confirming that from her expression; she was looking at the slender collar of her pale-blue blouse and fiddling with a loose button.

'If talking to the minister will reassure you,' I told her, 'then you—'

Ripping away her button, she threw it against the wall. It ricocheted to the ground and tap-danced across the floor.

'I know I'm intruding,' I said, 'but if we don't get this over now, I'll have to come back tomorrow.'

'Great idea, come back tomorrow!'

'If I do, you won't be able to stay here today or tonight. This is a crime scene.'

'You think you can kick me out of my own house?' she said with huffing outrage.

'Senhora Coutinho, that is exactly what I'm trying to avoid,' I assured her.

Her contemptuous laugh opened an ache in my gut, and I took a step back from her in my mind. 'If you want,' I said, careful to keep my true feelings out of my voice, 'call the minister and tell him you don't want me here.'

I offered her my phone, but she turned it down and showed me a withering look.

'If you'll sit down and answer my questions,' I continued, 'I promise to try to get this over with quickly.'

Pushing past me, she retrieved a black glass ashtray from the counter, stubbed out her cigarette vengefully and sat down at the kitchen table. She showed Luci and me a bored look. We sat down opposite her.

Sprinklers was what Fonseca and I called the victims' wives who sobbed through their first interrogation in order to convince us they were innocent. Senhora Coutinho was what we referred to as a *dry well*.

After lighting another cigarette, she took too quick a gulp of whisky and had a coughing fit. Watching her struggle for breath, I realized she'd get soused today and pass out in bed, probably under the belief that her loss would seem slightly less horrific in the morning. When I repeated my previous question, she replied, 'I was at our beach house. Sandi, our daughter, can vouch for that. And we also had a house guest – an old buddy of Pedro's from Paris – Jean Morel. We spent the day together.'

I asked for his number and she gave it to me without consulting her phone, adding in an annoyed tone, 'That's right, Inspector, I know Jean's number by heart!'

'Which means exactly what?' I asked, though I'd already caught the general design of the garden of earthly delights she was about to describe to me.

'My husband knew all about Jean and me,' she snapped, 'so you can spare me your show of moral indignation.'

'I'm rarely sufficiently sure of myself to be morally indignant about anything,' I said, hoping I might win back her good graces.

As though she hadn't heard me, she said, 'Pedro and I haven't been intimate in years. And he liked Jean. They're old friends . . . *were* old friends.'

She'd obviously needed to make that point right away, which gave me the idea that – despite her seeming ease – the angles of their triangle might have been painfully sharp on occasion. 'And when did Mr Morel get to Portugal?' I asked.

'A week ago.'

'Was he in Lisbon yesterday?'

She rolled her eyes at my implication. 'Jean is a furry little lamb. Besides, he flew off yesterday to Paris.'

This time she read my mind correctly and added, 'His flight left from Faro, Inspector, *not* Lisbon.'

'Does he smoke?' I asked.

'Yes, but as far as I know, that isn't yet considered a felony.' She took a long, defiant drag on her cigarette to emphasize her point. She had powerful lungs.

'Does he smoke Gauloise Blonde?' I asked.

She flinched; I seemed to have knocked her off the comfortable stoop in her mind. I explained about the cigarette butts we'd found.

'But Jean . . . I'm sure he left from Faro,' she told me, staring off into her doubts as if they were accumulating fast. 'He . . . he wouldn't have come back to Lisbon.'

Something in her stammer seemed artificial, and it occurred to me then that she was indeed putting on a performance, and doing her best to incriminate her boyfriend.

There were truths about ourselves that we only acknowledged when someone was trying to trick us; watching Senhora Coutinho gaze off as though needing to figure out what her best strategy to fool me might be, I realized that I was not very forgiving by nature.

'Oh, I get it now,' she said, as if she'd been silly not to understand earlier, and with false delight she said, 'One of Pedro's *lady friends* must have decided to visit him.'

Before I could ask if she knew any of their names, a slender, teenaged girl stepped inside.

Sandra had a drawn face and big, darkly shadowed eye sockets. Her thick blonde hair, clipped way too short, tufted up at spiky angles. She was wearing a man's cardigan sweater, powder blue with a white collar, with frayed, sagging elbows. It hung down to her knees. I guessed it still held her father's scent. She wore rose pink Converse sneakers with bright yellow laces and purple socks. She looked like a good athlete. And like a boy.

It seemed impossible that she was the demure girl nearing womanhood whom I'd seen in the victim's favourite photos. I started to introduce myself, but she cut me off. 'Someone went into my room!' she told her mother hotly, 'and whoever it was took off my sheets and looked through my drawers!'

'That was me,' I said.

Her eyes opened wide with rage. I looked to Senhora Coutinho for help, but she was gazing out of the back window again. She was extraordinarily good at not helping.

'We were searching for evidence,' I told the girl. 'I'm sorry.'

Luci cleared her throat and said, 'I'll help you put on fresh sheets.'

'I DON'T WANT FRESH ONES!' the girl shrieked, and so loudly that it raised gooseflesh on my arms.

Senhora Coutinho drizzled Scotch into her glass with practised ease. Watching her, a latch of panic opened in my chest and made me realize that my Valium was wearing off. 'I'm investigating what happened to your father,' I told Sandra. I took out the turquoise ring that Gabriel had found, and offered it to her. 'This must be yours.'

'You had no right to take that from my bed,' she told me, her voice fading to a frail whisper. She looked at me with a desolate expression. 'My dad . . . he always told me you can't just take other people's things.'

'I apologize,' I said.

Sandra closed her fist around her ring and faced her mother. Her need for forgiveness – and her fear that she no longer deserved it – hunched her shoulders, but her mother wouldn't look at her.

There's cruelty in this house, I thought. *And Senhora Coutinho doesn't mind my being aware of it. Maybe that's precisely what she wants me to understand without having to say it.*

'Sandra, is that sweater your dad's?' I asked gently, unwilling to venture on to more serious matters just yet.

'Yeah, it was his favourite,' she replied timidly. 'Mine, too.'

The glistening of a butterfly brooch pinned to her collar – red and blue enamel – caught my attention. 'And where did you get such a pretty butterfly brooch?'

'Oh this . . .' She turned her collar around and shrugged as if to diminish its importance. 'It was a gift from my parents. For my last birthday. Except . . . except it sometimes doesn't look like a butterfly to me any more.'

'What else could it be?'

She showed me a lost face. 'I don't have any idea.'

She seemed to need me to know that her father's death had changed the shape of everything in her life – had taken away the meaning of even small objects.

'Maybe we could talk a bit about your ring now,' I said. I wanted to ask her why she had hidden it but she thrust her hands over her face and broke down into tears.

Luci took a step toward her. 'I'll help you make your bed, if you—'

'Get away from my daughter!' Senhora Coutinho yelled, rushing around the table. When she pressed her lips to the top of Sandi's head, the girl threw her arms around her and hung on as if she were being swept out to sea.

It was an amazing thing to watch a teenaged girl weep, to cede to what she'd been struggling against, as if I were observing how the world would overwhelm all of us if we ever let our guard down. Susana managed to get her daughter to stop crying with whispered endearments. I gazed away from their intimacy. Luci gave me a long look that I took to mean, *I didn't expect it to get this bad so soon.*

'Come on, baby, you need to rest,' Senhora Coutinho told Sandi. She dried the girl's eyes with a tissue, smiling encouragingly.

Sandi hugged her hands around her belly as though she'd been abandoned. 'I'll never see Dad again, will I?' she asked her mother.

'Sssshhh. We'll talk upstairs after I get you into bed.' Senhora Coutinho took her daughter's arm.

'Mom, where did the bullet hit dad? Was it . . . in the back?'

'Oh, Sandi, why would you want to know something like that?'

'I don't know, it seems important.'

'We'll talk about it later.'

'I'll never have a chance now to tell him I'm sorry. It's all my fault, Mom!'

Senhora Coutinho gripped both her daughter's hands. 'Listen to me!' she said fiercely. 'What's happened has *nothing* to do with you!'

'If I'd have been nicer to him, then—'

'Daddy knew you loved him,' Senhora Coutinho cut in, her voice trembling. 'That's all that counts.'

Sandi turned to me as her mother led her from the room. Taking off her brooch, she laid it on the countertop near the door. To me and Luci, she said, 'If you take something away, you have to leave something behind in its place.'

'Why do you say that?' I asked.

'Because that's what my dad always told me.'

'And why are you telling me now?'

'Because you're investigating his death. You ought to know everything.'

Senhora Coutinho draped her arm over her daughter's shoulder and led her away. I imagined that many things her

84

father had told Sandi would pulse with hidden significance over the coming weeks. But the question for now was, what had she taken for which she was leaving behind her brooch?

After they'd left the room, Luci's eyes closed tight. She was pale, and her chin trembled.

'It's been a long day, and it's time you went home,' I told her.

I wasn't just being easy on a new recruit; I badly needed some time alone. I quashed Luci's protests by making my suggestion an order.

At the door, I told her to call headquarters on her way home and have someone check that Morel had been on one of the flights from Lisbon to Paris the day before.

Back in the kitchen, the silence in the house seemed too expectant – as if waiting for me to understand things I couldn't possibly know yet – so I cut a Valium through its centre and downed half. Senhora Coutinho swept into the room a few minutes later, barefoot, in a winged blue caftan with golden tracery embroidered on the collar. Her lipstick was pale pink and her honey-coloured hair was brushed into luscious swirls. Her earrings were shimmering black pearls the size of hazelnuts. She looked as though she'd made herself ready for paparazzi.

As she poured herself another whisky, her cell phone rang. She checked to see who it was, frowning nastily, then shut it off and stuffed it deep into her handbag. 'Bad news gets around quickly,' she told me disapprovingly. She sat down opposite me with a theatrical sigh and took a long sip of her Scotch.

'Is your daughter okay?' I asked.

She picked at the sponge cake. 'You'll forgive me,' she said, 'but I don't know what *okay* could possibly mean at this point.'

'I'm curious as to why she'd need to apologize to your husband.'

Senhora Coutinho lifted her eyebrows and gazed at me haughtily. 'Is that really any of your business?'

'I very much want to find out who killed your husband, and asking inconvenient questions is usually part of the process.'

'The *process?*' she asked, as if I'd said something absurd.

'The wrong word, perhaps. My Portuguese isn't perfect, as I'm sure you noticed.'

'Are you American or English?'

'American.'

Her eyes lit up. 'New York is my favourite city in the world!' she announced.

'I've never been,' I told her.

'No? Shame. Look, Monroe, teenagers get crazy ideas. And she's been rude to both Pedro and me of late. Besides, we all have regrets when a loved one dies.' She shook her head dejectedly. 'We think of all we could have done better.'

'Very true,' I agreed.

Senhora Coutinho sat up straight and stared at me with her head tilted, as if I were so odd that she might only be able to figure me out from a cockeyed angle. 'So what is it you regret, Inspector?'

Censoring my real reply, I said, 'Very little, these days. Regret has never taken me anywhere I wanted to go.'

I felt too clever as soon as I said that, but that was the reply I'd settled on long ago, when Ana and I first started dating.

Senhora Coutinho nodded bitterly, as though what I'd told her confirmed her own doubts about the possibility of redemption. Sensing a window of opportunity, I said, 'I'll need to have your full cooperation to solve this case.'

'Why do I get the feeling you're going to keep asking me difficult questions?' she asked, and her grimace seemed a request for me to treat her more gently than I might otherwise have.

'I'm betting you called Jean Morel after you helped your daughter into bed. That's okay with me, but I have to know what he told you.'

She reached for her cigarettes and tapped one out. 'I didn't call him,' she said, as if she'd expected more of me.

'Senhora Coutinho, you're not as good an actress as you might think,' I said, but I was bluffing, since I hadn't been able to read her expression.

She squinted at me as if measuring me for a noose.

'If you didn't call Morel to find out if he flew back from Faro or Lisbon,' I continued, 'then you should have. I certainly would have.'

'Your effort to be understanding just makes things worse, Monroe. It's *far* too American for my taste.'

As she stood up, I said, 'I don't want to quarrel with you. I'm no good at it. At the first sign of an argument, I run and hide.' When she gazed at me sceptically, I added, 'I'm a very fast runner, Senhora Coutinho.'

She laughed with a touch of admiration – as if I'd disarmed her adroitly – and said in apologetic tone, 'You might find this hard to believe after how I've spoken to you, but I don't like quarrelling either. Probably because I generally lose.' She stuck a cigarette in her lips and let it dangle. 'I've learned how to run pretty fast myself, Inspector.' With a trace of the bitter humour that I now recognized as a key part of her personality, she added, 'Though Pedro and Sandi were even faster, and usually managed to catch me.'

She wants me to know it had been two against one in this family, I thought. 'So what did Morel tell you?' I asked.

She lit her cigarette. In an impressive exhale of smoke, she said, 'He drove to Lisbon to talk to Pedro on Friday morning, early, and that when he left this house, my husband was very much alive.'

'What time did he leave?'

'Around ten thirty. There was a TAP flight to Paris at eleven forty and he was on it.'

'And what did he and your husband talk about?'

After a moment's hesitation, she reached for a chair. 'It's very simple,' she said. 'A few months ago, I told Pedro I wanted a divorce, but he convinced me to wait until Sandi turned eighteen. He was adamant about not hurting her any more than she already was.'

'Did your husband often get adamant?'

'I don't understand the question.'

'Did he often show his temper?'

'Doesn't everyone show their temper on occasion?'

'But not everyone makes enemies because of it. Judging from what's happened, he made a bad one.'

'Look, life wasn't as rosy as I implied before. Pedro and I felt trapped in our marriage sometimes. Once, after his hollering at me got out of hand, even Sandi told me – in confidence, of course – that it might be a good idea for us to separate. But in this particular case, as soon as I agreed to wait for a divorce, he became friendly again. He wasn't like me – he could change moods in an instant and be incredibly sure of himself.' She shrugged, as if she was resigned to her husband being a creature she'd never fathom. 'Anyway,' she continued, 'Jean told me that he drove to Lisbon yesterday morning to ask him to reconsider – to allow us to divorce, I mean. It was a spur of the moment thing.' In a voice pierced by regret, she added, 'Jean is in love with me, Monroe. He tells me it's the first time he's ever really fallen in love. And get this, he's sixty-two!' She rolled her eyes as if it were madness. 'But he didn't want us to get a divorce right away only because of his feelings about me. He felt strongly that Sandi was faring badly because we were staying together. He's her godfather, and very attached to her.'

'How did Pedro react to his suggestion?'

'Once again, he argued against a separation.'

'So Morel and he quarrelled.'

Annoyance sneaked back into her expression. 'Yes, but like I said, when Jean left here, Pedro was very much alive.'

'Did your daughter know about your affair with Morel?'

Senhora Coutinho glowered at me. 'I thought you said you liked to avoid quarrels?'

'I do, but I want to solve this case.'

88

'You get paid even if you don't find out who killed Pedro,' she said matter-of-factly.

'That's true,' I told her, 'but you deserve to know what happened to your husband.'

'Why?'

'Everyone deserves to know why bad things happen.'

She flashed me a probing look. 'Though you never found out.'

That remark evidenced such awareness of the little clues I'd dropped that it changed all I felt about her. And embarrassed me, as well, for I'd failed to see the true shape of what was taking place between us until now.

'No, I never really found out,' I admitted.

'And you don't always find the killers you're after, do you?'

Thinking of Moura, I said, 'For better or worse, this isn't TV.'

'I've been aware of that for a long time,' she said, with a disgusted little laugh. 'Look, Inspector, I had no idea Jean intended to come here or I'd have stopped him.'

'Did he say whether anyone else was here when he spoke to your husband?'

'He didn't mention it.'

I told Senhora Coutinho I wanted her to get Morel on the phone. After she explained to him who I was, she put me on the line. His English was pretty good. He confirmed that he'd met Coutinho at his home the day before, at just after ten in the morning, having driven up from the Algarve in his rental car. Pedro hadn't seemed nervous or ill at ease. He'd left without winning any concessions. He had no idea whether a girlfriend of Coutinho's might have been hiding in the house while they spoke.

Morel confirmed that he'd caught the TAP Air Portugal flight to Paris at eleven forty. He added that he'd called his old friend from Lisbon Airport to apologize for provoking a quarrel, but Coutinho's phone had been off. He tried again on reaching Paris but was still unable to reach him.

Was Morel devious enough to have called a dead man twice in order to throw a future police inquiry off the track?

I told him I wanted him to come to Lisbon as soon as possible, and he said he'd already booked a TAP Air Portugal flight for the next morning. He was scheduled to arrive in Lisbon at 12.45 p.m. On hanging up, I asked Senhora Coutinho if she knew where her husband's cell phones might be. She was picking a hole in the sponge cake with sloppy hand movements. 'If they weren't with him or on his desk in the library, I haven't a clue,' she told me. 'Haven't you found them?'

'No, the murderer seems to have taken them.'

'The murderer . . .' Tears squeezed through her lashes. After wiping her eyes, she jiggled her head, as though to make light of her grief, and smiled, an effort that seemed quietly heroic.

'I think you should drink something other than whisky,' I told her.

'And *I* think your wife must tell you fairly often to keep your opinions to yourself!' she declared, but with good humour in her expression.

When I admitted that she was right, she said, 'At this point, Inspector Monroe, I believe you're expected to give the grieving widow a few words of comfort.'

'Maybe you should call up a good friend as soon as I leave and ask her to stay with you.'

'If I had a good friend, I'd do just that.'

'There has to be someone you trust.'

'Christ, Monroe! Haven't you figured out yet that when people learn what it is you most need, they do their best *not* to provide you with it? Look, what if Jean and I are telling the truth?' A new possibility made her start, then hold her head in her hands. 'Oh, God – and what if Sandi keeps thinking she's responsible?'

Bent over her fears for her daughter, she began to cry silently. I went to the window. Out of the corner of my eye, I watched the ash curling on her cigarette. In profile, she seemed older – and to have just understood that she'd been carried too far away from all she'd ever dreamed of for herself to ever make it back to where she wanted to be.

As for me, while I watched Nero snoozing under the palm tree, I realized – in contrast – that I didn't want to be anywhere else. That might have seemed a strange conclusion to have reached, but I'd noticed before that I felt most at home when speaking to people at the worst moment of their lives. They seemed real to me then in a way they almost never otherwise did. Maybe it was even the most important reason I'd become a cop.

I sat down opposite her again. Her face – lost and helpless – moved me to speak. 'My mother died in a car accident when I was eleven,' I told her.

I surprised myself with that admission; in fact, it didn't seem to have come from me.

She nodded, as though hoping I'd say more.

'There are days, even now,' I told her, 'when I still can't believe it. I'll be walking down the street and the finality of it – and how it has determined the whole rest of my life – will stop me dead in my tracks. So you see, the truth is I'm the last person in the world who could give you advice on how to get past a trauma like this.'

'And yet you went on with your life.'

'I didn't have a choice. I had a younger brother.'

'And I've got Sandi. Is that what you're saying?'

'It wasn't my intent, but it's probably what I *would* say if I were to risk offering you any advice.'

'Life has so often been a disappointment,' she observed. 'And when it hasn't been a disappointment, Monroe, it's been even worse.' Holding my glance – as if to say *watch this!* – she pressed the back of her hand to her mouth and wiped off her lipstick, creating pink streaks across her cheek.

As she took off her earrings, time seemed to come to a halt, because I saw so clearly that she needed me to know that she'd never again be the same person she was before her husband's death. Tossing them to me, she said, 'Give

91

them to your wife.' With a wry smile, she added, 'She deserves a present now and again for putting up with you!'

I set them down on the table. The black pearls were slightly oval, like small dark eggs. 'We'll just keep them here for now,' I said.

'Avoid a quarrel, like a good boy, and put them in your pocket.'

I did as she asked, though I decided to keep them at my office in case she wanted them back in a week or two.

'Gosh, how I hated lipstick when I was a girl!' Senhora Coutinho told me. 'Took me years to get used to it.' She laughed in a reckless burst and joined her hands in prayer. 'May Susana Coutinho rest in peace. Long live Susana Lencastre.' She toasted her transformation back into the woman she'd been before marriage with her glass raised high. 'Which reminds me, Monroe, aren't I supposed to identify my husband?'

'Senhora Grimault identified him. But I can make arrangements for you to see the body when you feel up to it.'

She breathed in sharply. 'The body . . . God, that sounds awful!'

'I'm afraid the other possibilities sound even worse.'

She held up her hand to stop me from telling her what they were, though that hadn't been my intention. 'I don't think I'll ever believe what's happened unless I see Pedro.' She looked toward the wall tiles. At length, she asked, 'Was there a lot of blood?' She spoke as though from very far away.

'I'm afraid so, where the bullet entered.' I patted my gut.

'And that Japanese writing on the wall, was that made with Pedro's . . . ?'

'We think so.'

Senhora Coutinho winced. 'Do you think Pedro made it while he was dying? A last message?'

'You tell me – does it look like his writing?'

'I'm not familiar enough with how he wrote in Japanese

to identify his handwriting. Have you found out what it says yet?'

'No, but I'll research it today. Did Pedro ever mention anything bad happening to him in Japan – any enemies he might have made, business problems he got into?'

'No, nothing. He always spoke of his time there as if it had been his greatest adventure.' She shook her head. 'Jean couldn't possibly have killed him, you know,' she said, and softly, to imply that it was a simple fact. 'And I didn't either. I'm not only good at running away from an argument, Inspector. I also know how to wait if I have to, and waiting four more years for a divorce wouldn't have made my life any more difficult than it already was.'

'I believe you,' I said, and I did, but maybe Morel had lied to her about what he'd done. If he failed to fly in to Lisbon tomorrow, we'd know the truth.

'Tell me more about what the killer did to Pedro,' she requested. The tight, fearful hunch of her shoulders reminded me of her daughter.

'Maybe you should wait until tomorrow,' I suggested.

'So it was bad?'

I nodded. Letting out a moan, she dropped her drinking glass, which shattered. Ice streaked across the floor. When she looked up, I expected to see despair in her eyes, but anger was flashing. 'You make damn sure you question my husband's business associates,' she said.

'Anyone in particular?'

'Everyone in particular!' she shouted. She was vibrating with rage. 'Inspector, let me pass on one of the useful things that Pedro taught me – presume that every transaction in Portugal is shady until proven otherwise.'

'So did your husband make payoffs to get building contracts?' I asked.

'Don't be such an idiot! Of course he did! Talk to Rui Sottomayor, his accountant. He knew Pedro's business dealings back to front, and they've been friends since they were kids.' With savage amusement in her voice, she added,

'Though if you want to save some time, just write down the name of every politician whose signature is required to build a shopping mall in this fucking banana republic. The list of officials that Pedro had to bribe should be just about the same.'

She read me Sottomayor's number from her phone. In reply to my next questions, she said that she'd never seen any notes her husband might have written detailing his illegal transactions. And he'd never mentioned the names of anyone he'd bribed.

'He thought it safer for me not to know anything specific,' she said, and she went on to tell me that she had never given her front door key to anyone, not even Jean Morel. As far as she knew, Sandi hadn't either, but she'd ask her. We looked in the cabinet where the family kept their spare house keys, but none of them was missing.

She also told me she'd never seen her husband with another woman since their move to Lisbon and didn't know the names of any of his girlfriends. 'I learned to just look the other way,' she explained.

I asked her to follow me into the living room and showed her the Almeida drawing of Fernando Pessoa. 'Do you know if this was always here?' I asked.

'I'm not sure. Why?'

'I think the killer moved it.'

'Why would he do that?'

'I have no idea.'

'Look, Monroe, everything on the walls belonged to Pedro.' She gazed around the room in a teetering three-sixty. Her droopy eyes closed momentarily. 'All these beautiful things he bought, and now ... You know what it took me years to realize? That way back when, I was his most treasured *objet d'art*.' She snapped her fingers. 'But one day, just like that, Pedro traded me in for something more contemporary. When I figured that out, I stopped giving a shit about the beautiful things he brought home. Don't get me wrong – he was apologetic. Boy, was he ever! He cried like a baby when I first confronted him with his cheating on me. "Oh, sweetie, I'm sorry, I must be crazy to hurt you like this!" he told me. It took me a few months to figure out that he traded me in for good. Pretty stupid, right? Because it was simple – I was getting older. Men don't like women who have the bad taste to age. You can quote me on that, Monroe!'

She frowned at me as if I was part of a masculine conspiracy. I pointed to the Almeida drawing and asked, 'Would your daughter know what had been hanging here?'

'Probably. She and her father loved going to art galleries. I'll ask her when she's feeling better.'

'Please excuse another indelicate question, but the way your daughter shrieked ... Has she ever shouted like that before?'

'Monroe, her father has just been murdered. What do you expect from her?'

'True, but—'

'God, how Pedro loved that girl!' she cut in. 'He wanted so badly to get things right this time.'

'This time?'

'He was married once before. He had two kids – a boy and a girl. After the divorce, his wife turned the kids against him. He hasn't seen them in at least fifteen years, since the kids were teenagers. That's what he was most afraid of, I think – that I'd turn Sandi against him if we were divorced.'

'I'd like to know why Sandi felt she'd needed to hide her ring,' I said.

'Look, she's had a lot of difficulties lately. Among other things, the kids at school have been teasing her since she cut her hair. Maybe that had something to do with it.'

'Did she cut it herself?'

'Yeah, she just grabbed the scissors and ...' Senhora Coutinho made wild snipping motions in the air. 'Sandi said she wanted a more *edgy* look. I had to look up the damn word in a fucking English dictionary. *Edgy* – have you ever heard anything so stupid!'

95

'When did she do it?'

'About three months ago.' She rolled her eyes. 'And she insisted on trimming it again just a few weeks back. She also wanted to get a spike in her tongue, but I told her to forget it!'

'Did anything special happen to her three months ago?'

'Like what?'

'Any particularly bad quarrels with you or your husband?'

'No. Sandi never really quarrels, to tell you the truth. Not for long, anyway. Her technique is to stab you hard and deep enough to draw blood and then walk away while you're still in shock.'

'By any chance, did she spend any time away from you about three months ago, when something bad might have happened to her?'

'No.'

'Any trips at all?'

'Christ, you really don't give up, do you?' she asked. 'At Easter, she went to Jean's house just outside Paris with Pedro for a few days. I wasn't able to come. Jean has a big house in Normandy. It's lovely. Sandi went with two of her girlfriends.'

'And the trip went well?'

'She had a great time. She loves France – prefers it to Portugal. And given how depressed everyone is here, who wouldn't?' Senhora Coutinho combed her hand through her hair and teased out a snag. 'You have kids, Monroe?'

'Two boys.'

'How old?'

'Seven and thirteen.'

She whistled as though in warning. 'Boys mature a little later, so just wait till the older one hits fifteen or so. Then he'll start getting awkward and doing some really crazy things and forget how to talk to you nicely. Some of it is a generational thing, I'm told. Like vampires and YouTube and downloading crap like Lady Gaga.'

After announcing that she was thirsty, she led me back

into the kitchen. While she poured herself a glass of orange juice, I took out my two evidence bags. Once we were seated again, I showed her the honey dripper. 'This was tucked under the top sheet of your daughter's bed,' I told her.

'She has a sweet tooth. Inherited it from Pedro and me, so I can't deny our guilt.' She held out her hands. 'I'm ready for the handcuffs, Inspector.'

'Where'd she get it? I've never seen a honey dripper in Portugal.'

'New York, last summer. We had a brief vacation there.'

I took out the knife. 'I found this under her bed. Any idea why she kept it there?'

She studied it indifferently and dropped it to the table. 'I can't see what this could possibly have to do with Pedro's murder.'

'I'd still like to know.'

She swept the cake crumbs scattered across the table into a pile as she considered what to say. 'This is delicate. Please don't put this in any official reports.'

'That's fine.'

'Sandi started getting her period about . . . it must be eight months ago by now, and the blood really scared her.' She sat back, folding her arms over her chest as if to remind herself of the need for caution. 'The poor girl was very upset. She had nightmares – monsters sneaking into the house and coming after me and Pedro and her. Her shrink told us that all these TV shows and movies with trapped young women being tormented by psychopaths have created a kind of syndrome. Some girls live in a constant state of fear these days. It's crazy. Anyway, a few months after her nightmares started, Sandi told me she wanted to keep a knife with her in bed. I hated the idea, but her shrink thought it was all right – as a stopgap measure.'

'Did she ever tell you that someone real was threatening her?'

'No.'

'How long has she been in therapy?'

97

Senhora Coutinho looked away while doing the maths. 'Almost two months.'

'Are you certain no one hurt her just before that – physically, I mean? At school, maybe. One of the kids who's been teasing her? Or a teacher?'

'She would've mentioned that. At least to her father. He would've taken care of it. He was very good at taking care of things,' she added darkly.

'Just to be certain, would you ask her?'

'Sure, but keep in mind that whenever I try to have a serious conversation with her, she glares at me and pretends she's tapping on a keyboard. She calls it *pressing delete*.'

'That seems kind of—'

'Unnecessary?' she interrupted. 'And cruel?' She laughed caustically. 'That's what it's meant to be, Monroe. You asked why she needed to apologize to Pedro. That was why – she deleted him a lot of late. And me, too.' She jumped up, opened the refrigerator and took out an apple. 'Look,' she said, shaking it at me, 'I know you want me to care a lot about what Sandi is going through right now, and I do, but I also need a day or two for myself, just to go slightly insane.' She slammed the refrigerator door closed and kicked it hard.

I pictured her daughter lying in bed, in the dark, clutching her knife. 'It's a bad sign that Sandi hid the ring in her own room,' I said.

She took a big, determined bite of her apple. 'Why's that, Inspector?'

'Because it means that whoever she feared didn't respect normal limits and borders. There was no safe place. At least, Sandi didn't think so.'

'Then why in God's name didn't she talk to me or Pedro?'

'I'm getting the feeling it involved your husband's other life – with his girlfriends. And she couldn't very well bring that up with either of you.'

'And this is important to this case because . . . ?'

'What if the person threatening Sandi was the same one who killed your husband?'

'No one would ever threaten Sandi in this house. It's impossible.'

'You also said that Morel couldn't possibly have been in Lisbon yesterday. No parent knows everything that goes on with his or her kids. What if Pedro's girlfriend had a husband? Maybe he threatened Pedro while Sandi was with him. Or maybe the girlfriend made it clear she didn't want Sandi around.'

'I suppose it's possible, but it—'

'Was the ring a present from your husband?' I cut in.

'Yeah, Pedro gave it to Sandi for her twelfth birthday.'

'So she was keeping something from him extra safe. Maybe trying to keep *him* safe, too. Kids think like that – magically. I'm going to need to question her.'

My host reached for my hand. 'Please,' she whispered, 'give Sandi a couple of days to grieve without having to answer any questions.'

'I've generally found it's best to question the families of victims right away.'

'I know my daughter, Inspector. If you question her now, you'll push her deep inside herself. You won't get a word out of her.'

I felt the pleading tug of my empathy but also knew it would set a bad precedent to let Senhora Coutinho dictate the pace of my investigation. 'What time does your daughter usually get up?' I asked.

'About eight.'

'I'll be here tomorrow at nine thirty to talk to her, though I promise not to push her. Later in the day, I'll also send a lab tech over to talk to Jean Morel and get his DNA. He'll call you before he comes over.'

'All right. Thank you.'

'Also, I don't want her to sleep in her room tonight. I found what may be a bloodstain on one of her stuffed animals and, until I'm sure whose it is, I'd like her to sleep with you or in another room.'

'Okay, I'll tell her.'

'And neither of you are to touch anything in the library or the living room. If you don't think you can do that, I can't let you stay here.'

'It won't be a problem.'

On the back of one of my cards, I wrote out the phone number Senhora Coutinho would need to call when she was ready to see her husband's body. After handing it to her, I offered her earrings back to her, but she closed my fist around them and said, 'If you catch the killer, I'll give you the Almeida drawing, too.'

In her laboured, drunken handwriting, she then wrote me out a list of the friends and work colleagues who had visited their home over the last few months, though she still denied that it was possible that any of them had menaced Sandi. There were seventeen visitors in all, including Morel. Susana consulted her agenda and discovered that he'd slept over on two occasions in May when Pedro had been away on business.

On scanning my notes one last time, I rediscovered Sandi's cryptic comment to me: *If you take something away, you have to leave something behind in its place.* When I asked Senhora Coutinho what special meaning that might have had for her daughter, she replied that she had no idea. I asked her if Sandi had ever been caught stealing anything from her parents or anyone at school, but she rolled her eyes as if I were crazy. 'That wasn't her style, Monroe. She could be incredibly rude, but she wasn't a thief.'

I told her that I had no more questions for now and that it was time for me to leave, but she said, 'No, please, I need you to tell me how the murderer hurt Pedro – before I see him. I want to be prepared.' My reticence must have shown, because she added, 'I can handle it.'

I sat with her at the kitchen table. 'Your husband was

100

bound and gagged,' I began. 'Unfortunately, the gag was tied so tightly that he wasn't able to get enough air. And . . .'

As I explained the rest of what the killer had done to her husband, she faced the wall, her hands clasped together in her lap, her eyes dull, entranced by the immense proportions of this death. And certain – it seemed to me – that this was the worst thing that could ever happen to her. Though, in hindsight, it seems just possible that she had already caught a glimpse of much worse to come.

Chapter 9

It seemed possible that Coutinho had discussed his sexual conquests with Rui Sottomayor, his childhood friend and accountant, so on my taxi ride home, I decided to give him a call. This was the first he'd heard of his old friend's murder, and in a failing voice he told me he'd have to phone me back. When he did, he said that Coutinho hadn't told him the name of any of his girlfriends, and that he hadn't seemed ill at ease the last time they'd spoken, which had been two days earlier, on Wednesday. Sottomayor denied knowing anything about any bribes the victim may have made. When I informed him – exaggerating a bit – that Susana Coutinho had assured me he would give me names and figures, he told me coolly, 'I'm afraid she's overestimated my intimacy with her husband's business dealings.'

To pressure him, I told him to be at my office on Monday morning at ten sharp, and to be prepared for extensive questioning. I figured that if he worried all weekend about being interrogated, he might give up the name of at least one minor official whom Coutinho had bribed, and from there I could work my way up.

I next called Inspector Quintela, followed by Fonseca and Luci. Quintela told me that a couple of hours earlier he'd sent our report about the murder to Bruno Cerveira in the State Prosecutor's Office. Fonseca agreed to stop by Senhora Coutinho's house the next day to get Morel's DNA. He already knew, however, that the stain in Sandra's stuffed panda was indeed blood, but not the victim's. He promised to have all our evidence processed by mid-afternoon on Monday. Luci told me that Morel had indeed been on the TAP Air Portugal flight from Lisbon to Paris that he'd indicated. She'd also learned that he'd called the victim's cell phone twice that day, just as he'd said. I'd have to watch over my kids the next afternoon – while Ana was at her gallery – so Luci agreed to go to Senhora Coutinho's house early the next afternoon to question Morel. We went over what I wanted her to ask the Frenchman a couple of times. Next, David Zydowicz confirmed that Coutinho had choked to death. He pinpointed the time of his demise to between 9 a.m. and 11 a.m. the previous day. One bullet had entered his gut and exited his back without damaging any major organs. The deep bruise over his chest was from a kick so violent that it had fractured a rib. The contusion on his back indicated that the murderer had stomped on him, pressing him face-down to the living room rug; one of its white fibres had got stuck in his right eyelash. David promised to perform a full autopsy the next morning, but didn't expect to turn up anything else of interest.

I'd saved the call I dreaded for last and made it as soon as the taxi dropped me at home. Vaz told me that he'd be able to give me the brand of sneaker that had made the bloody imprint on the victim's shirt only on Tuesday afternoon. His icy tone made it clear that he'd recovered the full, malignant, senseless scope of his dislike for me.

A dry feeling of sadness swept through me as soon as I entered my apartment building. My head felt encased in thick glass; I'd taken too much Valium.

I sat on the shabby staircase with my hand muffling my mouth, hoping that none of our neighbours would hear me descending into purposeless grief. Remembering Moura's dull, unseeing eyes, I thought, *A crack opened in me the moment he died.*

As I stood up, I envisioned Ana's chilly reaction to my telling her I'd be putting in a few hours on the case

tomorrow; after having my salary slashed by the government in the fall of 2011, she'd made me promise not to work
weekends.

When I finally made it upstairs, our front door seemed
like a prop on a stage, just as everything waiting for me on
the other side – for the husband and father I'd learned to
become – seemed fake.

As I stepped inside, Jorge, my seven-year-old, ran to me,
belting out the theme song from *American Dad*, 'Gee it's good
to say, good morning U.S.A.!'

Since realizing a few months earlier that I grew up in
Colorado, he delights in every mention of America, even the
ones in cartoons.

Jorge crashed into my belly; he adores having an impact.
I probably would too if I was only three feet tall. I gasped;
holding his hummingbird quickness in my arms was like
being rescued. In a clear moment of revelation, I felt how his
little body was being shaped by the unstoppable will to
grow.

He was barefoot, since we didn't permit shoes in the
house, and his right big toe had been painted with red, white
and blue stripes. 'Great design!' I told him, pointing.

'Mom did it!'

Ana was hunched over her computer at her desk in the
living room, sloppy-sexy in her pink camisole and grey
sweatpants, concentrating hard, a yellow pencil clamped in
her mouth. She'd tied her shoulder-length brown hair into a
ponytail, except for the bright purple lock over her left ear
that she'd dyed on the day she'd turned forty and usually
let hang free.

I knew not to interrupt, and so did Jorge, so we held
hands and waited. When he started wriggling, I asked him
to please not wet himself, and he dashed to the bathroom.
Ana waved me over.

The touch of her hands and lips brought me feelings of
gratitude so overwhelming that I had no defence against
them. And, just like that, my life seemed my own again.

104

'I'll put the spaghetti on in a minute,' she said. 'The chestnut soup is already done.'

'Chestnut soup?'

'It's from Leonardo.'

'Are you sure it's edible?' I asked, grimacing like a gargoyle for full comic effect; Ana had been trying out recipes from *Leonardo da Vinci's Kitchen Notebooks* lately, and her previous creation – Lemon and Orange Soup – had defeated everyone but Jorge, who'd mixed in a heaping tablespoon of honey and slurped it up as a syrupy dessert.

'Don't start!' she warned me with her finger wagging, since becoming indignant was her half of our private vaudeville act. 'What time is it?' she asked.

I looked at my watch. 'Nearly seven. So how's the writing going?' I asked; she was in the third year of her PhD thesis about violence against transsexuals.

'I spoke on the phone today with Gena.'

Gena had been nearly beaten to death in Brooklyn a few months earlier, by two men who'd attacked her as she walked to the Public Library. She had been born in Pistoia, Italy, in 1972, though she grew up in Miami.

'She better?' I asked.

'Yeah, and she just visited her parents in Florida for the first time since the attack. They didn't ask her to stay over, so she had to get a room in a motel.'

'I wonder why she still tries to convince them to accept her.'

'She wonders the same thing!' Ana jerked her head back and eyed me sceptically. 'You don't look so bad,' she noted.

'Most people are good at faking illness; I'm good at faking being just fine.'

I took her hair out of the ponytail and breathed in on its warm scent.

Batting me away playfully, she said, 'Let me proofread a little more, and then I'll let you sniff me anywhere you want, Chief Inspector.'

105

I found Jorge finishing up in the bathroom. Eager to tell me about his art class at school, he turned around too soon and hosed down the wall and the cuff of my pants with a last, giddy arc. 'Hold on there, Mr Fireman!' I told him. I swivelled him back around and aimed his final drops into the toilet. A minute later, while I was mopping up his pee with paper towels, he ran back into the bathroom to show me the drawings he'd made that afternoon: three houses, all leaning to the left, as they always do, as if gale-force winds were always blowing in his head. And none of them had a roof. The one I liked best had what looked like a fox standing in the doorway and wearing a giant cowboy hat.

'Who's the fox?' I asked.

'The what?'

'The *raposa*,' I explained; my son knew animal names better in Portuguese.

'That's not a *raposa*! That's Ernie!' he said, as if it were obvious. Had he already figured out that my six-foot-two-inch-tall brother was a wily little creature of the forest at heart?

I washed my face with cold water and took off my bolo tie and wristwatch. On the dining table, I discovered a rejection letter from one of the twenty-one Portuguese art galleries to which I'd sent photographs of my brother's paintings two months earlier. I crushed it in a tight ball and tossed it in the garbage.

Upstairs, I changed into boxer shorts. I found Nati lying on his belly in bed, bare-chested, wearing the Wile E. Coyote boxer shorts I'd bought him for his thirteenth birthday, reading an old hardback. The fan on his dresser was lifting up his long, whip-like bangs of silky brown hair and tossing them over his forehead, but he didn't seem to notice. He looked like a boy on a solemn journey to himself.

As soon as he heard me, he slammed the cover of his book closed.

'Pornography?' I asked.

He rolled his eyes. 'Not funny, Dad.'

'Are you accepting visitors?' I asked.

'Sure, but don't mess anything up.'

Felt pens in rainbow colours were scattered across his rug, his blanket was nested on the floor and an apple core was sitting on his pillow, but he wasn't making a joke.

'Bad day?' he asked, and as I sat down, he turned on his side to face me, leaning his head on his hand.

'I hit the jackpot – a suicide *and* a murder, and a tormented teen to top it off. How about you? Grandma Vera commit any crimes against humanity today?'

'Almost. She took us to the café at the Gulbenkian Museum and pretended she was feeling faint from the heat so we wouldn't have to wait in line.' Nati imitated his grandmother, complete with a trembling hand over her heaving breast. He spoke in her heavily accented, nearly indecipherable Portuguese; she and her husband had emigrated to Portugal from Buenos Aires in 1978. Ana had been eight years old.

'Did you have the avocado mousse?' I asked.

'Two portions. And don't you dare tell Mom!'

It was another one of our running gags that her mother tried to limit our intake of sweets and we sneaked them on the sly. The avocado mousse at the Gulbenkian café was number one on our list of favourite Lisbon desserts.

I lay my head next to Nati's and resisted the urge to kiss him, since he'd become finicky of late about too much physical affection. It was reassuring to feel his breathing on me – Nathaniel John Monroe, the boy who'd made me a father. We have always understood each other, and even when we quarrelled – which was fairly frequently of late – we never seemed to forget we were on the same team. Illusion or miracle?

He picked at my eyebrows. He likes how some white hairs have sprouted amidst the brown. I imagined I was a small animal in his care, which brought up the question: would it be boring or wonderful to be reincarnated as a hamster? I decided to ask him.

'A real snooze,' he replied authoritatively. 'Binky had a gerbil once. All it did was eat and sniff around and take dumps all over its cage. And it dropped dead after only a year. Hamsters must be the same.'

Binky was Nati's best friend. Her parents were from Goa.

'Listen, Nati, a hamster's nose is orders of magnitude more sensitive than ours,' I pointed out. 'Every second offers them a universe of scents worth investigating.'

'Are you aware that when you talk about animals you sound like a brochure?'

'I need to take you to Colorado sometime – to see the squirrels and prairie dogs and eagles. And the turkeys! The wild turkeys alone are worth the price of admission.' I began making the squeaky-scratchy noises that baby turkeys make. Being touched by Nati can make me very silly.

'You want a back rub, don't you?' he questioned.

That hadn't been on my mind, but I accepted gratefully. While I slipped out of my shirt, he put his book on his night table upside-down, but I saw that it was a novel I'd recommended to him about a year earlier, *Moby Dick*. Having to sneak a look at the title made me feel right at home; my mother had been a secretive reader, too.

Nati scooted up behind me and kneaded my shoulders. Tennis lessons had given him powerful hands. Closing my eyes with an appreciative moan, I pictured him as a newborn, snoozing face-down on my belly. My son's trust in me – despite his naked and perfect fragility – meant that I'd arrived at the finish line of a race that I'd been running for nearly thirty years. I could finally stop running.

'You think that one day you'll want to press delete every time you see me?' I asked.

'What are you talking about?'

'The murdered man's daughter presses an imaginary delete button whenever her mother tries to talk to her,' I explained.

'I make no promises, Dad, but I'll try not to erase you in front of other people,' he replied dryly.

'Very kind of you,' I said in a sarcastic voice, but I knew I had only myself to blame for his sense of humour. 'Ever see a stuffed panda with big blue eyes, vaguely Japanese-looking?' I asked. 'There was one at the murder scene.'

'No, but I'll Google it for you later, if you want.'

'And why would a really pretty fourteen-year-old girl cut her hair to look like a boy?'

'The victim's daughter again?' he asked.

I groaned 'yes' as he pressed hard at the knots in my shoulders.

'Maybe she's a lesbo,' he said cheerfully.

We were speaking English, as I always do when I'm alone with my kids, but Nati used the word *fufa* in Portuguese. I turned around and shot him a questioning look.

'There are plenty of lesbians on TV these days, and you *occasionally* let me watch,' he informed me in a put-upon way. Of late, he never missed an opportunity to complain that he and his younger brother weren't permitted television on weekdays. It was a rule we'd adopted about a year before, when Jorge began repeating TV advertising slogans nearly all the time. And because the constant stream of bad news about our economy had started Ana panicking about our dwindling earnings.

'Young lesbians don't always want to look like boys,' I told him. 'That's a cliché.'

'No, it's a stereotype,' he corrected.

'Nati, are you aware that you might be too clever on occasion?'

He rolled his eyes. The timer in the kitchen buzzed and Jorge screamed, 'Dad!', as if I might have gone deaf over the last fifteen minutes.

'You could wake the dead!' Ana hollered at him.

I put my shirt back on. Jorge bounded up the staircase and appeared in the doorway, panting, tomato sauce splattered on his shirt. He was naked from the waist down.

Unfortunately, Nati is totally immune to his brother's Peter Pan charm and said, 'Where the hell are your pants, Dingo?'

He calls his brother Dingo, having concluded – accurately, I'm afraid – that the boy tended to eat like a wild dog.

'They got stained,' Jorge said. He was holding the spoon in his fist from which his mother had apparently given him a taste of the sauce. 'Dinner!' he added breathlessly.

Nati sat up. 'We figured that out, *meu cromo*,' he told him, meaning 'you idiot'.

'Shut up!' Jorge yelled back, and they started calling each other names in Portuguese.

At least the monsters I've raised are bilingual, I thought. 'If you're going to fight,' I said, jumping up, 'then I'll get your boxing gloves and sell tickets, so you nincompoops can at least earn me a few bucks.'

I hopped around like a kangaroo and made punching motions towards Jorge, who raced to me and crashed into my belly. Nati snorted. 'Dad, don't try so hard,' he said, which sounded so much like his mom that I had a good laugh. After I hoisted Jorge over my shoulder, Nati pushed us out of his room.

After dinner, Jorge got out his sketchbook, sat on my lap and drew his mom and me in the windows of his roofless, left-leaning fantasy mansions. At a quarter to nine, I awoke from a light nap to find Nati coming down the stairs. He was wearing his jeans that are ripped at the knees and the blue T-shirt with pink writing across the chest saying *Las Rosas Flour Company* that he ordered on the Internet and puts on for important outings. He was headed to the movies with Binky and two other friends. When Ana refused to let him stay out past midnight, Nati targeted me with a wide-open, expectant look, and that's when I realized that the back rub was meant to earn him a special dispensation for the evening.

'What would you do if you went out after the movie?' I asked, still so drowsy from my nap that I didn't think this could possibly result in a quarrel.

'We thought we might walk around the Bairro Alto for a while.'

The image of my son entering a dark, noisy, rancid-smelling bar made my stomach churn. Sensing defeat, Nati rushed to add, 'It's perfectly safe, and we'll be in a group. Or, if you want, we could walk around somewhere closer to home.'

'I'd rather we stick to our deal,' I told him. 'When you're fifteen you can stay out past midnight – but only in a group.'

'That's more than a year away!'

I tried to reason with him, but he called my arguments 'bogus' and 'irrelevant'. Before I had time to think up a compromise, he stormed out of the house to wait for Binky's mother on the street.

I carried Jorge up to bed. While I was undressing him, he sang, '*Sabe bem pagar tão pouco!*' It was the jingle for the Pingo Doce supermarket chain. 'It tastes great to pay so little!'

Only one jingle an evening was a big improvement, so I told him he was doing great and tucked him in. After I checked the locks on the front door, I collapsed in bed. Ana had nearly reached the end of Philip Roth's *I Married a Communist*.

'I'd like to visit Ernie over the weekend,' I told her as I fluffed my pillow. I sensed that this was the right moment to add that I'd be working on the case the next morning, but said nothing.

'Then go tomorrow,' Ana replied, 'because on Sunday I've got the Brazilian ceramicist whose show we've been arranging, and I'll need you for the dinner we're having for him. He only talks about himself. I won't survive it alone.'

I curled my feet around hers, since her toes were always cold. 'Don't get angry, but I may also have to put in a couple hours on my new case in the morning.'

She gave me a withering look. 'What's the weather like up there in cloud-cuckoo-land?'

'I know I shouldn't put in extra hours, but if you'd seen the wife and daughter of the guy who was murdered . . .'

111

I explained about Sandi Coutinho seeming so troubled. Ana started frowning when I told her how loudly the girl had shrieked, but I knew – after so many years together – that that meant she'd already given in.

'I don't suppose your mom or dad could watch the kids tomorrow for a few hours?' I asked.

'No, they're visiting friends in Cascais. I can hang around here until just before noon, but you'll have to come home after that. And King Kong and Godzilla will have to go with you to your brother's.'

'But I may want to stay over.'

'That's fine, it'll give me the night off from being a wife and mother. Just get home sometime Sunday afternoon.'

'You need a night off?' I said, offended.

She showed me a sceptical look, then kissed the tip of my nose to soften what she was about to say. 'Are you trying to tell me you don't need a night off from being a dad and hus-band now and then?'

'Yes, that's exactly what I'm saying.'

She rolled her eyes because she knew I was lying and returned to her reading. I rubbed my hand up the curve of her hip and down her leg, testing the shape of her against my memory. She always seemed more slender than I remembered.

'Ana . . . ?' I said, to get her attention.

'What?'

'Did you get upset when you started menstruating?' She put down her novel and looked at me questioningly, so I added, 'I need to know because of the victim's daughter.'

'Believe it or not, Chief Inspector, bleeding between your legs isn't a barrel of laughs. If men did it, there'd be encyclopedias written about every last aspect of it.'

'Right,' I said, uninterested for the moment in the feminist ramifications of my line of enquiry. 'Did you talk to your mom about it?' I asked.

She snorted. 'Are you crazy? My mom never discussed anything to do with sex! She'll be sixty-eight in October, and

112

I'm sure she *still* hasn't ever once taken a good look at her vagina. Jewish Argentinean women of her generation didn't do that.'

'Well, we can hope your poor dad has gotten a close-up on occasion.'

That earned me a reckless, hearty laugh, which made me feel better about her needing an occasional breather from the boys and me.

'How did you find out it was perfectly normal?' I asked.

'I asked some older girlfriends. They explained the mechanics of my ovaries. One of them drew me a diagram of a vagina, too, just in case I ever had reason to use mine. The clitoris she sketched looked like a piece of okra. It scared the hell out of me!'

I caressed my hand over her behind. She didn't mind. It was a continual surprise – and source of gratitude – that she let me touch her anywhere I wanted.

She took my penis in her hand and gave me a knowing look, but all the Valium I'd taken would prevent me from getting hard.

'Sorry, I'm pooped,' I told her.

'Surprises happen, so I'll just hold on to it for a while unless you mind,' she told me.

'*Mi casa es su casa.*'

While she jiggled me around in her hand, I explained about Sandra Coutinho getting scared by her period and about the bloody panties stuffed into the leg of her pants.

'Maybe she didn't want her parents to know she'd gotten her period,' she suggested.

'Could that make her want to look like a boy? I mean, she gave herself a haircut that was way too short. It looks really bad.'

'Perhaps she's got other girls on her mind.'

'That's what Nati said. But the thing is, Sandra Coutinho is only fourteen.'

'Kids are figuring out that sort of thing earlier these days. Or maybe she just got sick of long hair.' She gave my cock a hard squeeze. 'Sometimes a cigar is just a cigar, Dr Freud.'

'And is a stuffed doll always just a stuffed doll?'

'I don't get it.'

'There was blood on a stuffed panda I found on her bed.'

'The girl held it between her legs while she was menstruating and pressed down,' Ana said authoritatively.

'Did you used to do that?'

'I used a towel. A stuffed animal is a lot harder to wash without ruining it. I was a practical little girl.'

'So maybe she wanted her parents to notice how she'd stained her panda.'

'Sounds possible.' She dropped her hold on me and picked up her book. When she turned the page, a dried flower slipped out. She handed it to me, and I put it in the small pile I kept on my night table. It was a wild delphinium, faded from purple to pale blue. Ernie always slipped flowers in the books he gave us. You never knew when a paper-thin yellow hibiscus would tumble out of a history book or a jasmine blossom from a nineteenth-century novel.

I opened *Deaf People in Hitler's Europe*, since my latest reading project was on the Nazi war against disabled people. But I didn't get very far before Jorge took up all the room in my mind. I'd been thinking of late that he might turn out to be gay. Like his uncle. If that's what Ernie truly was, since I wasn't sure he'd ever had sex. What I'd decided previously and what I concluded again now was that I just didn't want my son to be in any hurry to grow up.

Ana turned off her reading light a few minutes later. It was pointless for me to try to fall asleep before Nati came back home, so I tiptoed downstairs and watched a baseball game on ESPN. Had hitting home runs for the Milwaukee Brewers really ever seemed like the future I wanted for myself?

The game was unable to hold my attention, so I moved my laptop to the dining table and attached Coutinho's flash

114

drive. It contained just one folder, *Christmas Vacations*. Inside it were twelve files: *Phuket 2011, London 2010, New York 2009, Egypt 2008, Cape Verde 2007, Brazil 2006, Japan 2005, Vietnam 2004, California 2003, Italy 2002, Prague 2001, St Barth's 2000*.

I started hunting for information about Coutinho's bribes with the Phuket file, but after an hour and a half I reached the conclusion that it and the eleven others held only the usual mind-numbing mix of posed portraits and postcard-pretty tourist shots.

Only two photos caught my attention. The older of the two had been taken in Japan in 2005, and it showed the victim leaning over a large sheet of blue paper, slashing a long brushstroke across its surface. Due to the slow exposure, his bamboo brush looked like an unfolding fan, and Coutinho's eyes were so intensely focused on his work that if life were a comic book instead of what it was, two lasers would have issued from his eyes.

The other photo had been taken in Trafalgar Square in 2010. Susana was wrapped in a luscious white fur coat with a dramatically dipping black collar. Her showy, sex-kitten smile looked too practised and phony. Pedro was sporting a black trilby circled by an emerald-green band and smoking a gargantuan cigar. Had they quarrelled just before the shot? A glint of seething malice shone in his eyes. They looked like a furious Al Capone and an ageing mom trying to pretend she was a Playboy bunny.

If Sandra took the picture, then she had an excellent eye for the macabre – a nascent Diane Arbus. Very likely she'd wanted to reveal what a failing marriage had done to her parents. Or maybe she'd turned away from a dozen other chances to document the decline of their family before permitting herself this shot. Maybe she'd spent years doing her best not to break the spell.

My son's key turned in the door while I was looking at a much younger version of Coutinho and his wife at a palm-shaded hideaway on St Barth's. It was Christmas of 2000.

Sandra had been a pudgy little Buddha, and Susana had been an achingly beautiful young mother.

Nati stumbled in at exactly 12.21 a.m., droopy-limbed and smelling faintly of beer, but I didn't say a word about him being late or about possibly falling prey to a bottle of Super Bock. I steered him to our spiral staircase.

'Louis Vuitton,' he told me as he started up.

'Come again?' I said.

'The fancy handbag designer. He made your panda. It's a collector's item. So steal it if you can. I'll sell it for you on eBay and we'll split the proceeds.'

'Thanks, I'll grab it after Forensics is through with it.'

Could Sandra have decided to ruin her most valuable doll as a way of making certain her parents would notice how troubled she was?

When I told Nati we'd be visiting my brother the next day and staying the night, I expected him to groan, but he just waved his hand in the air to acknowledge that he'd heard me and continued up towards his room.

I fell asleep shortly after getting into bed but woke up at 4 a.m. in Jorge's room. I was sitting on the deckchair onto which he tossed his dirty clothing. On my lap was a lit candle standing in the star-shaped silver holder that I'd inherited from Aunt Olivia. On the floor beside me was my laptop.

In my hand, G had drawn a tight circle of protective stars around two feathers and written, *H – it never hurts to make sure they're safe.*

Chapter 10

I remember Dad's first test as though a door slammed closed behind me the moment he dragged me out of bed. In fact, I'd guess I started separating from myself then, though Gabriel didn't write his first message to me until more than six months later. The way I figure it, it might take a while for a second person to come to life inside you.

It was Saturday 3 June 1978. I awoke into darkness, with a clasping weight over my mouth. Unable to breathe, I swung out and struck what felt like a padded wall. Dad's deep laugh made me shiver and his massive hand lifted away. I sat up, gulping for breath. The hammering against my ribs was the sound of a near escape.

My father's head tilted towards me. 'You've got to be ready for anything, son!'

His moist, rum-soaked whisper seemed like the start of a bad illness. 'Yes, sir,' I replied, still straining for air.

He flipped on the light. He wore a white T-shirt and faded jeans. He stretched his arms behind his back and bent far forward – a morning ritual. 'Son, you never know who might sneak up on you,' he told me, as if it were a great, protective truth, but what he said made no sense; our closest neighbours, the Johnsons, lived half a mile away and were in their eighties. Besides, we always locked all the doors at night.

I'd only just turned eight, but I already knew that something big was missing in Dad, though I had no idea what it could be. It wasn't obvious – like Ernie not being able to pronounce his name and saying *Eeenie* instead, or Mom not getting dressed all day. At some point in my childhood, I came to believe that no matter how long I lived, I'd never fail to understand as much about someone or something as what I failed to understand about my dad.

I found my brother's bed empty; his blanket was on the floor. I had a cramped-up feeling about him having vanished and the bed being a mess, the kind of dread that twists your gut when a teacher is about to call on you in class and you don't know the answer and you forgot to do your homework.

'Where's Ernie?' I asked.

'Waiting for us. Come on, get up!' He pounded my pillow.

'I'm really sleepy,' I told him, making my voice sound drowsy; there were days when Dad could be calm and forgiving. Though, if my theories about him are correct, he was just imitating the generous behaviour he observed in others.

Maybe that was why he married Mom, in fact; to have someone to study up close – so he could figure out how regular people behaved. In particular, I can easily imagine him practising how she smiled at me – in front of a mirror, hour after hour, till he developed a perfect imitation of the twinkling affection in her eyes.

'Get up, you little slob!' he ordered.

Swinging my legs over the side of the bed, my confusion seemed like a living thing inside me, chasing its own tail, because I never got any of the answers to my most important questions about how things could get so difficult.

I think now that Dad lacked the imagination to feel what others felt. Mom, Ernie and I were all props to him – everyone was; and the only reason he occasionally found us almost as engaging as his record collection or his old Plymouth was that he could make us – and not them – cry or smile or plead for him to stop.

'Hank, you can't possibly be that sleepy,' Dad said. 'You've had at least eight hours.' I could tell from his eyes – wide open and darting, like he'd been energized by a secret plan – that he'd taken some pills to ease his hangover.

By then, I'd figured out that Dad lived in an us-against-them world, though I couldn't have expressed it like that then. And it took me years to figure out that I was a member of *them*, even though he said I was part of *us*.

A cold wind was blasting in through the window, so Dad tossed me my cardigan sweater. It was lucky for him that Ernie wasn't old enough for school yet, because a teacher would've probably noticed what was about to happen to him and might not have been so easily convinced that I'd accidentally hurt him while playing cops and robbers. While *roughhousing*, as Dad put it when we went to the hospital, like I said. Though now that I think about it, Dad's timing must not have had anything to do with luck. He must have figured out that if he was going to steal something from Ernie and me that could never be returned, it had to be before his youngest son started first grade.

If you think that people can't plan years ahead to destroy a life, then you've never had to learn what I've tried a long time to forget. You got lucky.

Dad moved too purposefully to still be drunk. He'd slept off his bar-hopping in Gunnison on the couch in the living room.

I think he took amphetamines to cure his hangovers. It could even be that he pioneered the use of crystal meth; he told me once that one of Patsy Cline's musicians took it while on tour, though he could have been making that up. And it could be that I'm asking chemicals to explain what is a lot more complex.

My clock read 6.10 a.m. As I buttoned my sweater, I saw that the half-moon was playing tricks with the dusk – turning the early morning mist a ghostly white, and making the purple-black mountains seem soft and cottony. I figured that if I outlasted the darkness, then the sun peering over the hills in the east would make a bad ending impossible.

119

Maybe all children are born with a belief in a sun god. Maybe kids are the ones who created him in the first place.

Dad led me down the stairs. I was wearing my pyjama bottoms and slippers, and I'd put on my favourite scarf, too, so my memories of that morning seem filtered through a woolly and itchy scent. And through the deep brown colour of the scarf, too, though that doesn't make much sense.

'Where are we going?' I asked my father.

'Hold your horses!' he told me, and at the bottom of the stairs, he took my shoulders and gazed down at me amiably. 'It's like this, Hank. I've hidden Ernie. And you've got to find him. It's a new game we're going to play from now on.'

He stepped into the kitchen, opened the refrigerator door and peered in. His biceps stretched the fabric on the sleeves of his T-shirt. The plump Chinese lantern dangling from the ceiling above the kitchen table spread its reddish, under-water light around the room and made his back seem to glow like it was on fire.

Dad said clichés like *hold your horses* a lot. Maybe what was missing from him also made him lazy with the way he talked.

An old record was scratching away on the stereo in the living room. A clue, I'd later realize. Dad always left clues when he gave us his tests, but I wasn't much good at figuring them out at first.

'Who's singing?' he asked.

'The Andrews Sisters,' I shot back with show-off eager-ness. 'It's "Elmer's Tune".'

'Good boy. And what year did "Elmer's Tune" come out?'

I'm not sure what answer I gave, but it was wrong, and Dad grew disappointed in me because he liked for me to memorize all the details about his old records.

Listening to the herky-jerky singing of the Andrews Sisters and watching Dad peer into the refrigerator again made me tense with the need to run. But even if I managed to get to the main road and hitched a ride all the way to

Denver, it wouldn't do any good, because Ernie would then be alone with Dad. And wherever Ernie was, I was, too.

They say you can't be in two places at once, but that's not my experience. Maybe that's the main symptom of whatever it is that's wrong with me, in fact.

'Okay, enough stalling, it's time to find your brother!' he told me gruffly.

I shuffled up to him, trying to make myself seem real small and inoffensive. 'Why'd you hide him, Dad?'

The back of his hand caught me hard across my cheek.

'Ow!' I burst out. 'That hurt!'

'Shut up! This is no joke. If you don't find him, I'm going to do something that no one will be able to make better, and *you*, my friend, will be responsible.'

His lips were an angry slit. I could tell he was waiting for me to question him about what he'd do to Ernie, and I didn't want to, but I knew that if I didn't he might get even angrier, so I did.

'I'm going to cut off one of his thumbs!' Dad replied in a self-satisfied voice.

I don't remember what I said to that. I think I was too stunned to say anything.

'I told Ernie it would be the left one,' Dad added, 'but I might just surprise him and take the right. Or both!'

Dad had never done anything to us that needed to be x-rayed or required an operation, though Mom once had to go to the hospital emergency room in Grand Junction when he broke her nose. While I stood there wondering what to believe, and if he was telling the truth, I pictured myself racing all the way to Crawford. I'd go to the Black Cat Café and eat a sticky bun while hiding in the bathroom, which smelled like lavender and had wallpaper patterned with cowboy boots. I knew that if I could live in the bathroom of the Black Cat Café, I'd be happy for the rest of my life.

Dad took a quart of Tropicana orange juice out of the fridge and sat down at the kitchen table with a big sigh. He took a gulping swig out of the carton and wiped his mouth with his hand. Looking at his wristwatch, he said, 'Okay, Hank, you've got exactly two minutes to find your brother. Starting . . . now!'

My thoughts scattered out in a hundred different directions, trying to locate the point in what he was making me do.

Opening up his hunting knife, he started scraping out the dirt from under his fingernails. He wiped what he picked out on his jeans.

The knife had a mother-of-pearl handle that made you want to hold it up to the light to see it sparkle. He'd bought it at a store in Grand Junction that had rifles hanging on the walls.

Dad was forty-three years old in June of 1978, as wiry and strong as a wide receiver, with stiff, short brown hair like porcupine quills. He wore his Milwaukee Braves baseball cap nearly all the time, even when he napped. He said it was a collector's item, because the Braves moved to Atlanta shortly after he bought it. He had a big welcoming smile – and it had something manly and authoritative to it, too, like he was a policeman or a park ranger. He often went out drinking with friends from work, and they came over sometimes, but I never liked how they smelled of beer and called me *little man*, so I always ran out of the house when they came. We got a lot of phone calls from women wanting to speak to him, too, but they never came over. At the time, I didn't think it was weird that they called our home; I figured they worked with Dad at the sawmill.

He lit up a cigar after dinner every night. I didn't mind the choky smokiness around the house so much, but when he tucked us in at night, with those fingers of his stinking of dead tobacco, I'd close my eyes as tight as I could and think about being anywhere other than where I was.

'You've just wasted thirty seconds, Hank,' Dad told me. 'Come on, son, go on and find your brother.'

He started singing along with the Andrews Sisters. He had a handsome tenor voice that made me proud of him. Being asked to sing along with him always made me feel as if we'd touched down on the right planet after lots of false landings on the wrong ones. Dad said that he'd have ended up as a backing vocalist for Patsy Cline if she hadn't died in a plane crash. He even sometimes told that to tourists we met in town. He told me I should try to become a singer when I was older. He said I could form a duo with Ernie, like the Everly Brothers.

'What do you really want from me, Dad?' I asked.

He pointed his knife towards me. 'Keep your trap shut and find your brother!'

I looked in the kitchen cabinets. And then in the broom closet.

'You're so cold that your feet are turning to ice!' Dad told me, balancing on the back two legs of his chair, smirking at me like he was winning a contest.

I went to the living room. I searched behind the two arm-chairs and under the couch, and in the shiny folds of the yellow curtains my mom had bought because they were what she called 'Uma cor muito alegre.' A very cheerful colour.

Another thing I didn't know until it was too late was that buying curtains to cheer you up can be a real bad sign. It might even mean that you're not going to live much longer.

I ended up outside, crawling underneath the porch. The soil was moist there, and it smelled secretive, too, like some-one could hide there for a long time without anyone finding out. 'Ernie, you in there?' I whispered, because the space between the ground and the wooden slats of our porch went far back and got as dark as our closet got when we closed the door. I shivered, not because I was cold, but because Ernie and I had once spotted a big brown snake there that might have been a rattler.

No reply. I called his name a few more times. I even said, 'It's me, Hank,' though that seemed a stupid thing to say right after I said it. I told him that I'd figure out a way to get us out of this game without him getting hurt, but the truth was that I didn't have any idea what I was doing.

There was no answer, so on a hunch, I ran around to the garage. Almost right away, I spotted Ernie's stuffed cat Roxanne trapped in the passenger window of Dad's Plymouth. She was blue, with black beads for eyes, and Ernie had drawn big red lips on her with a felt pen. Her round, puffy face was peering out, as if she was trying to get my attention.

Ernie wasn't inside the car like I thought he'd be. And he wasn't underneath it either. Maybe he was inside one of the brown storage boxes. I figured time had almost run out on me, so I dashed back to Dad. 'He's got to be in the garage!' I announced, sure that my getting close to finding him would earn me another minute or two.

'Why do you think that, son?' Dad asked.

I held up Roxanne.

'I'm disappointed in you. You can be pretty dumb, you know. And your time was up twenty seconds ago, in any case.'

'That's not fair,' I protested. 'I should get another minute for nearly finding him!'

I could tell from the way he strode past me that Ernie and I were in big trouble. His chest got all puffed up like that when he was going to teach Mom a lesson, which was what he called punching her.

I caught up to him. 'How about some breakfast? I'm really hungry.'

He pushed me away and opened the cabinet with the cane-work front where he stored the 78s in his record collection. Ernie was inside, squatting on his haunches. Dad had gagged his mouth and bound his hands.

Seeing my brother all tied up and squashed like that, I felt something come undone in my chest – something important. Sometimes now, I think that was a signal that my world was about to change for the worse and would never be the same.

How many times have I asked myself if Dad really meant to hurt Ernie so badly? Maybe whatever drugs he took for his hangovers made all he did to us seem like one long, never-ending, competitive game, and forcing me to hunt for Ernie was just a small part of his strategy for achieving a lasting victory. It's possible that he didn't even know his own intentions.

I want to think that Dad later realized he went way too far on this occasion, and that he regretted what he did, but I'm pretty sure that's only because I want him to be like other people – and to be a person I'm not ashamed to love.

Ernie's eyes were terrified. But he wasn't moaning or trying to shout. That scared me the most – his silence. He was just four years old and already he'd learned it was best not to make a peep, even if he was about to have a thumb cut off.

I try not to visualize Ernie squatting in Dad's cabinet too often. Most of all, I try not to put myself in his place. Despite what the talk-show psychologists say on television, recovering certain memories does you no good at all.

Ernie had squeezed both his thumbs inside his fists. I caught his attention by waving at him and tried to tell him with my eyes that I'd make our father get so angry with me that he'd forget about him.

'Ernie's real scared, Dad!' I said, to buy some time.

'Yeah, son, he sure is!' he replied in the voice of a man gratified by his own success.

Did he really admire his own handiwork, or was that just the way his voice sounded to a kid who was learning how to hate?

'He's got to be hungry for breakfast, too,' I said.

I took a step towards my brother, and then another, and when Dad didn't stop me, I went straight up to Ernie and knelt down so that I could untie him. I prayed that if our father got so angry that he couldn't stop himself from hurting one of us, that he'd grab me and not my brother. But I hoped he wouldn't break my arm or leg, because then I'd be unable to play baseball all summer.

I started to undo the knot in the gag in Ernie's mouth. It was made of the same nylon rope Dad used to tie up the beans and tomatoes in his vegetable garden.

'I'm here, Ernie,' I whispered, and I squeezed his arm once so he'd know I wasn't going to go away.

But touching him turned out to be the wrong thing to do; he started to shiver and moan as though he'd fallen through the ice in a winter river.

'Shit!' Dad growled, and he grabbed me by my hair and yanked me back so hard that I crashed into the couch. I tasted blood on my lips as I got to my knees.

When Dad raised his hunting knife, the room seemed to grow dark around me.

'Leave him alone!' I yelled.

Did Mom hear me shout? She'd have had to. I suspect now that she was listening at her door, too afraid to make a sound and too high on Valium to come downstairs to help us, because a few minutes later, when I ran upstairs and told her we needed to get to the hospital right away, I found her sitting on her bed already dressed, and her eyes were so lifeless that I understood that she must have heard everything that had gone on.

About a year later, when I was home one day from school with a cold, she confessed that she was terrified of Dad, too. I'm not sure why she told me that. I guess I should have expected that she was afraid of him after all the lessons he'd taught her, but her words shocked me badly and then sat inside me like something rotten for weeks.

I can see now that I ought to have begged Dad to take me instead of Ernie. It might have made all the difference. But maybe the truth is that I was too terrified to substitute my brother. I've spent more than thirty years of my life ashamed of how I behaved that day.

Dad grabbed Ernie by the arm and dragged him to his feet. He cut off the gag and the bindings around his wrists. My brother started shrieking when Dad grabbed his arm and lifted him into the air, and he wriggled and kicked so

126

hard that our father put him back down and whacked him on the back of the head.

As I stood up, a glint of metal flashed in my eyes like a spray of acid, and there was blood – way too much – running down the side of Ernie's head and cheek.

Dad held up whatever he cut off and said, 'You see what I had to do because of you, Hank! You see how far you made me go! There's something evil in you, son!'

Chapter 11

I awoke on Saturday morning at 6 a.m. Despite having slept only a few hours, I felt refreshed and strong, and eager for the solitary silence of the living room. Easing my notebook out of my underwear drawer, I crept downstairs through the fragile darkness. Our breakfast table welcomed me inside a universe far beyond the ticks of any clock. While sipping my coffee, I held tight to my favourite illusion that everyone I had ever loved was safe. And inside the tight warm halo made by my overhead lamp, I worked on my secret project: *Haiku from a Colorado Childhood*. Only Ernie knew about it.

> *Springtime hummingbird*
> *Zooming between two brothers:*
> *Ruby pendulum.*

A man who knows he will not be watched can write what he wants – and risk seeming foolish. He can live in that part of his memory where good things have been stored and guarded, and write cryptic notes of exactly seventeen syllables to the boy he used to be.

When I heard the squeals of Ana turning on the tap in the shower, I took the stairs two at a time, crazy with my need to see her. She leaned away from me when I tried to kiss her, however. With the water pelting her back, she drew in her shoulders and said, 'Are you going to be friendly now?'

Her eyes revealed such misery that I reached out for her, but she batted my hand away.

'What did I do?' I asked desperately.

'Are you saying you don't remember?' she asked in disbelief.

'I must have been half asleep. I had a long day yesterday and—'

'I don't want to hear it!' she cut in. Her jaw was throbbing.

My heartbeat swayed me from side to side. Water pounded across her shoulders and glued her dark hair to her neck. I decided not to move; I'd outlast this quarrel, as I had so many times during the first years of our marriage, when G had tried to sabotage our relationship. At length, she turned back around to face me and took my hand. Her eyes were sad but forgiving.

'You know how I am when I'm half asleep,' I said. 'I say and do things that I don't recall in the morning. It's a form of sleepwalking. My mom had it. Now tell me what I did, please.'

'You were looking at photographs on your laptop. When I asked you what they were, you told me, "Mind your own fucking business!"'

After I apologized, she let me kiss her, and I explained about the victim's flash drive and how this new case was playing havoc with my mind. She nodded so glumly that I stepped into the shower in my boxer shorts and T-shirt and hugged her.

'Hank, what are you doing?' she exclaimed, horrified.

'I'm not sure,' I said, laughing.

The hot water soaking into me took away my inhibitions. I pressed my need into her hip and whispered what I wanted. Just after I'd entered her, Jorge called out to us. Through some deft contortions, Ana managed to poke her head around the shower curtain. 'Just a minute!' she yelled.

He stepped into the bathroom a moment later. 'I'm hungry!' he squealed.

'Go take yourself some bran flakes, baby,' she told him.

She wanted to say more but my unrelenting, slow persistence made her tremble. Lifting her up as quietly as I could, I drew her legs around me and pinned her back to the wall. She moaned, which seemed a triumph.

'Mom?' Jorge asked in a concerned voice.

Ana had closed her eyes by then and wasn't about to reply.

'Everything's okay,' I told my son. 'Mom and I are just having a shower.'

Ana pulled me as deeply into her as I could go. The scent of her neck was like warm wool. No one I'd ever known smelled as good as Ana.

'Dad?' Jorge asked.

'Yeah.'

'I'm hungry.'

'As soon as we're done here, I'll make you breakfast.'

'I want waffles!'

'You got it! Now let us have a few minutes alone, baby.'

Grunting loudly, he stamped out of the bathroom. And yet the determined force of his surliness only served to fill me with admiration for him – and also to change the direction of my lovemaking; I wanted to come so powerfully inside Ana that we'd make another kid – right here, right now.

Afterwards, we checked on Jorge but he'd already fallen back to sleep. While leaning my chin on Ana's shoulder, I gazed out the window, admiring the twittering exuberance of our Portuguese swallows and the pink haze that was painting the old houses of Santa Marinha Square with pastel colours. Lisbon was sacred at this hour, and its crumbling, emaciated charm made me feel as if I'd stepped into a fairy tale. 'It would be such a shame if our economic troubles destroyed all this,' I said, and for one slightly mad moment I thought that before conditions got any worse – and more people started emigrating – I ought to invite everyone who lived on the square over for tea.

I'd confessed to Ana that I might want to have another kid while we were getting dressed, and she said now, 'It wouldn't be fair to bring another baby into Portugal at a time like this. Besides, the world population is way too high.'

'Except that Ernie's not going to have any kids. We can have three and my family average will only be one and a half.'

She kissed my cheek as her way of saying no. 'We couldn't afford it,' she told me.

I held both her hands. 'Ernie's taking care of two other gardens now, so he's stopped using up our savings. We're going to be all right from now on.'

Back downstairs, I sat cross-legged on the sofa, quiet and warm, daydreaming about a new baby in my arms. Eager to pass on my good feelings, I called Ernie and told him that the kids and I would be coming over in the afternoon – maybe even for lunch, if I could finish up my work in time.

'Really – today?' he asked excitedly.

My brother and I had once watched a squirrel dash sixty feet to the top of a maple tree with an almond we'd handed him, ecstatic with his good fortune but also worried that one of his rivals would steal it from him. That little grey fur-ball, swaying on a slender branch, keeping one eye out for a thief, was Ernie on receiving any form of good news.

'Yeah, though Ana can't come. She's got too much work at her gallery – lots of tourists in the summer.'

'Too bad. When will you guys get here?' Then, regretting his inquisitiveness, he said, 'Though I don't want to force you into any specific time.'

'I'm hoping we can leave about noon, and in that case we'll be there around a quarter to two. And yes, I'll send you a message when we leave.'

Silence. My brother was considering all he'd have to do before our arrival: hide his medications from the kids, test his door locks, pick vegetables . . . Rushing him would only fluster him, so I crossed the room to the window overlooking the square. Lisa, the little dark-haired girl who lived on the first floor of our building, was walking her family's fluffy white Persian cat on a leash.

'Rico, do you think Jorge and Nati would eat eggplant and rice, and maybe some salad?'

'They'll eat anything you decide to make. You're an excellent cook.'

'They'll have to be a bit flexible.'

'Ernie, don't you think the kids have figured out what kind of meal to expect from you?'

'Sorry. I'm nervous. You scared me yesterday. Can we start over?'

That was what Ernie and I asked whenever the other got irritated.

'Done,' I agreed.

It was Aunt Olivia who'd invented the technique of beginning conversations over. She hadn't been prepared for an out-of-control fourteen-year-old and his morbidly quiet younger brother, and every time we overwhelmed her to tears, she learned to say, *Can we start over?* The amazing thing is that – after a year or two – Ernie and I developed the ability to rewind our emotions whenever she asked, as if she had spoken an incantation.

Maybe we all need at least one magician in our life. Aunt Olivia had been ours. What amazing luck we'd had that she was so eager to have us live with her!

'Oh, I need something!' Ernie exclaimed. 'When you turn off towards Quinta da Vidigueira, you'll see an abandoned farm with a few pomegranate trees. Pick me some flowers. If you don't mind, I mean.'

'Of course I don't mind.

'You know, Rico, pomegranate flowers are the *exact colour* of summer sunsets in Colorado!' In a whisper, he added, 'I hope Ana isn't angry at me for stealing you from her for a night. If she is, you don't have to stay over.'

Ernie needed me to know he was ambivalent about us staying the night. And he was testing me, too. Part of him wanted me to disappoint him – to prove to him the uselessness of wanting to be part of our family. 'Ana is only too happy to get rid of us once a week,' I told him.

He laughed. 'Okay, then look both ways before you cross the street.'

After hanging up, I took myself more coffee and went back to the breakfast table. I was thinking what a couple of loons Ernie and I were when a radio journalist from TSF called. It was still only ten minutes to eight. 'How did you get my number?' I asked.

'A friend.'

'Which friend?'

He passed over my question and told me he wanted just five minutes of my time to discuss Coutinho's murder. Startled, I replied in a ruder voice than I intended that our Public Relations department would give him a lot more than five and disconnected.

When Ana started down our staircase, I sat on my haiku notebook. At such times, I realized that I had more secrets than any one person should probably have.

While my wife was wolfing down her bran flakes and blueberries, Mesquita, the deputy head of the Judicial Police, phoned. 'Good morning, Chief Inspector,' he began. 'Have you seen the newspapers yet?' His tone was falsely cheerful.

'No, sir, sorry. I'm afraid I just woke up.'

Ana made an ugly face on hearing that I was on the phone with a superior.

'Tell me, have you ever been strung up by your balls?' Mesquita asked.

'No, but I'm guessing it might ruin my day.'

'I was warned you might try to be amusing.'

'It's a personality flaw, sir. Besides, my wife is here with me, and I like to keep her entertained.' I waved at her, and she waved back.

Ana mouthed: *Who is it?*

133

Mesquita.

She picked up her cereal and rushed into the living room. She hated overhearing my work calls because she thought I gave in to even the most outrageous demands of my bosses.

'Buy the *Correio da Manhã*,' Mesquita told me, 'then call me back.'

Two reporters were waiting for me just outside the door to our building, one from *Visão*, the other from Antenna 2. They pestered me all the way up to Graça Square. It appeared that my fifteen minutes of fame had finally come, but I made the stunning discovery that I no longer wanted them.

I bought the *Correio da Manhã* and went for coffee at the Concha, my usual café. The article on Coutinho was on page two and it noted that he had been shot with one bullet, gagged and left to die in his living room.

I was betting that Vaz had leaked this information. I called Mesquita to tell him I'd do some checking around, then get back to him.

As if that reply wasn't good enough for him, he said, 'I'm getting pressured to pick someone else to investigate the case.'

Stumbling backwards in my head, I stammered, 'I . . . I don't think that makes much sense, sir. We collected a great deal of evidence yesterday, and we're still—'

'No, you don't get it, Monroe,' he interrupted. 'I'm being pressured to find someone more easily . . . let's say, influenced. Not that they come out and say that. They just say that you're too much of a loner and, and that you hear voices, and that . . .'

'I really don't think—'

'Shut up and let me talk! Look, I want you to do whatever you need to do to solve the case quickly. *Anything!* Do you understand?'

Was he suggesting that I venture into illegal territory only a day after telling me to do everything by the book? I'd have asked him exactly what he meant, but he disconnected on me. For maybe the thousandth time since I'd become a cop, I wished I could have spoken to my colleagues in English, since I was far better at hearing what wasn't being said in that language.

At home, I found Jorge kneeling on the floor in the living room in his pyjamas, just two feet from the television, his face flickering bluish-white. Ana was at her desk, concentrating on her email. While I made my son strawberry waffles, his favourite meal, I figured out how to lay a trap for the person who'd leaked information to the press. I called Vaz first.

'It's Saturday, Monroe,' he said grumpily, as if I didn't know.

I explained that Coutinho's laptop contained details of the bribes he'd recently paid to a businessman from Madrid connected to the Spanish Interior Ministry. The payment was made to win a contract for a shopping mall near Salamanca. I'd just been warned that members of the Spanish government might try to alter the course of our investigation.

'And what in God's name does that have to do with me?' he questioned.

Our kitchen is open to the living room, and I was watching my son, who was walking around on all fours, imitating a cartoon lion, and he was so much more compelling than Vaz that I thought: *I've lost way too much time with this asshole over the years.*

'You're an unpleasant person,' I stated for the record.

'Why don't you just go back to America where you belong?' he shot back.

'So you've finally said it,' I told him.

'You think we're all a bunch of incompetent hicks in Portugal. You think the only sophisticated place in the world is where you come from!'

'You can't really be saying *I* think that rural Colorado was a sophisticated place to grow up!' I erupted into laughter without waiting for his reply.

By then, the waffle was done, so I slid it onto a plate. Jorge and Ana were looking at me with questioning faces because I was still laughing.

'What the hell is so funny?' Vaz demanded.

I took a few calming breaths. 'Despite what you've heard at Central Committee meetings, I wasn't responsible for the coup in Chile or electing George W. Bush one and a half times.'

'What are you talking about?'

When I put the breakfast plate down on the floor in front of my son, he brushed his head against my leg – a grateful lion cub. I said to Vaz, 'I didn't drop any bombs on Allende's presidential palace. I can't even fly a plane. Your inside information about me is all wrong. Though I will admit that I don't care much for his niece's writing.'

'His niece?'

'Isabel Allende. *The House of the Spirits?* My brother thought it was wonderful, but magic realism acts on me like a sleeping pill.'

I expected a huffing protest, or maybe a small, hesitant laugh, but Vaz disconnected without another word. If only he could have despised me for who I was instead of who I wasn't.

Jorge was nosing his strawberries around his plate with his make-believe snout and biting at them. When I waved at him, he growled ferociously, which was comforting under the circumstances. I called Fonseca next and identified the crooked businessman in my invented story as French. I made the construction project an office building in Toulouse. On each subsequent call, I gave the bribe-taker a different nationality and put the construction site in a different country.

Upstairs, while I was dressing, Nati came to me, sipping on a mug of peppermint tea. I was feeling optimistic about my plan to catch the snitch on my team and gave him a

136

quick kiss on his cheek. Since I'd caught him by surprise, he didn't moan or lean away from me – a small triumph.

'Can you make a file invisible?' I asked him while slipping into my jeans.

'Clarification, Chief Inspector.'

'I was looking at a flash drive. I need to know if it's easy to create a file that nobody can see unless they put in some sort of password or know exactly where to look for it?'

'It must be, but you better ask your computer expert.' Nati yawned. 'Listen, Dad, what time are we going to visit Tio Ernesto?'

Of late, Nati found it amusing to call Ernie by his Portuguese name, probably because my brother dressed like an American country music singer and seemed much more like an Ernie.

'Noonish,' I answered. 'And bring a change of clothing.'

'I don't suppose I could get out of sleeping over.'

'No, your *tio* is counting on it.' I eyed him closely. 'Believe it or not, he thinks you're still such a sweet little guy that you'd never even take a sip of beer without asking your dear old dad first.'

Nati made the cute-as-can-be grimace we called his turtle face. I wasn't falling for it. 'Remind me to talk to you about drinking on the way over to your uncle's,' I told him.

'You can skip the lecture,' he said, frowning. 'I just had one sip.'

'Is that why you smelled like a strip joint in Durango?'

'What's a strip joint?'

'A club where women are paid to take off their clothes and dance for the customers.'

'Sounds delightful,' he said, making a gagging sound.

'Nati, there are a lot of bored people in the world.'

'So did you used to go to a strip joint in Durango?'

'Amazingly enough, I had a life before you were born.'

'Yeah, only you never tell me about it,' he said resentfully. He gazed off. He looked too adult in profile for my liking. 'Do you ever regret having me?' he asked.

I felt as if I'd been thrown from a speeding car. 'Where'd that come from?' I asked.

'You never tell us about Colorado. And ... and I said something mean yesterday.'

'What did you say?'

'I said I might press delete on you.'

'That wasn't mean! That's what kids all do sooner or later. Besides,' I winked, 'it won't work. I'm un-deletable.' I took his hands and swung them between us like a bridge. It was a game we'd often played when he was little. 'Listen up, Nati, I never regret having you. That would be impossible. I don't talk about Colorado because nothing of interest ever happened there.'

'But what were your parents like?'

'Like everybody else's.'

'Like everybody else's how?'

I looked through the stack of Holocaust books on my night table to take the pressure of his gaze off me. 'Mom stayed home and cooked,' I said. 'Dad worked at a sawmill. Ernie and I ended up on our own most of the time.'

'Do you have any photographs of your parents?'

I picked out *The War Against the Jews* because it had statistics at the end that I could pretend to be studying. 'I really hope not,' I said.

He rolled his eyes. 'Who do you look like, your mom or your dad?'

'I have my mom's nose and hair, my dad's mouth and eyes. An unfortunate mix – my modelling career would have taken off if it were the other way around.'

'So Ernie must have your mom's mouth and eyes.'

'Ernie doesn't look like either of them.' Untrue, but the very last thing I needed was my eldest son suspecting just what Dad had suspected.

'And you're sure you have no photos of your parents? I mean, you've looked?'

'I didn't bring any to Portugal. Besides, vampires don't show up on film.'

'Not funny,' he said.

I went to the window and stuck my head outside. The breeze was already warm. When I turned around, I discovered Nati was still waiting for me to provide him with grandparents. I'd always suspected this day would one day come, but I'd have preferred putting it off for a few more years.

'You must have pictures of your house, at least,' he said optimistically.

'Not me. Ernie may have a couple. We'll ask him today.'

'And both your parents are dead?'

'I am absolutely certain I've told you all this before.'

'Tell me again. I must have been too little to remember.'

'You weren't too little.'

'If I want to hear it all again,' he said angrily, 'then what's it to you?'

'Mom died first. I was eleven. Ernie was seven.'

'A car accident, right?'

'Yeah, she crashed head-on into a tree – a cottonwood tree. The biggest one on the road to the nearest town.'

He wrinkled his nose. 'That must have been awful.'

'It was, especially for Ernie,' I replied.

'What about you?'

I hated the idea of Nati feeling sorry for me. 'Me? I did the best I could.'

'And what about your dad?'

'Oh, he was upset at first, but he did fine in the end. I took over doing the laundry, so I don't think he even noticed she was gone.'

'No, I mean when did your father die?'

I almost told Nati the truth, just to get it over with once and for all, but that would have led to questions about the police and how they'd located my father's car but never found him, and how a forty-nine-year-old man could vanish without a trace. 'Dad died three years after Mom,' I told him.

'In the same month, I think you once said.'

'So you do remember, after all.'

'Dad, just tell me!'

'They died on the very same day in May – May the second,' I said. 'But three years apart.'

'That seems impossible.'

It would have made sense to him if could have said, *He decided to disappear on the day Mom died*, but I was too deep inside my lie. 'Strange things have happened to me my whole life,' I said instead. 'Me and Ernie both. You might even say we're a magnet for the odd and unlikely. Though, to tell you the truth, I've always thought that Dad worked it out so he could die on the same day as Mom.'

'How would he have done that?'

'Doctors sometimes give people a morphine overdose if they're in a lot of pain. On the sly, of course. I think my father may have asked for that.'

'What did he die of?'

'Pancreatic cancer.' I'd heard it was always fatal and unbearably painful.

'And that's when you and Ernie came to live with Aunt Olivia?'

'Bingo.'

Nati took a quick sip of his tea. 'And where did you go to school when you were growing up?'

'Five miles from our house, inside a little brick building. It's all a blur except for gym class. I liked baseball. I was a real good pitcher.' Actually, I never pitched, but I was enjoying how well I could lie. 'So, was it really just one sip of beer?' I asked.

'It was half a bottle. But it made me feel sick. You don't have to worry.'

'Good, because we have some violent drunks in our family.'

'Who?'

'My father.'

'My grandfather was a drunk?' he asked in an astonished tone.

'Yeah, except he wasn't your grandfather.'

'If he was your father, that makes him my grandfather. *Ipso facto*.'

'*Ipso facto*?'

'Senhora Laredo teaches us Latin to help us with our Portuguese.'

'You can tell Senhora Laredo that it takes more than biology to make someone your grandfather.' In the coded language that Ernie and I had invented, I added, '*Can you sure be didn't he us deserve*.'

'I'm not Tio Ernesto,' he said resentfully.

I translated for him: 'You can be sure he didn't deserve us.'

'Because he was a drunk?'

'Among other things.'

'But you just said your parents were just like everybody else's!'

He was sure he'd caught me out, but I was ready for him. 'Half the people in our neck of the woods were alcoholics,' I told him happily. 'Hell, Mayor Anderson couldn't stand up straight from September through May. They had to pad his office with bubble wrap!'

He gave me a sceptical look; maybe he guessed that I'd used those lines before – as it happens, I'd first tried them out on his mother on our second date. Although Mayor Anderson was real enough. Our dad used to go elk hunting with him in the San Juan National Forest. *Two Drunks Shooting Anything That Moves* – I always thought it would make a good title for their travel guide to Colorado.

'Was your father violent?' Nati asked.

'He yelled a lot.'

'At you and Ernie?'

'And at our mother. She got the worst of it.'

'What did he yell at her?'

'Nati, what exactly is the point of this?' I demanded.

'Just tell me!'

'He used to call her a slob.' Another lie, but I wouldn't say what he'd called our mother; I'd vowed never to repeat those words aloud.

141

'Did your mom yell back?'

'No.'

'Did you and Ernie?'

'No.'

'That's weird.'

'Maybe. It seemed normal at the time. I learned very young that normal can be the weirdest thing of all.'

'Dad, you don't always have to try to be amusing,' he informed me, as if he were doing me a favour.

'A playwright named Oscar Wilde once wrote, "If you want to tell people the truth, make them laugh, otherwise they'll kill you." Astonishingly enough, I came to the same conclusion that Mr Wilde did when I was just a little kid.'

'Was it your father who had the record collection?'

'What record collection?' I asked, going for my Oscar award.

'Mom once said that you know all those old songs because your father had a thousand record albums, even some . . . I forget what they're called. When they're played at a different speed.'

'Seventy-eights. Yeah, he had seventy-eights of a lot of amazing people.'

'Like who?'

'The big bands, all the best blues singers . . . But I loved Eddie Cantor and Al Jolson the best. I used to imitate Jolson pretty well.' I knelt down, spread my arms as if to summon my son into my arms and tossed off a bit of 'Swanee'.

'Sounds awful,' Nati said with a disappointed frown – because I'd performed for him instead of confiding in him.

I was a bit disappointed in myself, too. 'Awful was very popular during the 1930s,' I replied. As a concession, I added, 'We used to listen to Dad's records all winter. Sometimes we'd dance, too.'

'Dance?'

'Yeah, me and Ernie and Dad. He taught us to jitterbug and foxtrot and tango. We had a great time. Dad may have been a drunk but he had *style!* Mom would sometimes dance with me and Ernie, too – but only when my father wasn't home.'

'But you *never* dance.'

'I was a kid, Nati! I did lots of things I don't do now.'

'Did you save any of the records?'

'No. I'm not sure what happened to them.' *We poured gasoline on them and had ourselves a vinyl fire so big that the prairie dogs smelled it all the way over in Utah*, was the reply I kept hidden under my tongue; if I'd said that, Nati would have asked why we didn't just donate them to a charity or a school, and I wasn't sure he'd buy the excuse that we were just kids. And maybe I'd have had to explain, too, about my brother not wanting to set them ablaze and crying for three straight days afterward.

By then, I figured I'd used up my daily allocation of lies, so I produced the long sigh I was famous for in our family and said, 'Have you eaten breakfast yet?'

'No.'

'I can scramble you some eggs with piri-piri just like you like.'

'Nah, I'll just have Weetabix.' He started away, looking miserable, then turned back. 'I'm sorry I was mean to you yesterday.'

I wanted to hug him for being so kind to me, but he would have squirmed. 'It's okay,' I said. 'Listen, Nati, I may not recall much about the way my life was before you came along, but I remember *everything* about you.'

He nodded, trying to hide his continued disappointment behind a smile that seemed so generous that I almost regretted not telling him the truth.

On checking my email, I discovered that Fonseca had sent me a photo of the Asian characters written in blood on the wall of Coutinho's living room, as well as a link where I could download every page of his address book. Given the victim's background, I presumed for the moment that the writing was Japanese. On the site for Lisbon's New University, I located the office number and email for the Japanese language teacher, Yosoi Kimura. When he didn't answer my call, I left a brief message and asked him to phone me back. I also sent him an email and attached Fonseca's photograph.

It was nearly nine by then, and I had to leave to interview Sandi.

Susana Coutinho answered my knocks on her front door in khaki trousers and a T-shirt, wearing neither lipstick nor make-up – still convinced, it seemed, she'd fare better by impersonating the woman she used to be. Crescents of skin under her eyes betrayed a bad night, however. After inviting me in with a peeved swirl of her hands, she said, 'I had a hell of a time getting Sandi to agree to talk to you, Monroe.'

Her nasty frown was an attempt to make me feel guilty. 'I'll try to be quick,' I assured her.

Sandi was seated by the table on the garden deck, in the slanting shade of the palm tree, rigid and glum, as if she'd been punished unfairly. She turned away the moment she spotted me coming out to her. She must have showered just before my arrival: her hair was wet and parted on the side, which made her look like a studious young boy. I suspected her mother had insisted that she comb it. She was still wearing her father's blue sweater, which hung down from her shoulders to her knees. On her feet were bright pink sneakers with yellow laces. Her socks were emerald green.

At that moment, her need for colour meant that she and Ernie had a lot in common.

I whispered to Senhora Coutinho, 'I'd like to talk to your daughter alone, if you don't mind.'

'Out of the question!' she shot back.

'She'll express herself more freely without you listening in.'

'Maybe so, but I won't leave her alone.'

144

'You can watch us out the kitchen window. If you see any-thing you don't like, you can come right out.'

She heaved a sigh. 'This is absurd. Sandi doesn't know anything about her father's murder. You're wasting your time.'

'People are often unaware of what they know.'

She snorted as if I'd spoken an embarrassing platitude. 'All I know,' she told me, 'is that if you upset her, I'll have the Minister of Justice fire your ass!'

I took her arm, hoping to regain a little of the solidarity we'd achieved the day before. She looked at me long and hard with her bruised eyes – trying to come to terms with the unwelcome surprises I provoked in her, it seemed to me. 'Tell me, Monroe, are you like this with everyone you've just met?' she asked.

'Like what?'

'Invasive. And unpredictable.'

'I hope so, but I'll ask my wife just to make sure.'

She showed me a grudging smile – amused and irritated at the same time. Without my asking again, she returned to the kitchen.

'Good morning,' I said to Sandi on sitting down at the deck.

She faced me with dull eyes, as if to show me she had no intention of participating actively in our conversation. While driving over, I'd decided to ask her first about hiding her turquoise ring and keeping a knife under her bed, because such protective measures implied that she'd been threat-ened. To my questions about them, however, she replied, 'That's none of your business.' She used the tone of a teenager trying – and failing – to sound haughty.

'Maybe we should start over,' I told her. 'Did your father seem nervous or worried over the last few days?'

She rolled her eyes. I could easily imagine her deleting me in her mind.

'I take it that means you noticed no difference in his behaviour,' I tried.

'No, none.'

'Did you ever overhear him being threatened by anyone?'

'No.'

'Did you ever lend out your front door key to a friend or to someone who was doing work at your house – carpenter, plumber . . . ?'

'No, never.'

While scanning my notes, I found something that I hoped would jar her out of her defensive pose. 'Why did you ask your mother yesterday if the bullet hit your father in the back?'

She gazed down as though I'd caught her in a trap. 'I . . . I don't remember,' she said hesitantly.

'Does a bullet in the back have some special meaning for you?'

'No, how could it?' she said.

'Maybe it would mean your father was betrayed by someone he knew.'

'But my mother told me he wasn't shot in the back, so what difference could it make?'

While I was searching for the right way to squeeze past this stalemate, she said in a frail, fading voice, making a first fearful step towards me: 'I always thought that my father was so strong that nothing could hurt him.'

'You thought he'd always be able to defend himself. But a person who is shot in the back doesn't get that chance. Is that what you meant?'

'I'm not sure – probably.'

'Do you have any idea why someone might have wanted to hurt your father?' I asked.

'No.'

'Can you think of anyone who might have hated him?'

'No one could hate my father,' she said, as if stating an obvious fact. 'He wasn't that kind of person.'

Out of the corner of my eye, I noticed Senhora Coutinho staring at us out of the kitchen window. She was smoking hard.

'So you don't have any idea who might have hurt him?' I asked.

'None. I'm sorry. I'd help if I could.'

Anxious to put her more at ease before I asked her another question she might resent, I said, 'You can sleep back in your own bed tonight, if you want.'

'Thanks.'

'There's something else I need you to tell me,' I continued. 'But I'm afraid you'll get angry at me again, like you did yesterday.'

'Mom always says I get too angry and upset about things. But I'll try not to.'

'I need to know if someone has been threatening you,' I said.

She shook her head bravely. 'No, no one.'

'Sandi, it's important for me to know if someone has been making your life difficult,' I said.

'That's just it,' she burst out, moaning. 'No one was! I wish there had been, but there hadn't! It was all in my head!'

'What was?'

'Terrible dreams! And they wouldn't stop!'

'Your mother mentioned them. Someone breaks into your house and hurts you and your parents.'

'That's right.'

'Have you ever been able to see who it is?'

'No, it's always at night. I can only see a vague shape entering the house.'

'A man?'

'I'm not sure.'

'A ghost – something supernatural?'

'I don't know.'

Her face peeled open to misery again, and I suddenly understood more about her guilt. 'You told your mother about your nightmares, but not your father. Is that right?'

She nodded through her tears. 'I never had a chance to warn him what might happen to him.'

'Are you sure your mother never told him about your nightmares?'

'Yes. She said she didn't want to upset him.' Sandi spoke as if she had been trying hard to forgive her mother. And failing.

'Is there anything else you can tell me about your nightmares?'

'No, I try not to remember them.' She began tracing a finger over the wooden grain in the table. I sensed she wanted to ask me something but didn't dare.

'I'll tell you anything you want to know,' I said.

'Are you going to catch the person who killed my father?'

'I'm going to try.'

'So you're not sure you'll be able to do it?'

'No. I can never be sure.'

'Do you have any idea yet who it might be?'

'I suspect it's someone your father knew. And maybe you and your mother, too. That's one of the reasons I needed to speak with you right away.'

I was hoping she'd suggest a name without my asking, but she began to trace her finger more determinedly over the table. I looked over my notes in order to give her a pause from the pressure I was putting her under. 'There was a painting that might have been moved in your living room,' I finally said. 'A drawing by Julio Almeida is there now – of Fernando Pessoa. Do you know what artwork was in that spot before?'

She looked up, surprised. 'The Almeida drawing has always been there,' she said definitively.

'You're sure?'

'Yeah, Dad loved it in that spot,' she said, as though rising to his defence.

'It's just that the rectangle of darker paint on the wall behind the Almeida would indicate that a larger painting had been there. Your mother said you sometimes went to art galleries with your father, so I thought that you might be able to identify it.'

148

'I can't see why it's important,' she told me, trying to sound superior again.

'Anything moved at a crime scene is important.'

'But nothing was moved!' she hollered.

Susana Coutinho came rushing toward us. 'That's enough!' she called ahead.

Turning to Sandi, I decided to risk sounding ridiculous. 'You deserve protection from whoever was menacing you. I'll be back to talk to you. And I promise to do everything I can to help you.' I handed her my card. 'I don't let vague shapes stop me. Or bad dreams. Or people who get pleasure from hurting young girls!'

On the way out, I asked Senhora Coutinho to think again about what painting might have gone missing and she said, 'I have the feeling it was a portrait, but that's really just a guess.'

'A portrait of who?'

'An old woman . . . ?' she said, as if it were an open-ended question.

'Someone your husband knew? A family member?'

'I don't think so. Look, Monroe, maybe it wasn't even an old woman. Like I said, I'm mostly just guessing.'

'Do you have any photos taken in your living room that might show what the painting was?'

'Why are you making such a big deal of this one little thing?'

'I think the killer took it – and for a very specific reason. Because if he was just after artwork he could sell for lots of money, he'd have taken the Paula Rego and the Almeida. And I also think that Sandi is lying about not knowing what was there.'

'Why would she lie?'

'I thought maybe you'd be able to tell me.'

'I'm just her mother, not a mind-reader,' she said in an irritated voice. In a more conciliatory tone, she added, 'But I promise to check for photos. And to find out if Sandi lied to you.'

149

After I thanked her, my phone rang; it was David Zydowicz. He told me he'd just completed his full autopsy and had confirmed all his findings from the day before. He agreed that Coutinho's body could be released to his wife.

On hanging up, I gave Senhora Coutinho that news and reminded her that Luci and Fonseca would be coming over in the afternoon. I told her I'd be speaking to her again Monday morning, if not earlier. It was five to ten when I stepped again onto the Rua do Vale. I phoned Luci to tell her to question Morel and Senhora Grimault about the painting in the living room that had been moved. With the time left to me, I decided to visit those apartments on the street where no one had answered our knocks the day before, but none of the neighbours now at home had ever met Pedro Coutinho, or heard any gunshot on Thursday morning.

I got home at twenty to noon. Jorge ran to me at the door with his little red backpack already on. He told me his mother had just left. As soon as we were all buckled up in Ana's Passat, which was more reliable than my old Ford, I sent Ernie an SMS saying we were leaving. Nati sat up front with me as my co-pilot, our Automobile Club map of Portugal spread across his legs. He seemed to have gotten over his disappointment in me and filled me in breathlessly – as if running downhill – on the latest comic and tragic absurdities at his school. As we entered the freeway, he confessed he was worried about a project on Brazilian music he'd been assigned. Yet beneath even his apprehension and doubt, he seemed to be telling me he felt at home inside the intricate complexity of his life.

Jorge sat in the back seat with his wooden giraffe, whose name was Francisco. On the bridge over the Tagus, he jiggled Francisco up and down behind my head and asked questions in his giraffe voice, which was high-pitched and squeaky: 'Do we need to worry about lions around here?'; 'When can we stop to eat from the treetops?'

150

Our ongoing gag was that Francisco always had the opposite opinion as me about everything, and I kept telling him in a furious voice to *put a lid on it!* That expression made Jorge squeal with laughter. Today, I kept panting with my tongue out and complaining about the heat and Francisco kept telling me in a chill-induced stutter that it was *f-f-f-freezing!*

We ended up caught in heavy traffic on our way south to Setúbal. Still, it charmed me the way Nati traced his finger along the line of freeway to show me where we had to go. I loved how serious he could get about almost anything. But only when we spotted the hilltop castle of Montemor-o-Novo coming into view did I let myself feel the freedom of the hinterland. *No one in Colorado has ever heard of this place,* I thought, tingling with gratitude. Soon the horizon widened into reassuring vistas of rolling hills dotted with silvery-branched olive trees. I lowered my window for the earthy, extravagant, sensual scent of summer flowers and drying grasses. When we stopped for gas, the kids bought snacks while I filled up the tank, then sat on the kerb by the tyre-pressure meter as I washed the windshield. Nati nibbled on potato chips while Jorge gobbled down his chocolate bar. They shared a Coke. I waved. They waved back. The absurdity of waving to my kids even when they were only a few feet away from me never ceased to make me feel as though I'd stolen somehow into an affectionate universe.

The Alentejo had nothing monumental about it, no snow-capped mountains or towering buttes like the American West, but the whitewashed houses and cobblestone streets were so ordered and neat, and the varied greens of its land-scapes so sweetly comforting – like a child's dream given form – that it seemed to be just the right place for me and the boys.

About ten minutes after leaving the gas station, I noticed that a battered white Fiat seemed to be following us, however. It refused to pass me even when I slowed way down. With my heart jumping in my chest, I eased onto the gravel shoulder of the road. When the Fiat came to a halt fifty yards behind us, my apprehension came out as anger.

'Don't move!' I told Nati. 'And you stay put too!' I said, turning to Jorge.

'What is it, Dad?' Nati asked anxiously.

I patted his leg. 'Everything will be fine. Just stay here.'

There are moments when you become little more than a single overriding emotion. I got my handgun out of the trunk. And this I knew: I'd feel no remorse about killing anyone who threatened my kids.

A young man with short dark hair was driving the Fiat. I strode toward him with my gun drawn. He shifted into gear and began to turn in a tight circle, so I fired in the air.

He screeched to a halt. He had a gaunt face and unshaven cheeks. He yelled something out his window, but I didn't catch it; blood was throbbing in my ears.

'Get out of your car!' I shouted.

He pushed out on his door and stepped outside with his hands over his head. He was tall and lanky. He looked to be in his early thirties. 'Don't shoot me! I'm a journalist.' He tried to laugh off his terror but it came out more like a moan.

'What do you want?' I asked.

'I wanted to talk to you about Pedro Coutinho. I expected you to drop your kids somewhere and drive to police headquarters. When you got on the freeway, I didn't know what to do, so I followed you. I'm sorry.'

I lowered my gun. He lowered his hands.

'I want to interview you,' he said. 'I work for *Record*.'

'What the hell has a sports newspaper got to do with Coutinho?' I asked.

'He was a big supporter of Sporting.'

Sporting was one of Lisbon's two main soccer teams. 'Tell me, do journalists in this country think they can do anything they like?'

'It's an important story. If I don't get it, I could lose my job. Times are tough.'

'You think you can use the economic crisis to justify scaring me and my kids!'

'Look,' he said, a plea for solidarity in his voice, 'how about if we talk for just a few minutes? It would really help.'

He flashed what he must have regarded as a winning smile. Worse, he took my stunned silence as assent. 'I think it'd be best if I record our conversation,' he said.

'Forget it!' I told him.

'Then I'll just take notes,' he said amiably, and this time I was sure he misunderstood my meaning on purpose. My head was pounding by then; G had stepped up right behind me. I breathed deeply to hold him off. 'Listen, don't ever follow me again or I *will* shoot you!' I said. 'Now get in your car and get out of here!'

After he'd started off in the direction of Lisbon, I stowed my gun back in the trunk. Jorge pushed open on his door and ran to me. By the time he reached me, G was gone.

'He was just a journalist,' I told the boy as I embraced him, but he must have scented my distress and began to tear up. The passenger door opened, then slammed closed. Nati scowled at me from the shoulder of the road. I dried Jorge's eyes and ushered him back into the car. Nati got in as well. After sliding in behind the wheel, I apologized to them both.

'Why was he following us?' Nati demanded.

'The guy whose murder I'm investigating knows a lot of important people.'

Thinking of the bad things that could happen to me, I fell into a dark silence as we got under way. Nati gazed at our map convincingly, but I could tell he was still panicked – and furious at me. Thankfully, Jorge had Francisco to keep him company in the back and was holding an animated conversation with him about their friends at school.

'Hey, how big are the mountains in Colorado?' Jorge squeaked in Francisco's voice as we turned off N354 onto the nowhere-land road that would take us to Ernie's house.

'I need to think about that,' I replied; I was still jittery.

A little later, I spotted the abandoned pomegranate trees Ernie had mentioned. I figured we could use a few minutes in the sunshine. Nati waited in the car, talking on his cell phone to his friend Binky. While Jorge and I picked the glowing orange flowers, I told him, 'Sometimes, baby, the mountains in Colorado are as big as the whole sky.'

'So there's no sun?'

'Nope, it just vanishes. And no moon and no stars either. The mountains are everything. But the strange thing is, that kind of everything has two sides.'

My father used to tell me and Ernie and Mom that. I was never sure what he meant until now.

Jorge dropped the last of his flowers into my wicker basket. 'Which two sides?' he asked.

'The side you can see and the side you can't.'

On which side did you and Uncle Ernie live?

Jorge didn't ask me that. But if he had, I would have replied, 'That's just it – on the side that no one could see.'

Chapter 12

The down-payment on Ernie's house used up a third of what we'd saved from the sale of our home in Colorado. I got it cheap because the walls and roof were in ruins. Also, the property's five acres of overgrown olive fields and weedy vineyards were scattered with trash – broken bottles, oil drums, even a rusted bed frame. On my first visit there, when I stepped through what had been the front doorway, a feral cat – white, with a grey tail – poked his head out from under some shattered roof tiles, hissed at me satanically, then tore off, doing his best to convince me that he was a bad omen. Still, I knew right away, with the easy certainty of a reader turning a page, that I'd already decided to buy it; from this high corner of the hinterland, Ernie would be able to gaze out at the horizon in all directions. In the spring, a sea of wildflowers would guard him – and keep him supplied with blossoms for his artwork.

Rebuilding began on 9 December 1996. I remember the exact date because I'd met Ana three days earlier and was already crazy in love. Workers knocked down all the inner walls after putting in steel pylons, and on Saturday 4 April 1997, I spotted a small, fraying sack peeking out of some rubble. Inside it were greenish-brown coins with uneven edges and a sour smell. Ernie and I counted fifty-four of them, all of them the same, with a portrait of a wreathed monarch on one side and an angel on the other. Later that week, a coin dealer in Lisbon identified them as Roman sestertii dating from the fourth century. They were bronze and had been minted in Constantinople. The regal portrait on the front was of the Emperor Constantine. What we'd guessed was an angel was actually Winged Victory, the Roman equivalent of the Greek goddess Nike. Unfortunately, they were worth a lot less than we thought – only a few thousand dollars – so we ended up holding on to them.

Signing the papers on a house that had been occupied for at least 1,600 years meant many things to me, but most of all that I was now part of a history way beyond my time and place. On the day Ernie moved in, I realized that I'd wanted to be part of something bigger than myself since he and I were small. Almost right away, we began calling the house the Villa Ernesto – after Ernie, of course.

After the builders had completed their work, in March of 1998, I hired a stone dealer to haul in six hundred pounds of smooth-surfaced grey and white pebbles, like the river stones we used to collect in Colorado. Ernie and I shovelled them into a three-foot-wide moat around the house. As a last touch, we planted twenty-four shoulder-high orange trees to flank the scabby road leading up to the house, which my brother insisted we call the Via Enrico. We had plans for a fountain of Pan playing the flute outside the front door, but by then we'd used up all but two thousand dollars of our savings.

I still regretted we'd never had Pan welcoming visitors to the house, however, and I started sculpting him in my head again while passing the tiny whitewashed houses of Quinta da Vidigueira, the last village before Ernie's house. A phone call tugged me out of my daydream. I pulled over on seeing it was from Luci. She told me she was already at the victim's house. Morel was there, as well, and Fonseca had called to say he was on his way over. To me, Morel's willingness to return to Lisbon meant it was unlikely he'd had anything to do with the murder, but it was still possible that he'd menaced Sandi in some way. For now, I was hoping that Luci could jog his memory and that he'd recall having seen a jacket or some other item of clothing that would help us identify Coutinho's last lover.

After we hung up, I called Susana Coutinho. She had a bad hangover. In a hoarse, gravelly voice, she told me she had remembered that Pedro had taken photos of the living room that might show some of the paintings, but that she couldn't find them.

After I hung up, Nati said, 'Who were you talking to?'

'The victim's wife.' I patted his leg. 'We'll be at Ernie's place in a few minutes. I'd like to talk to you about drinking before we get there.'

'I'd prefer it if you didn't give me a long lecture,' he said, frowning.

'I'll try to be quick. In two months, when you turn fourteen, you can start with half a glass of wine with dinner. Or the same amount of beer. That would seem pretty fair to me. And prudent, given our family history.'

'Prudent?'

'Appropriately cautious.'

'I know what it means, Dad.' He rolled his eyes.

He must have decided that making this difficult for me was equally fair. 'In other words,' I continued, 'I'm asking you to refrain from drinking for a little more than a year.' I used *refrain* to make it clear I wasn't about to limit my vocabulary just to keep him from making fun of me. 'Do we have a deal?'

He gazed down, considering his options.

'Francisco is hungry,' Jorge chirped, and he poked his head around my seat to get my reply. 'He wants a tuna fish sandwich.'

'I'm having an important talk with your brother. Put your seat belt back on, please.'

He obeyed me grudgingly, folding his arms over his chest. '*Quero uma sanduíche de atum*,' he grumbled in Portuguese, in case his English hadn't made sufficient impact on me. To reinforce my uselessness, he exclaimed, 'The way Mom makes it!'

157

Nati whipped around to face him. 'Give it a rest, you little idiot!'

Jorge erupted in tears; he must have still been upset from my confrontation with the reporter. 'Thanks a lot!' I told Nati.

'*Não tem de quê,*' he replied, glaring. *Think nothing of it.*

Jorge was sobbing. We'd descended into hell. And I hadn't even felt myself falling.

I summoned the poor kid out of the car, swooped him up into my arms and placed his head against my chest. Hot tears were sliding down his cheeks and he was having trouble catching his breath. A couple of cars whooshed past. I took his pulse and discovered his heartbeat was racing. I carried him into the shade of a cork tree, sat him down on the grass and instructed him to look at me. 'Just watch my eyes,' I told him, smiling encouragingly. He was panting with worry, but I did my best to tell him with my expression that I'd never let anything bad happen to him. After a minute or so, his breathing slowed and his face brightened. But sweat was running down his cheeks. 'Good work,' I told him. I wiped his face with a tissue. His pulse was back to normal. With any luck, mine would soon be, too.

At just before two we pulled into the gravel clearing next to Ernie's house, beside his rusted Chevrolet Impala. Rosie, Ernie's wire-haired mutt, raced towards us from out of the scrub beyond our orange trees, lunging and biting at my front tyres.

When Jorge pushed out on his door and opened his arms to Rosie, she twirled around in tight, ecstatic circles, then jumped up on him, yelping. A moment later, Ernie stepped out of his house with his hands tucked into the front pockets of his faded jeans. He was wearing his leather vest and a white T-shirt. A green feather stuck up at the back of his cowboy hat. It was a Native American touch that seemed just right on him, maybe because it seemed a reminder that he and I were from far away – another world entirely, in fact.

His shaggy brown hair fell across his shoulders. He was barefoot, and he'd already put on his surgical gloves.

Gazing at me as though hiding a smile, he reminded me, as he often did, of Albrecht Dürer's self-portrait – the one we'd seen with Aunt Olivia in the Prado, in Madrid, and which he'd bought as a poster. I know for a fact that Ernie realized something important about who he wanted to be that day, while communing with the long-dead German artist, because he later told me what it was: *I can inhabit my own country.*

Before I was aware of even opening my car door, I was walking towards my little brother. Seeing him emptied me of everything except the need to hold him in my arms. He took off his hat and smiled his sideways smile for me. We embraced, and I breathed in on the warm oatmeal scent of him. I rubbed my cheek hard against his so that the sandpaper of his stubble could remind me that he'd become a man. He rubbed me back, which always made me feel as if we were brothers in a myth or dream, children of the forest getting to know each other again through their skin.

Having Ernie safe and whole, and all grown up, with an independent life amidst his flowers and trees, was so wide and deep – with emotions too complex for me to ever try to name – that it contained all I had ever accomplished in my life, and all I could ever hope to accomplish, too. We hugged for longer than most people would consider appropriate because that was how long it took for us to be ready to separate.

When we finally let go, Jorge ran forward and crashed into his uncle's belly. Ernie gasped, since that's what the boy wanted, then kissed the top of his head.

'Francisco's hungry!' Jorge declared, holding up his giraffe. 'He wants tuna!'

'Sorry, I made eggplant stew and a big salad. But everything is fresh, fresh, fresh – picked this morning from the garden!'

Ernie was hoping that his enthusiasm might make up for

the wrong menu. But over the past few months, Jorge had discovered the joy – and power – of being inflexible. 'Francisco wants tuna!' he whined, and he began to stamp around like he does when he's overtired, so I grabbed him up with a growl and folded him over my shoulder, which got him giggling; he was still a sponge for love, thank goodness.

Rosie barked irately because we were having fun without her.

'*Olá, Tio*,' Nati told Ernie, coming around the car to him.

'*Olá, Nathaniel*,' my brother replied.

Nati leaned in for a kiss while trying to maintain his distance. With my brother, he often looked as though he didn't know where to put his hands and feet.

'You got any photos of the Ponderosa?' I asked Ernie. 'Nati wants a look. And if you have any shots of the old folks, you can show him those, too.' I was hoping Nati might give me points for remembering his request right away, but he avoided my glance to show me he hadn't yet forgiven me for whatever I'd done wrong.

'I might be able to scare up one or two photos of where we lived,' Ernie told his nephew, playing up his Colorado twang for comic effect, 'but I don't have any of your grandparents.'

After I put Jorge down, he turned in a wobbly circle, getting the most out of his dizziness, in order to keep my attention. I grabbed a hold of him and scissor-gripped him between my legs, which was what he wanted. While Rosie licked at his hands, the boy looked up at me and whispered, 'Dad, the flowers!'

'Go get 'em!' I whispered back, pushing him off.

The basket in which we'd collected the pomegranate flowers was in the back seat. Jorge crawled in and came back out so excitedly that he spilled half of them on the ground. Rosie started nosing them around, her black nostrils flaring and huffing. Jorge, Ernie and I kneeled down and picked them up.

'Thanks, Sweet Pea,' Ernie said as he took the flowers

from his little nephew. 'You get my Most Valuable Player award today!'

The kids and I carried our bags into the house while Ernie put the basket of flowers on his work table, an old oaken door we'd rescued from a dumpster in Évora a few years back. Rosie remained outside, scratching at the screen door, staring in with the loneliest face she could come up with, but a few seconds later – not having any gift for melodrama – she gave up and ran off.

The Villa Ernesto had no divisions – no rooms, cabinets, or closets. No place where an intruder could hide. And no mirrors.

The July sunshine had turned the yellow curtains to gold, and the earthen scent of the fields swept into the house through the open windows. The boys and I removed our shoes. Jorge slid across the wooden floor over to the rose-bushes surrounding Ernie's bed. He sniffed at a clump of red blossoms. Turning to us, he said in an announcer's voice, *'Mais perto do que pode pensar!' A lot closer than you might think!* It was a billboard advertisement for the Corte Inglés department store that he must have spotted on the way out of Lisbon.

Ernie said, 'Try the flame-coloured ones, Sweet Pea.'

Jorge sniffed hard at the showiest of the blossoms and twirled his head as if he were about to faint from its perfume, then collapsed back on the bed. Whenever my brother was nearby, he turned into a circus performer, ever eager to earn his uncle's spotlight.

Ernie had hung our framed photograph of Patsy Cline above his headboard. I read the dedication to myself: *To Bill's kids, Kisses, Patsy.* She was wearing a plaid shirt and white cowboy hat, seducing the camera with that sassy, rodeo-queen look she'd perfected. Touching my fingertip to the heart she'd drawn above the *i* in *Kisses,* I remembered how Dad told us that he'd charmed Mom *off her feet* at Joe's Steaks in Washington DC. Mom had been a freshman at

161

Marymount College. She'd won a scholarship sponsored by the church back in Portugal.

If Dad hadn't delighted her with his gossip about Patsy's latest tour, and kissed her with such wild-hearted passion at the door to her dormitory, Ernie and I would've never been born. And Mom would still be alive. Which is proof, you might say, of an astonishing thing: that everything that has happened to you in your life has meant that a thousand other things never would.

Mom told me that before they were married Dad had been *maravilhoso* – wonderful. Once, she and I made a list in Portuguese of words she'd have used to describe him when they'd first met: *elegante, espirituoso, charmante, maluco . . .* He'd crooned songs to her by Cole Porter. And he was the first man whose hands seemed sure enough to lead her around a dance floor, too. It was only after they were married that he started to brutalize her. She never understood why he changed. My theory was that he never had; he just faked being wonderful wonderfully well.

My brother studied Patsy's photo while looking over my shoulder.

'Patsy drew a heart,' I told him, pointing. 'I hadn't remembered.'

'Our one brush with fame,' he replied, 'and it came before we were born!'

'I don't get it,' Nati said.

I handed him the picture. 'Dad was one of Patsy's roadies,' I told him. 'She signed this picture for him in 1962. He and Mom only married in 1966, and I came along four years later. He asked her to sign it for his future kids – for me and Ernie.'

'Wow, Grandpa sounds kinda cool!'

I was certain Nati said *Grandpa* to defy me, so I said in a tone of warning, 'If he sounds cool, then there's something badly wrong with your hearing.'

'Whatever,' Nati said dismissively. 'Who's Patsy Cline anyway?' He handed the photo back to his uncle.

'In my opinion, the best country singer of all time,' Ernie told him. 'But she died in a plane crash in 1963.'

'And that was the end of Dad's music career,' I announced happily.

'Why was that?' Nati asked.

'He had a reputation by then. No one would hire him after Patsy died.'

'A reputation for what?'

'For fucking up all the time.'

Nati eyed me because I'd only said the word *fuck* in front of him a handful of times. I slung my bag onto the middle futon. Sensing my emotions were about to go haywire, I started to add up the pluses and minuses of taking a Valium.

Ernie jarred me out of my calculations by clapping his hands. 'That's enough talk! Everybody to the dining table.'

On my way over, I stopped at Ernie's desk to study his latest painting. A slender yellow figure with emaciated arms was climbing up a black, ominous, pyramid-shaped mountain made of burnt twigs and seeds. The sun – a soft circle of fire-coloured leonotis blossoms – was melting over its peak in waves of violet and blue. At the corner of the landscape, in a lush, cup-shaped valley that was both protective and imprisoning, were two tiny men and an elderly woman. With their heads raised and mouths agape, they seemed astonished by the view – and hemmed in by the perilous wall of darkness they faced. They stood with their hands touching, like paper cut-outs – wanting to help one another, but intimidated.

I knew I was the blue man with an orange head; Ernie always made me with wild delphiniums and California poppies. He'd told me once that they were the flowers that appeared to him whenever he thought of me.

The climbing woman's slight build and angular awkwardness implied that she'd never make it to the summit.

'This is the first time you've put Mom in one of your paintings,' I called to Ernie, who was carrying a tall vase of pink gladioli to his dining table.

'Did you know it was her right away?' he asked, smiling gratefully.

'Of course,' I assured him.

My brother called the kids to the table. In his black ceramic salad bowl were home-grown greens crowned by yellow and orange nasturtiums. There was a big bottle of Coke for Nati and Jorge, and a carafe of carrot juice for Ernie and me.

Our place settings – from Thailand – were made of shimmering pink silk, and our glasses – Mexican – were thick and blue, with greenish air bubbles caught in the glass. It often seemed to me that Ernie was like a man recently cured of blindness – always seeking to surround himself with colour.

Jorge and I took our usual places but Nati said he'd wait until the food was served. He stood by the window overlooking his uncle's rose garden.

'Sure thing,' Ernie told him. Putting on Aunt Olivia's Christmas-tree potholder gloves, he clanged open the door to the oven and lifted out a white ceramic casserole of stewed eggplant. At the table, he eased it down on top of a tile trivet and stood back to check on its position. Finding that it wasn't in the right place, he slid it closer to the salad bowl. That didn't work either, so he moved it nearer the edge.

Life for Ernie often came down to a chess match against himself. Rushing him only caused him to lose, so I told him it wasn't a problem when he apologized for taking so much time to get everything ready. Nati gazed out the window. I imagined he was picturing himself walking on the main road to Évora and catching a bus home.

After my brother's seventh move, Jorge asked me what his uncle was doing. I'd explained before about Ernie's compulsive behaviours, but the little boy had forgotten. 'He needs to get things lined up just right.'

Finally, when Ernie had everything in the right position, he sat next to Jorge, and Nati dropped down next to me on the other side of the table. My brother asked me to say grace. I used it as an opportunity to broker a truce with Nati. 'We

164

thank the soil of the Alentejo and the plants themselves for the gifts they've given us today,' I began. 'We are grateful to Ernie for his gardening and cooking, and to Jorge and Nati for giving up a Saturday in front of the television and on the Internet. And we solemnly apologize for any wrongs we've committed since we were last together.'

Solemnly was Aunt Olivia's word. *Solenemente.* I could still hear the abundant roundness of that word as she pronounced it. She had made it part of many an incantation meant to turn two lost boys into something like men.

'Amen,' Ernie said, smiling at me for having thanked our aunt in code.

I was hoping for an all-is-forgiven expression on my eldest's face, but he turned away from me as though I were intruding into his thoughts. Nati's taut silence during the rest of the meal was like a neon sign flashing *I'm Miserable And It's All My Dad's Fault!* When it came time for dessert, Ernie's famous chocolate and cinnamon brownies, the sulking young man patted his belly, said he was stuffed, and found refuge on the screened-in porch with *Moby Dick.*

Jorge grew sleepy halfway through his third brownie, leaned his head down on the table and closed his eyes. 'Time for your nap,' Ernie told him, taking the rest of the brownie from his limp fingers and handing it to me. He cradled Jorge in his arms and hoisted him up, then showed me a concerned look. 'Is it okay?' he whispered.

'Jesus, Ernie, you know you don't have to ask,' I told him in a frustrated voice.

He carried Jorge to his futon and tucked him in with quick and precise hand movements. I realized I admired my brother more than anyone I knew, and watching the delight in his eyes as he slipped a pillow underneath my son's head salvaged my day. It was as if I'd managed to give both him and Jorge the gift they'd most needed. I'd already made Ana promise that if I died before the kids were adults, she'd make sure that Ernie was a constant presence in Jorge's life. From my brother, my son would learn to surround himself

165

with simple and beautiful things – and maybe even stop running from silence. And my brother wouldn't be broken by my death if he knew the boy was counting on him.

After we'd done the dishes, Ernie fetched his photos of our ranch. He took off his latex gloves, reasoning that his nephew would feel more at ease with him if he looked *a little less deranged*, as he put it to me with a wily grin.

I peeked at the two of them from behind the curtain. Nati sat on the old bench that we'd painted yellow a few years back. Ernie sat in one of his wicker chairs. He let my son flip through the pictures in silence, then talked to him about how we used to look for scorpions on the rim of Black Canyon, and how the hinterlands of Colorado had been our true home. 'Everything we saw in the wild accepted your dad and me just as we were,' he said.

'And your parents didn't?' Nati asked.

'Not our dad.'

'He yelled bad things at you, didn't he?'

Ernie gripped his bolo tie – a silver Kokopelli, the trickster god of the American Southwest – and gazed out towards the horizon. 'He didn't want to, Nati, but he did.'

Guilt at invading their privacy took hold of me, so I moved to Ernie's desk and traced my finger around the petals forming our mom's outlines in his latest painting. When he came back inside, he told me that their talk seemed to go well, then scrubbed his hands at the sink. When he was done, I retrieved my evidence bags and asked him to come for a walk with me.

On the way to his grove of broad, heavy-limbed carob trees, we detoured into the rose garden, and he picked a praying mantis off a leaf. The insect was stick-like and greenish-brown, with long prickly legs and a serene, noble, upright head – the ballet dancer of the invertebrate world. Ernie told me he'd distributed two thousand baby mantises around his garden a month before. He'd ordered them from Spain. They'd devour aphids and other insect pests all

166

summer long. Sometimes they managed to sneak into the house, even into his bed, but he didn't mind.

Under the shade of the oldest and shaggiest of Ernie's carob trees, seated together on the green blanket Ernie had brought along, I handed him the bag containing Sandra's knife and explained about finding it under her bed. His eyes widened with apprehension. 'Why show it to me, Rico?'

I had a lie prepared. 'You remember how we used to hide our dinner plates under your bed until we were ready to wash them? I thought maybe you'd have some idea why she'd have hidden the knife.'

He shook his head. I could tell he was keeping something from me. And he knew I knew, which made him fidgety. After a while, he stood up and walked down the lazy hillside toward the dry stream bed where we sometimes found edible mushrooms. I caught up with him while he was searching behind a fallen oak. I showed him the honey dripper. 'I discovered this, too – tucked into a corner of the girl's bed.'

'Why do you care so much what's wrong with the vic's daughter?' he asked.

'Because she won't tell me or anyone else about how she's being threatened or hurt. All she's got to hold onto is her own silence. And Ernie, you and I both know it isn't going to be enough to save her.'

When my brother walked off this time, I didn't follow him. I went back to his house and sat on my futon with our bag of Roman coins on my lap. At that moment, their jangly weight meant to me that the past sometimes sent us messages, and that some of them could change our lives in the present.

Ernie stepped inside a half-hour later. The knees of his trousers were grimy. Had he been praying?

He caught the Roman coin I tossed him and nodded knowingly, as if he knew I'd been communing with lesser gods in my own way.

'Give me a little while and I'll tell you what I know,' he said.

Chapter 13

'Don't try to trick me,' Ernie said resentfully. He was kneading a scuffed old baseball in both his hands.

We were seated on his stone patio, under his trellis of kiwi fruit, which were dangling down out of the thick vine like furry brown earrings. Jorge was still snoozing. Nati was reading *Moby Dick* under the shade of an orange tree on the Via Enrico.

'I'm not trying to trick you!' I snapped, though I was. 'I had a flash of memory about you hiding a knife around our room when you were little.'

He tossed me the ball and turned over his left arm to show me his jagged scars. 'How did you think I got these?'

'I assumed Dad made them when I wasn't around.'

'No, they're not deep enough for his work.'

He gazed back at his house, apprehensive, the same silent boy with the ever-watchful eyes who fumbled his replies at school and who never trusted words – which was another way of saying that they'd never done him any good. There were moments one was never prepared for, and I sensed this was going to be one of them.

'Tell me what you're thinking,' I told him.

'I started cutting myself when I was a kid,' he said.

My heart took a sharp dive. 'With a knife?'

'Yes.'

'Why?'

'Sometimes my chest felt like it would explode. Cutting myself helped.'

'So it didn't hurt?'

'Of course it hurt!' He kicked his head back and had a good laugh. 'But when it hurt badly enough, I'd go all numb.'

He held his hands open and jiggled them, so I threw the baseball back to him. 'How often did you do it?' I asked.

'Maybe once a week.' He tossed the ball high in the air and caught it in one hand.

'Even when you were real little?'

'No, only after Dad disappeared. I started worrying that he'd come back and take me away with him, and that you'd never be able to find me.'

'Do you still cut yourself?' I asked. My hope that he didn't was clenched inside me, afraid to breathe.

'No, never,' he declared.

I didn't believe him; he'd spoken too definitively. Still, we had an unspoken agreement not to pursue each other into our hiding places, so I kept quiet. He balanced the ball on top of his shoulder and, leaning slowly to the side, set it rolling down his arm into his hand. It was a trick Dad had taught us and that Ernie had mastered. I was certain he was telling me in the language of our past that he could be just as secretive as I was.

'Listen, Rico,' he finally said, 'have a paediatrician check the daughter's arms and legs. And in more . . . intimate places, too.'

While I considered what might have made Sandra Coutinho hurt herself, Jorge shouted 'Dad!' He was waving from around the side of the house and wearing his pyjamas.

'Don't come out here barefoot!' I hollered back. 'Change into real clothes!'

He went back inside. Ernie and I pretended to study different areas of the horizon; sometimes our intimacy was too much for us.

Jorge came out in shorts and a T-shirt, wearing his beloved Puma sneakers – red high-tops with blue emblems on the side. My brother asked him to take care not to step on any of the mantises, then sat the boy on his knee so they could play Rodeo Star. Ernie was a wildly bucking stallion named Pillsbury and Jorge a grizzled rodeo veteran named Ferndale Hawkins, which was the name Ernie and I had invented as kids.

Ferndale kept tumbling off and dusting himself off and getting right back on Pillsbury, though he complained that Ernie bucked too hard. My brother whinnied and shook his head to express his disagreement. He made a fine horse.

Watching Jorge jerking up and down, his arms flailing, laughing crazily, I realized he was a tough little guy.

When Ernie and Jorge headed off to see how the olive trees were enjoying the summer, I went back into to the house to make some calls. My cell phone rang just after I turned it on. It was Yosoi Kimura. He had a clipped Japanese accent but his Portuguese was very good. 'The writing you sent me is the name *Diana*,' he told me.

'And does the name *Diana* have any special significance in Japanese culture?'

'Well, it can mean *big hole*. Except that then it would be written with Chinese-style characters. The way it has been written is just a name.'

After thanking Kimura and disconnecting, I turned on my laptop and consulted Fonseca's photographs of Coutinho's address book. Two Dianas were listed, one with a Lisbon address, the other in Coimbra. I wrote their full names and phone numbers in my notepad, then called Inspector Quintela.

He told me he had with him a list of the victim's incoming and outgoing calls over the last two weeks. He checked the numbers I read him and soon confirmed that Coutinho hadn't spoken with either of the two Dianas. He'd spoken to only two women other than his wife and daughter over the last week: Fernanda Aleixo, his secretary, and an architect named Maria Teresa Sanderson. He'd called Aleixo once on Tuesday and Sanderson twice on Wednesday, the day before he was murdered.

'How long were the calls to Sanderson?' I asked.

'Close to six minutes on the first, and a little more than two on the second.'

'Her name rings a bell,' I said.

'She married into one of the Port wine families. I'm told she gets herself into those god-awful gossip magazines on occasion, just like our dead man.'

'What else have you found out about her?'

'So far, all I've got is that she was designing a housing project that Coutinho was building along the Sado Estuary.'

'Isn't that protected land?' I questioned.

'Some of it is – there's part of it that's in the Sado Estuary National Reserve.'

'Do you know if Coutinho's development is inside the reserve?'

'No, but wouldn't that be against the law?'

'Exactly,' I said, 'so get a map of its boundaries and another one indicating exactly where the housing project is. Did you get the address of Sanderson's office, by any chance?'

'Yeah, it's here in my notes somewhere.'

He read it to me. It was on the Rua Alexandre Herculano. She could have walked to the Rua do Vale from her office in less than half an hour.

I phoned Sanderson from the porch. As soon as I introduced myself, she said she'd been expecting to hear from the police. Hearing my accent, she switched to English. She told me that she'd done all her schooling in London.

'So you read about the murder?' I asked.

'Yes, this morning. I figured that sooner or later you'd get around to Pedro's business associates.'

'Is that all you were to him?'

'What's that supposed to mean?' she said in an affronted tone.

'Excuse me for being direct, but were you sleeping with him?'

'Inspector, I don't sleep with married men. I made that mistake once when I was young and stupid, and I swore I'd never make it again.'

'So what did you and the deceased speak about in your last calls?'

'Fountains.'

'What kind of fountains?'

'Decorative ones – for the grounds of the housing project. He told me that wealthy people think they're classy. Which is true, except that they're usually too cheap to keep them running properly. Between you and me, it often seems as if people build beautiful things just so they can let them fall apart. Anyway, Pedro and I quarrelled.'

'Who won?'

'Here's a clue – he pays the bills. But I talked him down from four to two.'

'So is this housing development inside the National Reserve?'

She replied with silence.

'I'm going to find out sooner or later, so you might as well tell me.'

'We've added an access road that's just inside the park,' she admitted grudgingly.

'That's it?'

'And a very small shopping centre.'

I laughed because she said 'very small', as if that kept her crime well within the bounds of good taste.

'Listen, Inspector,' she said as if I'd offended her, 'the marshland there had already been compromised by a factory that closed years ago and that was falling apart!'

'You can explain all that in court,' I told her.

'I assure you we obtained all the necessary approvals.'

'You didn't get mine!'

'I'm pretty certain we didn't need it, Inspector.'

Her condescending retort lit a flare in my chest. 'Let me

172

explain how a democracy works,' I said acidly. 'My taxes pay for the upkeep of public lands. Every foot of every reserve and park in Portugal belongs to me and my wife and every other citizen of this country!'

'Maybe that line of reasoning makes sense in America, but nothing is going to stop the project here. Pedro has already put in the foundations.'

'Who signed off on it?'

'Pedro dealt with the signatures.'

I changed the subject to keep from giving her another angry lecture. She claimed she didn't know Coutinho well and had never met him outside his office. She'd never spoken to his wife or daughter. She agreed to messenger over the plans for the housing development to my office first thing on Monday morning. Her frustrated and bored tone, which was meant to convince me I was wasting my time, only convinced me I wasn't.

I called Luci next. She said that Jean Morel seemed genuinely shaken by Coutinho's murder. He claimed to have never held a gun in his life, and she believed him.

'What size shoe does he wear?' I asked.

'Forty-one. I made him take one of them off and show me, just to be sure.'

Luci added that Morel hadn't any idea who'd been sleeping with his old friend. He'd spotted no women's clothing on his last visit to the victim's house, and he knew nothing about any enemies Pedro Coutinho might have made when he lived in Japan. Coutinho had never spoken to him about anyone named Diana.

Reading carefully from her notes, Luci told me that Morel had identified the painting missing from the living room as a small, unsigned, nineteenth-century portrait of an aristocratic young woman that Coutinho had found in an antique shop in New York City about a year earlier. He said that his friend had fallen in love with the portrait at first sight and bought it on the spot. He wasn't sure if Sandi had been with her father when he'd purchased it. As for the Almeida

173

drawing, it had been hanging in Coutinho's library, which meant that I could now be sure that the killer had taken the time to go upstairs.

Had the killer known about the nineteenth-century portrait beforehand and intended to steal it all along? If so, then he'd probably been to the house before.

After Luci had finished reading me her notes, I called Senhora Coutinho. Her cold was worse. In a constricted whisper, she told me that Pedro had never discussed anyone named Diana with her.

She didn't remember any details about the woman in the portrait that Morel had identified and hadn't any idea why anyone would steal an anonymous painting.

'How about Maria Teresa Sanderson?' I asked. 'Ever hear of her?'

'No.'

'Then tell me about Fernanda Aleixo,' I said.

'Christ, you really are lost, aren't you?' she said, as though she were losing hope in me. 'Fernanda is in her fifties, and shaped like a beefsteak tomato, and the woman you're looking for is younger and cuter than I am, Monroe. Or haven't you even figured out yet what gets ageing Portuguese men singing in the shower?'

That evening, Jorge had two helpings of our beet and basil risotto, but Nati picked over his food as if I'd poisoned it. Every time I tried speaking to him, he gave me a withering look. Still, at bedtime, he allowed me to wish him goodnight without turning away or groaning. Or pressing delete on me. A minor triumph.

I awoke once in the night needing to pee and discovered the taste of chocolate in my mouth. A sheet of paper was folded in two on my belly. I tiptoed out to the porch and pulled the cord of the Chinese lantern hanging from the ceiling.

Opening the paper, I discovered it had been printed with

174

one of the photographs from Coutinho's vacation in Phuket over Christmas of 2011: at the left was a crescent-shaped beach bordered by slender palms; at the right, a turquoise sea with a sailboat in the distance. A circle had been drawn in green ink around a bright patch of sky. Inside it were several lines of minute writing, too small to read. The writing seemed to be in the photo itself.

Turning over my hand, I read: *H – The tiny red lights ended up giving the game away.*

I found my laptop still open on Ernie's desk. An Arcadia chocolate bar wrapper was scrunched into a ball by the keyboard. Carrying the computer outside, I opened the Phuket file and found the picture G had printed out. It was the nineteenth in the series, and a tight cluster of minute red sparks showed up in the area that he'd circled on the photo. On zooming in a thousand per cent, the lights became a string of numbers, as well as values in euros and dates. The first line read: *8 2 12 5 10 14 6 1 10 10 4 6 11 2 6 – ten thousand euros – June 1.* There were twelve such lines.

If they were payoffs – as I guessed – then the numbers were probably coded names.

I opened the file of pictures taken a year before, during Christmas of 2010, when Coutinho and his family had vacationed in London. The nineteenth photo showed Sandi standing outside a clothing shop, shading her eyes from the sun. Above her left shoulder floated a similar cluster of sparks. When enlarged, the list indicated values ranging from four thousand euros up to twenty-two thousand.

On hearing footsteps, I turned around. Ernie pushed open the screen door and shuffled out to me. 'Hey there, what's up?' he asked sleepily.

'Just finishing some homework.'

'You sound cheerful.'

'I think I found what I was looking for.'

Rosie pushed out on the screen door with her nose and padded out to us. She dropped down by my feet with a snuffling sigh.

'Just lock the door securely behind you when you go to bed,' my brother told me, and he kissed the top of my head before going back inside. Rosie stayed. She was already snoring softly.

The earliest vacation in the folder was 2000. If I was right, I'd just found Coutinho's register of bribes for the last twelve years. I'd have to contact a specialist to work on decoding the names.

A few minutes later, while I was checking the list for 2008, the screen door opened again and Nati zombie-walked out in his T-shirt and boxers. 'You okay?' he asked.

'Great. Listen, I've got a question – how would you paste tiny writing onto a photograph?'

'You got top secret information you want to conceal?'

'Not me, the vic.'

He yawned and scratched under his arm. Rosie stepped to him and looked up with a pleading face. As he picked her up, he said, 'You copy any text you want, outline the area on the photo where you'd like the text to go and then paste it down. How could you not know these things?'

'I was born eons ago, Nati. Dinosaurs still roamed the earth.'

He waved goodbye.

'Wait a minute,' I pleaded in a whisper. 'Why were you angry at me?'

He turned, unsure of what to say. 'You didn't listen to anything I said in the car driving over here.'

'That's not true. I remember all about your food fight in the school lunchroom, and the girl who fell asleep and started snoring in your mathematics class, and—'

'No,' he interrupted, 'you hear half of what I say and then you say something you think is amusing. It's not the same thing as listening.'

'All right, I'm listening now,' I replied.

He sat down beside me and told me he was worried about his project on bossa nova music. He'd become muddled in unfamiliar chords and harmonies. He had only until Friday to complete it and every minute away from home was putting him in danger of failing. He had started to panic on the drive here.

Everything has been a potential disaster for this boy since he was five years old, I thought, and I assured him that I knew – by heart – every album recorded by João Gilberto from 1959 till 1977. 'Son, you're looking at a true bossa nova expert!'

He didn't look convinced, so I sang the first bars of 'Corcovado' to him softly.

'Sounds pretty good,' he said, fighting a smile, not quite ready to give up his anxieties.

I told I'd start helping him the next day, and though he didn't fall into my arms, as I'd hoped he would, he at least let me walk him back to bed. Once he was tucked in, I stroked his hair so he'd fall asleep knowing I was beside him in my thoughts, but I wasn't. I was wondering what might have caused Sandi Coutinho to cut herself with her knife – at night, when she was alone. And if Ernie still did.

Chapter 14

I awoke cradling my pillow over my eyes. Sitting up into the soft, slanting light of dawn, I spotted Jorge asleep in my brother's bed. The two of them had kicked off the sheets. Ernie had spooned up behind my son, his nose buried in the little boy's soft brown hair, his big, coarse hand curled around his waist. Jorge's arm hung over the side of the bed, reaching toward Rosie, who was snoring away on her little red rug, her head on her forepaws. The boy was wearing his beloved Tweety Bird pyjamas – big-hearted canaries paddling rowboats across cottony clouds. Ernie was naked except for the beaded Sioux headband he wore to keep his hair in place when the kids were around.

If I'd have become an artist like Ernie, this is what I'd paint, I thought.

Then, a hand seemed to whack me on the head from behind, and a moment later, I was kneeling before Jorge, who was sobbing. We were outside Ernie's house. My son was naked, and his pyjamas were on the gravel beside him. Nati was pleading with me to stop terrifying his brother. Rosie was snarling at me and barking as if I'd walloped her.

I'd been moved through time and space.

Nati tugged hard on my arm. 'You're scaring him, Dad! Leave him alone!'

Standing up, I lifted Jorge into my arms and pressed my lips to his cheek, which was moist with tears. The dog scuttled around me, growling, baring her teeth.

'Do something about Rosie before she bites me!' I told Nati.

He snatched her up. As Jorge's weeping eased, I asked Nati what had happened.

'You don't know?' His face was drawn and hopeless. Rosie wriggled in his arms.

'No, just tell me.'

'You grabbed Dingo and you started hollering at him, asking him to tell you what your brother had done to him, and he started crying. You ran outside with him in your arms, and stripped off his pyjamas and examined him all over, and . . .' Nati, breathless, lost the trail of his words.

'Okay, I get it,' I told him. 'Now, tell me where your uncle is.'

'In the house.'

The front door was ajar. To Jorge, I said, 'I'll be right back. Nati will take care of you and get you dressed again.'

'No!' the little boy shouted through his tears. I handed him to my eldest son before my guilt could surround me completely.

Ernie was sitting on the floor between his bed and the wall, his knees drawn up to his chest, hidden behind a rosebush. He'd blindfolded his eyes with his hands. He was naked. I closed the front door behind me to keep Rosie out.

'Hank, don't come near me!' he yelled as I approached.

I knelt next to him. 'I'm sorry,' I said.

'I shouldn't have let Jorge climb into my bed!'

Blood was seeping out under his hands and dripping to the floor.

I began hiccupping. It happened sometimes – an overflow of emotions. 'You've hit your head,' I said, and I started to lift him to his feet but he shoved me so hard I fell on my behind.

Ernie was trembling with rage. I didn't dare touch him again.

Two men sit together, sensing that all they have – and will ever have – is each other. 'I need to look at your cut,' I whispered.

179

'No, you might catch something from me!' he warned.

'What are you talking about?'

'I could have a bad disease. I could even have HIV.'

'How could you have HIV?' I felt the entire world turning around his reply.

'I've been with women.'

'What women? Where?'

'In Évora.'

'Prostitutes?'

He nodded.

'Did you protect yourself?'

'Of course, but that's no guarantee.'

Time slowed to a halt. My body was heavy with the need to remain just where I was. We'd have to keep as still as possible – and not make any noise – if we were going to outlast everything that could go wrong.

Outside, Jorge had started sobbing again. My need to hold him made my hands ache. 'Nati, bring your brother in here!' I hollered.

Nati appeared in the doorway. 'Dingo will be okay,' he said. 'I know the drill.' He spoke with an adult determination I'd never seen in him before. He must have studied how I calmed down his brother without my knowing.

'Call me if you need help,' I told him gratefully. 'I'll come right out.'

Ernie had started rocking back and forth. I prised his hands from his eyes, which flooded with tears as soon as he saw me, so that mine did, too.

With my brother, it has always been important for me to assume command at the right moment, so I took off my T-shirt, wrapped it around my hand and pressed down hard over his cut. My movements were quick and sure. I should have realized you don't forget how to care for a wound.

'Go away!' Ernie snapped, and he pushed me hard again.

'I don't give a damn if I catch what you have!' I yelled back, and I pressed the palm of my hand over his cut. Ernie shrank away and refused to speak, seeming to back into that

180

closed space inside himself where no one could find him, so I took his blood on my fingertips and painted streaks across my cheek and down my neck onto my chest. 'Look at me!' I ordered him. 'We're in this together. We always have been and always will be.'

His eyes fluttered close and he went limp in my arms. He might have been six years old again.

'Nothing is any good in my life unless you're okay,' I told him. 'I wish it could be otherwise, but it can't be. I'm sure it's the same for you.'

Summoned back to me by the uncomfortable truth we tried never to voice, he reached out for my hand. Joining through our fingers meant that we had passed another test. At length, I said, 'You might need a couple of stitches.'

'I'm not going to the hospital. I'll sew myself up if I have to.'

'You don't know how to do that.'

'I do. I've done it before. You've done it before, too.'

'I don't remember.'

'Still, you know how to do it.'

'Did I make the gash?' I asked.

'No, I banged my head into the wall.'

'Why?'

'I saw the way you were inspecting Jorge.' He showed me a sharp, resentful look.

'I got frantic. It was the suicide yesterday, and then the murder. When I'm really upset, I sometimes I lose myself and . . .' This was when I should have told my brother about G, but a fist seemed to close around my neck. I drew his attention away from me by saying, 'I hate it when you hurt yourself!'

He shook his head disappointedly. 'Don't you get it? This is nothing – I'm on my best behaviour while you and the kids are here. The moment you leave . . .'

I held up my hand to stop him from giving me the details just now. 'Tell me where your first-aid kit is. We'll figure the rest out later.'

He pointed to a box under his desk. Before retrieving it, I scrubbed my hands at the sink and took a peek outside. Jorge had his pyjama bottoms back on and Nati was tying a bow in their cord. I realized – as if having just added up a simple column of figures – that I'd never leave Portugal. Ernie and I would die here. We'd never make it home.

Giving up America for good would require me to think out a lot of things. But I was glad to have finally learned the truth: that the life Ernie and I now had was the only one we'd ever have, even if it wasn't the one we ought to have inherited.

Underground rivers can carry us to unexpected regions of the heart, and as I watched my sons starting to play cat's cradle with a long white string that Nati must have found around the house, I pictured the two of them hunting for fossils with me on the rim of Black Canyon. I waved at them because I needed them to sense in the way I watched them that Portugal would be enough for me as long as they were here.

'Look, Dad!' Jorge said excitedly, holding up the parachute design Nati had helped him make with the string.

'It's great! I'll be out to watch in a few minutes.'

Nati twisted around to face me. His eyes were so worried that I knew that Ernie had been right; I couldn't let him see his uncle – or me – at our worst.

Back inside, I discovered Ernie's old stuffed cat Roxanne next to his first-aid kit. When I held her over my nose, I expected the oatmeal scent of my brother, but her short stiff fur had soaked up the scent of the camphor inside his box. On putting her back, I noticed a stack of Dad's 78 records wrapped in clear plastic.

I dribbled rubbing alcohol onto a cotton ball and dabbed Ernie's cut.

'*Merda!*' he whispered.

'I spotted Roxanne,' I told him, adding a smile so he'd know I didn't mind.

'Yeah, I rescued her from the flames when you went back

into the house for more lighter fluid.' Under his offhand reply, I detected his nervous curiosity about whether I'd spotted the records, too.

'Good for you,' I said, and in our childhood code, I added, 'Glad I'm saved you you what wanted' – which meant, I'm glad you saved what you wanted.

Ernie nodded his appreciation and squeezed my hand.

'Listen,' I said, 'I'll put on a bandage after it stops bleeding.' In truth, I was still worried we'd have to go to the hospital.

The silence we made together – while listening to a car zooming down the main road – was also our thanks. 'How could you believe I'd hurt Jorge like that?' he finally asked, and he shook his head to let me know his question was really a reprimand.

Only one reply seemed serious enough. 'Listen, did Dad ever . . . make you do anything you never told me about?'

'No. And you?' He grimaced to show me that he'd long suspected the worst.

'No. In some things we got lucky.' One disclosure led to another and I said, 'Listen, Ernie, I . . . don't know anything about what you do in bed. Though you don't have to tell me if you don't want to.'

He gazed straight down – an angle that seemed another small part of our inheritance.

'Have you ever had a girlfriend?' I asked. When he didn't reply, I lifted open the latch of a high gate that had been waiting for us for years. 'Or a boyfriend. I don't care which.'

He began twisting a lock of hair behind his half-an-ear.

'Ernie, if there's one thing I've learned in my life, it's that we have to take love wherever it comes from, and in whatever form it chooses to take.'

Understanding the ambivalent ups and downs of my brother's hopes made me then confess something I never thought I'd say: 'I played with other boys when I was in my teens. It embarrassed me for a long time. Maybe it still does. But that's my problem – it's not because what I did was

183

wrong. In fact, I know it was right. Because every crazy mess I made on myself, every kiss, led me to Ana, and that was a very good thing.'

'No boyfriend, no girlfriend,' he whispered. He showed me a crooked, self-conscious smile – as though pushing away defeat – and looked at me hard. 'But despite everything, I've had moments of real love.'

I turned away because *moments of real love* was what I'd long wished for him – but without any faith that I'd ever hear those words anywhere but in my daydreams. To find a place inside myself for so large a gratitude before it faded, I asked him to hold my shirt to his cut and stepped to the window. Outside, Nati had lifted Jorge up around his waist so he could pick a lemon from the tree we'd planted by the chimney. Back on the ground, Jorge cupped the fruit in both his hands, electric with glee, as though he'd stolen the goose's golden egg. I was charmed by my sons' wildly differing temperaments. And I realized I could have spared myself a thousand grief-stricken, sleepless nights if I'd have had more trust in my brother and his resilience. As for the conversation he and I were having, and the cautious care we showed each other, it was a part of life I'd not have wanted to miss for anything.

And then the true miracle: Aunt Olivia seemed to enter the house behind the earth-scented breeze and ease past me, on her way to my brother. *She'd want to be here with us*, I thought, as if spirits and ghosts behaved by the standards of the living, and I only shivered the moment her presence no longer seemed perfectly reasonable. I told Ernie what she'd have said had she been with us: 'You deserve love more than anyone I know.'

'*Deserve* doesn't count for much of anything in this world,' he said.

'Consider my words an incantation,' I told him, surprised that I'd happened on a reply that matched my intention so completely.

Ernie accepted my shift of interpretation with a wry smile: change the wrapping paper and the gift also changes.

184

When I returned to him, a green mantis – about the size of a toothpick – was standing on his thigh. It had grabbed his fingertip in its burred, L-shaped forelegs. Ernie's eyes were watchful and serious – the studious gaze of the amateur naturalist he'd been since he was a three-year-old drawn to the red and yellow gravity of Colorado wildflowers.

'I'm too scared of being touched to make sex much good for me or anyone else,' he volunteered.

'Everybody's first efforts are the stuff of nightmares,' I assured him.

'Rico, I *apologize* afterward. And just about everyone I've ever slept with *accepts* my apology. Do you know what that means?' He rolled his eyes. 'I'm a disaster.'

We were squashed between his bed and the wall, behind a resplendent red rosebush, and he was shifting his finger back and forth to test the seemingly imperturbable goodwill of a creature that looked as though it had inhabited the earth for a hundred million years before human beings had come along. I was painted in blood with Cherokee stripes, and he was naked and bleeding. We looked at each other with our familiar *we've-crash-landed-again* irony, because we often seemed to end up where we could have never predicted.

I pressed the tip of my index finger to a patch of blood on the shirt he still held to his forehead and drew stripes down his cheeks. 'Now everyone will know we're kin.'

'Members of the Rivermouth tribe,' he observed, because the original meaning of Monroe was 'river mouth' in Gaelic.

'And proud members of the Rabbit clan,' I added, since our mother's family name – Coelho – was Portuguese for rabbit.

At length, he whispered, 'Listen, Rico, I know that someone else takes you over.'

Like me, maybe he sensed that the time had come to talk about Gabriel. Still, the way he gazed off meant I wasn't obliged to reply.

'How long have you known?' I asked, trying in vain to keep my sense of shame from listening in on our conversation.

'Since we were little. You go away and someone takes you over, though I don't know who it is.'

I studied the muscles slanting across his shoulders and arms, and how his hands seemed too big for his body. He was strong and fit – the self-effacing hero of the low-budget, Portuguese Western that his life had become.

I lifted my shirt from Ernie's forehead to take a look at the cut, which had nearly stopped bleeding. I pinched out a strand of hair that had gotten caught. 'Tie up that mane of yours and come talk to me on your bed.'

Sitting on Ernie's mattress, I stuffed a pillow behind me and leaned back against the wall. Ernie took a hairband from his night table, made a tight ponytail and dropped down beside me.

Slowly, cautiously, in unsure stops and starts, with my voice sounding as though it belonged to someone else, I explained to my brother about the first message written on the palm of my hand. I went on to talk about G taking Dad's tests for me, watching my brother's eyes for any sign of scepticism, but none appeared. I realized that by telling him all I knew, I was fulfilling a promise I'd made long ago without even knowing it. Because I was finally giving G credit for all the times he'd saved my brother's life.

I explained to Ernie that I thought that everything he had suffered had made G more observant than me. 'He's excellent at identifying the essential features of a landscape, a room, a photograph – or, more to the point, a murder scene. He had to become that way. And he's helped me solve a lot of cases.'

'Does he ever make mistakes?' Ernie asked.

'He's given me some false leads on occasion, but even when he does, I don't mind. Because the thing is, Ernie, he sees things I don't – subtle connections. He separates the meaningful from the insignificant very quickly. He had to develop that talent because time was always running out for us whenever he appeared. I think he may have a photographic memory, too. And an uncanny aptitude for finding what's been lost. It used to astonish me.'

'But not any longer?'

'No. When you live with something extraordinary for thirty years, I guess you get used to it.'

'Maybe he's so focused because he doesn't get detoured by the kind of complex feelings regular people have. Maybe he's too worried about coping with disaster to think about much else.'

'Could be,' I agreed. 'I'm not even sure he ever sleeps. I have the feeling that when *I'm* asleep, he's still trying to solve my cases.'

'Sometimes when you found me, Rico, I knew it wasn't you,' Ernie confessed. 'You were too controlled, too purposeful. And once you told me that Dad wasn't my father.'

'How did you reply to that?'

'I asked you how you knew, and you said, "There's no resemblance, kid."'

'No physical resemblance? Or did he mean your personality wasn't like Dad's?'

'I'm not sure.'

'Did I call you *kid* a lot?' I asked.

'Yeah, like you were an adult. And your voice had a depth that yours doesn't have.

'What else did I tell you?'

'Never to trust grown-ups – to trust only Hank.'

'That didn't scare you?'

'Nope. By then, I'd had ample evidence that Gabriel was there to help us both.'

My brother went on to tell me that he'd assumed that G had vanished from my life because he hadn't seen him in years – and because he, Ernie, no longer needed saving. When I told him that neither the kids nor Ana knew about how he shared my body, my brother licked his tongue over his lips like he did when he was forced to decide between bad options.

187

'I couldn't tell Ana about G without also saying a whole hell of a lot about Dad,' I explained, and I made him promise never to reveal anything to her or my sons without my permission. Then I told him about Coutinho's murder and my conversation with his wife and daughter, and how the case seemed to be playing havoc with both my emotions and G's. 'I think Sandi was being threatened or hurt by someone she knew,' I said. 'And I'm getting the feeling her father was murdered for defending her.'

My brother gave me a look that meant he wasn't sure his opinion would receive a fair hearing. He stood up and fetched his jeans.

'Go ahead, I'm listening,' I told him.

After slipping on his pants, he sat down beside me again. 'Look, Rico, if the victim's daughter is cutting herself, then someone or something *is* tormenting her. It's her only way of . . .' Ernie stopped in mid-sentence because Jorge and Nati had appeared in the doorway, holding hands, anxious – children in need of adults. As soon as I opened my arms, Jorge ran to me. I gave him the little kisses he called *pipocas* – popcorn – and he snuggled his head into my lap.

Nati waited by the door. He looked frazzled and exhausted, as if he'd been hit by lightning. 'You saved the day, son,' I told him. When he didn't step forward, I said, 'How about some of your uncle's Colorado French toast?' I turned to my brother. 'Ready for action, chef?'

'Jus' lemme rustle us up some eggs!' he said in his finest Western drawl.

Nati didn't smile. He was staring at my brother with his hands over his mouth.

'*Shit!*' Ernie whisper-screamed, and the way he ripped his hairband off his ponytail and shook out his hair made me understand that Nati had spotted what our father had done to him after I'd failed our first test. By the time I turned towards my son to reassure him, he'd run away.

188

Chapter 15

I found Nati seated in the back seat of our car. From the ambivalent way he turned away from my probing eyes, I was sure he wanted me to come to him but wouldn't let himself say so. As though I'd finally made sense of an obscure poem, I realized that for weeks he'd been trying to prove he was no longer a little boy and that our relationship had to change. Only thirteen, and so impatient to walk into the sunrise of adulthood.

When I joined him, I managed to resist the urge to pull him close. Denying myself that physical reassurance reminded me of being his age, and the helpless, dead-end feel of having all my most fervent questions about myself go unanswered.

'I know you're growing up,' I whispered. 'Forgive me if it's sometimes hard for me.'

He replied by leaning his head on my shoulder.

'I often dream of when I was your age,' I told him. 'Thirty years vanish and I'm wondering if I'll ever start shaving or be able to make love.'

'What do you dream about when you dream you're my age?' he asked.

'I picture landscapes a lot – the mountains blanketed with snow, the wisteria climbing up our patio . . . Often I'm standing on the main street of the town near where we lived. And though it's just like I remember it, it seems too perfect to be real.'

He sat up. 'The town was Crawford, right?'

'Yeah. You know, a few weeks ago, I wrote down one of the dreams I had. I was in the general store buying a post-card to send to Portugal. The thing is, I didn't know anyone here when I lived there.'

'Who did you want to send it to?'

'To Aunt Olivia, I guess. Or maybe to you and Jorge and your mom.'

'But we weren't born yet – you said you were a kid.'

'You saw our photograph of Patsy Cline – the one she autographed for me and Ernie before we were born. Nati, the heart isn't as time-bound as we think.'

He nodded as if he understood, and I realized with a start that I'd have preferred for him not to; maybe it would have been better if he didn't yet sense the length and breadth of his life. If I could have been totally honest with my son at that moment, I'd have said, *Being a father surprises me all the time. Maybe because everything seems to go by too fast.*

'Dad, what happened to Ernie's ear?' he asked.

The thing about a big lie about your past is that once you've given it a really solid façade, you can pretty much describe all the rest as it really was.

'We had tons of farm machinery,' I answered casually, 'and Ernie's ear got caught in a rototiller.'

'What's a rototiller?'

'It turns over the soil to make it ready for seeding.'

I lowered my window. A hot gust of wind pressed against my face. 'We'd better start watering Ernie's garden soon,' I said. 'All the plants are panting with their tongues out.'

'Did your parents take Ernie to a hospital?' Nati asked.

'Yeah, we ended up in an emergency room in Grand Junction.'

'The wound must have bled a lot.'

'You got that right!' I shrugged as if it was just a minor nuisance. 'Dad made us put an old blanket down to protect the upholstery in his car.'

'He did what?' Nati asked in a shocked voice.

190

'His Plymouth had fancy white seats – real leather. He loved them. He'd have been furious if Ernie had bled on them.'

'Was your father crazy or something?'

'His car was a '56 Belvedere. It was red and white, and it had wings at the back. It was beautiful! Wow! Your uncle and I used to feel like celebrities in it – like astronauts in a parade! I was Neil Armstrong and Ernie was Buzz Aldrin.' I waved at the make-believe crowd around us as though I were in a slow-motion newsreel.

'So what happened at the hospital?' Nati asked.

'Ernie was in shock by the time we got there. He almost bled out. The doctors said he was so young that the part of his ear that was lost would mostly grow back.'

'But it didn't.'

'It started to, but then it got infected and that ruined everything.'

'How old was Ernie?'

'He was four.'

'He must have been really scared.'

'Yup. We all were.' Nati seemed to want more drama and emotion from me, but I had used up my allotment years before. 'Your uncle and I cried for years over what happened,' I told him. 'But then we realized that things were the way they were and weren't going to change. The ink dried and could never be erased.' I patted my son's leg. 'Though it's easy for me to imagine a parallel universe – an unforgiving one – in which Ernie died that day. I'll tell you a secret, Nati – I feel the chill of that universe in my bones every day of my life.'

'You should stay here in the real world, Dad,' Nati told me, as if that were as simple as having a conversation with me in his mom's car.

'I do – most of the time. But knowing what could have happened to Ernie . . . That's why I'm so glad you have the chance to know him. I know he's weird, and that you . . .'

191

'It's okay, Dad, I like him – I like him a lot. He just makes me impatient sometimes.'

'He often has that effect on people.'

'So how did his head get caught in a rototiller?'

'He was a curious kid – and always wandering away from me.'

Thankfully, Nati didn't ask how a boy barely four years old had figured out how to start an engine.

'Dad,' he said, 'Uncle Ernie can wear his hair in a pony-tail if he wants to. I wouldn't mind.'

'Tell him that. He'll appreciate it. But we'll also have to be sure Dingo is prepared.'

We sat inside the easy quiet we made together. Nati was assimilating the new information about his father and uncle. And maybe, like me, he was thinking about the way this present moment was hurtling as fast as it could into the past. To stop time – even for just a day – would be the magic trick I'd most want to be able to perform.

'Sorry for scaring you before,' I said.

'You went pretty berserk.'

'I saw Jorge in Ernie's bed, and for a second I thought that Ernie was my father. I must have still been half-asleep.'

'Your father was *that* scary?'

'Yes, Nati, he was. Though every once in a while he was really great, too.'

'I don't get it.'

'Neither do I. And I don't think I ever will.'

Breakfast was Colorado French toast, which called for mashed apple to be added to the egg. While the kids did the dishes and Ernie got down to work on his latest painting, I dragged the hose over to the azalea garden – twenty-seven bushes, and all of them shaded by red and yellow umbrellas that Ernie and I had bought at the market in Évora and tied to stakes, since the flowers tended to burn on the hottest days of summer. I gave the bushes all the water they could handle, creating the muddy mess their roots seemed to love.

About a half hour later, after I'd started sprinkling the herb garden, Luci called.

'Good news!' she told me excitedly. 'Remember the building being remodelled on the Rua do Vale, with the scaffolding? One of the construction workers there spotted a woman coming out of the victim's house on the morning he was murdered – at about ten o'clock. He tried to start a conversation with her, but she told him to fuck off. Just this morning, he saw an article in the paper about the case and went to the police station in the Restauradores. I've got a portrait of her made from his description right in front of me.'

'I'm at my brother's house. He has a fax. Send it to me.'

'Of course, sir, but listen, the portrait isn't so great. She was wearing a hat pulled down over her forehead and the guy only got a good look at her face for a second, when she glared at him. But he noticed she had a strange tattoo on the back of her hand.'

'What's it of?'

'The number thirty. I'll fax you our drawing of it.'

Chapter 16

Throughout dinner with Ana's self-obsessed Brazilian ceramicist, I sneaked glances at the angry eyes of the woman who might have been Coutinho's lover. Since she'd chosen the back of her hand for her tattoo, she clearly intended the numeral 30 to be visible to herself and others. Had something life-changing happened when she was thirty?

Everything changed that year because I . . .

I excused myself just after we'd ordered dessert and ducked out to the street to call the only person I knew who might be able to help me narrow my list of possibilities for the end of that sentence. David Zydowicz told me that he'd had his father's concentration camp number tattooed on his arm before the old man's heart bypass surgery back in 1982. 'Papa fled the room whenever I tried to discuss his experiences back in Poland,' David told me, 'so it was the only way I could think of telling him what I needed to say without actually saying it.'

'What kinds of things did you need to tell him?'

'That I'd never let him suffer alone again. And that there was nothing he couldn't say to me. Other things, too, but I don't want to speak of them. They're too important.'

As to the number thirty, David told me, 'It's a numeral, so maybe what she needed to say was also beyond words.'

Back at the dinner table, I caught each of my wife's cues for me to say something humorous or memorable to her artist, but I couldn't think of anything that wouldn't have sounded forced. Later, at home, Ana told me that I could have at least *looked* interested in him. Happily, she didn't stay angry with me.

Unusually for me, I fell asleep nearly as soon as my head hit my pillow. I awoke to the ringing of our home phone. I jumped out of bed, sure that something was wrong with Ernie.

'Sorry to wake you, Henrique.'

To my relief, the voice belonged to Chief Inspector Romão, who was on call this week. I sneaked a look at the clock; it was 7.14 a.m.

'It's okay,' I said. 'What's up?'

'Bad news,' he said, and he explained that Susana Coutinho had phoned 112 two hours earlier, having found Sandra unconscious in bed. 'The kid took a handful of her mother's sleeping pills.'

'Oh, Christ. Where is she now?' I asked. I sensed myself standing on a fragile pinnacle high above this conversation.

'The hospital. And please don't freak out on me, Henrique, but the doctors were unable to stabilize her blood pressure. She was pronounced dead at six forty-seven.'

I made no reply. I had fallen into a cold ocean, and the miles of sea leading out to the horizon were everything I should have been able to predict.

Ana stirred behind me. 'What's wrong?' she asked sleepily.

I held up my hand to have her wait. The fatal heaviness in my arm made me realize I'd carry around this moment for many years to come. 'I really hate this case,' I said to myself more than to Romão.

'Hang in there, Henrique.'

'Did the girl leave any note?' I asked.

'Not a thing. Listen, I just tried to question her mother, but she'll only talk to you.'

Susana wants to tell me that she'll never recover, I thought. *She'll want me to know the truth even if she lies to her family.*

'Monroe, don't you disappear on me!' Romão said impatiently.

195

'I'll go see Senhora Coutinho,' I told him, realizing that all he wanted was for me to take him off the hook.

'What's happened?' Ana asked as soon as I hung up.

I'd sat down on the edge of our bed without realizing it. Her arms slipped around me. I told her about Sandi's overdose in a clenched whisper. I was holding back a scream; if I let it out, I figured I might not stop for a long time.

Being touched when I was jittery made me feel trapped, so I lay back down and put my pillow on top of my eyes. Not ever getting up seemed my best option.

A man imagines he will never say another word – not to his colleagues, his wife, his children or his brother. He tells himself he will go on strike against the unfairness hiding under everything, but he knows it will really be against his own loss of control.

Ana whispered that she'd call in to work to say she'd be coming in late so that she could sit and talk with me, but kindness was the second most important thing I didn't deserve at that moment, so I didn't answer.

The phone started beeping; I must have put the receiver down badly. 'Smash it with a hammer!' I snarled.

After Ana had clicked the receiver back in place, she opened our window all the way. The dry breeze came in, trailing the chattering of swallows. It was reassuring to be reminded that there was a world beyond all of our human concerns, but I didn't want any comfort; surely we should allow ourselves to feel the torment that compelled a young girl to take her own life, if nothing else.

Tears came, but only for the selfish reason that I couldn't bear having to slip back inside my professional demeanour and face Susana Coutinho. Ana rested her hand on my back as if to ask for my thoughts, but I didn't tell her what they were because it would have seemed crazy: *if a swallow darts in through the window and perches on me or even on the bed, I will believe in God, and I will believe that eternal life awaits us all, and I will learn to pray again. And maybe, if I'm feeling generous, I'll even forgive myself for all I could have done and didn't.*

None of the swallows took my challenge, of course. It was just one of the impossible-to-win games I invented when I wanted to be certain I was powerless to stop bad things from happening. And to remind myself that there was no God, even if Aunt Olivia had been sure He was watching over us.

After I gave Ana the terrible news about Sandi, she spoke to me in a sympathetic whisper, but I didn't listen to her advice after the words, *You have to learn how to* ... Instead, I got up and started to put on my shirt and underwear. I assured her I was better. I did a silly little jig to prove it, too – which I hated myself for even as I was doing it, because it made a joke out of what had happened.

Ana flashed with irritation. 'Stop it! I don't like it when you belittle yourself.' She pulled me down onto the bed and had me sit with her. Combing my hair out of my eyes, she said, 'You have a beautiful profile.' Squinting for comic effect, she added, 'Worthy of a Roman statue.'

'I wouldn't like not being able to move.'

'Ssshhh! You know, sometimes I make believe you were a Roman nobleman in a past life. It's those ancient coins you and Ernie found. I've made up a whole story about you.'

Not for the first time, I wondered if Ana's secret life was as vast as my own. 'What's the story?' I asked.

'You lived with Ernie and the rest of your family in the Villa Ernesto in the fourth century. You had a huge formal garden with the most beautiful roses. And a farm with olive trees and grapevines and fig trees. You made olive oil that you sent back to Rome.' Her face lit up. 'You and Ernie were famous for it! Enrico and Ernesto's Portuguese Olive Oil!' She fixed me with a cheeky look. 'You were drawn to those old ruins because a part of you remembered that you two nutcases used to live there.'

'Was I a cop back then, too?'

'No, I told you,' she groaned, 'you were a nobleman. You supervised production of your world-famous olive oil! Anyway, that sack of coins you found ... You yourself hid them away sixteen hundred years ago, and that's why you were able to find them.'

At that moment, the unlikeness of my having been alive sixteen hundred years ago didn't seem so different from being who I really was. The arc of my life – of all I had seen and done – seemed impossible.

Ana took both of my hands in hers. 'Now tell my why Sandi meant so much to you.'

'You can't return the gifts you get in childhood,' I murmured by way of reply – and without exactly intending to.

My wife showed me a confused look. I stood up to fetch my trousers. 'I need to get to work,' I said.

'First, tell me what gifts you're referring to,' she said.

She pursed her lips and gazed at me with such hopeful interest that I decided to reveal a little more about what it was like to live on the side of the mountain that no one could see, but while slipping on my pants, my car keys tumbled out. Ana snatched them up and wouldn't give them back. She said I was in no condition to drive. She insisted on taking me to Coutinho's house.

I fought her in a mean-spirited voice, but she waved off my arguments and went off to tell Nati to look after Jorge. I was secretly grateful to her for ordering me around. At such times, Ana seemed like a chess champion who nearly always knew how to counter my cagiest moves.

From outside my son's bedroom door, I listened to her and Nati whispering together, but not their actual words, and I thought: *These are the people I love most, but I'm too obsessed with this case even to listen to what they're saying to each other.*

As we drove across town, I practised how I'd express my condolences to Susana Coutinho, but I didn't have any idea what the Portuguese expected to hear in such circumstances. Ana was still wearing a blue-striped pyjama bottom and one of my old white T-shirts. She adored going out in her bedclothes. She always said it made her feel as if she were living in a tiny village instead of a big city. I told her I was sure to make grammatical errors in what I said – I always did when I was upset. She didn't answer me until we parked. Then, she caressed my cheek and said, 'You're a good person. And Senhora Coutinho will see that.'

If I'd have replied, I'd have said that being *good* was precisely how you ended up so broken along a mountain road in Colorado that all the king's horses and all the king's men could never put you together again.

Sensing her first probe hadn't landed anywhere useful, she said, 'Listening to what people need to tell you is more important than being grammatically correct.'

'Except that I didn't hear what Sandi was trying to tell me.'

'Probably because she didn't yet know what she wanted to say!'

'But I should have been able to figure things out by the way she looked at me.'

Ana's eyes burned. 'When did you become clairvoyant?'

'I'm talking about being sensitive to what people in trouble won't permit themselves to say.'

'Look, I've got news for you: you couldn't have changed that girl's mind even if you'd read her thoughts. You were a stranger to her!'

'You can't possibly know that!' I said in desperation. 'You can't know what positive effect we can have even on people we meet just for a few minutes. It's one of the best things in life – that strangers can help us.'

I closed my eyes, squeezing hard on the darkness because I'd spoken rudely. 'There are places in Colorado where you can look twenty miles in each direction and you won't see anything but ancient rock and reflected sunlight,' I said. 'And those places are still in me.'

I wasn't sure why I'd told her that. But maybe she knew. 'Black Canyon might be a dangerous place for a foreigner like me,' she said.

'I'd never let anything bad happen to you.'

'No, I can see you wouldn't.' She took my bolo tie of a kachina – a Native American goddess – out of her backpack. It was silver and inlaid with red coral, and it was the most powerful talisman I owned. Nathan had given it to me just before I left Colorado. He'd told me that the kachina had been made by his father, who had studied with Black Elk.

Nathan also told me that it would prevent even the most *ornery* demon – *ornery* was one of his favourite words – from learning the secret name he'd given me. 'And remember, Hank,' he added, his big, sun-darkened hand resting on my head, 'a demon who doesn't know your name can't hurt you!'

I reached out to take the bolo from Ana, but she said, 'Let me put Debbie on you.'

Debbie was the name that Ernie and I had given the kachina, because it seemed the single most unlikely name for a Native American goddess – and therefore of no use to anyone who might want to harm her or us.

I bent my head down to Ana, and as she spread the tie's leather cord around my head, I sensed her taut, purposeful, creative power – and the confidence in herself that had first attracted me to her because I found it such a mystery.

For a moment, it seemed as if we'd grown up together – and that we were taking part in a ritual far beyond our time and place.

'I thought you didn't believe in magic,' I said when I rose back up.

'But you do,' she told me.

I slid Debbie's crown up into the V of my collar. Her sharp silver edges pressing into my palm seemed to be points of contact between me and all that I'd never understand about the world but would forever be thankful for.

My wife grinned as she did when she saw me as a challenge. 'You see awful things, Hank,' she said, 'but you keep going back. You try everything to make things turn out right. That's what I meant by being a good man.'

'But maybe that has nothing to do with courage or anything else that could be considered ... praiseworthy.'

'No? Then what's it got to do with?'

I stated the truth for the first time, though I had no idea why. 'Because only people in pain seem absolutely real to me. And I need to be with them to be sure I'm real, too.'

Eyeing me sceptically, she said, 'And that's the only reason you try to solve these terrible crimes?'

'Maybe not the only one. I think maybe the other reasons are why I live on Valium.'

She smiled, as I'd hoped, and pressed her lips to mine, and I thought what I have nearly always thought when Ana kisses me: *I could never have predicted that I wouldn't have to spend my life alone.*

When I kissed her back, it was the ease and warmth of our bodies coming together – like wintering animals seeking each other's comfort – that allowed me to leave her.

She took my shoulder as I started to get out of the car. 'Give me a ring if you need more magic, Chief Inspector.'

As she drove off, I took the kachina in my hand again. When I turned around to face Coutinho's house, I saw myself as though on a bridge leading straight from Colorado to Lisbon. I wondered what Nathan would think of the man I'd become, which was probably why I heard him whisper to me, *Hank, you've got to find out which demon was able to learn Sandi's real name.*

Chapter 17

An elderly man with a gaunt face answered my knocks on Coutinho's door. His thick silver hair was neatly combed. His blue eyes were weary.

'Jean Morel?' I asked.

'*Oui. Et qui êtes-vous?*'

When I told him, he said in resentful, heavily accented English, 'You come too late!'

After a brief search for how to reduce all I felt to a single sentence, I said, 'I made the mistake of underestimating how bad things were. I'm sorry. How is Senhora Coutinho holding up?'

'Holding up? She's not *holding up* at all!' he told me, obviously regarding my phrasing as unfit for the circumstances. He didn't invite me in.

'I need to talk to her,' I said.

'No, no, no,' he replied, wagging his finger as if I were a schoolboy.

'I'm on official police business,' I said. The authoritative tone of my voice made me aware that his animosity had transformed me back into a police officer again.

He barred my way with his hands crossed over his chest – a gesture that earned my respect even as it narrowed my options. I could have pushed past him easily enough, but instead I looked up the street towards the Jesus Church, searching its deeply shadowed archways for the right words to prevent two strangers from quarrelling at a bad moment.

I didn't find them, but a slender elderly woman with shiny, copper-coloured hair cut in severe bangs and a long, flowing, hippyish white dress came to the door and broke the impasse. She wore black-rimmed sunglasses held together by tape, a knee-length strand of amber beads and an embroidered peasant shirt. She reminded Morel in precise, carefully worded French that Susana wanted me there.

After I'd followed her inside, she removed her dark glasses and introduced herself as Pedro Coutinho's elder sister, Sylvie Freitas. She had big leaky eyes – red-rimmed and puffy. Bending over the coffee table, she picked up a closed fan. The tendons straining in her hand as she pressed it to her chest told me that she wasn't going to let go of it again for a while.

She told me she'd come over the night before to help take care of Sandi and Susana. She lived in Cascais.

Sitting around the kitchen table, Sylvie explained to me – with despairing hesitations and pauses – what had happened the night before. She fluttered her fan by her face whenever she lost her voice. It was painted with black and gold geese flying against a blue sky. It looked Japanese – a present from her brother, perhaps.

Sandi had been doing surprisingly well, Sylvie said – had even let her poodle Nero chase her around the garden for a while and had managed to eat some spaghetti for supper. She'd gone to bed early. Susana sat with her until she'd fallen asleep.

Sylvie spoke in a voice that had been scraped raw by grief. She spoke in English because Morel couldn't follow our Portuguese. A Scottish lilt played over her vowels, and when I asked her about that, she told me that she'd studied art history at the University of Edinburgh in the 1960s. She made a point of telling me she'd spent her student years in a commune, much to her parents' embarrassment. I had the feeling she needed me to know that she'd been the black sheep in her family. Maybe she was trying to distance herself from her brother and his troubles.

I asked her and Morel if Sandi had been wearing her turquoise ring, since I wanted to know if she'd thought she needed to keep it hidden, even though she would soon be dead. Neither of them had noticed, however. 'We saw nothing out of the ordinary with her,' Sylvie told me in summation.

'This is not quite true,' the Frenchman corrected with an apologetic tilt to his head. He stood up, took a pack of Gauloise Blondes from his shirt pocket and pinched one out. Reaching into his pants' pocket, he took out his lighter, which was sleek and gold, and which reminded me I'd entered a world I usually only glimpsed on magazine covers.

'Sandi gives me a gift after dinner,' Morel explained. 'And later, before bed, she kisses me goodnight.'

'That was unusual?' I asked.

Tearing up, he replied, 'Yes. She is not . . .' He tapped a fist against his head and looked to Sylvie for help.

'Affectionate,' she suggested.

'She is not affectionate with me for some months.'

'What was the gift?'

He lit his cigarette. 'A cookbook. I fetch him.'

Morel headed into the living room and returned with a huge volume entitled, *Cozinha Tradicional Portuguesa.* 'Sandi tells me that her mother does not cook – not even eggs – so I will have to. She says her grandparents give her the book but she wants me to have it. I refuse but she insists. You understand, Inspector? It is her way to say she accepts me.' Morel made a Gallic puffing sound with his lips. 'You cannot know the relief this means to me. And yet the story ends in the worst possible manner.'

I decided not to mention that people who intended to kill themselves often gave away their prized possessions, but Sylvie must have already had her suspicions and made a tight, strangulated sound while running her hand down her neck. When Morel looked at her worriedly, she told him she needed more coffee. Maybe she feared he might break down if he learned the truth. I asked for a cup, as well; my participating in their small ritual might help me gain their confidence.

While filling the kettle, Morel told me that Susana had come downstairs at four in the morning because she'd been unable to sleep. She'd discovered Nero sitting in the kitchen – 'looking miserable' – and let him out into the garden. He'd joined her shortly afterward. They'd conversed in the living room. Susana had checked on Sandi at about 5.15 a.m. and saw the box of sleeping pills – Victan – on her night table, along with a half-empty bottle of vodka. Her breathing was dangerously shallow.

'Susana called 112,' Sylvie told me.

Morel began to pour the boiling water through the coffee filter.

'Have either of you moved anything in Sandi's bedroom?' I asked.

'We search for a note,' Morel replied, 'but we not find it. We remove nothing.'

'Good. I'll need to look around. Later, someone from Forensics will come over. Where's Susana?'

'In bed,' Sylvie replied. 'Unfortunately, we'll have to get her up later.'

'Why's that?'

'Pedro's funeral. It's today – at two in the afternoon.' Noting my surprise, she shrugged and added, 'It was too late to alter the date. Friends are coming from Paris.'

I pressed on my temples because the word *funeral* had started an insistent pulsing in my head. Gabriel was already standing behind me – watching and waiting.

'I need to show Susana something,' I told Sylvie, hoping that an active conversation would keep G from taking me over. I took out my portrait of the woman who'd been seen leaving the house on the morning of Coutinho's death and explained why I was so keen on identifying her, but neither Sylvie nor Morel recognized her. Nor had they ever seen a tattoo of the number thirty. 'I don't think it will do any good to show the sketch to Susana now,' Sylvie added. 'Her doctor was here and gave her sedatives.'

Morel held up my coffee cup. 'Milk or sugar?' he asked.

'Inspector . . . ?' Sylvie raised her eyebrows in a questioning fashion.

I was facing her, which seemed wrong. I was holding my pen, too.

'If you want paper, I can get you some,' Sylvie said.

It took me a moment to realize what she meant. When I did, I said, 'I often write on my hand when I don't want to risk losing an important thought.'

'Milk or sugar?' Morel repeated.

'Neither,' I answered. I took the cup from him and sat back down.

What was scribbled on my palm had been written in the code Ernie and I had made up as kids. Deciphered, it read, *The good wife wanted you to understand that cruelties have taken place in this house. So did . . .*

The message stopped abruptly – probably because Sylvie had interrupted G.

After a first sip of my coffee, I told Sylvie, 'I want you to take the drawings upstairs to Susana. Wake her if you have to. Tell her that Monroe needs her help. And ask her if her daughter was wearing her turquoise ring.'

As soon as Sylvie had left, Morel sat down beside me and offered me a cigarette. For the first time in years, I accepted. Maybe I just wanted a brief escape from my usual patterns of behaviour, or was hoping for the comfort of an old vice, but it was possible, too, that G had slipped soundlessly across the border between us and influenced my decision.

Smoking made me feel as though I were standing at the edge of a deep precipice – one false move away from losing everything.

Morel stood up and ran his finger along a row of ornamental tiles on the wall, tracing the contours of the bright yellow and blue glazes. Watching him, I realized that as men grew older their very way of moving – the faltering grace – became a test of one's own solidarity and fear of death.

When he noticed my staring, he turned to me, tearing up again – as though he'd spotted more empathy in my face than he'd expected.

Moved by the loneliness in his eyes, I said, 'You've lost a lot.'

'I know Sandi since she is born,' he told me. 'I am her godfather.'

'Do you think that Susana will be able to talk to me later today?'

'I doubt this very much.' Instead of elaborating, he gazed at the tiles again.

'Any ideas on who might have murdered your friend?' I asked. I tried a second puff of my cigarette, but it was worse even than the first.

'No, none.'

'At first, I thought you might have killed him.'

He shook his head as though he were disappointed in me, and sat back down. At length, he closed his eyes as if listening to far-off music. Taking a deep drag on his cigarette, he let the smoke curl out through his nose. His distance seemed a kind of perfection, which made me wonder if he had also been sedated by Susana's physician.

When I asked about that, he replied, 'I take a pill Sylvie gives me.' He held up both his hands as though he'd had no other choice. 'The same pill that Sandi takes,' he added in an embittered voice. The way he stubbed out his cigarette – absently and, because of that, overly persistently – gave me the impression he was considering how much else to tell me about his feelings. He said, 'You know, what happens is very unfair, Inspector. Pedro has too much sadness in his life – more than one man should have,' he replied.

'What exactly are you referring to?'

'The first marriage is a very big sorrow.'

Why is he telling me this? I thought, though later that week, while daydreaming in my hospital room, I came to the

207

conclusion that Morel might have been giving me a clue –
perhaps below his level of conscious thought – as to why his
friend had been killed.

'So what happened during his first marriage?' I asked.

'Frederique, his wife ... she turns the children against
Pedro. She says he cheats on her, which is true, and they
make a divorce. She tells the kids that Pedro does not wish
to give her any money, and that he tries to steal their house.'
Morel waved a dismissive hand in the air. 'This is not true.
But everyone is *so* angry. It is a bad French opera – worse
even than Offenbach! So Pedro gives up. He gives
Frederique all she wants. He pays for Marie and Pierre to
have a good education, but still, they do not speak to him.
He sees them for the last time ... it must be fifteen years ago.
The kids at that time are adolescents. This is why he is so
always together with Sandi.'

'A second chance,' I observed.

'*Exactement.*'

'Is Frederique still alive?'

'Probably, but I do not speak with her for years.'

'Would she be in Paris?'

'Or Bordeaux. She is from there.'

'And Marie and Pierre?'

'I have no idea.'

Morel's eyes fluttered closed and he drifted off again. Or
pretended to. It seemed to me that he'd said what he needed
to and was anxious to let go of this time and place.

A copy of the *Público* newspaper lay folded on the counter
by the oven. I took it and went to the window. Maybe
Morel's view of the divorce was distorted and Coutinho had
tried to ruin his first wife's life. Perhaps some recent trauma
had brought all the pain back to her and made her take
revenge against her ex-husband all these many years later.

A crystal ashtray sat on the sill, and in it were two butts
from the night before. I added a third.

I found no article about the murder in the paper, which
meant that whoever had leaked information to the press

hadn't taken my bait. On hearing footsteps from the staircase, I gazed at the doorway and discovered the room circling slowly around me. When I reached out for the windowsill to steady myself, the newspaper I'd been holding fell to the floor. Sylvie stepped into the kitchen while I was picking it up. I was holding my pen now in my left hand.

'Inspector, are you all right?' she asked.

'Just a momentary loss of balance,' I told her. 'What about Susana?'

'She's never seen the woman in your sketch or the tattoo. She also said that Sandi was not wearing her ring. She has no idea where it could be. And she says she'll do her best to talk to you this evening. But no promises.'

As I took back the sketch from her, I noticed that the message on my hand had been completed. G had written, *So did the kid really cash in her chips all by her little self?*

Chapter 18

Standing in the foyer, I called David Zydowicz and told him what had happened to Sandi, adding that he was the only person I wanted to do the autopsy. Muffling my voice, I said that he was to check for bruises and other signs that she had been forced to swallow an overdose. After he agreed, I called Luci and asked her to join me right away.

I was wiping G's message off my hand when the doorbell rang. Sylvie rushed in from the kitchen, clutching her fan to her chest, and opened the door to two teenaged girls.

'*Bom dia*, Senhora Freitas,' the younger-looking of the two said in Portuguese. *Good morning.* Her black bangs fell straight to her eyebrows. She looked like a pop star from the 1960s – a hopeful, fourteen-year-old Cher.

The second girl was tall and slender, and she had pulled her long blonde hair around to the front. She gripped it as though it were a rope she were clinging to, and her lips were sealed tight. She wore a billowy white shirt with long bell sleeves, which seemed to give a balletic grace to her stance.

Both girls stayed where they were, held back by timidity.

'Come in, come in!' Sylvie told them eagerly, and she introduced them to me as Sandi's best friends.

Monica – the would-be Cher – exchanged kisses on the cheek with me. Joana – the tense ballerina – extended her arm as far out as she could to shake hands.

'Is Sandi . . . is she all right, Senhora?' Monica asked in a hesitant voice.

'Let's get comfortable in the kitchen and I'll explain,' Sylvie told them. Steering the girls forward, she looked at me as though she were walking a gangplank in her head.

Joana stepped into the kitchen first. Morel stood at the back of the room, by the open window, rubbing his hand over his stubble. 'Joana!' he exclaimed with eager surprise.

On seeing him, the girl gasped and thrust her hands over her mouth. Monica, stepping beside her friend to see what had terrified her, burst into tears.

'*Oh, mes petites, qu'est-ce qu'il y a?*' Morel asked in a troubled voice. *What's wrong, my little ones?*

Monica drew in her shoulders and pressed a hand over her heart. 'It's just ... just you startled us,' she said in French, though that struck me as an obvious lie. Joana must also have heard how false it sounded and, to make up for her slip, she added, 'We had no idea you were here. And I've been really nervous lately. I'm sorry – so sorry.'

'It's all right, don't worry,' he assured her.

He stepped towards the girls with open arms and embraced them. As he separated from Joana, he cupped her chin and looked at her with fatherly radiance. She smiled back appreciatively. She was an accomplished actress.

Nothing between them will be what it seems, I thought, and yet the need to decipher all their interactions made me feel certain that I had a small advantage over them – after all, I was prepared now for their attempts to fool each other and me.

'How do you all know each other?' I asked.

'We meet last time Sandi comes to France,' he replied. 'Joana and Monica ... they come with her. They make a weekend with me at my country house in Normandy. They even ride my horses! We have a nice time, no?'

'Very nice,' Joana said, and she gave me a big nod to convince me she was telling the truth. *It is important for her to fool everyone in this room, even me,* I thought, which meant that the danger Morel represented – either real or perceived – was so grave that even the police couldn't protect her.

211

Sylvie took a chair for herself and asked the girls to sit next to her, one on each side. She gripped their hands tightly. She told them they had to be strong.

On hearing what had happened, Joana jumped up, fighting for air, and Monica burst into sobs. Sylvie signalled for Morel to help Joana while she comforted Monica. He convinced the girl to sit again and knelt beside her, but when he tried to warm her frigid hands in his, she pushed free of him and rushed to the far corner of the room, by the garden door. Squeezing herself into the angle between the two walls – a small child trying to push through brick and plaster to safety – she began to weep. Sylvie went to her and gripped her shoulders from behind.

Morel took a cigarette from his pack but fumbled his lighter. After he scooped it up from the floor, his eyes caught mine.

Two men mirror their uselessness, acknowledging that only Sylvie will be able to help Sandi's best friends, because she is a woman.

Morel raised his hands and let them fall to signal our mutual defeat, and in the second it took to do that I seemed to understand more about him – about his being caught in events way beyond his control or authority – than I had over the previous half-hour.

Unfortunately, my newfound clarity about how lost he was made the girls' reaction to him seem inexplicable.

Once Joana's tears had subsided, she shuffled back to the table with her head down, apologizing, saying in a thin, frail, self-conscious voice – clinging to smallness for safety – that she hadn't been herself since learning of the murder of Sandi's father.

Joana explained to us that Sandi had called both of them the previous afternoon. Sniffling into a tissue, she said that the girl had told them about her father's death but refused to discuss how she felt.

The three friends agreed to speak again yesterday evening, but Sandi never called either of them. Monica and

Joana had both tried to reach her but her cell phone had always been off, so they'd decided to come over.

'Where's Sandi's cell phone now?' I asked Sylvie.

'Susana has it with her,' she told me.

When I asked the girls why Sandi had been so troubled over the last few months, Monica replied that she'd been viciously teased by kids at school for being what they called a 'spoiled little rich girl'. She'd apparently become an easy target for classmates whose parents had lost their jobs or who'd had their salaries cut since the start of our economic crisis. Sandi began to regard herself as an outcast. She'd decided to make her image more rebellious.

'Is that why she cut her hair so short?' I asked.

'Yeah, she figured it might stop the teasing,' Monica said. 'Though it didn't work,' she added bitterly. 'Kids just started teasing her for looking so weird.' For Morel's benefit, Sylvie repeated Monica's words to him in French.

'Do you agree, Joana?' I asked. 'Was the teasing how Sandi's problems started?'

The girl folded her lips inside her mouth and nodded. Morel must have jumped to the same conclusion I had; he joined his hands into a position of prayer and pleaded in French, *'Ma petite*, if you know something we don't know, then I beg of you to tell us.'

Joana opened her eyes wide and drew back her head, as if he'd cornered her, and I thought she might just shout an accusation of his having planned the murder of Sandi's father and menaced her friend. Instead, with an air of abject defeat, she laid her head onto the table and wept.

The look of dashed hope she showed me in the moment before tears washed her eyes made me realize that she needed me to know that Morel was an enemy so far beyond her capabilities that there was no hope for her. To distance myself from her despair and think things out, I said I needed to make another call and went out to the garden. Had Sandi hated the idea of a divorce so much that she'd begged her father not to permit a separation? If so, then Morel would

213

have discovered her responsibility sooner or later, and when he did, he might have threatened her. When the girl still wouldn't give up her objections to a divorce, he decided to free Susana in the only way that seemed possible: by having her husband killed.

While circling the lawn, I realized that – if all that were true – Sandi would have also concluded that Morel was responsible for her father's death. She might have told him last night that she suspected him of having planned – or even carried out – his old friend's murder. Maybe he overpowered her and forced her to swallow an overdose.

When I entered the kitchen, Sylvie was stroking Monica's hair. The girl's eyes were glazed with disbelief. Joana was resting with her head on the table; her eyes were closed.

Morel stood by the back window, smoking absently. Nothing in his face or posture indicated that he might be worried about what the girls could tell me about him. I sat next to Joana and placed my hand on her shoulder. When she opened her eyes, I told her I was grateful for her help. Feeling the reticent rise and fall of her back, I saw myself as though I'd entered one of those dreams where you do something you could never do in real life.

When the doorbell rang, Morel volunteered to see who it was. A few seconds later, Luci stepped into the kitchen behind him. The stiff, artificial way she smiled at me made me believe she was having second thoughts about her police career.

I asked Sylvie and the girls to wait in the kitchen while Luci and I examined Sandi's bedroom. To draw Morel away from Joana and Monica, I asked him to join us.

We found a bottle of Absolut vodka and an empty box of Victan still on the girl's night table, along with the vampire novel she'd been reading – *Queimada* – and two of the three CDs I'd spotted there the day before: *Day & Age* by The Killers and *Let England Shake*, by P J Harvey. A young woman with pale skin had been pictured on the cover of the missing CD but, for the moment, I couldn't remember its title or the name of the group.

I could see that Luci was waiting for me to ask her to speak her mind, but there wasn't time. 'If you start to feel like you won't be able to cope,' I told her, 'step out of the room for a while.'

'No, sir, that won't be necessary,' she replied in a business-like tone. 'I'm okay.'

I put on my gloves and gave *Queimada* a shake, but no suicide note or anything else fluttered out. Neither of the two CDs contained anything unusual.

According to the blurb on the book's back cover, it was about a young vampire named Zoey Redbird with a broken heart and 'shattered soul'.

The bed was unmade. Sandi's dolls and stuffed animals were grouped neatly on her desk. I took a quick look through them while Luci went through her dresser drawers. I also checked under the bed, but there was no jumble of clothing this time, and no knife taped to the corner of the mattress.

When I emerged from under the bedframe, Morel asked me if he could check on Susana. 'Fine, but this is an official investigation now,' I told him sternly, 'so I don't want you to talk to Joana or Monica without me around. And bring Sandi's cell phone with you when you go back downstairs.'

On a hunch, thinking that Sandi had left her ring – or perhaps even a suicide note – where I'd found something valuable of hers before, I lifted the mattress off its platform. Her laptop was in the corner. It seemed to have been wait- ing for me, which gave me the tingling notion that Sandi knew I'd lift off her mattress after her death because I'd done it once before. I'd underestimated her intelligence.

'Maybe she wrote her suicide note on her laptop,' Luci said.

'My thoughts exactly.' I handed her the computer. 'Have a look, but if you don't find anything useful right away, get it to Joaquim. I want him to check all the files created since Friday.'

While Luci sat at Sandi's desk with the laptop, I looked through the shelves for the third record she'd had on her night table. A sudden constriction at the back of my head made me realize that Gabriel wanted me.

I didn't turn up the missing CD. By then, the girl's clock read 9.47. I checked in the hallway. There was no sign of Morel. 'Get out your notebook,' I told Luci.

When I awoke to myself, I was downstairs in the living room. I was holding the CD that had been missing from Sandi's night table: *Lungs*, by Florence + the Machine. I realized that it had been night inside me a moment earlier, long after midnight, and I had been running with my brother.

Luci was seated on the couch, holding out Sandi's turquoise ring to me. She spoke, but I only caught fragments of what she told me. I asked her to wait with a shake of my hand and closed my eyes till I could form words. When I opened them, she said, 'You asked me to hold the ring for you, sir.'

I took it from her and examined it. 'Where did I find it?'

'In the medicine cabinet in her parents' bathroom. Apparently, it was where Sandi found her mother's sleeping pills.'

I held up *Lungs*. 'And this?'

'In the liquor cabinet. Where Sandi found the vodka.'

If you take something away, you have to leave something behind in its place . . .

Sandi had been counting on me to remember her last words to me after she was gone – and to find her hidden treasures. Which meant that she'd already decided to end her life when we'd talked in the kitchen on Friday – and probably already formed a plan. Amazing girl. If only I'd heard what she didn't dare tell me.

216

I expected to find a note for me or her mother inside the CD, but not even the lyrics were there. She must have wanted whoever found the record to have to listen to it. She or someone else had scribbled the title of the record on a blank disc, which probably meant that it had been downloaded.

Back in the kitchen, Monica told me that *Lungs* had been Sandi's favourite record, and she often used to quote its lyrics, but neither she nor Joana remembered any of the verses their friend had liked so much. Both girls looked miserable and tense. I instructed them not to leave until we'd had an opportunity to talk and asked Luci to walk them outside.

Alone with Sylvie and Morel, I warned them that reporters might start calling them and asked them not to talk with anyone about the case.

'They've already started,' Syvlie told me with an irritated frown. 'Though I've no idea how they get my number.'

'It's a small country. A friend gives out your number on Friday and by Monday half of Portugal has it.'

Outside, Luci was holding Sandi's laptop under her arm and conversing with the girls. I'd already decided by then to talk to Joana alone, since she'd made her silent despair so clear to me.

'Where do you live? I asked Monica.

'On the Alameda.'

I flagged down a taxi for her on the Calçada do Combro, handed the driver a ten-euro note and told him to give the change to the girl. Before leaving, she returned to Joana and engaged her in a brief, whispered conversation. I told Luci to summon someone from headquarters to pick up Sandi's computer and cell phone because I'd decided she should follow Morel wherever he went. As she walked back up the street toward the house, Monica's taxi started off.

As soon as I faced Joana, she brought her hair around to her front and held on with both hands. Her eyes were suspicious and apprehensive.

'Do you live far from here?' I asked gently.

'In Estoril, Chief Inspector. I'll walk to the Cais de Sodré and catch the train.'

'We'll take a taxi together,' I said. 'It'll give us time to talk.'

'I'd prefer to be alone, if you don't mind.'

'How about this – on the way to the station, I'll tell you what I've figured out, and you can tell me where I've gone wrong.'

I tried to sound inviting, and to make it clear with my expression that I badly needed her help, but she folded her lips inside her mouth once more and looked at me guiltily. 'Inspector, I don't live in Estoril,' she said.

My phone rang. I didn't recognize the number and turned it off. 'No, I didn't think so.'

'Walk with me,' she said, and she headed off down the street without waiting for my reply. Her sudden resolve astonished me.

When we were out of view of the Coutinhos' house, Joana told me her address. It was in the Lapa. 'Ring the bell in a half-hour,' she instructed me.

Without waiting for my reply, she walked east, down the hill. She never looked back, though she stopped and shuddered once, as though tossing off an unwanted emotion.

As soon as I turned my phone back on, Mesquita, the head of the Judicial Police, called. 'Did you disconnect on me, *Monroy*?' he snarled.

'I was interviewing someone.'

'Don't do it again! You hear me?'

'Yes, sir, I'm sorry.'

'So did you learn anything interesting in your interview?'

'Possibly. I've one more person to talk to, then I'll know.'

'Listen, it seems you stopped the press leaks,' he noted approvingly.

'I did my best.'

'Have you received any pressure from anybody important yet?'

'No, maybe everyone is waiting to see what I come up with.'

'Could be,' he replied, but he sounded doubtful.

Exhaustion seemed to weigh me down after I disconnected on Mesquita, and my mouth was very dry, so I decided to drink a quick orange juice. Out front of a cramped café along the Rua da Esperança, a stocky beggar wearing a Yankees baseball cap, with the knotted grey beard of a fairy-tale gnome, was standing guard. After he took my fifty cents, he saluted me. Had he recognized me as a cop?

A black kitten was sleeping on a white pillow on the counter, unsanitary but charming, as though posing for a photograph never to be taken, like half of Portugal. I sipped my juice while petting her cashmere belly, and ordered a cheese and tomato sandwich from the young Brazilian woman at the counter.

In the bathroom, I soaked my head with cold water and slicked back my hair. While I was peeing, the unlikely Elvis I created in the cracked mirror suggested a Valium would cure what was ailing me, but I managed to leave him behind without taking his advice. Back at the counter, I called Joaquim. Luci had already told him that he'd be receiving Sandi's computer and cell phone. I asked him to start with files from the last three days, then go back one week at a time, all the way to Easter, if necessary. In addition to the suicide note, he was to look for anything the girl might have written about being molested by Morel or anyone else.

Outside, the homeless gnome took the sandwich I'd bought him with another salute. As soon as I passed the next cross street, a hand seemed to grab my coat from behind, and I began to fall . . .

I was kneeling on the sidewalk when I came to myself. I'd lost seven minutes – enough time for Gabriel to enjoy a smoke, judging from the taste in my mouth. I wondered where this would end. And would I be there when it did?

My phone rang. Ernie's number showed up on the screen. 'What's going on?' he asked as soon as I answered.

'I wish I knew,' I replied.

My brother explained that I'd just called him and told him to come to Lisbon. 'Were you making fun of me?' he demanded.

'Why would I make fun of you?'

'You know I can't go all the way to Lisbon! Why do you make me say it out loud?'

'It wasn't me, it was G,' I confessed.

'What do you mean?'

'*He* told you to get here! It wasn't me. Now tell me exactly what he said to you.'

'He said, "Come to Lisbon where I can watch over you!" And then he hung up.'

'He's taking over more often than ever before,' I explained. 'The border between us is vanishing.'

My brother made no reply, probably thinking of how to reassure me, but my head filled with all the terrible things that could happen to him when we were apart. I asked him to load the pistol I'd bought him and keep it by his bed. 'If Dad shows up, you have to shoot him!' I ordered.

'Jesus, Rico, stay calm. He's not ever coming to Portugal. It's over.'

'Ernie, haven't you figured out yet, it'll never be over?'

'We're talking about two different things,' he said.

'We're not! Load the gun like I showed you. And shoot. A second will be all he needs.'

I disconnected before he could disagree. My shirt was drenched with sweat, so I bought a bottle of water in a tiny Indian grocery shop. I downed a Valium with the last sip. I reached Joana's apartment a few minutes later. She buzzed me in. While I was exiting the cramped elevator at the top floor, Inspector Quintela called and told me that the victim's accountant, Sottomayor, had just shown up at headquarters. 'When can you get here?' he asked.

'I can't. You talk to him. And I want you to get me the

220

name of at least one person that Coutinho bribed. With one we'll be able to get more. Threaten him with arrest if you have to.'

'Can I hit him?'

That was Quintela's sense of humour, and I tried to laugh, but it came out hollow. When I knocked at Joana's door, Monica opened it.

'Hey, I thought I sent you home!' I exclaimed.

She smiled cheekily. 'We figured it was best to stick together!'

I realized she and Joana would have been up to summer mischief under more favourable circumstances. I also knew that the sad calculation of three minus one would probably keep them in close touch for the rest of their lives.

Monica handed me a ten-euro bill. 'I can't let you pay for my taxi.'

I tried to give her the money back, saying I was the one who insisted on a cab, but she refused to take it.

'Stand firm!' Joana exhorted her friend in a mock-heroic voice. She was rushing into the room through the door at the back, playfully eager to win this small battle.

Joana was still in her billowy shirt but had put on plaid shorts that would have looked more appropriate on a middle-aged golfer. She was barefoot and was drying her face with a towel. We kissed cheeks. 'I was roasting,' she said. Her hair was dripping wet. She was creating a puddle on the carpet by her feet but didn't care. *The confidence of a girl who has top billing in the story of her own life*, I thought.

She invited me into the living room, which was decorated like a desert tent: Oriental rugs in orange and red covered the walls, and hanging from the ceiling was a yellow fabric printed with black and white stars. The cool blast from the air conditioner made me shiver agreeably. I peeled off my jacket and loosened my collar. 'I'm sorry,' I told the girls, 'but Lisbon and I have differing ideas about the ideal climate.'

While Joana fetched mineral water from the kitchen, I gazed up at the stars.

'Her mom and dad go a lot to North Africa,' Monica explained. 'I went with them once – to Marrakech. Sandi came, too. We ate in that big square they have and even rode camels!'

When Joana returned with our drinks, she pointed me to a battered red-velvet armchair. She and Monica sat opposite me, on an equally worn sofa.

'Listen, Chief Inspector,' Joana began, 'I want you to know that I wouldn't tell you any of this if Sandi were still alive.'

Her self-assurance startled me again. 'You sometimes seem older than you are,' I told her.

'My parents say the same thing,' she replied with a pleased grin.

She seemed a girl who revelled in defying the expectations of adults. Maybe the three friends had had that in common.

'Tell me exactly what happened at Morel's house in Normandy,' I said. 'From the beginning.'

Joana shifted her legs and sat forward eagerly. 'Sandi, Monica and I stayed there for four days over Easter. We slept in the same room, Sandi and me in a big old bed and Monica on a cot.'

Joana told me that no one but Sandi's father and Morel stayed in the house while they were visiting, though an elderly French cook came twice to make dinner, and two young men who worked part-time in the stables had helped the girls go horseback riding.

'On our second night,' Joana continued, 'I woke up at two thirty in the morning and Sandi wasn't next to me. I figured she'd woken up and gone downstairs for something to eat. Or got scared and went to her dad's room.'

'Why would she have been scared?' I asked.

'Monsieur Morel's house is gigantic. And ancient.'

'The floors groan wherever you step,' Monica added with a grimace.

'It didn't help any that Sandi's dad and Monsieur Morel joked with us over dinner about the house being haunted,'

222

Joana continued in a critical tone. 'Dr Coutinho even talked about having once seen a ghost in the kitchen with blood dripping from his mouth.'

'Her dad was trying to keep us entertained,' Monica added, rolling her eyes.

'Sometimes,' Joana said, 'he didn't seem to have a clue that Sandi wasn't like him.'

'Not like him how?'

'Not sure of herself.'

She spoke as if that had been Sandi's fatal flaw.

'About a half-hour after I noticed Sandi was gone,' Joana continued, 'she tiptoed back into our room and sat down on the end of our bed. She started whimpering as soon as I sat up. She wouldn't tell us what was wrong. We put a blanket over her because she was shivering, and she finally said that Monsieur Morel had . . . had hurt her.'

Both girls looked at me darkly, so I said, 'You won't shock me. I've heard nearly everything over the course of seventeen years of police work.'

'She . . . she was bleeding between her legs,' Joana told me, gazing down like a little girl who's revealed something that might get her punished.

'Had Morel raped her?' I asked.

Saying the word 'raped' seemed to leave me alone in my own half of the room, across an invisible barrier from the girls.

Joana tried to reply, but her voice broke. Covering her eyes with her hand, she ceded to despair. While Monica comforted her, I stood up and traced my gaze back and forth over one of the Oriental rugs, dark red and brilliant orange, thinking of all the things I wanted to tell the two of them but not daring to intrude on their intimacy.

After the girls had regained a measure of their composure, Joana looked up at me with red-rimmed eyes. Her breathing seemed dangerously hesitant. 'I was fine and then, suddenly, I wasn't,' she told me. 'I'm really sorry, Inspector.'

'There's nothing to apologize for,' I replied, sitting back down. 'I only wish I could tell you something that would help.'

'I'm not sure anything could help us now that Sandi . . .' Monica shook her head rather than end her sentence.

'I hate to put you through this, but it's very important that you go on with your story.'

'Of course – we know we have to,' she said. To Joana, she added, 'I'll start, and you just catch your breath.' After taking a quick sip of water, she said, 'Sandi told us that Monsieur Morel was reading in his room with the door open a crack, so he heard her walking to her father's room. He came out to her in the hallway and invited her into the kitchen, and he heated her some milk. It was supposed to help her fall back to sleep, he said. Later, Sandi figured out that maybe he'd put some drug in the milk, because she started to feel really weak. He told her he'd help her back to her bedroom, but instead she ended up . . .' Monica took a long deep breath. 'She ended up in his room, and he . . . he did it to her.'

'Sandi swore us to silence,' Joana continued, disapproval in her voice. The stern way she frowned gave me the idea she was remembering – bitterly – how she'd failed her friend. 'She said that her mom and dad would never believe her, because Morel was her mother's lover and her father's best friend.'

'And he also threatened her,' Monica added disgustedly. 'He told her he knew about her father's affairs with other women and would make sure the gossip magazines wrote about them.'

'He even claimed Sandi was at fault – that she'd seduced him!' Joana said, seething with contempt.

'But she hadn't!' Monica exclaimed. 'Sandi wasn't like that!'

When Joana kissed her cheek, I thought with admiration, *This friendship is far deeper than any I could have entered into at their age.* And I sensed that they would not have formed so strong a bond with Sandi unless she, too, had been beyond her age in terms of loyalty.

Joana said, 'Monsieur Morel also told Sandi he'd wanted to take her virginity and, now that he had, he was no longer interested in her. He said she didn't have to worry about him doing it again to her.'

My gaze turned inward as I realized that Sandi had given a present – a cookbook – to the man who'd raped her. Had she needed to feel her debasement so deeply that she'd be able to carry out her plan and kill herself?

That question seemed to solve a riddle that had confounded me for thirty-two years: why a woman sentenced to death would spend her final hours knitting a six-foot long, rainbow-colored scarf for her jailer.

'Inspector?' Joana asked.

'I'm here,' I said. 'So do you think that Sandi ended up telling her parents what Morel had done to her?'

'She claimed she didn't, but I figured she was lying. In any case, they didn't do anything about it. Dr Coutinho must have regarded Morel's threat as real.' Frowning disdainfully, she added, 'He'd have hated for something bad to get into those stupid gossip magazines.'

'I don't suppose Sandi was able to sneak off to a doctor or clinic the day after she was hurt by Morel? I mean, to have herself examined.'

'No, but I kept something that'll prove what he did to her!' Joana said with vengeful triumph. She reached into the pocket of her shorts, took out an amber phial and stood up to hand it to me. Inside was a sliver of stained white fabric. 'It's a piece of a bloody towel,' she said.

'Whose blood is it?'

'Morel's!' She sat back down. 'While trying to fight him off, Sandi scratched his back really badly. Once she was safe in our room, she wiped her hands on a towel. She couldn't stand the feel of him on her. While she was showering, I snipped off a piece.'

'That was smart,' I said, though I knew already that her guile wouldn't do us any good.

'You can get Morel's DNA from it, can't you?' she asked.

She leaned towards me and made fists. Three months of hope must have been inside them, because the moment I promised I'd give her phial to Forensics, tears flooded her eyes. Struggling to find the right words, she whispered, 'Thank you, Chief Inspector. Thank you for helping Sandi.'

Her face was luminous. I realized it would have a disastrous effect on her to learn that it would be impossible to prove in court that Sandi had got Morel's blood under her nails while being raped. Sandi's testimony would have made that connection. But now that she was dead, there'd never be a trial.

After the girls had fetched a carton of apple juice from the kitchen and passed it between them, I asked if Morel had tried to hurt Sandi ever again, either in his home or at her own house. Monica had begun braiding Joana's hair by then, with an impressive, sure-fingered seriousness.

'She didn't mention anything like that,' Joana said, 'but I'm not sure she'd have told us. She said she felt dirty all the time. But I know she didn't trust what he said about not being interested in her any more. So she did everything she could to make sure he wouldn't find her attractive.'

'That was the real reason she chopped her hair off, wasn't it?'

'Yeah, and she started starving herself, too, to make herself even more unattractive.' In a disapproving tone, she added, 'She started wearing long shirts and trousers to hide that she was all skin and bones.'

I remembered that Sandi had worn her father's sweater both times I'd spoken to her. I'd thought it was to comfort herself with his scent. She'd clearly become very skilled at subterfuge by the time I met her.

'Did you ever see her throw up after a meal?' I asked, thinking that I now knew why she'd kept a honey dripper in her bed.

226

'Yeah, she told me she had started vomiting to keep from gaining weight. And she said it as if it were a fantastic new talent. It was crazy!'

'And did you ever see her cut herself?'

Joana showed me a puzzled face. 'Cut herself how?'

'With a knife? On her arms. Or somewhere else on her body.'

Neither girl knew anything about that, which probably meant that Sandi intended to stick her blade into Morel if he ever dared step into her bedroom. Nor had they been aware of any suicidal feelings Sandi might have had. 'Though she told us her dad's death was her fault,' Joana told me. 'Maybe that was why she did it.'

Did she think it was her fault because she'd failed to tell her father about the deadly content of her nightmares, as she'd originally led me to believe? When I asked the girls, Joana said she was convinced it was quite the opposite – that it was what Sandi had confessed to her father that had ended up overwhelming her with guilt.

'She must have told her dad that Morel had hurt her,' the girl said. 'And he must have confronted Morel. To silence Sandi's father, to keep him from going public with an accusation, Morel paid someone to kill him.'

That was a logical enough explanation. Except that such a possibility would have required an unlikely series of events to have taken place at the Coutinho's vacation house in the Algarve. And for Susana Coutinho to have lied to me about something crucial to her daughter's life.

Monica stopped braiding her friend's hair and said in a distraught voice, 'Sandi might even have started believing that Morel was right when he claimed she'd seduced him. It seemed to me that she was way too upset to think clearly.'

'You know, Inspector,' Joana added, 'Sandi also stopped getting her period. Because she wasn't eating enough. And she was glad that happened.'

'Glad? Why?'

'She figured that no man would want her if she wasn't getting her periods. Maybe it doesn't make much sense now, but it made sense when she told us.'

Monica finished off her braiding with an elastic hair tie. Joana pulled the braid around to her front and inspected the neat, tight weave closely, obviously pleased. After thanking Monica, she leaned forward and grabbed a copy of *Visão* from the coffee table between us. She twisted the magazine into a tight scroll. I had the feeling she needed to feel her own strength.

'I'll stop Morel from getting anywhere near you,' I told her, guessing at her fear.

She looked down at me with anxious eyes. 'How can you do that?'

'Because he knows I consider him a suspect, so he'll be on his best behaviour. Also, I've got him under surveillance.'

'You do?' Monica asked, stunned.

When I confirmed that he'd be followed day and night if necessary, Joana tapped her scroll on Monica's head and giggled.

I hoped that the girls' devotion to each other would see them safely past this trauma.

To my next question, the girls told me that they didn't know if Sandi had spoken to her therapist about being molested.

'Did she say if Morel had tried to steal anything of hers?' I asked; I was thinking of her turquoise ring.

'No, she said nothing like that,' Joana told me, and Monica agreed.

So maybe starving herself made her fingers so slender that the ring kept slipping off.

'I've got it!' Monica suddenly burst out.

'What?' Joana questioned.

'The line from *Lungs* that Sandi liked best. It was something like, "Happiness crashed into her like a train rushing down the track."'

Monica sang the verse as best she could remember. We retreated into silence after that. Joanna gazed away for a while, clearly fighting another wave of despair. It seemed almost certain that both girls were thinking – like me – that Sandi's first sexual encounter had run her over. And been meant to.

'Inspector,' Joana asked, 'when are you going to arrest Monsieur Morel? Can't you do it right away?'

'We need to talk about that,' I replied.

'Why is that?'

'The problem is that there's only one way I can think of that could make Morel the killer and keep things logical. And it'll take some checking on my part. Mostly with Senhora Coutinho, and she's not yet in any condition to answer my questions.'

'We told you exactly what Sandi told us!' Monica exclaimed in a hurt voice.

'I'm sure you did, but your story only makes sense if Sandi's father learned what had happened to his daughter on his last day in the Algarve. Because if Sandi said anything to him earlier, he'd never have let Morel stay in his vacation house with her. Not to mention that Morel wouldn't have accepted an invitation to stay in the same house with a girl he'd raped three months earlier.'

'Unless he's a sick and evil person!' Joana exclaimed.

'Yes, there are people like that, it's true. But if Sandi told her father she'd been raped, he'd have probably had a violent quarrel with Morel in the Algarve.'

'That's probably just what happened,' Joana said.

'Except that Sandi's mother told me that everything was friendly there.'

'It's possible she wasn't there to see what happened.'

'Even if she wasn't, she'd have found out about any bad argument that took place in her house.'

'Maybe there was no fight because Morel told Dr Coutinho he regretted what he did,' Joana said. 'He agreed never to go anywhere near Sandi or Senhora Coutinho again

229

and left right away. He told everyone he was headed for the airport, but he lied. He surprised Dr Coutinho at his house and shot him. Or he hired someone who did.'

'And what was his motive?'

'To prevent Dr Coutinho from going to the police.'

'So to avoid a rape charge that might not stick, he paid for a murder? Not very likely. Besides, you told me yourself that Sandi's father would have hated for something to come out in the press, so he wouldn't have gone to the police. He'd have remained with Sandi at their vacation house. He'd have wanted to help her.'

'Maybe he had something really important to do in Lisbon,' Joana said, desperate to salvage her theory. 'You didn't know him. He was *always* working. Right, Monica?'

'Yeah, there'd be whole weeks when he'd come home late every night.'

'Besides,' Joana added, 'he was leaving Sandi with her mom. She'd be safe.'

'Except we all know now that she wasn't safe with her or anyone else,' I told them.

I stood up and stepped away from the girls to think things out. Maybe Sandi had told her mother exactly what happened, but Susana refused to believe her story because that would have meant having to give up her boyfriend – and face a public scandal. She might have convinced herself that Sandi was lying about being raped in order to prevent her from leaving Pedro and marrying Morel. If she thought that Sandi had resorted to lying about something that serious – and something for which Morel could face criminal charges – then she might not have shown her daughter much sympathy. Which might explain why I sensed so much tension between them when we first met.

Not being believed is like having all that's good about you murdered.

Ernie and I had never needed to say that to each other – every time we looked at each other, we knew it; but maybe that was exactly what I needed to tell Susana in order to find out what had happened between her and Sandi. Unless . . .

Another possibility turned me back towards Joana and Monica: Sandi had indeed lied, but not about being raped. 'Tell me more about the men who worked in Morel's stables,' I said.

'What do you want to know?' Joana asked.

'How old were they? Where did they live?'

'They looked like they were in their twenties. They were from the nearest town. They were at university and only worked part-time for Monsieur Morel.'

'Did they flirt with you?'

'They joked around with us,' Monica said. Sensing the direction of my thoughts, she added, 'It was harmless – really.'

'Did they go riding with you?'

'One of them did.'

'Do you remember his name?'

Monica turned to Joana. 'Was it Bernard?'

'I think that's right,' Joana said, adding, 'do you think he'll be able to confirm that Sandi was hurt by Monsieur Morel?'

'That's not the point,' I said.

'Then what is?'

'I'm beginning to think that Morel didn't hurt her – that this Bernard did.'

'That's impossible!' Joana declared with that disarming assurance of hers. 'Sandi wouldn't have named Morel if he didn't do it.'

'No, not unless she thought she could swear you two to silence more easily if she convinced you that he was the man who had attacked her. She told you that he had secrets on her father that would ruin her parents' marriage. That was to force you to keep quiet. And her plan worked – you didn't say a thing until now. If she told you it was one of the young men from the stables, it would have been nearly impossible to guarantee your silence.'

'I suppose it's possible,' Joana said, 'but would Sandi really have—'

'You saw the way Morel acted with you,' I cut in. 'He wasn't at all worried about what Sandi might have told you about him, or about what you might tell me.'

I said nothing more. I didn't want to add that Sandi might have been eager to meet Bernard or his friend that night. Or even both of them. To her, it must have seemed a thrilling adventure – a chance to journey further towards herself.

After they were done with her, the young men probably convinced her that her flirting – and her coming to meet them in the stables or somewhere else on Morel's property – made what they'd done acceptable. They'd have told her she'd been asking for it.

But what could have prompted them to travel a thousand miles to Portugal and murder Coutinho three months later?

Chapter 19

Ernie and I ran away from home on 23 June 1979, a Saturday.
I was nine and my brother was five. School had just ended
for the year. It was late morning, near noon, and Dad had
woken up with a killer hangover.

We were on the porch eating breakfast when Dad started
hollering for Ernie and me. The dread falling like a shadow
over my brother's face told me I'd better do something fast.
I grabbed him, and we raced hard in the direction of
Crawford. I guess Dad was too groggy to come after us, and
once we climbed over the rickety wooden fence bordering
the Johnsons' property, we took their trail to town.

Ernie and I hardly said a word to each other. During a war
you tend to keep pretty quiet. You save your energy.

I was hoping that Nathan, who worked at the general
store, would drive us to Grand Junction or anywhere else
where Dad couldn't find us. Or, if he couldn't take us, we'd
hitchhike. But Ernie slipped at a bend in the trail that had
been badly eroded by the spring rains. He tumbled over and
slid down a hillside covered with weeds, maybe forty feet.
When I reached him, his shoulder and one of his knees
were bleeding. I cleaned out most of the dirt with my hand.
Ernie was in favour of going on, but while I was blotting the
blood on his knee with my shirt, I realized what should have
been obvious – that Dad would end up blaming Mom for us
running away and she might not survive the lesson he'd
teach her.

When I looked ahead to see where Ernie and I would never go, I realized that we were standing in the shade of a big woolly tree, every branch bending under the weight of hundreds of filigree earrings. They were bright emerald. I hadn't even noticed. I was so astounded that I took a step back.

Beauty that unusual might be dangerous, I was thinking, though I couldn't have put it into a neat sentence like that back then.

Later, I learned that the tree was a black walnut. The earrings were called catkins.

To this day, whenever I see something towering above me, even just the side of a building, that walnut tree rises up before me and a shooting star of surprise and wonder flashes across the whole length of my mind.

We trudged back home. Dad wasn't there, but Mom was on her bed holding a bag of frozen peas to her cheek.

After my mother died, I pleaded with Dad to build a bridge over the stream that ran through our property, though it was easy to walk across except when it rained a lot. I no longer remember why.

Before Dad cleaned out Mom's drawers, I stole her deck of cards from her night table – the ones with landmarks of Lisbon on the back. I gave twenty-six cards to Ernie and kept twenty-six for myself. I liked the idea that Ernie and I would only ever be able to play rummy or poker if we played together.

I'm not supposed to know where my brother keeps his half of the deck, but I do. They're in a plastic storage box under his bed with his maps of Colorado and his CDs of corny crooners like Carlos Gardel and Bing Crosby.

Ernie does a very good imitation of Carlos Gardel, but his hair is way too long for there to be any physical resemblance, so you have to close your eyes to get the full impact of being in the same room with a dramatic Argentinian superstar belting out *Por Una Cabeza*.

I remember sitting with Dad after the funeral and bending his fingers back really far, mostly to make Ernie laugh. Dad was double-jointed, and the freedom of doing whatever I wanted with his hand was like being able to fly.

I also remember Dad dancing a slow tango with Ernie in his arms after Mom was gone, and Mieczysław Fogg singing his heart out in Polish on our old KLH record player, and I was clapping in time with the sneaky beat, and though I couldn't have put my thoughts into words at the time, I know now that I was thinking, *Despite everything, Ernie and I lucked out, because I wouldn't want to have any other father, even though I hate who he becomes when he's angry and will never understand why he does the things he does.*

It was a moment I knew I'd always carry with me, in a secret place where no one would ever find it, because thinking good things about Dad was an unforgivable betrayal of both Ernie and me. And of Mom, too, of course.

I loved moving the tiny lever on our KLH record player that shifted between 33, 45 and 78 RPMs because of the definitive, ratcheting sound it made. I think it gave me the idea that you could change anything in your life if you could just figure out where to concentrate your energy and what direction to push in.

Dad had LPs by Mieczysław Fogg, Hanka Ordonówna, Sefcia Górska, Zula Pogozelska and lots of other Polish singers. Before I was born, he bought the record collection of a Polish house painter who'd advertised in the *Denver Post*.

Whenever my father danced with Ernie, he'd close his eyes and let the melody take him over. Spinning and twisting like Fred Astaire didn't seem any harder for him than breathing. He was a graceful man. And handsome. I was proud to be his son.

Dad had those aw-shucks good looks – with his hair always mussed up and two days' worth of dusty-looking whiskers on his cheeks – that seems to me to be typical of the West, though maybe that's because I live thousands of miles away from Colorado now and don't know how men there really look. If our life together had been the big-budget production he'd have preferred it to be, Dad would have had slicked-back, movie-star hair and would have tangoed his way into Ginger Rogers' heart in the most dramatic scene. And honeymooned with her under the full moon in Acapulco.

He – and not Ernie, of course – would have sung *Por Una Cabeza* in the climactic scene. His life in Colorado – along with me, my brother and our mom – would have ended up on the cutting-room floor.

Mom told me she was in a choir back in Portugal but I don't think I ever heard her sing. She was from Évora, a small city about an inch to the east of Lisbon on the map of Portugal in our Collier's Atlas. When I was alone in the house, I'd sometimes touch my fingertip to Évora and imagine the whitewashed buildings of the central square.

Dad was touchy and mean when he was drunk, but he was dangerous when he had a hangover. Is that odd for alcoholics? I've never found out; there are some things I'd rather not know.

If Mom was alone with me and Ernie, she'd sometimes speak Portuguese. But if Dad was around and had been drinking, she didn't dare. He'd slap her right across the face if she didn't speak English.

'You're always putting me down to my kids with that god-damn gibberish – and right in front of me!' he'd holler at her, sneering like she was dirt.

But I never once heard Mom say anything mean enough about him to be accurate. Not in English, and not in Portuguese either.

Now that I'm an adult, I can see that his slaps and punches took most of the fight out of her, and that Valium took the rest. Maybe having to care for Ernie and me helped weigh her down, too. Sometimes I think that having us around just dragged her right out into the deepest part of her lonely sea and dunked her under, straight to the bottom.

Or, more to the point, having Ernie and I to raise tugged her into Dad's old Plymouth and sent her driving off to her appointment with a cottonwood tree.

Then again, when I'm watching my own kids playing together, I become certain that we were the only light that ever reached her down there on that seabed she lived on. Would she have left Dad if we hadn't been born? That's a question I don't think about too often because it adds too much black depth to my insomnia.

I think that our running away and her getting punched for it was the end for her. After that, she stopped leaving the house, even to go to church or collect wildflowers. She hardly ever even got dressed. Maybe it was while holding the frozen peas up to her face that she figured out how to free herself forever.

She probably thought that if she wasn't around, then we could run away. And we'd make it this time. In a way, she was right, though it took four more years for us to make it out of Colorado. And we managed that only after Dad left us.

Dad's drinking got worse just before he disappeared – so bad that he sometimes woke up not knowing where he was and thinking that Mom was still alive.

One afternoon, when Dad was really hammered and went upstairs to sleep, Mom told me – translating badly from Portuguese – that Dad had downed so much rum that *he couldn't stand himself and went to make a nap.* She meant that he couldn't stand upright, and had made the verb *to stand* reflexive because she was nervous, but I wished it were true and that Dad hated himself when he got drunk.

I didn't dare hate my father until I got to Portugal. When I was living at our ranch, I was convinced he could read my thoughts, and if he located something in my head he didn't like, he'd make Ernie and me take one of his tests.

The Sioux regard the cottonwood tree as sacred. Nathan told me that after Mom died. I think he meant that she had chosen that tree because she knew it was holy. Not that I

237

think he had any expectations of easing my suffering by telling me that. I suppose that I'd need to be raised as a Sioux to understand why the kind of tree she crashed into was important.

Nathan was in his fifties by then, I'd guess. Ernie and I used to visit him at the general store in town. He sold us Chiclets and liquorice. When no one else was around, he told us about Black Elk, the great Sioux holy man – about his schooling and travels to England with Buffalo Bill's Wild West Show, his visions and writings. But if anyone entered the store, he'd always make-believe we were discussing baseball or football. He believed that I'd been blessed by a Thunderbird at birth. I don't know how he figured that out. Sometimes he'd sit me down on top of the wooden counter where the cash register was and let me take a little puff on his pipe. He said the pipe was what gave him the power to prophesy the future and that was why he was sure that Ernie and I were going to need a lot of help to make it to adulthood.

Nathan had cinnamon-coloured skin and deep wrinkles around his eyes and black-black hair that he grew long and separated into two tight braids. He had small, sunken eyes – like obsidian beads. He didn't wear traditional Sioux clothing. He wore jeans and T-shirts. He had thick calluses on his hands because he was a wood carver.

There was a blazing sun inside Nathan, though most people couldn't see it, of course.

Once, he sat Ernie down on his chair and danced around him seven times, whispering a Sioux prayer. 'That'll help keep him protected even when you're not around, Rico,' he told me.

Ernie and Nathan and Mom were the only people I let call me Rico.

Nathan would sometimes go around town in the evening with his hair down, wearing garlands of flowers around his neck. Some of the townspeople laughed at him and said he wanted to be a woman. They didn't know – or care – what a *winkte* was. And they didn't like Indians.

We didn't call people like Nathan Native Americans at the time. The townspeople would have laughed at anyone who used that term.

Back then it was perfectly okay to dislike someone just for being Sioux. And you could say it out loud, too, and expect a lot of people to agree with you. And cops could arrest a Native American for just walking down the street. Nathan got picked up by the police whenever he left Crawford. He once spent a week in jail in Denver. When he made it back to Crawford, he told me, 'Always remember, Rico, in Denver, they can arrest you for just sitting in a garden and thinking!'

When I was just five or six, Nathan told me he was a *winkte*. That's a clown who's also a wise man – and who does everything upside down when he's performing. A *winkte* is blessed at birth with a double spirit: a masculine one and a feminine one.

I think now that he'd known a lot about what Ernie and I were going through at home. At the time, I didn't realize it. Did he make my father vanish? Maybe there are things that *winktes* can do that go way beyond what white policemen think they can do.

I wish he had helped Mom with some of his magic. Though maybe he tried and I never found out about it.

Life must have seemed such a daily struggle to Mom when she first got to Colorado. She must have clung to my father – a powerful man who seemed to know all the secret cultural codes in her new country – as if he were a catcher in a trapeze act.

Second of May 1981, a Saturday. I had a Little League baseball game that morning in Crawford. Ernie walked to town with me and watched me from the top row of the stands, sitting next to Nathan. Dad might have come, but he was sleeping off a night out with his buddies. Mom was also at home, knitting in bed. She said she wanted to finish the scarf she was making for Dad, since she only had one more foot to go.

The scarf was rainbow-coloured. She'd ordered naturally dyed wool from a store called Art Fibers in Santa Fe.

'Sorry, sweetie,' she said to me when she said she couldn't watch me play. 'Maybe next time.' Except she said it in Portuguese: '*Desculpa, Amor. Talvez a próxima vez.*' She kissed me and breathed in deep on whatever scent was in my neck. 'Better than wildflowers!' she told me.

Then she held Ernie's head in both her hands and told him that he was the most beautiful boy in the world, which might have made me jealous except that she was acting so oddly that I was more worried about her than anything else.

I should have figured things out but I didn't.

After the game, Ernie and I were walking back home on 92, the road that passed in front of our ranch, when we spotted Dad's beautiful old Plymouth Belvedere up ahead, just passed Mayor Anderson's rickety old house. Only it wasn't parked. It was smashed up against a big tall tree. The front end had been pushed back into the windshield and moulded around the trunk. There was a big tow truck just behind it and a Colorado State Patrol car on the other side of the road, and our father was talking to a trooper. Dad was gesturing a lot with his Milwaukee Braves cap in his hand.

I'd already guessed what had happened but I didn't let myself think it.

Maybe Mom thought that destroying Dad's beloved Plymouth would be part of her revenge. Or maybe she took the only way out that seemed reasonable and it never occurred to her that she was wrecking what he most cherished.

Ernie ran ahead. I didn't. I didn't want to enter what would be my life from now on any sooner than I had to.

As soon as Dad picked Ernie up, he must have told him what had happened. My brother started shrieking as if he was being murdered.

240

The state trooper told Dad there'd been a witness to the accident – a hunter from Boulder. The man said that Mom sped up as she raced towards the tree. She was going at least fifty miles an hour.

When we got back home, we found the rainbow scarf Mom had made folded on the kitchen table. It was sitting under a letter addressed to Dad. I never learned what she wrote. Dad snatched the letter up and refused to show me when I asked for it. The only thing he told me was that she apologized for leaving Ernie and me.

I've never forgiven him for not showing me Mom's letter. I can't see how I ever could. I get the feeling sometimes that I should forgive him, for my own peace of mind if nothing else, but I won't ever do it.

Though maybe it's true that she wrote nothing more to me and Ernie than she was sorry.

Dad never wore the scarf. I don't know what happened to it. I looked for it every now and then over the next few years, but I never found it.

It's just possible that too much Valium made Mom fall back to sleep after she started towards town in Dad's car. Maybe she meant to drive all the way to Denver and fly from there to New York and then head on to Lisbon. Or maybe she took an extra dozen pills so she wouldn't feel the pain of having her back broken when she hit the holy tree she'd picked out. I like to think she'd planned so far ahead that she was able to avoid feeling anything at the moment of impact. Though when I'm desperate with the need to talk to her and be kissed by her, I occasionally hope that she was in really bad pain for two or three seconds. I know that you should never think such things about someone you love, of course, but being left behind when you're only a little kid will put cruel thoughts like that in your head.

Chapter 20

Before leaving Joana and Monica, they told me they'd never seen Sandi's father with a woman other than his wife and didn't recognize the face in the police sketch. They'd never seen the number thirty tattooed on the back of anyone's hand.

That morning, Sylvie had given me the phone number of Sandi's therapist, Benjamin Loureiro, and I called him while walking to the Rato Metro station. He'd been expecting to hear from the police. He told me that Sylvie had already informed him of the girl's death.

Dr Loureiro answered my questions guardedly, explaining that he was obliged by his professional code to withhold the specifics of what Sandi had confided to him. He told me that he had been treating the teenager for psychological difficulties that were compromising her physical health, as well as acute feelings of self-hatred.

'Did her parents know about her bulimia?' I asked.

'So you think she had bulimia?' he questioned.

'She kept a wooden honey dripper in her bed for provoking her gag reflex,' I told him. 'And she told her friends that she was throwing up after meals.'

Dr Loureiro hesitated for a moment, then confirmed my suspicions. In response to my next question, he told me that Sandi had never mentioned any instances of sexual abuse. In fact, she had told him she was still a virgin. They had had their first session on the third Friday in May. Her eating disorder had begun a few weeks earlier. Loureiro was under the impression that her parents' marital difficulties – along with a very poor adjustment to her move from France – had undermined her self-confidence. Additionally, Sandi had begun menstruating about six months before and the hormonal changes in her body had badly affected her stability. She had never spoken of suicide, but he wasn't shocked that she'd ended her own life; her lack of nutrition had caused dangerous mood swings. He had spent much of his time with her simply devising strategies for eating healthily.

He confirmed that she'd indeed had dreams of a violent intruder entering her house and hurting her family.

Loureiro added that he'd called Sandi on Saturday. She'd sounded depressed but stable. They'd scheduled a special session for this afternoon.

After Loureiro read me the dates of his sessions with Sandi, I called David Zydowicz and convinced him to do the girl's autopsy as soon as possible. When I mentioned the additional information I wanted, he asked how old she'd been, and on telling him, he said in a critical tone, 'I thought it was only in Brazil that girls started that young.'

'Unfortunately, she had no choice,' I told him.

Next, I tried Senhora Coutinho's cell phone, but it was off. I reached Morel, however, and asked him to put her on the line.

She cut off my attempt to express my condolences. 'Oh, Monroe, are you still in Lisbon?' she asked. Her voice sounded merry and heavily drugged. 'But this connection is terrible! You'd think you were on the moon!'

'Look, Senhora Coutinho, I need to know if—'

'I'm all ears,' she interrupted in English, and she heaved a throaty, smoker's laugh.

'I'm sorry to ask you this, but did Sandi ever tell you about any sexual abuse she might have suffered at Monsieur Morel's house in France?'

Silence.

243

'Senhora Coutinho, this is important,' I said. 'Try to concentrate, please.'

'Call me Susana. I feel like we're old friends by now. I mean, if I had any friends, you'd be one of them!' She laughed again.

'Susana, try to hear what I'm saying. Did your daughter ever talk about any sexual experiences she'd had – violent experiences that would have upset her badly?'

'I really do like you, but your Portuguese is abominable!' To Morel, she said, 'Can you understand his Portuguese?'

Morel got on the line. 'Susana is not well. Call back later!'

'Sandi might have been raped, so put Susana back on now!'

'Raped? What do you mean?'

'Susana can explain to you when I'm done. Give her the damn phone!'

After a moment, Susana asked, 'Is that you again, Monroe?'

'Yes. Now listen closely, Susana. Did Sandi ever tell you about what happened at Morel's house – about her being hurt or molested?'

After a moment of silence, she pounced. 'I want the name of the person who told you such a crazy thing!'

'Two of her friends told me.'

'Which two?'

'Joana and Monica. They were with her at Morel's house in Normandy.'

'Were they . . . molested?'

'No, but Sandi told them what happened to her.'

'Look, Monroe, you've got me thinking things that don't make sense. And I don't know what you're trying to say.'

'Joana and Monica told me that Sandi was attacked while she was staying at Morel's house – at his house in Normandy.'

Susana lowered the phone and spoke to Morel in French, but I couldn't make out what she was saying. When her sobbing started, he came back on the line. 'Monroe, you are a madman!' he shouted. 'You make things worse!'

'Something terrible happened to Sandi at your house. I need to know everything you know.'

'Wait a moment.'

Morel spoke to Susana in French, as though giving an order, then told me to hold on a few more seconds while he left her bedroom. When her crying faded to silence, he said, 'Listen closely, Monroe. We have a nice vacation together at my home. I do not know what you are talking about.'

'So nothing bad happened with Bernard?'

'Who is Bernard?'

'One of the young men who works at your stables.'

'Bernard Mercier? You think he hurt Sandi?' Morel asked in an astonished voice.

'Yes. You never suspected anything like that?'

'No, never.'

'What about the other man at your stables? What's his name?'

'François Savarin.'

'Did you ever suspect that he was capable of violence?'

'No, he is a good young man. I know his family for many years.'

'Are both of them still working for you?'

'François is. I send Bernard away.'

'Why?'

'He steals from me.'

'When?'

'At Easter – while Sandi and Pedro visit.'

'I thought you said nothing bad happened then?' I said angrily.

'Nothing bad happened with Sandi and the other girls! That is what I say!'

'So what exactly happened with Bernard Mercier?'

'Pedro Coutinho sees him stealing.'

'What did he steal?'

'An important book. I have a valuable library. He steals the first edition of *Les Confessions,* by Rousseau. He still not return it. He tells me he never steal it.'

'But Pedro saw him taking it?'

'Exactly.'

'And you fired Bernard?'

'What else should I do?'

'Did Bernard know that Pedro accused him of stealing?'

'Yes. I must tell him because I am not there when he steals it.'

'How long had Bernard worked for you?'

'Since he is a boy.'

'How long in years?'

'Maybe . . . maybe ten years.'

Before disconnecting, Morel read me the cell-phone numbers of his two stable hands. By the time I'd hung up, I'd formed a possible scenario of what could have happened.

Sandi had been raped by one or both of the young stable hands. What she told Joana and Monica about being drugged was probably true, since that was not the kind of detail a young girl would make up. Whoever raped her must also have told her that now that she'd lost her virginity, he was no longer interested in her; again, I couldn't imagine a fourteen-year-old thinking up such a cruel remark. And I knew from many years of experience that telling truthful details made the overall lie much easier to sustain.

If I was right, then Sandi had told her father the truth. If she hadn't been coerced into meeting her attackers, her father would have concluded that the police would have no basis on which to make an arrest. Maybe he even held his daughter partially responsible. In any case, he probably ordered her to keep what had happened a secret. She was not even to tell her mother, since Susana might go to the police, which would mean that the press would find out. In order to make Bernard Mercier pay for his crime, and in order to be sure that Sandi would never have to see him again, Coutinho found a way to have him fired. My guess was that he took the first edition of Rousseau's *Les Confessions* from Morel's library and said he'd spotted

246

Mercier stealing it. To Coutinho, it must have seemed the ideal – and discreet – solution.

Mercier found himself out of a job after ten years of loyalty to Morel. He'd have been furious at Coutinho for lying – and ruining his reputation. And maybe at Sandi, as well.

Very possibly he believed that he had nothing to be ashamed of – after all, the girl had agreed to meet him. He used the last three months to plan his vengeance. Perhaps he'd only planned to scare Coutinho and things had got out of hand.

As for Sandi, she must have been shattered by her father failing to defend her. She fluttered desperately for three months against the flame of her own shame, and then her resistance gave out and she fell.

To check my theory, I called Luci and told her to go upstairs to Coutinho's library and look in his locked case for *Les Confesssions*. I also called Inspector Quintela and asked him to turn on his computer so he could find me the date of the first edition. A minute or so later, he had it: 1782.

Luci called as I reached my office. She was holding a leather-bound edition of *Les Confessions* that had been published in 1782.

That it was a first edition still wasn't absolute proof that Coutinho had stolen it from Morel, but inside the front cover she discovered a badly faded nameplate that read: *J. Morel, rue du Floquet, Sacquenville*.

'What do you want me to do with it, sir?' Luci asked.

'Bring it to me,' I replied, but as soon as I said that I realized that Morel might have lied to me and been in on the plot to fire Mercier. And in on the cover-up. If so, then he knew the book was locked in Coutinho's case. 'I've changed my mind,' I told Luci. 'Put *Les Confessions* back on the shelf where you found it. I don't want to give away that we're aware that it might have special importance.'

I could see through my side window that Inspector Quintela was in his office, so I handed him Joana's phial and asked him to bring it to Forensics. If I was right, the blood on the sliver of towel would be Mercier's or Savarin's. Or, in the worst possible case, both men's. I also told him to get the passenger lists for all flights to and from Paris over the last two weeks and to check if Mercier or Savarin were on any of them.

After Quintela left, it occurred to me that Sandi might have told her mother about being raped even if her father had instructed her not to. At the very least, Susana would have sensed a change in her daughter's behaviour and probably forced a confession out of her. In that case, she might have disagreed with her husband about how to handle the problem. She'd have been aware that her husband had denied Sandi the help and compassion she deserved. She might have been in favour of informing the police and been overruled by Pedro. Very possibly there'd have been a violent quarrel. All of which would explain why she'd implied to me that there had been great cruelty in her house. Did her sense of guilt make her hope that I'd catch on? After all, she'd gone along with her husband's plan to keep silent about their daughter's rape.

Everything seemed to be coming together, but I sensed there was something else that no one wanted me to see – something I was missing, and that had to do with the need to make the very worst crimes disappear as if they'd never happened.

Back at my desk, I navigated to the Florence + the Machine website and found the lyrics for the *Lungs* CD. The song 'Dog Days Are Over' caught my attention right away because it spoke of a girl whose happiness hit her like a runaway train. It also contained a reference to menacing horses and, near the end of the song, a comparison between happiness and getting shot in the back.

We often searched for narratives that would help us make sense of our lives, and it seemed clear to me now that this particular song had provided one for Sandi.

I watched the video of 'Dog Days Are Over' twice on YouTube. The female singer wore a gauzy white dress, and her face and hands were painted white. Her hair was a frizzy red helmet. Her singing started breathy and soft, and her awkward, sinuous hand movements gave her dancing an unrehearsed, youthful, amateurish feel. A minute or so into the song, however, when syncopated clapping started up in the background, she began to belt out the lyrics as though she'd grown enraged.

As I was going over the list of calls to and from Coutinho's phone to see if he'd heard from either of the two young Frenchmen over the past few weeks, David rang me on my office phone. He told me that he'd just finished Sandi's autopsy and there were no signs that she'd been forced to take an overdose and no self-inflicted cuts. He would wait for the results of the toxic substance tests to classify her death as suicide, but he saw no reason to suspect it was anything else.

When he told me she'd been dangerously underweight, I explained that she'd suffered from bulimia.

'There's one last thing, Henrique,' he added darkly. 'The girl had been pregnant.'

David's revelation fixed me in place. 'How far along was she?' I finally asked.

'About three months, though the foetus was only sixteen millimetres long. It would have developed more fully if she'd eaten better.'

There were twists of fortune that could make continuing to struggle on seem pointless, and this had proved to be one of them. I knew I'd always remember the hard roundness of my coffee mug in my hand because it was while squeezing it that I realized that Sandi had stopped eating so no one could tell she was pregnant. Which meant she'd starved her unborn baby, as well – a crime she had only been able to live with for as long as it took to take her own life.

On completing my scan of Coutinho's outgoing and incoming calls, I confirmed that he hadn't spoken to either

249

Mercier or Savarin over the last two weeks. Fonseca appeared in my doorway while I was wondering if I should put in a request for the French police to interview both young men. He gave me a rundown on the evidence that he and Vaz had collected on Friday. After excluding the fingerprints of family members and Senhora Grimault, they'd obtained prints for six other individuals, but none of them had turned up in our database. No matches had come up for the bullet either, which meant that the killer's gun hadn't been used to commit any other crime in Portugal. Fonseca had identified it as a Browning semi-automatic pistol, but had found no fingerprints. Curiously, it was a model that we'd used in the police until about ten years before.

As I expected, Sandi's own blood had created the stains on the stuffed panda and her underwear I'd found under her bed. Morel's prints had been all over the living room, and his DNA was on the Gauloise cigarette butts. *Diana* in Japanese had indeed been written in Coutinho's blood. A fibre caught in the second character indicated that the brush used had been rabbit hair.

'We'll need to check the victim's paintbrushes,' I told Fonseca.

He eyed me cagily. 'I'm way ahead of you again, Henrique! His brushes are cat and marten.'

'Cat?'

'I checked on the Internet. The Japanese use it to make brushes all the time.'

'So the killer brought his own rabbit-hair brush to the festivities.'

'Right, which means he expected to make enough blood for his calligraphy. He thought ahead.'

'What about that small piece of towel? Whose blood did you find on it?'

'No results yet. Sudoku promised me he'd analyse it this afternoon. He'll call you.'

Fonseca went on to say that Joaquim had found nothing

of interest on Coutinho's computer, neither threatening emails nor evidence of bribes he'd paid, but he still had several hundred files to consult. As for Sandi's laptop, he hadn't been able to start on it yet. He knew I was in a rush and had promised Fonseca that he'd take it home with him.

'What about the sneaker print?' I asked.

'A size forty-three Converse,' Fonseca replied.

'Anything unusual about them?'

'Vaz says the tread showed no signs of wear.'

'So the killer bought them for the murder – he's a clever guy,' I said, because even if we'd found them, we'd have been unable to learn anything about his daily routine from what we tweezered out of their tread.

Before Fonseca left, I asked him to go to Coutinho's house and search Sandi's room for evidence, and he promised he'd get there by the end of the day.

Our receptionist Filipa called while I was going over the lyrics to the other songs on *Lungs*. 'A pretty young lady named Joana is here asking for you,' she told me cheerfully.

I met the girl at the top of the stairs. She smiled with relief on seeing me.

'Are you all right?' I asked.

'Fine, thanks.' We kissed cheeks. 'Listen, Chief Inspector, what if thirty isn't really the thirty?' she asked.

Her riddle brought nothing to mind. 'I don't get it,' I said.

'One of our French professors teaches yoga twice a week after school. She has a tattoo on her right hand. It's Sanskrit for Om, the syllable that Hindus chant. I should have figured out that that's what it was, but I must have been too upset. Om looks pretty much like thirty if you only get a quick look. If you have a computer, I'll show you.'

Back in my office, she dropped down in my desk chair and starting tapping away on the keyboard. I leaned over her shoulder, but the father–daughter feel of our positions felt too intimate and I took a step back. A moment later, Google Images presented us with six million, two hundred thousand pictures of Om. Joana picked one that was stylishly drawn.

'Am I a genius, or what?' she asked me, laughing.

'You're an amazing girl!' I agreed. Giving her shoulder a little squeeze, I stepped around my desk so that I could face her.

'So what's this teacher's name?' I asked.

Joana lifted up her lip like a donkey. 'Your sketch doesn't look much like her,' she said, 'and I wouldn't want to get her into trouble.'

'She might have been in Sandi's house when her father was murdered. Which means she might have seen or heard the killer.'

'It's just . . . just that I don't want her to hate me.'

'If she hates anyone, it'll be me, not you. I promise.'

'Her name Maria Dias,' Joana said and, as I jotted that down, she took out her cell phone and read me her phone number and address.

'How did you get her contacts?' I asked.

'Miss Dias invited me, Joana and Sandi over for lunch one Saturday just after the spring break. She especially liked Sandi.'

Chapter 21

Maria Dias lived in the Chiado, across the street from Nood, an Asian noodle restaurant that Jorge adored because the African and Brazilian waiters gave him piggyback rides if he pleaded with them shamelessly enough. The intercom for her apartment house was defaced with jagged red script reading FUCK MOODY'S. It was a reference to the American ratings agency that had downgraded Portugal's credit rating to the level of 'junk' almost exactly a year earlier. I buzzed Dias's third-floor apartment, fully expecting her to have escaped the dusty, overheated city for the beach, but after a few seconds, she asked who it was, and I explained why I needed to speak with her. She buzzed me in right away.

On opening her front door to me, she said, 'You found me much quicker than I thought you would, Inspector.'

'I got lucky – someone helped me identify you just a little while ago.'

'Come on in.' She smiled shyly.

The apartment was small and crowded with figurative paintings on the walls; she had that in common with her murdered boyfriend. The floor was tatami. A waist-high stone statue of the Buddha – meditating serenely – sat in the corner. The furniture was sleek, contemporary and uni-formly white.

A handsome, well-worn leather quiver that hung over the door to the kitchen caught my attention. Its feather fletchings were slender and grey – not so different from the ones Nathan used to make.

Dias was barefoot and asked me to remove my shoes. I lined them up with the two other pairs by the door. She wore loose-fitting black trousers and a pink tank top. Her arms were lithe and tan, her waist slender – a gazelle with long-lashed green eyes. Her dark hair was clipped short and spiky. She must have had it cut over the weekend to avoid being identified. I'd have guessed she was thirty, but there was an authority in the way she carried herself that made me believe she might be older.

I was surprised that she was so different in style from Susana, but that was likely one of her attractions to Coutinho.

'So, what can I get you?' she asked, once again showing me a timid, reticent smile.

'Nothing, thanks. I just had breakfast.'

She clasped her hands together as if she wanted me to give her a chance to play hostess, which gave me the idea that she didn't often have visitors. 'How about just some tea?' she asked.

'Good idea. With a little lemon if you have it.'

'Come into the kitchen and we'll talk. You look desperate for answers.'

Her kitchen was small and well organized. In the middle of her white marble table were twelve canary-yellow ceramic cups, arranged as though they were the petals of a lotus flower. Inside each cup were powdered spices – turmeric, paprika and others in varying shades of red, yellow and brown that I was unable to identify. Not surprisingly, the air was heavy with the scent of curry.

'Beautiful,' I said, pointing to her ceramic flower.

'I'm glad you like it,' she replied gently.

After filling her kettle, she got out our mugs – black with blue frost glazed on the rim – and set them on the counter. She hesitated for an instant when she reached for the handle of her silverware drawer and then nearly fumbled the small spoons she took out. That, together with the constrained, purposeful slant of her jaw told me she might prefer a few minutes of small talk before being questioned.

'How long have you been doing yoga?' I asked.

'Since I was a kid. It was my father who got me started, as a matter of fact – yoga and judo.'

'And how long have you taught at the French high school?'

'Eight years.'

'A good place to teach?'

'I love it. The kids are great.' She pointed to two tins of Twinings tea on a high shelf. 'English Breakfast or Earl Grey?'

'English Breakfast.'

Standing on her tiptoes, she knocked the tin off the shelf and caught it securely.

'I'm guessing you're bilingual, French and Portuguese,' I said.

She nodded. 'Though I'm more at home in French.'

'Were you born in France to Portuguese parents?'

'Exactly.' She opened the lid of the tin and took a long, grateful inhale. She had a handsome profile. I'd have bet her students did their best to please her – and that she was a talented teacher.

'I'm told that Sandi was in your class,' I said.

'Yeah, she's a wonderful girl.' On setting down the tin, she asked, 'So how did you find me?'

'A construction worker spotted you leaving Coutinho's apartment. Though you don't look much like the sketch he helped us make. It was your hand that gave you away. At first, we thought the tattoo was the number thirty.'

She turned her hand over to show me her Om in wine-coloured lettering.

'It looks good,' I said. 'But why did you choose your hand?'

'To be *mindful*,' she said.

In Portuguese, she used the word *consciente*.

'*Consciente de quê?*' I asked.

255

'Of myself – the functioning of my body and my mind. And of my effort to lead the life I wish to lead.'

'Which is?'

'Centred and calm, Inspector. And alone. On my own.'

'Attachments lead to suffering,' I said – a paraphrase of one of the Buddha's Four Noble Truths, at least as Ernie had told them to me during his Eastern Philosophy stage.

'I'm impressed!' she said. Her eyes twinkled with humour. She probably assumed – like most of the Portuguese – that all cops were ignorant and interested mainly in soccer.

'I'm the kind of person who knows a little bit about a lot of things,' I told her.

'A fact collector.' She nodded as if she knew all about them and didn't much appreciate their ways. 'What I meant, Inspector, was that I don't believe in a God who watches over us. Buddhists don't believe that sort of crap.' She used the word *tretas* for crap. It sounded harsh and out of place coming from her.

'We're born alone and we die alone,' she added, and she looked at me as if daring me to defy her. 'Once you accept that, the real work begins.'

She seemed to believe that human existence was one long, purposeless winter.

'So what's the real work?' I asked.

'Perfecting yourself. The Buddha is a perfect soul. He's our model.'

'Like Jesus,' I said, thinking of Aunt Olivia.

She pounced on that. 'No, not at all! There is no God like the one in the Bible. And no son of God! We don't pray to the Buddha, Inspector. That would be laughable. It's not at all like Christianity!'

Her superior manner irritated me – and seemed provincial in a typically Portuguese way; all my acquaintances in Portugal who'd discovered Eastern beliefs tended to act as though they were the first Westerners ever to do so. I found I had nothing to say. I clasped my hands behind my back and gazed around the room, thinking now that it was very possible that we'd quarrel during my interrogation. And dreading it.

She didn't seem to notice my discomfort. After lifting a black ceramic teapot out of a cabinet, she set it on her counter and added three heaped teaspoons of tea leaves. 'I suppose you're a believing Christian,' she said. Disapproval continued to be woven into the tone of her voice.

'Lapsed,' I replied as she took a lemon out of her refrigerator. 'My parents and aunt were. Maybe my brother still is.'

'And your wife?' She cut a slice of lemon and placed in a tiny, blue-glass cup.

'Jewish. I think our kids are too, but I'm not entirely sure.'

'Not sure?

'My wife thinks God was invented to keep women in their place, but my mother-in-law has made a point of telling me that Judaism passes through the mother. Which, in my case, makes our kids Jewish.'

When the water came to a boil, she poured it atop the tea leaves in a diminishing spiral, enjoying her own precision. I asked, 'So how long had you and Coutinho been involved – amorously, I mean? Did you just meet recently?'

She started, then smiled ironically and gave a bursting laugh. She put down the kettle.

'What's the joke?' I asked, suspecting it was my Portuguese again; I'd used the word *envolvidos* for *involved*, and maybe it was an awkward translation.

She looked off as though she hadn't heard me. 'The world is nearly always at its most beautiful when we least expect it to be,' she said, clearly addressing only herself. Then, to me, she added, 'It gives us gifts, too, if we make ourselves ready to receive them.' She smiled gratefully.

'Right,' I said, but without feeling; at that moment, my receptivity to her poetic observations was close to zero.

Still smiling to herself, she placed the teapot, along with our mugs, onto a black lacquer tray. I had the feeling that daily life was a series of small meaningful rituals for

257

her – an attempt to maintain order in a world that seemed too focused on superficial matters.

'Let's talk in the living room,' she told me, and she carried the tray to her dining table, which was an old wagon wheel covered by a circle of thick, green-tinted glass. I ran my hand over the age-darkened wood around the side and, on a hunch, asked if Pedro Coutinho had given it to her, but she told me it had been her grandmother's.

Dias excused herself to go to the bathroom while the tea was steeping. Once she was out of the room, I tiptoed across the tatami and pressed down on the Buddha's shoulders to feel his solidity of purpose, thinking that in another life Ernie would have decorated his place like this. It pleased me – this possibility of taking a peek at what might have been.

After Dias returned and we took our seats, I asked, 'Was Coutinho a Buddhist, too?'

'No, but he'd studied Zen when he lived in Japan. He still chanted and meditated on occasion.'

It began to seem that she and Coutinho had been an excellent match.

'And how did you two first meet?' I asked.

'Pedro spotted me at a gathering of teachers and parents about nine months ago. His wife had been unable to come. After the presentations, he asked for my number. He called a few days later. I knew I shouldn't see him, since he was married, but I was curious. And he was bright, funny, affectionate . . . I ended up falling in love with him, though I made it clear that I couldn't see him as often as he liked. As I told you, I need a lot of time to myself.'

She filled my mug and her own, sitting rigidly, as though remembering that good posture was part of mindfulness. As she was blowing on her tea, she fixed me with an inquisitive look, and I thought she might ask me about how close we were to finding her lover's killer. Instead, she said, 'This moment is very different from how I'd expected it to be.'

I couldn't tell whether she regarded that as good or bad,

which made me realize I was unable to read her expressions very well – perhaps because we were both talking in our second languages. It was even possible – I granted reluctantly – that she hadn't meant to be condescending to me a few minutes earlier.

'How is this moment different?' I asked, squeezing lemon into my tea.

'I figured that when you found me, I'd panic. And I almost did, but I didn't.'

'For selfish reasons, I'm glad you didn't,' I said.

'Selfish?'

'It makes talking to you easier. Can we get started now?'

'I thought we had,' she replied, and she showed me a devilish, childlike smile. She seemed at ease all of a sudden, as though a gear had shifted inside her.

I took my notebook out of my coat pocket. 'Were you in Pedro Coutinho's house when he was murdered?' I asked.

'No. I left early that morning. The killer hadn't come yet.'

I tried to hide my disappointment, but she said, 'Sorry. I wish I'd seen him. What he did to Pedro was awful.'

'How did you know what he did to Pedro?'

'I read about it in the newspaper.'

'It must have been a shock.'

'It was horrible – my heart seemed to stop. I was just about to give a class, which was lucky, because my students helped me.'

'A class? I thought you'd be off for July and August.'

'Over the summer, I teach yoga at the Chiado Health Club. It's only twice a week – on Tuesdays and Fridays. I was about to give my first class of the morning and there it was in the paper.'

'You must have realized we'd want to talk with you, but you didn't come forward.'

'I almost did, but an affair with a married man . . . And I knew I couldn't help. My coming forward would have only created problems for me at school. And also for Pedro's family.'

Once again she eyed me as though defying me to disagree. I had the feeling that she didn't much like me or trust me. 'Cutting your hair makes me conclude you were determined that we wouldn't find you,' I said.

I spoke more judgementally than I'd intended. She brushed a tense hand back through her hair, as though to check that it was still as short as she remembered. 'If you think it was the police I was afraid of, then you're wrong,' she told me resentfully.

'Who then?'

Her eyes targeted me. 'Inspector, hasn't it occurred to you that the murderer might want to find me? He may think that I was there when he killed Pedro – which means he'll want to make sure I can never identify him.'

'I didn't consider that because I was under the impression that no one knew about you and—'

'Of course, you didn't consider it!' she cut in acidly. 'But I've been a nervous wreck! And yes, I cut my hair. If you were in my position, wouldn't you try to change your appearance?'

'Yes, but what I was trying to say was that I didn't realize that anyone knew about you and Pedro Coutinho. Senhora Coutinho certainly didn't.'

'I can't be sure what Pedro told his buddies. You know how men can be.'

'So do you have any idea who might have wanted to hurt him?'

She shook her head. 'Pedro didn't ever talk about business with me.'

'You're assuming that he made an enemy in the business world,' I observed.

'That's the only thing that makes sense to me.'

'Does anyone in particular come to mind?'

'I told you, he didn't discuss that side of his life with me.'

'On your last evening together, did he mention an old French friend named Jean Morel?'

'No.'

'Did he ever mention the names Bernard Mercier or François Savarin to you?'

'Not that I recall.'

'Did he ever talk about his daughter Sandi in the context of anything – let's say *violent* – happening to her about three months ago?'

Dias jerked her head back. 'What happened to Sandi then?'

'I'm not at liberty to say. But did Pedro ever tell you anything that led you to believe she'd been hurt?'

'No, but he wasn't very comfortable talking about Sandi with me. I was her teacher, and that made things awkward.'

'Did he seem nervous or worried on the morning of his murder?'

'No. He seemed . . .' She reached a hand to her temple. I had the feeling that my mentioning that Sandi had been a victim of violence had had a delayed effect on her. Turning over her hand, she stared at the Om with a determined expression. At length, she said, 'Give me a moment.' Standing up, she rested her hands on her thighs, crouched forward and took a series of ten sharp breaths. Then, standing on her toes, she stretched her arms over her head – with her palms together – and lowered them ever so slowly to her sides, as though closing her wings.

I could easily imagine Coutinho painting her with his Japanese brushes and then summoning her into bed with him. I took a long sip of my tea, wondering how a Buddhist would react to the suicide of a young woman she cared about.

'What?' Dias said, seeing me hesitate.

'I'm sorry to tell you this, but Sandi took her own life last night.'

She tilted her head, as though she hadn't heard me right.

'Sandi took an overdose of pills,' I said. 'She was pronounced dead early this morning. I'm sorry to have to tell you.'

She jumped up, her jaw clenched, her expression suspicious. 'You're lying!' she yelled. 'And now I see what you're trying to do! You must think I'm a fool!'

'No, I'm telling you the truth. Sandi took a handful of her mother's sleeping pills. She downed them with vodka.'

Dias leaned towards me, pressing her hands to the table. The wild fury in her eyes made me believe she might come at me.

'Tell me what's really happened, you bastard!' she hollered.

'Sandi died at seven o'clock this morning,' I said, opening my hands and keeping my voice even, as I'd learned to do with violent people. 'And we've no reason to suspect anything other than suicide.'

Her tightly focused stare unnerved me. Counting on the accumulation of details to weigh down her rage, I said, 'I was told that doctors couldn't get her blood pressure stabilized. She took Victan – twenty tablets. She took the pills from her mother's medicine cabinet.'

She gazed past me and tugged at her hair. 'This . . . it's impossible,' she whispered absently.

'I'm sorry to have given you such a shock. I realize—'

'*Merde!*' she hollered.

As I looked for what else to say that might be of some small help to her, she turned her back to me and whisper-screamed *merde* three more times.

Rushing to her bedroom, she banged the door closed and clicked the lock in place. Her sobs set me pacing across her living room. I ended up at her window facing the square below. The hazy light slanting over the rooftops brought tears to my eyes. When I opened them again, I was standing by the kitchen door, in front of a small portrait. There had been no throbbing in my head or any other warning signal.

The painting was of a young woman in a shimmering white gown standing before a mirror, her dark tresses – swirled on top of her head – held in place by a long purple ribbon. She was looking left, and her eyes showed exultant surprise – as if an unexpected friend or family member had just entered her room after a long absence. From the slightly downward angle of her eyes, I guessed that her visitor was her son or daughter. The painting was executed in the style of Goya. And the woman had Dias's slender face and intelligent eyes. They could have been sisters. Which meant that this work of art hadn't been stolen from Coutinho's living room, after all; he must have given it to her as a gift.

I looked down into my hand, but nothing was written there.

Dias came back into the room holding a tissue. Her eyes were rimmed red. Shuffling to a small desk near the Buddha, she took a stick of incense from the top drawer and inserted it into the palm of a white ceramic hand sitting on one of her bookshelves. Once it was lit, she wafted the smoke towards her and inhaled gratefully.

'I'm sorry to have left you alone,' she said on returning to me, her voice unsteady.

'It's all right, I understand,' I said.

She sat down and started tearing her tissue into small pieces – but carefully, as though it were important not to lose control again.

'I like the painting Pedro Coutinho gave you, I said, pointing to the portrait.

'Yes, it's lovely,' she said, but without feeling.

'The woman might be you – if you had lived in the nineteenth century.'

'Yes, Pedro thought the resemblance was . . .' Failing to find the word she wanted, she gave up with a shrug.

'When did he give it to you?' I asked.

'About month ago.' Tears squeezed through her lashes.

'I'll get you another tissue,' I said, standing up.

'No, it's better to let them fall.'

To give her a pause, I studied the painting again. I decided that the woman was about to dash towards her unseen child. The artist had wanted to capture the moment before she rushed away. In so doing, he had also painted her about to go back to her real life and abandon her status as the subject of a painting. It seemed a theme worth telling Ernie about.

263

At length, she said, 'I'm ready for more questions.' Her effort to smile reminded me of Senhora Coutinho. *We are a country of brave women, if nothing else*, I thought.

'Did you have any idea that Sandi had suicidal feelings?' I asked.

'No.'

'But you noticed she was troubled?'

'Of course, but I didn't question her. Like I told you, my affair with her father made things very awkward.'

'You didn't even ask her what was wrong when you had her over to this apartment just after spring break?'

She started. 'How did you know she came here?'

'Her friends Joana and Monica told me.'

'No, I didn't question her about herself, though I obviously should have,' she said remorsefully. Standing up, she added, 'Sometimes I think I'll become a monk and never talk to another human being for the rest of my life.' Challenging me to doubt her frankness, she added, 'What do you think of that?'

'I think this has been the worst week of your life.'

She looked at me as though she'd just realized I wasn't the insensitive fool she'd taken me for. After gazing again at the Om on her hand, she closed her eyes and whispered a brief chant. Stepping quickly to the same window I'd stood at, she hid herself in the folds of the gauzy white curtain and looked out.

'I'm betting he's long gone,' I said, guessing at her concern.

'Why do you think that?'

'I suspect he came from France to kill Pedro. By now, he's probably back home. I'll let you know for sure after I get the names of the passengers on all the flights to Paris since last Thursday.'

'Thank you. That would be very helpful.'

On scanning my notes, I came up with a final question: 'On your last morning together, did you notice whether Pedro had either of his cell phones with him?'

'No, I'm sorry.'

264

'So, is there anything more you can tell me about the murder?'

She shook her head.

'Just to be safe,' I said, 'if you see anything suspicious, call me right away, day or night.' I held up my card, saying, 'My number is here,' then put it down on her table. 'Maybe you should ask a friend to stay with you for a few days. There's no need for you to go through this all alone.'

'But that's just it!' she shot back. 'We are *all* alone – always. And this just proves there's nothing we can do to help one another!'

Dias and I shook hands at the door. Hers was frozen.

On walking down the stairs, I heard the shattering of pottery. A life with Ernie gave me a good idea of what she was breaking – her lotus flower of spices – and why: because it was the most beautiful thing she owned.

Chapter 22

Inspector Quintela met me at my office with the news that there was no record of either a Bernard Mercier or a François Savarin on any of the flights to or from Paris over the last two weeks. He leaned against my doorframe, gnawing at his thumbnail. Eager to check my logic, I said, 'Listen, Manuel, if you wanted to murder someone in Paris, how would you get there?'

Manuel's eyes shone with the competitive eagerness of a young man accepting an older man's challenge. 'Who am I going to kill this time?' he asked, since we'd played this game before.

'A wealthy builder you met a few months ago.'

'And why am I going to murder him?'

'He got you fired from your job by lying about you stealing a valuable book.'

'That's not very nice.'

His naiveté seemed sweet rather than infuriating, as it usually did. 'No,' I agreed. 'So how would you get to Paris?'

'I'd drive – there are no border crossings these days, so nobody could later prove where I'd been.' He dropped down in the chair in front of my desk. 'I wouldn't use any credit cards and I'd avoid the Spanish and French teller machines. I'd take out plenty of cash in Portugal, but slowly, over a period of weeks, so nobody who went over my bank statements would spot anything fishy.'

'Maybe even over a period of three months,' I said.

'Sounds about right to me.'

'You've obviously thought about this before,' I said with a perverse lilt in my voice.

He picked up the large smooth stone from Ernie's garden that I used as a paperweight and squeezed it hard. 'I think a lot about finding the asshole who hit my brother,' he told me.

His older brother, Luis, had been run down by a speeding Spanish lawyer about a decade earlier, in Sitges, a resort town near Barcelona.

'And where would you buy the gun you'd need to shoot him?' I asked.

'On the black market. And in Portugal, where I speak the language well enough to not say anything that would give away my identity.'

'Anything else?'

'Yeah, I'd dye my hair black and buy a really nice Basque beret. The Catalans would assume the murder was carried out by an ETA separatist.' With his hands, he showed me how he'd angle the beret at a jaunty angle over his right eye.

'I'm beginning to think all cops have at least one murder filed in the back of their head,' I said. 'Maybe it's even why we pick this profession.'

'You mean, to prevent ourselves from actually doing it?'

'No, to learn how to do it and not get caught.'

His laugh indicated that he didn't think I was serious, but my unswerving stare changed his mind.

'So who would you want to kill, Monroe?' he asked.

Manuel often seemed oblivious to a great many of the most obvious human desires – in this case, my desire for secrecy. But I told him the truth; wearing a mask in front of him no longer seemed as necessary as it once had.

'You'd kill your dad?' he replied in a stunned voice.

'Or he'd kill me first.'

He rubbed his pink, youthful cheek, considering a possibility that had never occurred to him before. 'You know what bothers me most, Monroe? It's that that bastard didn't spend a single day in jail. I keep his name and address in my wallet, you know.'

'Was he ever tried?'

'Nope. A Catalan detective told me off the record that the guy was good friends with Juan Antonio Samaranch. Remember him?' Manuel sneered. 'He was the Fascist asshole who ran the Olympics. The Catalan also told me that the Spanish courts were the most corrupt in Europe.' He licked his fleshy lips with malicious glee. 'I told the guy he obviously knew nothing about Portugal!'

I asked Manuel to get me a list of the names of passengers on all the international train routes in and out of Lisbon over the past two weeks. I also told him to look for credit card records for Mercier or Savarin at any Portuguese gas stations on the route to Paris.

Once I was alone again, it occurred to me that the killer – or killers – might have bought their brand-new Converse sneakers in Lisbon. It was just possible that they'd slipped up and paid for them with a credit card.

After I'd eliminated the first three sporting goods shops on the list I'd Googled, I got a call from Sottomayor, Coutinho's accountant. 'I missed you today,' he said.

'Sorry, I couldn't help it.'

'I've been having second thoughts. I'll talk to you about bribes, but only in person.'

'When can we meet?' I asked.

'I'm right outside your headquarters building.'

Sottomayor had a closely cropped beard dyed such a deep shade of brown that it made his face appear cadaverously pale. Possibly because of that, his dark eyes seemed to have the suffering appeal of a Christ in a Russian icon. His blazer was blue, but both his trousers and vest were cream-coloured linen. He wore black leather driving gloves and carried a wooden cane with a silver duck-head as a handle.

Eccentricity seemed to be the way he'd chosen to make his way through the world.

As we shook hands, he said in a determined voice, 'I won't ever testify in court to anything of what I'm about to tell you.'

I invited him to take the chair in front of my desk. 'Then why come here in the first place?' I asked.

He tugged on his earlobe as though considering his options. 'Although I don't want you to involve me directly, I'm hoping you can use what I tell you to prosecute one or more of the corrupt officials Pedro paid off.' He smiled sympathetically. 'Not that I think that you'll be successful.'

'No?'

'When did anyone get convicted of corruption in this country?'

'How about Isaltino Morais?' I pointed out. He'd been the mayor of Oeiras and had been prosecuted successfully a few years back.

Sottomayor sighed while peeling off his gloves. 'You obviously haven't followed the case.'

'Not lately.'

He placed his gloves down neatly on my desk, taking his time, pleased to show me his aristocratic manners, which I found curiously relaxing, as though we'd been carried back to a previous century. 'As you may recall,' he began, 'Morais was convicted in 2009 of corruption, fraud and money-laundering, and sentenced to seven years in prison. This was for acts he committed in 1996. He appealed, of course, and his sentence was reduced to two years. In the meantime, he ran again for mayor of Oeiras. Do you remember the outcome, by any chance?'

'He won.'

'Thereby proving to all of us,' he said in a delighted voice, 'how few people in this country care about either corruption or their own self-respect! He'll never be brought to justice. He'll never spend any time in jail.'

'Did Morais ever accept a bribe from Pedro?'

269

'Forget Morais! He's a pipsqueak, an upstart, a . . . pro-vincial zero who can barely read and write!' he said contemptuously. With his dismissive vocabulary, Sottomayor seemed eager to let me know that his was the contempt of Old Money for New. Regaining his calm, he said, 'I am try-ing, Chief Inspector, to make a very different point.' He took out a handsome pipe and a silver lighter. 'Do you mind?'

'It's against the law.'

'Come on, have a little compassion for an old man,' he said with a sweet, apologetic look.

'All right, go ahead,' I told him.

I opened my window and retrieved the clamshell I'd used as an ashtray before our anti-smoking law came into effect. Once he had his pipe lit, he undid the buttons of his blazer. Then, clenching his pipe between his teeth, he leaned back, joined his hands behind his head and asked, 'Do you play soccer, Chief Inspector?'

'No.'

'But you watch a game now and then?'

'Not if I can help it.'

He laughed, 'I'm beginning to think very highly of you.' Clearly enjoying his tutorial role, he said, 'My point is, men like you and me, who believe that everyone should play by the same rules . . . We are in a small minority. Most people are very happy to win a job through a friend, or to get authorization to add an extra bedroom to their house by paying a bribe.' He leaned towards me anxiously. 'So are we off the record?'

I found Sottomayor entertaining but overwhelming – like too grand a fireworks display. When I gave my agreement, his eyes grew deadly serious. 'Pedro made all his payments himself and nearly all in cash,' he began. 'He wore gloves, so as not to leave fingerprints. But occasionally he made a bank transfer. Start with those, Chief Inspector.' His pipe had gone out. He lit it again, sucking in on the smoke with greedy determination. 'The last transfers I recall were made to win a housing contract in Coimbra. Pedro made at least

270

two payments to a corporate account in the Cayman Islands. This is in the spring of 2010.' He jabbed the stem of his pipe at me and squinted through a cloud of smoke. 'Check Pedro's bank records in Portugal and France and you'll find the name of the bank. Or check Susana's and Sandi's records. He might have used one of their bank accounts so he could avoid any direct association with the transfer.'

'Did he use that strategy often?'

'Only when a transaction required special . . . care. Now, the name on the account receiving the transfers in the Caymans should be Alcino Lima. But try to convince someone at the bank that received the money to confirm that.' His mood of urgency broke and he winked at me. 'If your charming American accent doesn't get you the information you need, offer a bribe. It's expected there. That may mean you have to fly there, of course, but it's a lovely place. Great snorkelling! And excellent fresh fish. Try the conch salad – it's my favourite. They marinate it in lime juice. Who would have guessed? Anyway, bring your wife and kids – they'll love it.'

'How do you know I have a wife and kids?'

'Would I talk so openly to a shady cop? I did a little checking on you. A thousand euros ought to get you the documentation you need. I'll give you the cash now if you'll agree to go.' He took a thick envelope from the inside pocket of his coat and offered it to me.

Was he offering me money for something more than following the trail of a couple of bank transfers? Maybe he thought he could buy my promise to leave his name out of any investigation. I waved his money away.

'Please don't be offended, Chief Inspector. We're all facing lean times, and who could begrudge a hardworking officer a few days in a tropical Eden?'

'Who's Alcino Lima?' I asked, anxious to move into safer territory.

'Quite right!' he said, putting the envelope back in his pocket. 'But if you change your mind, let me know. I'll make you a special gift of your airfare. As for Senhor Lima, at the time, he was the councillor in Coimbra in charge of Housing. Though it's possible, of course, that his account in the Caymans is in a relative's name. I'm told he has a nephew studying in Lisbon who passes money along to him.'

I got out my notebook and wrote down the names he'd given me. 'About the payments that Pedro made in cash, do you have any records?' I asked.

'No, Pedro kept them.'

'Where?'

'I don't know. He often discussed the amounts with me and who he was about to bribe, but he never gave me any information about his records.'

'Then how can we be sure he kept any?'

'Because he told me he did. I've always assumed he had them in his house. I've no idea where, though if a handsome police officer like you were to try a little mild torture on me,' he said with an amused twist to his lips, 'I'd hold out for a while just to please him and then I'd suggest Pedro's library.'

Sottomayor had clearly found it useful to let me know he was gay – perhaps to prove he trusted me and that I ought to trust him. But I was beginning to get the idea that he was a member of the elite who had ruined this country's economy.

'Why his library?' I asked.

'Because he was the only one who ever went in there. Except for Senhora Grimault.'

'His wife never went in?'

He tapped the tip of his cane on the ground and gave me a displeased look. 'Have you met Susana, Chief Inspector?'

'Yes.'

'And did you come away with the impression that she was an admirer of classic French literature – Proust, Zola, Anatole France . . . ?'

'She struck me as intelligent,' I told him.

'Then you didn't spend much time with her.'

'Are you always so mean-spirited?' I asked.

'Mean-spirited?' He laughed at the idea. 'You have me completely wrong, Chief Inspector. I *like* Susana. I like her enormously! And she was one hell of a sexy woman when Pedro married her, I can assure you.'

He eyed me as though he were challenging me to disagree.

'Okay,' I said, unable to keep the irritation out of my voice, 'so why did Coutinho tell you anything at all about his bribes? What did he get out of it?'

'He liked to have someone with whom he could share his amusement. We've been friends since we were little. And we have a similar sense of humour.'

'So he was amused by the bribes he made?'

'When he started his business, having to pay off politicians turned his stomach. As a defensive strategy, you might say, he learned to make it into a game. He ended up getting a kick out of making absurdly low offers and watching a mayor or minister haggle for more. It pleased him to bring out their greed. Best of all was seeing every pretence of public service fall apart. Inspector, are you familiar with a certain kind of Portuguese politician who wears Italian suits and who needs a Mercedes or BMW to give him the class that he has always lacked? I once called a particularly loathsome one of them a cheap whore, and Pedro grew furious with me. He said such men had nothing in common with whores, even the cheapest ones, because a woman who offers sex for a price provides a useful service to society.'

'So who did Pedro buy off?'

'Anyone whose approval we needed and who took Pedro's hint that he would be happy to help *his favourite political cause* – every politician's favourite cause being himself, you understand.'

Sottomayor grinned at his witticism, but I was so far out to sea – with no sign of the landmarks I might recognize as Portugal – that I didn't find anything he said the least bit funny. Had bribes been offered me many times over the past seventeen years without my even realizing it?

273

'I'd like some names,' I said.

'Where do you want me to start?'

'Who got the biggest bribes?'

'Ministers and secretaries of State. Mayors received less, and city councillors were usually only the price of a week at a four-star hotel in Madeira. These days, however, everyone is on sale. You can get bargains if you shop around.'

'Did Coutinho pay them directly?'

'He'd usually pay a relative. Cousins are popular, especially if they have accounts abroad. Pedro made many payments in France for projects he was building in Portugal, and vice-versa.'

Sottomayor went on to name two of the last four mayors of Lisbon and three current city councillors. He also named a former Minster of the Interior and a current Secretary of State. He told me that a former president of a Lisbon football team held the record for Pedro's largest bribe: forty thousand euros. By way of explanation, he said, 'The man was a close friend of several well-placed members of the Socialist Party, at a time when they controlled most of the important city halls.'

'How about the shopping mall Coutinho was building in the Sado National Reserve?'

'What about it?'

'Who'd he pay off?'

'A local city councillor received fifteen thousand euros, as I recall – Jorge something-or-other. But the man was going to use that sum to pay off other officials. Alas, I have no idea who they were or how much they got.'

'Fifteen thousand is all they received?'

Sottomayor laughed. 'Tell me, Chief Inspector, how much are *you* paid for your signature?'

'But fifteen thousand isn't much for a multimillion-dollar project.'

'Like I said, there are bargains out there if you'll just do a little comparison shopping.'

My next move seemed risky, but his tone of bemusement – with an undercurrent of real contempt – led me to believe that he was telling the absolute truth. 'What if I were to say that I had your old friend's entire list of bribes for the last twelve years,' I told him, 'but that it was in code.'

'Neither of those two pieces of information would surprise me.'

'Because?'

Sottomayor's pipe had gone out again. As he knocked out the spent tobacco from the bowl into my clamshell, he said, 'Because I've been told you're competent, and because Pedro was a cautious person. He wouldn't have wanted the police to find out what he was up to – especially not an upstanding officer like you. You might spoil all his fun!'

'Do you know anything about the code?'

'I might. Is it all numbers?'

'Yes.'

'It's a system we figured out as kids. All you need is what we used to call a master sentence. Imagine the following, 'My pipe has just gone out.' The first letter, M is assigned the number one, the second, Y, is given the number two, the third letter becomes three, and so on. It's easy.' He took out his tobacco pouch and began filling his pipe. 'Without the master sentence, it's extremely hard to crack the code. And we developed ways of distorting it so that it would be virtually impossible for anyone to figure it out.'

'What was the sentence you used when you were kids?'

'The first verse of the *Lusíadas*.' He sat upright and unfurled his arms to embrace the epic scope of his words: '*As armas e os barões assinalados, que da ocidental praia Lusitana* ... Arms and heroes, who from Lisbon's shore ...'

After declaiming the first verse in triumphant Portuguese, as though playing to the back row of a theatre, Sottomayor leaned back and let out an exhausted sigh. 'If it's not that sentence, Inspector,' he said, 'then I'm afraid I can't help you. My advice – forget the code and forget the bribes he

275

made in cash. Track down the transfers to the Caymans. It's the only way forward.' He lit his pipe and funnelled the smoke towards the ceiling. 'Anything more I can do for you?' he asked.

'One last thing,' I said. 'To your knowledge, had Pedro conducted any business in Japan lately?'

'Japan?'

'His killer forced him to write the name "Diana" in Japanese characters on his living-room wall.'

'Diana? Whatever for?'

'I don't know. So did he have any deals in Japan in the works?'

'Not to my knowledge.'

'Are you aware of any connection the name Diana might have to his stay in Japan when he was a young man?'

'No, none at all.'

'How about a connection to his present life?'

He shook his head. I consulted my notes one last time and found a gap I needed to fill in. 'Where did your old friend get the cash to make his payoffs?'

'He kept a stash at home.'

'Where did he keep it?'

'I've no idea.'

'And how'd he put together so much cash?'

'Everybody keeps cash around for emergencies, Inspector.'

'I don't.'

He laughed again. 'Yes, but how many shopping malls or soccer stadiums have you built lately?'

Luci called me shortly after Sottomayor had left to tell me that a limousine service had picked up Susana, Sylvie and Morel, and was taking them to the Ajuda Cemetery for Pedro Coutinho's funeral. An hour and a half later, I'd just finished with my twelfth sporting goods store – with no leads on the sneakers the killers might have bought – when she rang again to tell me that the limousine had just dropped them at home. 'And I've got some disturbing news,' she added. 'Burglars broke in to her house while we were gone. It's been trashed.'

Getting to my feet, I asked, 'Has anything obvious been stolen?'

'No.'

I gazed out through my window as though I were peering through my stunned silence. Then I remembered Coutinho's French–Farsi dictionary; it was possible that the burglars had been after the flash drive I'd found in its cubbyhole.

'Did they mess up the library?' I asked.

'Yes, the books are all over the place.'

'And Sandi's room?' I was hoping we hadn't lost the evidence of how she'd spent her last hours.

'Ever see what a tornado does to a small town?'

'Any idea how they got in?'

'No. No doors were forced and no windows were broken. Sir, if I can be perfectly frank, I don't see how this fits in with your theory about the Frenchmen at Morel's stables. I mean, if they were responsible, then they did what they came to Lisbon to do – Coutinho is dead. There was no need for them to go back to the house.'

All I could think of was that we were dealing with two separate cases – a murder committed by one or both of the Frenchmen who had raped Sandi, and a burglary ordered by a shady politician. As I explained my theory to Luci, I decided we'd better make sure that the burglars hadn't merely been petty criminals taking advantage of a grieving family's absence.

'Luci, are you in the living room?'

'The kitchen.'

'Go to the living room and see if any of the paintings there have been stolen.'

A few seconds later, she told me that the only one missing was the Almeida drawing that Fonseca had taken back to the lab for fingerprinting.

'Check to see if any of Susana's jewellery is missing,' I told her.

Shortly after hanging up on Luci, I realized there was still a chance the crimes were connected and called her back. I told her to look for *Les Confessions* in Coutinho's library. 'I should have had you hold onto it,' I confessed. 'If Savarin and Mercier burgled the house, then they probably took it.'

'But why would they want it?' she asked.

'Coutinho got Mercier fired by removing it from Morel's shelves and claiming the Frenchman stole it. If that had happened to me, I'd have grabbed it the first chance I got. That would have seemed fair to me – like rectifying an injustice. Not to mention that the book must be worth a small fortune. I wouldn't be surprised if a suitcase full of Coutinho's first editions are missing.'

'But Mercier could have taken *Les Confessions* on the day of the murder.'

'He didn't want to hang around long enough to locate it – not with Coutinho choking to death in the living room. First-time murderers often lose their cool, Luci.'

'But why trash the rest of the house?' she asked.

'Expect one big goddamn mess where there's hatred,' I replied, and for once I didn't mind sounding like a private eye from the 1940s.

'So if it was Mercier, then he must have been watching the house,' she said.

As the consequences of her revelation became clear to me, a shiver shook me hard. 'Very true, Luci. So don't waste time on the jewellery for now. Go to the library and look for *Les Confessions*. It's the only book that we can be sure was there and that should now be missing.'

'Locating it is going to take a while, sir,' she replied in a dispirited voice.

'Cheer up – this is the best thing that could have happened!' I told her.

'Why's that, sir?'

'Because if Mercier did this, then he was still in Lisbon as of an hour ago, and he probably hasn't managed to flee the country yet.'

On the way to Coutinho's house, I instructed Inspector Quintela to call our contacts at the airlines and at the Portuguese National Railway and to instruct them to stop any passenger named Bernard Mercier or François Savarin from leaving Lisbon. Luci called soon after that. She was in the library, searching for *Les Confessions*, but had asked Sylvie to check on Susana's jewellery; none of it was missing.

Twenty minutes later, Sylvie answered my knocks on Coutinho's front door. She held a tall, pink-tinted flute of champagne and was stirring it with the slender arm of a pair of metal-rimmed eyeglasses. She was barefoot and wore thick gold anklets. Spotting my interest in them, she said, 'Susana and I travelled to India last year.' Holding up her champagne, she added with bitter irony, 'Here's to taking advantage of the poverty of others!' She downed it in a single gulp. It was clearly her turn to get smashed.

'Any ideas what the burglars were after?' I asked.

'That's what I was about to ask you, Inspector.'

'I see the living room hasn't been touched.'

'Is that important?'

'It leaves two possibilities: either they already knew that whatever they were hunting for wasn't here, or they found what they wanted before starting to look here.'

'I see. Any idea how they got in?'

'I'm betting they had a key.'

'Except that we had the front door lock changed yesterday.'

'How about the back door? Did you have the lock changed?'

'No, not yet, we scheduled that for today. But could they have come through there?'

'Why not?'

279

'The garden is enclosed by a ten-foot wall.'

'One of the properties behind the garden looks like it has been abandoned for years. With a ladder, climbing over the wall would be easy. I'll have my Forensics people check for footprints and other evidence.

'Do you think the same person who murdered my brother is responsible?'

'That's certainly a possibility.'

'And where did he get the keys to the house?'

'It's easy enough to make copies. All anyone would have to do is get hold of the key chain belonging to your brother – or Susana or Sandra – for a little while.'

As I said that, I realized that Mercier could have stolen Sandi's keys after he'd hurt her. She'd have been too upset to notice them missing, which would have given him time to make copies and for them to appear *mysteriously* somewhere around the house the next day. Even if she'd realized her key chain had gone missing, she wouldn't have wanted to admit it, because she'd have then been forced to explain how Mercier had had a chance to steal it.

I found Luci sitting on the floor of the library, gazing down into the wings of a leather-bound volume, surrounded by a sea of lost books. It was easy enough to see her as a little kid seated in a sandbox, lost in a children's mystery.

She pointed to the shelves, where a couple of hundred books were already neatly lined up. She told me that she was arranging them in alphabetical order. She hadn't yet come upon *Les Confessions*.

'What are you reading?' I asked.

'Oh, this? It's the collected stories of Sherlock Holmes in Portuguese – an edition I've never seen before. I'm sorry for taking a break, sir.'

'You're forgiven, Luci.'

'There was a time when I'd have given anything to be Dr Watson,' she said, shaking her head as if to dismiss a silly fantasy.

'And here you are, just a few years later, impersonating Holmes himself!'

'Unfortunately, sir, I don't think Mr Holmes and I have much in common. Everything he finds elementary, I find a mystery.'

'Maybe so, but we all have moments of insight, Luci. And I'll need you to tell me when you have yours. I'm counting on you, in fact.'

She smiled gratefully. 'Yes, sir. Thank you, sir.'

'So what story are you looking at?' I asked.

'The Adventure of the Speckled Band.'

'A favourite of yours?'

'When I was a girl, it terrified me that the villain used a poisonous snake to commit his murders.'

'Yes, an Indian swamp adder,' I observed.

'You even remember the species!'

'When you grow up in Colorado, Luci, identifying snakes can be a matter of life and death. Though for better or for worse, Conan Doyle invented the Indian swamp adder.' I sounded as though I were trying to impress her, which made me uncomfortable, so I added, 'Enough of my tricks of memory. Let's get back to work.'

Luci closed her book and stood up. A pile of swept glass crowded the corner of the room, near to where the locked case had been smashed open. The classical CDs were missing but it didn't appear that any of the first editions were gone. When I pointed that out, she said, 'Yeah, it makes no sense. Unless there was something secretly valuable about the CDs.'

'Maybe they didn't contain music,' I speculated.

'You think they had some secret information on them, don't you?'

'A few decades' worth of details about bank transfers and payoffs, I'm guessing – maybe direct evidence of criminal behaviour, rather than just a list. Possibly even recordings of conversations with crooked politicians. He probably kept a lot of information for his own protection. I'm getting the

281

feeling that the flash drive we found was just for quick consultation.'

'The Frenchmen wouldn't have cared about information on Coutinho's illegal transactions, so we're back to your theory about two separate crimes.'

'At least for now,' I agreed.

While we were both searching for *Les Confessons*, Morel stopped by. He was on his way to the kitchen to make more coffee.

'Is Susana any better?' I asked.

'What do you think?' he said with a sour look.

'Can she talk to me yet?'

'No.'

The front door opened and closed. A moment later, Sylvie called upstairs, 'Your technicians have arrived, Inspector.'

I had Fonseca and Vaz start on the top floor, in Sandi's room, and instructed them to take a careful look around the garden after that. About an hour later, at exactly 5.49, I found *Les Confessions*.

Chapter 23

Finding *Les Confessions* seemed to rule out my theory that the Frenchmen had burgled the Coutinhos' home, which left the possibility that a corrupt politician had been after records of shady business deals. He or she might have somehow learned that Coutinho's flash drive was kept in the French–Farsi dictionary. And it now seemed possible that they also wanted to get their hands on the dictionary itself, which was why I asked Luci to go to the evidence room at headquarters after she was done in the library and to check if any words or sentences in the book had been highlighted in any way.

I left her in the library, intending to ask Fonseca and Vaz if they'd come to any conclusion about how many burglars had been in on the job, but on reaching the staircase, I heard Sudoku conversing in the living room with Sylvie. I started down just as he appeared at the bottom step of the staircase.

He waved, then started up. We met halfway. Since I'd last seen him, he'd cut his hair so short that he looked like an army recruit.

'Is your cold all better?' I said.

'It's not me, Henrique,' he whispered. 'I just told the others that to avoid problems. Maria is back on chemo.'

'I'm sorry, Sudoku. I hope you get some good results quickly.'

'One day at a time,' he replied.

I slapped his arm playfully. 'Hey, you were supposed to call me about the piece of bloody towel!'

'I would have, Henrique, but I got a weird result the first time I analysed the sample, so I went back to the beginning. But I got the same result. So I figured I'd better talk to you in person. I just got here.'

'What'd you find out?'

'You're not going to be happy about it.'

'I'm not happy about anything having to do with this case.'

'The DNA is the victim's.'

'*Which* victim?'

'Pedro Coutinho.'

When I came to myself, I was sitting on a bench in a small, shady park circled by a waist-high black railing. I was sweating hard. I'd been in a dark hot room only a moment before – humid and nearly airless.

My lungs felt as though they were flecked with rust, and I was having difficulty breathing. My mouth and tongue tasted of tobacco; three cigarette butts were stubbed out on the pavement near my right foot. I was gripping my kachina. The goddess's crown had made three perforations in my right palm. I realized I'd been waiting for Nathan to tell me where to hide Ernie.

A tiny old woman with brittle-looking grey hair and opera glasses around her neck stood nearby, dropping bread-crumbs onto the ground from a plastic bag, cornered by a knot of greedy pigeons. I looked from her to my left hand.

I can see now that maybe we didn't want to know that this was possible.

Gabriel had underlined that message twice, but I didn't know what he was referring to; for the moment, I'd forgotten what Sudoku had told me.

It was 6.27 p.m. Turning around, I recognized the towering silk-cotton tree behind me. I was in Alegria Square. The tree had a massive trunk that was creased like elephant hide

284

and spiked with thorns. Their brittle sharpness against my fingertips confirmed what I needed to know – that the world outside my head was real.

I turned on my cell phone.

Fonseca: *Where the hell are you?*

Luci: *I need to speak with you.*

Mesquita: *Turn your damn phone on!*

Ana: *I send you lots of kisses.*

When I checked my outgoing calls, I discovered that G had made two. The first was to Maria Dias. It had only lasted four seconds, which meant that he hadn't been able to speak with her and had decided not to leave a message. I suspected that he didn't want to risk another person hearing what he had to tell her, but why not let me know what he wanted from her?

I didn't recognize the second number. On calling it, I discovered it was the Chiado Health Club. G's call had lasted seven minutes. He must have been anxious for Maria Dias to tell him more about Sandi.

After speaking with the receptionist at the health club, I remembered my conversation with Sudoku. So many scattered bits of information made sense now. It was as though I could see a complex constellation – in the exact shape of this case – where before I'd only seen points of light. I even knew now why Coutinho had been so desperate to stay married; he couldn't bear losing Sandi just when he wanted her most.

I was struck then by the odd certainty that this case must have picked me; unlike most people, I knew – in my flesh and heart – that there were men who were able to plan for a very long time to hurt the people they loved. The strategizing gave them purpose.

Coutinho must have scared Sandi with a bloody ghost story at Morel's house in the hope that she'd come to him in the night. Though it's possible he lured her to him some other way, of course. He had probably been undermining her confidence for months.

Sandi had tried to make herself as unattractive as she could over the weeks that followed his attack. But the knife she kept in her bed told me that that strategy had not worked. Did she become pregnant on that first night or only later?

She had taken off the ring he'd given her as a birthday present, but she couldn't bear to throw it away. She must have wanted her mother to ask her why she no longer wore it and to insist on a reply. She wanted her mother to tell her that she'd listen to anything Sandi needed to say to her – and to promise that she'd believe anything the girl told her.

Was it a paradox that truths left unspoken ended up taking away your voice?

Sandi never made it back home after her Easter vacation in France. That girl only existed in a before-time that was no longer within her reach.

It had long seemed unforgivable to me that I continued to miss my father every day of my life, and I'd guess that Sandi had felt the same, at least for a while – that she continued to miss the dad she knew in the before-time. And yet, like me, it's possible that she also prayed every night for her father to die – even to be murdered. And with a bullet in the back.

Sandi cut her hair and purged what she ate down the toilet. She stopped having her periods. Maybe she figured her mom had to put the clues together sooner or later.

And maybe she had. Was Susana Coutinho the greatest actress I'd ever encountered?

If so, then she would probably have told any professional killer she hired to be gentle with her husband. Though maybe he'd just disregarded her orders. Or perhaps she'd given in to her rage and told the man she'd hired that she wanted the son of a bitch to die in a lot of pain. Once I managed to obtain Susana's bank statements, maybe I'd find that she'd taken out a large sum of cash in the weeks prior to the murder. But given what her husband did to her daughter, did I really want to try to prove that she was guilty?

Chapter 24

On taking out Gabriel's pack of Marlboros from my coat pocket, I also discovered a list of Sandi's incoming and outgoing calls over the past week. Sudoku must have handed it to me during our conversation – after G was already in control of me.

A quick call to Inspector Quintela confirmed that he'd given it to Sudoku to give to me.

On Saturday afternoon, Sandi had received three unanswered phone calls from Dias, and one more on Sunday. There was no record of the girl having made any attempt to call Dias back. There was a total of eleven unanswered calls from two other numbers; I suspected they belonged to Joana and Monica.

When I phoned Fonseca, he hollered, 'You just vanished, Monroe! You can't do that!'

'Sorry, Ana called to tell me Jorge was sick.'

'Does he have a fever?'

'No, stomach problems. He ate a spoiled hot dog.' Lying gave my words an easy, confident arc. 'He's better now but for a while he was really bad.'

'Give him a kiss from Uncle Eduardo. So where are you?'

'I've just left my apartment. I'll be there soon. What have you got for me about the burglary?'

Fonseca confirmed that the intruders had climbed over the back wall to the garden; two small branches on the ruby-red bougainvillea snaking over the wall had recently been snapped. Also, he'd retraced the burglars' route into the adjoining property and discovered what looked like imprints from the base of a ladder. Unfortunately, he held out little hope that he'd turn up any evidence more useful than that: the intruder or intruders had worn gloves and must have had the back door key, just as I'd suspected. The only evidence that he, Vaz and Sudoku had managed to find in the house was a faint shoeprint stamped on a CD cover in Sandi's room. It appeared to have been made by a man's sneaker – size forty or forty-one, according to Vaz. 'Too small for our murderer,' Fonseca reminded me.

'Where would you say the burglar started hunting around?' I asked.

'The girl's room. It was messed up the worst.'

'And do you think there might have been more than one of them?'

'That's my working theory – a lot of damage was done.'

'Which rooms weren't hit?'

'The living room, parents' bedroom, kitchen and pantry. And the storage room on the top floor.'

We both knew that the burglars must have known that whatever they wanted wasn't in those rooms. Which meant that either they were working with someone who'd visited the Coutinhos' house before, or they had been there themselves.

'You hear about Sudoku's result?' I asked him.

'Yeah, Coutinho was a real piece of work.'

'Maybe his wife had him killed and paid somebody to destroy whatever evidence the guy may have left behind.'

'If that's what happened, she deserves the Fonseca Medal of Honour!'

'Yeah, except that she should have planned things a whole lot better – Sandi ended up killing herself. Anyway, first thing tomorrow, I'll try to interview the neighbours we haven't managed to speak to yet. I'm also going to try to get copies of Susana Coutinho's bank records and talk to

Coutinho's employees. Depending on what I learn, I may need you again.'

'Fine. Oh, I almost forgot . . . Luci wanted you to know that nothing was highlighted or dog-eared in the French–Farsi dictionary.'

I left the park in the direction of the Avenida da Liberdade. I was planning on going to the taxi stand in front of the Tivoli Hotel but I never made it there.

When I came to myself I was sitting with Jorge on my lap, in our living room. It was 9.20 p.m. I'd lost almost three hours.

Jorge was drawing on his sketchpad, concentrating hard. I was in my pyjama bottoms and my Colorado Rockies baseball shirt. I was wearing my red slippers, too. I'd misplaced them maybe a year before. I'd thought they were lost.

The Chordettes were harmonizing on *Mr Sandman*, which was playing softly on the CD player; Ernie and I had sung along with those eerie, harp-like voices when we were kids.

Lifting Jorge off me and standing him up, I got to my feet. A desperate shout seemed to be curled in my chest, waiting for a chance to get out.

I wanted to find Ana and Nati. I figured they were upstairs.

'Hey, you made me make a mistake!' Jorge whined, frowning in that puffy-lipped way he does when he wanted me to know he was being treated unfairly. 'My drawing is all wrong now!'

He looked as if he might throw the blue crayon he was holding at me, so I made a shield with my hands. 'Where's your mom?' I asked.

He sat back down in a huff. 'She went to bed.'

'And Nati?'

'I don't know. Maybe he's reading. He's always reading!'

'Did you have dinner?'

He squinted at me as if I had interrupted him one too many times.

'Jorge, be nice to me, please,' I said.

289

'I'm not Jorge, I'm Francisco.' He lifted his toy giraffe out from between the cushions of the sofa and jiggled him.

I rolled my eyes, so he rolled his. My miniature clone again. As I started off for the kitchen, he yelled, 'I want a cookie – chocolate! And cherry juice!'

I stopped, turned around and glared at him. 'You have five minutes for your juice and a cookie, and then I'm putting you and Francisco to bed.'

'That's not fair!'

'Jorge, I've had a very long day and you're just making it longer.'

He flapped his hands at me, impersonating Roger the cross-dressing alien from *American Dad*. He was eager to get one of my laughing reprieves but I shook my head in warning. He grunted and went back to his drawing.

In the kitchen, I discovered that G hadn't written me any message. Just as I grabbed the container of cherry juice, *Mr Sandman* came to an end. And so did I.

I awoke in bed with Ana. She was sleeping on her side, facing away from me. *It has finally happened*, I thought. *I've come to the end of the slow, uphill race that I'd been running since I was eight.* The hollow sense of loss in me seemed linked to my not having anyone to turn to. I wanted to ask my wife for help, but feeling the restful rise and fall of her in my fingertips – her physical separateness from me – only reminded me that she might not believe me and that, in any case, I'd sworn to Ernie that I'd never tell her the truth. I leaned away from her and sat up.

I knew I needed a plan I could carry out quickly. I took a pen from my night-table drawer and wrote a message to G on my hand for the first time in my life, though as I was scribbling I realized I'd always known that this would happen one day: *You need to let go of me. Ernie and I will be all right. Don't wreck my life.*

I stood up, tiptoed downstairs and sat at Ana's desk. I took a sheet of paper from her printer tray. I wanted to write a note that would explain what was happening to me, but I soon realized that anything I told her now would only confuse her. I had to speak to Ernie, because proving to Gabriel that he was safe was my only hope of remaining who I was – and of re-establishing the borders around myself.

I intended to call my brother from the small laundry room off our kitchen so that I wouldn't wake Ana or the kids, but a few seconds after I stood up I found myself seated again. I was in the armchair in Jorge's room, and he was fast asleep, naked from the waist down and wearing only one of his socks. His Tweety Bird pyjama bottoms and his second sock were lying on the floor. Francisco was standing guard on his night table. In my lap, a long red candle pointed up out of Aunt Olivia's star-shaped holder. Cottony circles of light contracted on the ceiling when I stood up.

I was panting with a fear that seemed to cling to my breathing. The clock said 3.40 a.m. I looked at my hand; Gabriel had washed off my message.

When I closed my eyes to think things out, the world shifted again.

Jorge was now seated on his bed, fully awake, glaring at Ana, who was standing in the doorway, barefoot, draped in her orange Denver Broncos nightshirt, looking impatient and upset.

'Don't yell at him, Mom!' Jorge hollered.

I was standing behind my son's armchair as though for protection. My candle had burned down another inch. I sneaked a look at the clock: it was 4.17.

My wife looked from the boy to me. Her face swelled with rage. 'Hank, what the hell were you thinking?' she demanded.

Before I could make a reply, Nati came up behind her, bare-chested, scratching his belly. 'What's going on?' he asked in a sleepy voice.

'I need a minute,' I said. I cringed on hearing the puny, useless sound of my voice.

'You can have all the time you want!' Ana snarled, each word a threat. 'But I want you out of this house!'

Jorge burst into tears. I knelt down and opened my arms, and he ran to me. Feeling his solidity – and the quick pulsing of so much need for me in his little body – brought me back to myself. 'Everything is okay,' I told him, but he spotted the doubt in my eyes and began to sob.

'You don't even know what you did wrong, do you?' Ana said contemptuously.

I shook my head. 'I'm sorry. I'm confused. Let me just help Jorge and then we'll talk.'

Nati pushed past her to me. 'So did you vanish for a while, Dad?'

He spoke calmly, which was odd. I lifted Jorge into my arms and stood up. I pressed my lips to his cheek. 'It's okay, baby, I'm here now.'

Nati exclaimed, 'Dad, listen to me! What happened?'

As he glared at me, I said, 'I was gone for a little while.'

'And you're back now? It's you?'

'It's me.'

He turned to his mother. 'It's okay, Mom. He's back.'

'I don't get it,' she told him.

'The excitement is over, folks, keep on moving,' Nati said, imitating a TV cop urging onlookers to leave the scene of an accident. It was one of his comedy routines. When no one laughed, he snorted. 'You're a great audience, folks, but I'm going to the kitchen now to get myself a doughnut.'

'Nati, are you crazy?' Ana asked. She looked from him to me to Jorge as if we'd formed a united front against her. I held Jorge tightly because he'd started to shiver.

'I'm sorry for whatever I did,' I told her.

She frowned coldly.

'What did Dad do?' Nati asked her.

Ana hugged her arms around her waist protectively. 'This is between me and your father,' she said darkly.

Nati shrugged, as if his mother were unfathomable. The four of us seemed to be cut off from the rest of the world – on an island I'd made for us. Or that G had.

'I thought you were going to the kitchen,' Ana told Nati.

'Look, Dad just disappears sometimes,' he said, choosing his words carefully. He looked at her, then at me, trying not to take sides. 'I thought you knew, Mom.'

'Nati, you're not making any sense,' she said.

He turned to me with an astonished expression. 'You never told her?'

'No,' I replied, because lying – for the first time in recent memory – seemed a bad idea.

To his mother, Nati said, 'Dad goes away and someone else comes.' Biting his lip, he looked unable to come up with the right words. Facing Jorge, he said, 'Dingo, do us all a favour and stop crying, and tell Mom what happens!'

Jorge dried his eyes with his fists.

'*Força, diz lá,*' Nati said more gently, since Portuguese often had a calming effect on the little boy. *Go on, tell her.*

'Dad watches me sometimes,' he replied, wriggling in my arms so he could face his mother.

'When?' she asked.

I'd have liked to disappear into my little boy at that moment.

'I don't know,' he said. 'Whenever he does.'

'And what does he do?'

'He sits and watches me.' The boy pointed to the armchair on which he tossed his dirty clothing. 'He sits right there.'

Neither Jorge nor Nati had ever said a word to me about Gabriel. I didn't dare move for fear my legs would give way.

Nati said, 'He used to watch me, too – when I was younger. He'd always sit with that star-shaped candlestick he has. Dad, you inherited it from Aunt Olivia, right?'

I nodded.

'Once or twice he said hello to me. But mostly, he never talked. Sometimes, when I was little, he'd pick me up and stroke my hair. And kiss me all over. We had a game where we'd count my toes together, one by one. He'd cry, too, at least at first – but I could tell it wasn't because he was unhappy. Although he never told me why.'

293

Turning to me, he smiled the same generous, amused smile he'd had since he was a baby. Now, it made me go stiff.

'What's wrong?' he asked me.

'Many good things have happened to me, but I don't know why,' I whispered. 'There's so much I can't explain.' I looked at Ana and mouthed *I love you.*

She looked away, as though measuring her options.

'You know, Dad, sometimes I don't get you at all,' Nati said.

'Maybe you're not supposed to. You're only thirteen.'

'Whatever,' he said, with the ease that kids show when dismissing the oddness of adults. 'Sometimes I caught him smoking, too,' he told Ana. 'He'd just sit there watching me and smoke. Dingo and I call him the Night Watchman.'

'Okay, Hank, so you pretend to be someone else,' Ana told me definitively, as if she'd finally heard something that made sense. 'But would you mind telling me what the point is? If it's just so you can smoke in the house . . . Because, if that's all it is, then—'

'Ana, it's hard to explain,' I cut in, 'but I don't pretend. I swear.'

'The Night Watchman isn't the same person as Dad,' Nati told her. 'When he comes, Dad disappears.'

'I've heard enough!' Ana hollered. She swirled her hand towards Jorge, as if she were reeling him in. 'Come here, you're going back to bed with me.'

'He needs both of us right now,' I told Ana in a pleading voice, but I really meant, *We need our kids with us or our marriage might not survive this.*

'Just put him down, Hank.'

I did as she asked but the little boy clung to my leg.

'Jorge,' she hollered, 'get over here right now!'

He looked up at me and grimaced like Roger the alien.

'We'll talk later, baby,' I told him. 'Everything will be okay.'

The boy took a deep breath and started singing the theme song from *American Dad* as he stepped to Ana. He didn't make it to the chorus because she snatched his hand like it might fly off.

'Ow!' he yelled.

'Yeah, ow!' she snarled. 'And you,' she said, glaring at Nati, 'go to your room!'

'I just assumed you knew all about the Night Watchman,' he told her, shrugging.

'I would have if you'd told me!'

'Don't make this about me, Mom! That's not fair!'

'Nati, please,' I said, 'just go to your room. We'll talk later.'

'But I'm hungry,' he whined. 'I wasn't kidding about that.'

'Then go to the kitchen and stay there until your mother and I are done.'

Before heading downstairs, my son gave me a withering look that meant he'd never understand adults. There was amusement in his glance, as well; he was delighted with himself for keeping his calm when his parents were out of control. Was that a sign of hard-won maturity, or his way of pretending that our quarrel wasn't important?

After Ana led Jorge off to our bedroom, she came back to me with my trousers and shoes. She put them on the floor and took two steps back, as if they might explode.

'Get dressed,' she said. She faced me like a prison guard, cold and impenetrable. I'd have never believed it possible.

My thoughts scattered, and I somehow latched on to the idea that she was testing me – trying to force me to tell her the truth about myself and my childhood. And testing me, too, for whether I loved her more than anything or anyone.

At length, I said, 'I'd choose you. You and the kids.'

'What are you talking about?' she demanded.

'You've always wanted to know if I'd pick Ernie over you.'

'Jesus, Hank, I'd never make you choose,' she said in a frustrated voice. Her words hung in the air, as if I'd misunderstood all that was essential about her. 'Why would I do that?'

'Because making a person choose between the people he loves is the surest way to destroy him.'

'Maybe that's true,' she replied. 'I don't know. But in any case, I can't get back into bed with you tonight, so . . . so put on your clothes.'

'I don't have anywhere to go,' I told her. 'And I'm going to fall a very long way.'

'Hank, you hurt me!' she hollered. Her eyes gushed with tears.

I stepped towards her, slowly, my hands open. I sensed our future teetering just in front of me. My body ached with the need to embrace her. 'Ana . . .'

She backed away. 'Don't come near me. I don't know who you are! After thirteen years of marriage, I just realized I don't know who you are!'

'I'm sorry. I didn't mean to hurt you. I promise.'

'You meant to hurt me! "*Just shut up and take it!*" How could you say that to me?'

'It wasn't me.'

'Oh, Christ, not again!'

Contempt creased her face. And I realized something that seemed nearly impossible: that I'd failed to notice the steady accumulation of grievances inside her heart. Layers of ice . . . Thirteen years of telling her lies had created this freeze between us.

'Can we start over?' I asked.

'That doesn't work with me like it does for you and Ernie and Aunt Olivia.'

'Ana, listen. I don't think he meant to hurt you. I don't know all that much about him, but I'm sure he doesn't know how to behave with other people. I call him Gabriel. I've called him that since I was little. I think he may never have been with a woman before. He must have seen this as his one chance to . . .' I stopped speaking because her impatient expression showed me how ridiculous I sounded. But I had to say it. 'Try to imagine that you have just one chance to be intimate with another person. Maybe you'd risk everything for it?'

She heaved a sigh. 'Hank, do you think I'm a total idiot?'

'Of course not. I'm trying to tell you that it wasn't what you think, that he—'

'Don't make me shout at you again,' she cut in. 'It'll upset the kids.'

I started making a list in my head of all the things I couldn't let happen. At the top was that I couldn't let Jorge and Nati grow up without my protection.

'But I want to be with you and the kids,' I said. 'That's all I've ever wanted.'

'Right now, I don't care what you want. I may care a lot tomorrow – I probably will, but not right now.' She showed me a disappointed look.

Something more than shame made me turn away – something born of the hundred scars that Ernie carried on his body, and the hundred others that I carried inside me.

'Stay with Ernie,' Ana said more gently. 'He'll take care of you while I figure out what to do.'

I put my trousers on. The compressed urgency in her face told me she wanted to cry but wouldn't. I sensed an opening, yet my thoughts seemed to be scattering around me. My one chance at a good life was turning around this moment and I couldn't put a single coherent sentence together.

'If you give me just fifteen minutes,' I told her, 'I'll explain everything. I'm trying to handle way too much right now, Ana. It's this case. It seems like it chose me. And I see myself in Sandi. I don't—'

'Why should I believe you?' she interrupted.

Time was ticking down loudly inside my head. If I could only make it stop, I might figure out the incantation that would permit me to stay.

I patted the air between us. It was an awkward gesture, but I was hoping she'd understand that I meant that if we took this very slowly, I might yet be able to make her understand. 'Because I'm backed up to the wall of everything I've done wrong,' I told her. I took another step towards her but she held up her hands to block me. When I realized she'd become frightened of me, all my hopes collapsed inside me.

A man watches his feet meet the pavement of a Lisbon street, listening to each step as though it might be a clue about his future. Cobbling together the fate of his adopted homeland with his own, he thinks, *We've been undone by our lies.*

I crouched around the corner from headquarters, as though I were a criminal in a B-movie waiting to give myself up at daybreak. For a time, I watched a pigeon ripping at a crust of pizza. When my phone rang, I knew it would be Ana, and my heart leapt, but it was Ernie's name that appeared on my screen.

'Nati called me,' he said breathlessly. 'He told me what happened. He was very upset.'

My son must have reconsidered his amusement or faked it in order to convince us not to move our argument behind closed doors.

I answered all of Ernie's questions about what had taken place between Ana and me, though I wasn't able to explain the quarrel in anything resembling a coherent order.

'Look, just come to my house,' he finally interrupted.

'I've got to stay in Lisbon. That's where Ana and my kids are.'

'But you shouldn't be alone,' Ernie said.

I lowered my phone to my side; there seemed no point in speaking if I couldn't be with Ana when I most needed her.

Ernie shouted my name and, when I didn't reply, continued hollering it until I had no choice but to lift up my phone again. 'I'll be fine,' I told him.

'You won't be! Drive here. Please, Rico!'

'I've been trained to cope, so just go back to sleep.'

'Okay, listen, Rico. Go to your office and call me from there. I need to know you're somewhere safe.'

'Ernie,' I said, 'where I am on your GPS won't change anything.'

298

'Christ, Rico, do what I tell you for once in your life!'

I could see no point in quarrelling. 'I'll call you when I get to my office,' I told him.

That was a lie when I said it, but for lack of anywhere else to go, I ended up at headquarters a few minutes later. Filipe, our night guard, always brought apples to work as a snack. I caught the big Granny Smith he tossed me in one hand, which gave him a respectful grin.

At my desk, I sent Ernie an SMS saying I was in my office. He didn't call back, which was a relief. With any luck, he'd already drifted off to sleep again.

I watched the video of 'Dog Days Are Over' on YouTube over and over, studying the singer's hands as she danced, trying to catch the hidden messages she'd given to Sandi, but all I could think of was how stupid it was of me not to have realized that I needed Ana more even than I needed my secrets. Eager to escape the corner I'd backed myself into, I shifted over to Google Maps and looked at images of Black Canyon.

I pictured myself sitting between the canyon walls, listening to the Gunnison River rushing by in torrents, then gazing up to the blue scratch of sky two thousand feet above me. I held my Walther semi-automatic pistol in my hand. It seemed the perfect partner for a last magic act – silver and black, and absolutely certain of its own expertise.

For the second time in my life, I counted to ten with a gun barrel in my mouth. Dad had put it there the first time. He'd pulled the trigger, too, but surprise of surprises, he hadn't loaded it. Back then, I'd passed out before finding out that I wasn't going to die. And when I came to, Ernie was lying next to me. We were under an overheated clump of blankets. I didn't understand why, until he told me that I'd turned to ice after passing out. What neither of us yet knew was that a part of me would never completely thaw.

This time, an important realization surged through me while I was counting down towards death: that Mom's killing herself meant that I'd never do to my kids what she did

299

to me and Ernie; I could never do to Jorge and Nati what she had done to my brother and me when she crashed Dad's Plymouth into a tree on the road to Crawford on a warm spring day in 1981.

More than thirty years after her death, Mom had saved me from putting a bullet in my head.

After I stopped counting, I realized a second thing that seemed even more important: that my mother hadn't been scared of dying. Everything about that day must have felt just right to her. *Foi canja, Hank,* she'd have told me if she could have. *Easy as pie.*

Though maybe that was just what I wanted most to believe. With the dead, it seemed you could never get definitive answers.

Footsteps awakened me. Lifting my head off my desk, I saw a tall, slender silhouette in the doorway. The cowboy hat in his hand told me it was Ernie, and yet I knew he'd never travel this far from home.

'Is that really you?' I heard myself ask, and although it seemed impossible, I saw my voice flutter down from the ceiling and land on the floor. A butterfly of sound.

And then I was awake for sure, and Ernie was stepping into my office. His face was older than I remembered it, and his eyes a softer shade of green.

'You're way too far from home,' I told him.

I didn't stand up and go to him. I wanted to feel the urgent tension of needing to hug him before I let it go. Or maybe, for the first time in my life, I needed him to come to me. I put my head back down on the desk and closed my eyes.

By the time I'd counted to seven, I sensed him squatting beside me. At twelve, he put his hand atop my head. I lost count then, because the oatmeal smell of him became a deep well that I was tumbling into. Down there in the dark, sitting with my brother, he rubbed his cheek against mine, and the scratch of his whiskers convinced me that we had made it to adulthood – and that there was still hope for me.

'I won't let anything bad happen to you,' he whispered. It was our incantation of incantations, though by now we both knew it came with no guarantee.

He caressed my hair. My gratitude for that simple kindness was so wide that it held forty years of our shared past and still had room for the present moment. I sat up and let Ernie wrap his lean, strong arms around me because I was sure now I was made out of things I'd never wanted – broken things that I didn't want to hold onto any longer.

'I fucked up badly,' I confessed.

'We'll make things right,' he told me, and his voice sounded so confident that I was able to let myself go. When my tears finally ended, I leaned back in my chair, but he held onto my hand. Our entwined fingers were our bridge – and always had been.

He took two big, gulping breaths. Beads of sweat trailed down his cheek.

'Is it bad?' I asked.

'It's just that I left so quickly that I forgot to bring any medications with me. I may need to sit in the dark a while or . . . Do you have a spare Valium with you?'

'You never take Valium.'

He held out his hand. 'I do now.'

After he downed the pill, he sat on the chair in front of my desk and bent forward with his head between his legs. I turned off the lights and rubbed his back.

When he finally sat back up, he said, 'Everything is okay. I'll be fine now.' His voice was strangely secure. 'Maybe you should call Ana,' he added.

He put his cowboy hat down between us. Its feather looked like a thick black arrow in the darkness.

'Later,' I told him. 'I wouldn't survive another quarrel right now.'

'And Nati – you'll need to speak to him,' he added.

'I'll call him.' I put Ernie's cowboy hat on. He said I looked like Alan Ladd in *Shane*. 'I'm feeling very odd,' I said, just so he'd know.

'Tell me.'

'I feel like we've finally managed to escape from time. You and I . . . We're living between ticks of a clock. It's always going to be now.'

I realized I was no longer afraid of what would happen with me and Ana – not because everything would be all right but because I knew that nothing would ever be good again unless I risked everything to get her back.

Ernie gazed over my shoulder at the parking lot. 'Your view really sucks,' he said.

'Thanks. How did you get past reception?'

'I was here once before, years ago. Remember?'

'Not really,' I said.

'Well, anyway, the guy from Cape Verde at reception remembered I was your brother. He thinks we look alike.'

'But we don't.'

'Our eyes are our Mom's, even though they're different colours.'

'Yours are nicer.'

'You think?'

I nodded. He picked up my apple. 'You going to eat this?'

'Maybe.'

'Can we split it?'

'Sure.'

He took a bite and handed it to me. It was good to pass it back and forth between us. After he'd nibbled down to the core, I held up my garbage can and he tossed it inside.

'Thanks for crossing the Continental Divide,' I said. That was what we called the imaginary line west of Évora that he hadn't driven beyond since Aunt Olivia's death in April of 2006.

'I almost didn't,' he said. 'My heart froze the moment I started visualizing the drive. But then I figured the worst that could happen is I'd have a heart attack and drop dead

302

on the freeway. Which wasn't so bad when compared to what not coming here would mean.'

'What would it mean?'

'That my whole life was a failure.'

'I don't see how that could be true.'

'Because I've prepared all my life for this – to help you when no one else could. If I didn't come here now, I couldn't go on. I couldn't look at myself in the mirror.'

'You have no mirrors,' I pointed out.

'You can stop trying to be witty. It's just the two of us.'

'What if I don't want to? Listen, Ernie, you don't owe me anything. I want you to live your life anyway you want and not care what I think.'

The forced way he gazed down told me that something I said put Colorado on the horizon of his thoughts.

'There are some things you can't help me with,' I added. 'Nobody could.'

'But at least I can take you home,' he said.

'No, I've got to stay in Lisbon. I've just started to understand that this case has a lot more to do with you and me than I thought. It's like some sort of test.'

'I meant I could take you to *your* home,' he said.

I turned to face the doorway, because time would start up again the moment I left my office.

'I'll talk to Ana,' my brother told me.

Ernie being assertive made me suspicious. 'What'll you tell her?' I asked.

'The truth.'

'But you've always said that was the one thing we could never reveal!' I said resentfully.

'I was wrong. I realize that now – though I needed to have Évora in my rear-view mirror to realize it.'

'Ernie, what's going on?'

'We know who we are now, Rico. When we arrived in Portugal, we were just kids. We were lost, we needed rules. Dad had just been killed, and I was—'

303

'Killed?' I pounced – because for thirty years I'd suspected that he knew more than me. 'Ernie, what's the truth about Dad?'

'You know what I know, Rico – he vanished. And if he hasn't shown up by now, he must be dead.'

'You don't know any more than that?'

'No.'

I didn't believe him. Maybe he'd heard from an investigator in Colorado. 'Have the police finally found what was left of him?' I asked.

'No. At least, not that I know of.'

Another lie – I was sure of it. But Ernie's profile hardened. From experience, I knew I'd get nothing more out of him.

'And this is what you're going to tell Ana?' I asked, incredulous. 'She's not going to buy it, Ernie. She's going to get angry at you.'

I realized I wanted my wife to holler at my brother because I couldn't.

'What happened in Colorado happened to both of us,' he said. 'So we need to tell Ana together. It's the only way. She deserves to know.'

Could my past become hers, too? I realized now that in the world I wanted to live in, the people who loved you wanted to inherit all that had made you who you were.

'And if she doesn't believe us?' I asked.

He lifted his hair off his sliced-off ear. 'I'll show her my scars.'

'You can't do that,' I said. 'It would be—'

'Rico, I'll do anything I have to do!' he declared. 'I'm going to tell her what it was like when Dad took out his knife that first time and I realized that he'd never let me reach adulthood! And to know that I was the reason that he'd never allow you to grow up either.'

Before we left my office, I turned on my phone and found more messages, from Mesquita, Fonseca, Sudoku and Luci.

Luci's was the only one I opened: *Sir, I'm worried about you. Please call.*

After I apologized for waking her, she told me to wait a moment so she could leave her bedroom. 'Where are you?' she asked.

'At headquarters.'

'Are you all right, sir? I can't stop thinking that you're in bad trouble.'

'Thank you, Luci, but you needn't worry – I've been at this since you were ten years old. So there was nothing high-lighted in the dictionary?

'No – nothing at all. Is that important?'

'I'm not sure. I've been thinking that the dictionary might contain the code for deciphering the names in the list of bribes Coutinho kept in his vacation pictures. It would make sense for him to have somehow indicated it there. But if nothing is highlighted, we have no way of finding it. The problem is, Coutinho would only have told someone conspiring with him that he kept a flash drive with incrimin-ating information on it in his library. And I don't see how the burglar could be both a close confidant of his *and* someone he bribed. When things make no sense like that, Luci, it means we're being fooled – or failing to understand something obvious.'

'We don't know who he bribed, but we *do* know a couple of his good friends – Morel and Sottomayor.'

'Yes, except that Morel lives in France. I find it hard to believe he'd be involved in the victim's day-to-day business dealings in Portugal. And Sottomayor told me he didn't know anything about where Coutinho kept his records.'

'But did you believe him, sir?'

As Ernie and I walked to his car, I checked my outgoing calls and discovered that G had phoned Maria Dias again, just before my quarrel with Ana. Their conversation had lasted almost twelve minutes. To wake up Dias the middle of the

305

night, G must have had something essential to ask her – or tell her.

When she answered my call, she said as though pleading, 'I really hope you aren't having second thoughts.'

'No second thoughts,' I assured her, to go along with whatever G had agreed with her, 'but we need to talk in person.'

'All right, come over. We'll talk while I pack.'

G must have told her something that would make her leave Lisbon in a hurry. All I could think of was that he'd figured out who the murderer was and was certain that the man would try to hurt her. But why keep me in the dark as to his identity?

Dias surprised me by hanging up before I had a chance to say goodbye. That must have also caught someone else off guard; a man's voice – barely audible – said something about being hungry. With my hand over the mouthpiece, I told Ernie that someone careless was apparently listening in on my phone call and asked him to try to make out what he was saying, since my brother could eavesdrop in Portuguese better than I could.

Ernie listened, angling his head down, exactly as he's done since he was a toddler, then handed the phone back. 'I heard a man talking as if he were conversing with someone next to him. But the only thing I heard clearly was, *Monroy isn't easy to predict.* After he said that, the line went dead.'

Chapter 25

Having my cell phone tapped might have meant that my investigation had been seriously compromised, but it also pleased me that whoever had murdered Coutinho and robbed his house feared me and what I could do. And now that I knew I was being observed, I could play a trick or two on them.

I turned off my phone to keep its signal from giving away our position and rejoined Ernie. His hulking Chevrolet was parked just down the street. Rosie was curled in the driver's seat. With her straining to lick my face, I lifted her up and put her in the back.

I headed to Dias's apartment along the Rua da Escola Politécnica. Twenty minutes later, I squeezed into a parking spot by the São Carlos Theatre.

'Stay here,' I told my brother. 'I'm going to take a quick look around.'

I didn't dare tell him that whoever had been listening to my calls might confront me, but he must have figured that out, because he touched his index finger to his forehead, which was our sign for: *Be very, very careful.*

'Always,' I replied. 'But listen, I'm going to call you in a few minutes and tell you I'm headed somewhere crazy.'

'Where are you going?' he asked suspiciously.

Hearing the discomfort in Ernie's voice, Rosie sat up in the back seat and barked.

'Nowhere. I want to confuse whoever has bugged my phone – keep him running around. After we speak, join me in Camões Square.'

After walking some way down the street, I shifted my gun to my coat pocket, calmed by the feel of death inside my fingers.

As I turned onto the Rua Serpa Pinto, a fist-sized piece of cement smashed into the sidewalk across the street. The explosion made me jump back and sent my heartbeat racing. It also put a dismayed look on a walnut-faced old lady leaning out from a second-storey window. I looked up past her to see where the cement had come from and discovered a tell-tale gap in the moulding below the roof tiles.

'*Mais um meteoróide lisboeta,*' the old woman called out to me, outraged. *Another Lisbon meteorite.* 'Nobody cares that the city is falling apart,' she added with a sneer.

Up ahead, in the slender divide of pavement at the centre of Bordalo Pinheiro Square, a young woman in skintight snakeskin pants and a halter top was checking messages on her phone while waiting for her shrunken-looking, hairless chihuahua to squeeze a dump out of its shivering behind. Out front of Dias's apartment house, two shaggy-looking young men – their thick hair combed forward over their eyes – were leaning against an old BMW with a coat hanger for an antenna.

The orange and yellow light blazing off the tile façade of the building at the top of the square made me look up again, where I discovered a perfect dome of cerulean sky. Under other circumstances, I'd have dragged Ana and the kids hiking in some nowhereland out past Ernie's house.

While crossing to the other side of the street, it occurred to me that the same guy who'd bugged my phone might have leaked Coutinho's murder to the press on Friday. After all, who couldn't use a little extra cash during an economic meltdown? He'd probably been hired by one or more of the politicians bribed by Coutinho. Maybe he hadn't provided his friends in the press with any further details on subsequent days because his employers had discovered what he'd been up to. I also had a possible answer as to why no ministers or their assistants had called to question me about my progress; the ones with the most to lose must have already had transcripts of all the phone conversations I'd had since the start of this case!

Whoever was tracing my movements had counted on my naiveté. And if Coutinho had bought ministers, then he might also have passed some cash to high-ranking cops. For all I knew, Mesquita might have made it seem as though he were doing me a favour by keeping me on the case so I wouldn't begin to wonder about him.

And then it hit me: Mesquita had regarded turning my phone off as a personal affront because he'd been tracking me!

That revelation stopped me dead in the street. I sensed that I was standing below a tower that had been invisible to me until now. Without knowing it, I'd been circling its base since Friday morning, down here on the overheated pavement with the old beggars and dog-walkers and Lisbon meteorites. There, at the top, thousands of feet above us, were the men who bought and traded people like me. And who were following every move I made.

If I tried to bring their tower crashing down, they'd have me fired and blacklisted.

Tingling, alert, feeling as though I'd just jumped on a train heading where I'd long wanted to go, I rushed back down the street to Camões Square, scattering a group of pigeons pecking through a pile of sand outside an eyeglass shop. Turning on my phone, I took the steps of the Carmo Church two at a time and told Ernie that I was about to leave for the train station in Santarém, where a witness who could identify the burglar who'd trashed Coutinho's house was going to meet me at nine thirty. I also said I'd have Coutinho's flash drive with me.

Santarém was at least an hour from Lisbon. It was now 8.05. Even if whoever was tracking me figured out sometime after nine thirty that I'd tricked him, and even if he called

309

friends in Lisbon for backup, Ernie and I would be able to move around freely for an hour and a half.

After my brother joined me, I asked him to take off his surgical gloves before meeting Dias. She buzzed us in as soon as I gave her my name. My brother took one look at the rusted handle of the elevator and started up the stairs.

'Okay, we'll give Anselmo a break,' I told him; we always joked that these homemade-looking Portuguese elevators were actually pulled up and down by a poor old slob named Anselmo who slaved all day at the bottom of the shaft.

I climbed ahead of Ernie, picturing Ana lying alone in the dark, regretting the years she'd wasted with me. My brother could often see things in my eyes that no one else could, so when I turned around to check on him, he said, 'Stay calm. I've got a secret plan.'

'What kind of plan?'

'If I told you, it wouldn't be a secret!' He smiled his mischievous smile, which annoyed me, but there wasn't time for a quarrel.

We found Dias's door already open. I knocked twice and identified myself.

'Come on in,' she called.

She wore loose-fitting black sweatpants and a silvery camisole. Her muscular arms and shoulders glistened with sweat. She stood beside two metallic suitcases neatly packed with clothing, dark colours in the smaller one, lighter ones in the larger. Behind them, her statue of the Buddha had been wrapped with towels and tied with nylon cord. The glass top and wagon-wheel of her dining table were leaning together against the wall. On top of the base – a column of white marble – was a roll of packing paper and a small stapler. Her books were in three large brown boxes with *Jumbo* – the name of one of our supermarket chains – printed on the side.

I introduced my brother to her and said he was visiting me from Évora. 'He knows what we've agreed on,' I told her.

As Dias and I shook hands, suspicion narrowed her eyes. 'Look, Monroe,' she said, 'I don't want problems.'

'We're not going to have any,' I assured her. 'I just need to get some things straight.'

Ernie would have preferred never to shake hands with anyone, but when Dias reached out, she gave him no other choice. After the worst was over, he moved his hand behind his back, where he wouldn't be tempted to touch himself.

His jaw was throbbing. If he were home, he'd have crawled into bed and curled into a tight ball.

Our host didn't notice the discomfort in his face. In fact, she seemed amused by him. Maybe drugs made her unobservant. There was a stiff abruptness to her hand movements that made amphetamines seem a possibility – and that made it seem as if there was some dense, tangled underbrush inside her that allowed her precious little freedom of movement.

'Are you a real cowboy?' she asked Ernie with girlish curiosity.

'My brother and I are from Colorado,' he replied.

'Which means exactly what?' Dias asked.

'Lots of people wear cowboy hats in Colorado,' he told her.

'But you're in Portugal now.'

'Yes and no.'

She kept her eyes on him as if he were a riddle needing solving. Anxious to draw her attention from him, I said, 'You aren't planning on returning to Lisbon, are you?'

She scowled at me. 'Inspector, *you're* the one who told me to leave and not come back. What the hell are you trying to pull?'

'Nothing. How could I be sure you'd do what I suggested? You're obviously a woman who likes to do things her own way.'

I expected she'd be gratified by my compliment. Instead, the displeased way she licked her lips gave me the impression that she'd just remembered why she didn't like me.

'You look like you've been up all night working on this case,' she said, but without any sympathy.

I realized that my shirt was rumpled and that I hadn't shaved. Unable to come up with a lie that seemed plausible, I said, 'I had a quarrel with my wife.'

'Not over helping me, I hope.'

Her green eyes shimmered with amusement. Perhaps that was her way of warning me that there was a great deal more underbrush inside her than I'd even guessed, and that I'd better not try to cross it.

'Our quarrel was personal,' I said. 'So when do you plan on leaving?'

'I'll leave by noon even if I don't have everything packed,' she told me. Turning in a circle, she took in the disorder in the room, as though assessing what next needed her attention. 'A friend will come by and ship whatever I don't take with me,' she added.

'Where will you cross the border?'

'At Valença. I'll sleep somewhere near Bilbao tonight, then head up to Bordeaux. I spoke to my mother last night – she's expecting me the day after tomorrow.'

'She lives in Bordeaux?'

'Yes, that's where I grew up.'

A jarring sense of finality made me withdraw inside myself. I pictured Morel sitting in Coutinho's kitchen, smoking languidly. He'd just told me about his old friend's first marriage to a woman from Bordeaux and how the acrimonious divorce had ruined his relationship with his teenaged children. One of them had been named Marie . . .

'Everybody must call you Marie in France,' I said. 'Rather than Maria, I mean.'

'Yes, of course.'

Coutinho must have ruined his relationship with his first daughter long before his divorce, at the time she started becoming a woman. Gabriel had figured that out long before me. And he'd plotted against me in order to assure her escape.

312

'Is your brother Pierre also in Bordeaux?' I asked, anxious to check my reasoning.

Her eyes opened wide. 'How do you know about my brother?' she asked roughly.

'Jean Morel told me about the two of you,' I replied, trying to keep all inflection out of my voice, as I did with violent suspects.

She smiled bitterly, but with a coquettish slant of her head. 'So, how is dear Monsieur Morel?'

'He seems to be in love with your father's second wife.'

'Now that *is* interesting,' she said with slow, drawn-out irony, but a moment later she gazed past me as though a dangerous figure had just appeared in the distance.

Ernie looked at me questioningly. He seemed confused by her.

'Miss Dias,' I said to call her back to us, and as she turned to me, I asked, 'When was the last time you saw Monsieur Morel?'

'At the time of the divorce. He came to the courthouse with Coutinho a few times.'

'How old were you?'

'Sixteen.'

'And if you don't mind my asking, when did your father start . . . hurting you?'

'When I was thirteen – thirteen and three months and six days. He came into my room one night when my mother was away and told me he had something special for his *big girl* – now that she was all grown up.'

Dias looked between Ernie and me, challenging us to doubt her story.

'I'm sorry,' I told her, though the sympathy I felt was largely subdued by my fear of her.

She stared at her Om tattoo. 'You know what troubled me the most, Inspector? He got off watching us in the big mirror in his room – seeing what he was doing to me. And do you know what saved me? You'll laugh when you hear it.'

'I doubt that very much.'

313

'The transcendence in me that would survive no matter what – my Buddha nature.'

I didn't know what she meant by that, and though I had no doubt that she was sincere, it also seemed a declaration she'd memorized long ago. Her Buddhism seemed to be her strategy for maintaining her wild rage under strict control.

'Did his abuse come out at the divorce hearing?' I asked.

She shook her head. 'We had no proof, and Coutinho would have claimed that our lawyer was just trying to get my mom and me more sympathy and money. He'd have humiliated me in public. He had no qualms about that, I can assure you.'

'You call your father Coutinho,' I pointed out.

'A suggestion my therapist made years ago, back in Paris. We decided it was best for me not to consider him my father.'

'And you believe that Monsieur Morel knew what he'd done to you?'

'He was Coutinho's best friend,' she said, sneering. 'What do you think?'

'I think that some men are experts at fooling people. They're charming and clever – great joke-tellers, excellent singers or dancers. They're the star of every dinner party.'

She laughed mirthlessly. 'You talk like you know my father well.'

'I'm familiar with men like him.'

'I expect you've arrested a few.'

'Whenever I get the chance.'

Something odd happened then. I was sure that Gabriel had just entered the room, but not to take me over. He wished to observe us. I looked towards the front door, as though expecting to see exactly what he looked like for the first time.

'Something wrong?' Dias asked.

'I was just thinking of an old friend. You're an excellent actress, you know. All that fear you showed at being pursued by the murderer during our last conversation – I was certain you were terrified.'

314

'What happened with Coutinho taught me the usefulness of giving a standout performance.' Gesturing towards a small white sofa against the wall, she added, 'Listen, you two can sit down if you like. I can see this might take a while. I'll be right back. I remembered something I need to pack.'

'Is it all right if I use your bathroom?' Ernie asked.

Dias pointed towards the door, just past her bookshelves. While they were both out of the room, I realized that my key mistake was assuming that Dias had been Coutinho's last lover. And it was clever of her to have worn men's sneakers just long enough to make a bloody shoeprint. She must have just finished watching her father choke to death when the construction worker bumped into her on the Rua do Vale.

Dead moths clouded the translucent bottom of her circular ceiling lamp. It seemed a telling oversight. Staring at the accumulation of so many small deaths, I pictured Dias meditating in her prison cell, and lived out ten years of her life in just a few seconds. Tattoos of Buddhist symbols wrapped around her arms and climbed up her neck as the need to hide her anger and despair grew stronger. Her hair greyed and her eyes shone with the strange, isolated light of the ascetic who has renounced all attachments to the world.

She would tell other prisoners that she had chosen this life, had embraced the path she had been on since she was a girl.

Ten years hence, in July of 2022, would I still be wondering if arresting her had been the right thing to do?

I stepped up to the nineteenth-century portrait of the young mother that had been hanging in Coutinho's house until Friday. It was leaning against the wall by the front door. Dias must have spotted it on the day she murdered her father; she'd have hated the idea of him keeping a likeness of her. It must have seemed as if a symbolic part of her were still his prisoner.

Ernie sauntered back into the room. His right hand was red; he'd scrubbed it with scalding water. Waving away my concern, he sat down beside me and pointed towards a one-euro coin he'd spotted between the cushions. I retrieved it and offered it to him to give to Dias, but he told me he wouldn't touch anything more unless he had to. 'She seems high on something,' he whispered.

'She probably is,' I said, and I touched my fingertip to my forehead, which he agreed to with a nod.

After crossing his arms, Ernie leaned over himself. I patted his leg encouragingly. 'We'll leave soon,' I said.

'It's okay, the Valium just kicked in.'

After Dias darted back into the room, she tucked a small black bag into the larger of her suitcases. I guessed it contained her gun, but I didn't ask. She drew up one of the wooden chairs that had been around her dining table. I handed her the euro coin. 'My brother found it in your couch,' I said.

'Thanks.' She took it in her fist and sculpted a quick-worded prayer. On noticing Ernie's awkward posture, she spoke gently for the first time since we'd arrived. 'Are you feeling all right?'

'Just a little dizziness – I got up too early this morning,' he replied, sitting back up.

She looked at Ernie sympathetically, but I didn't want Dias anywhere near the hole in his heart left by our mother.

'Are you taking the portrait you stole from your father?' I asked.

'Absolutely. As far as I was concerned, he had no right to it.'

'Why did you have Coutinho write *Diana* in Japanese lettering with his blood?'

'He didn't write it – *I* wrote it!' she exclaimed vengefully. 'It was his pet name for me. He taught me how to write it in Japanese when I was a kid. It seemed fun at the time. The thrill of having him move my arm around the paper so that I could write those beautiful characters . . . I thought he was amazing!'

'Why the name Diana?'

316

'I'm not sure – he just started calling me it when I was little.'

'But why write it on the wall after the murder?'

'I wanted to assume responsibility for what I'd done. Think of it as a part of my mindfulness, Inspector. I needed the world to know that I'd achieved justice – me, the little stupid girl he'd abused, the fool who'd trusted him, who'd worshipped him.' Her eyes radiated amusement again. 'I knew you'd assume he'd written it. And no one in Portugal knew it was his private name for me. So it put me at no extra risk.'

'Do you know who your father was sleeping with – his final lover?'

'Inspector, you can be certain he had more than one,' she said, as though I still didn't understand anything about him. 'All the time he was abusing me, he had other girls. One of them was even my closest friend, though neither of us knew it until years later.' She looked towards the window as though the past were there. 'My friend thought Coutinho was in love with her. Maybe he even was – for a time. But who knows what a man like him feels and thinks?'

'So you have no idea who slept with him on the night before you killed him?' I asked.

'No, but I'd look for a girl between the ages of thirteen and eighteen, slender, blonde, pretty and . . . what?' She looked for the word. She seemed eager to help me now.

'Lacking in self-esteem,' I suggested.

She tossed off a bitter laugh and said, 'Yes, he was a master at destroying the confidence of the girls he wanted.' She carved the air with imaginary brushstrokes. 'An artist whose medium was the promise of a deeper love from a very special man.'

'Do you know the names of any girls he might have molested here in Lisbon?'

'No. When I first found out that he had moved here, I wanted nothing to do with him. And I sure as hell didn't want him recognizing me! I cut my hair short and dyed it,

317

and I avoided any meetings with parents, when I might have had to see him.' She tossed the coin up and caught it, then turned it over. 'Heads,' she said, and she looked at me as if expecting my view on the importance of chance in our lives, but I had no opinion at the moment. 'If he hadn't returned to Portugal,' she continued, 'then none of this would have happened. Or was it completely predictable that we'd meet again one day? What do you think, Inspector?'

She needed to test me for a belief in destiny – or some Buddhist concept of fate with which I wasn't familiar. 'I have no idea,' I told her.

'I think you do,' she insisted.

'I don't believe there is any plan, if that's what you're asking,' I told her.

She sighed as if I were being stubborn. 'You know, when I learned he had moved back to Lisbon, I didn't think of killing him – at least, not right away. He forced me to make that decision.'

What I didn't then dare ask was, *And were you also forced to kill him in such a painful way?*

'We'll get to what happened last Friday,' I said instead, 'but first tell me if anyone found out about your father's abuse and did nothing to stop it.' I was thinking again of Morel – wondering if he had any responsibility for Sandi's death.

She shifted uncomfortably in her chair and turned away from me. 'I'm not sure,' she said. 'I *do* know that Coutinho had other friends with the same . . . inclinations. I found a photograph he had of himself with two young girls and a group of other men. This was before he started abusing me.'

'Was Morel one of the men?'

'No, he wasn't there.'

'Did you know any of the girls?'

'No.'

'So who were the men? Friends of your father's?'

'I assumed they were businessmen and politicians he knew.'

'From France or Portugal?'

'I don't know.'

'Where did you find it?'

'In Coutinho's agenda. This one time, he left it right on the kitchen table – just forgot about it. When I picked it up, the picture fell out.'

'Did you save it?'

'No. I made the mistake of bringing it to my mother. She burned it.' Sneering, she added, 'She said she wanted to protect the girls.'

'But you thought she burned it to protect your father.'

'Let's just say that my mother was too often a woman of misguided loyalties.'

She looked at Ernie, so I did, too. His eyes were closed, with his head angled down; he was trying to burrow into that part of himself with no doors or windows.

'So who wrecked your childhood, Inspector?' Dias asked.

We looked at each other. I don't know what she saw, but I saw a woman who was far too pleased by her own intuition.

'Our childhood wasn't wrecked by anyone,' I told her.

'No?' she asked, her ironic tone indicating that she knew better. Maybe she had a kind of radar for people like my brother and me. Most of us with bad childhoods did, I'd learned since joining the police.

'It was our father,' Ernie told her. He was sitting up, and he'd put on his cowboy hat. I hadn't noticed him changing positions. I checked my hands, but nothing was written on either palm.

'But he's gone now,' Ernie said insistently, 'and we're still here.' He looked over at me, anxious for my confirmation.

As I nodded, it seemed that my life was made of the thousand times I'd noticed that Ernie and I were sitting together in our own dimension, no matter what we were doing or how far away we were from each other.

'When did you find out that Coutinho had moved from Paris to Lisbon?' I asked Dias. 'Did you even know he had a second family?'

'I spotted him at a meeting with parents last September,' she said, 'just after the start of school. He was with his wife. It was a shock to see him. I hadn't seen him in nearly twenty years. I thought he was still in Paris. I'd heard he'd married again, from my mother. She'd spotted an article about his wedding in some gossip magazine. But I didn't know he had a daughter. Part of why *I* moved to Lisbon was to get away from any chance of ever running into him. And then he was here, and Sandi was in my class . . .' She shook her head at her bad luck. Or perhaps at the impossibility of fighting fate. 'Inspector, if I hadn't slipped up, would you have caught me?' she asked anxiously, as though desperate to confirm how clever she'd been.

'What do you think?' I asked, hoping her reply would give away what she meant – and how G had figured things out.

'I have no idea. I don't know what evidence you turned up.'

'Your sneaker print – a men's size forty-three.'

She laughed girlishly and said, 'You'd never have found me with just that.' She turned to the window facing the square once again. I sensed she was looking out into an alternative world in which she hadn't been caught. There, in a city whose buildings and streets were constructed according to her wishes, Sandi must still have been alive, and overflowing with tearful thanks for what her half-sister had done for her.

'So you figured out how my brother ended up knowing the killer was you?' Ernie asked, realizing it was a question I couldn't ask.

'Yeah. I knew right away I'd made a bad slip. He didn't tell you?' she asked in a surprised voice.

'No. Henrique doesn't always like to share the details of his police work – at least not with me.'

Dias smiled at him knowingly, as though she and my brother had just formed a team that excluded me. In a confidential tone, she said, 'I told your brother I'd read about how Coutinho was murdered at my health club, and that I

320

worked there on Tuesdays and Fridays. It was Monday when I told him that, so he knew I was claiming that I'd read about it on Friday. But the newspapers only carried the news of Coutinho's death on *Saturday*. I couldn't have known he was dead on Friday unless I'd been involved. Pretty stupid, right?'

So G had called the Chiado Health Club to double-check that she hadn't given any special yoga classes on Saturday.

Dias turned to me. 'I started watching you very closely to see if you'd picked up on my mistake, but you gave nothing away. You're a pretty good actor yourself, Inspector!'

Standing up, she went to the window. After pulling back the curtain and opening it a bit further, she flipped the one-euro coin outside. Facing me again, she said, 'When you came to see me the first time, I was sure you'd caught me. Then, when you assumed I was Coutinho's girlfriend, it was ...' She raised her hands in thanks. 'Like the universe was smiling down on me.'

Unwilling to let her get away with such a self-serving belief, but not wanting to set her off, I said gently, 'Until you found out about Sandi.'

'Yes, till then.' She swiped a tense hand back across her hair.

If her conscience were as stunted by all she'd suffered as I thought it was, then she'd soon recover her composure and convince herself that Sandi's death was an unfortunate – but necessary – consequence of her achieving justice.

'When did you realize Sandi was being hurt by Coutinho?' I asked.

'After she stopped eating. I tried the opposite technique to keep Coutinho away from me, you know. I ate all I could!' She puffed out her cheeks. 'He hated how fat I got!' With her eyes twinkling, she turned to Ernie, so her new friend could share her glee. 'He couldn't get it up with a chubby thirteen-year-old in his arms. That's how my mom figured things out. He was a bit too insistent that I go on a diet – and too angry when I refused.'

'You were smart,' my brother told her admiringly.

'Yeah, except I looked *hideous!*' She hid her face in her hands – a little girl craving reassurance.

'You did what you had to do.'

I didn't like Dias prompting Ernie's reactions. He probably didn't either, but he gave her what she wanted for the same reason that I didn't dare mention that her half-sister had been pregnant.

'Did Sandi know how concerned you were about her?' I asked.

She sat back up very straight, as though to reclaim her adulthood. 'Yes, I went to her and told her I knew what was going on. She told me there was nothing I could do – at least, at first. She was feeling hopeless. And guilty.'

'Guilty because her father convinced her she'd seduced him?'

'And because she was torn between wanting to please him and kill him. Yes, Inspector, please him *in bed!*'

She bit down hard on her last words as though to shock me but, given my past, Sandi's confused and tragic hopes didn't surprise me in the least.

'Did you know that she kept a knife below her mattress?' I asked.

'No, but it makes sense.' She looked off, considering this new detail. 'I think that not using it . . . might have been what she found hardest to forgive about herself.'

'Why didn't you want Sandi to know you were related?' I asked.

'Because I was scared she'd reject me. I suspected that Coutinho had told her awful things about me; what a selfish monster I was for refusing to ever speak to our *sweet, generous* daddy – our *handsome, youthful-looking* daddy!' With a vicious, triumphant smile, she added, 'You know he had a face-lift, didn't you?'

'Yes, I spotted the scars.'

'Probably more than one,' she said contemptuously.

'So did you end up telling Sandi you were half-sisters?'

322

'Yes, and she confirmed that Coutinho told her I was mean-spirited and spoiled, and that I'd made his life miserable during the divorce.'

'When did you first talk to her about the abuse she was suffering?'

'A couple of weeks or so after she cut her hair, she started getting dangerously thin. Looking at her bamboo arms made me sick – physically sick! What was amazing was that at first I didn't know why I had such a visceral reaction to her losing weight. The mind is a funny thing . . . And then it hit me one day at school.' Dias flexed her arms over her head, needing to be reminded, perhaps, that she was strong and determined – no longer a hopeless, overweight teenager. 'I'd called on Sandi in class, to analyse a poem by Baudelaire. She answered with such . . . what would I call it? Timid hesitation? She'd always loved being called on before, so it shocked me. When the meaning of the grief I spotted in her eyes hit me, it hit me *really hard*. There were many nights when I didn't sleep at all. All my fear of him was back – the absolute terror!' She focused on me with predatory eyes. 'Do you know what it's like to be hallucinating your father's voice while you're giving a class? My God, how I hated that voice of his!'

'Is that why you gagged him?'

'He started ordering me around. Imagine, he has a bullet in his gut, and I'm still holding my gun, and he thought he could tell me what to do!'

'When did you first start planning to kill him?'

'In early June. After a week or two of panic-filled insomnia. I only started sleeping again when I bought a gun.' She put a hand atop her heart as though needing to make a vow. 'He gave me no choice, Inspector,' she told me. 'If I didn't kill him, I'd have failed Sandi. And myself.' She turned away when tears washed her eyes.

'Where did you get your gun?' I asked.

'I have an old friend from Paris who lives now in Madrid. When we were younger and a lot stupider, we robbed houses in Neuilly and other fancy suburbs of Paris. He's cleaned up his act by now, but he still knows some resourceful people.'

'Was there any special point to your using a Browning semi-automatic?'

'My friend told me that you cops used to use them. So the choice seemed right to me – a kind of symmetry.'

I didn't believe she could have had anything to do with the burglary at Coutinho's house, but given what she'd just told me, I had to ask.

'No, I don't want anything of his – anything he's touched,' she replied. 'So what'd they get – the oil paintings?'

'No. We're not sure what they took just yet. Do you still have your gun?'

'It's with my sneakers – under fifty feet of water.'

'In the Tagus?'

'Yeah. There's a lovely boardwalk in Vila Franca de Xira now. I went there on Saturday. You can see a lot of birds if you go early – herons, egrets . . .'

She spoke as if she were talking about a relaxing day in the country. And with her father no longer stalking her thoughts, it probably had been. I could easily imagine her watching her gun sinking into the jade-coloured water and whispering to herself, *If we follow our destiny far enough, we are rewarded with the world's beauty.*

'The key to Coutinho's house – where did you get it?' I asked.

'I took it from Sandi's backpack when she came here for lunch with Monica and Joana. I told the girls I'd forgotten a bottle of wine in my car. There's a tiny shop around the corner for making keys. I was gone only a few minutes.' She gazed down and laughed to herself. On looking up, she steeled herself for another battle. 'You can't imagine how I hoped that Coutinho wouldn't have more children. Or would change. If I hadn't killed him, he'd still be molesting Sandi.'

She looked at Ernie as though needing his agreement,

but he'd had enough of her pressured glances by then and turned away. Reading his wariness as a criticism, she shouted, 'Sandi killing herself wasn't supposed to happen! I was trying to prevent that! I was the only one helping her!' She pointed a damning finger at me. 'What do you ever do to help the kids who are being abused in this fucking country? The police do nothing.' Turning to Ernie, she shouted, 'Your brother does nothing!'

Ernie jumped up, his anger in the ferocious depth of his eyes and the wide set of his shoulders. 'You have no idea how many bad people my brother has put in prison,' he told our host in a quivering voice. 'And you have no idea what we've been through.'

Looking up at him, she took a sharp intake of breath and shrank back. Did she realize she'd understood nothing about the depth of complicity between my brother and me? Maybe she simply felt the more basic terror of being outnumbered by men.

Although Dias seemed keenly intelligent, she also seemed to me to be unable to see the shape and scope of what others were thinking about her. Later that week, it would occur to me that she'd only glimpsed the vaguest outlines of Sandi's tormented feelings and had mistaken them for her own need for vengeance. Maybe she even thought that Sandi had given her unspoken permission to murder their father.

In a wounded voice, trying to win us back to her, Dias said, 'I only meant that it's impossible to prosecute child abusers in Portugal.'

I couldn't tell if her remorse was genuine. I didn't even want to make the effort. I wanted to leave and see my kids, and ask Ana to let me back into her life. Ernie's gaze had turned inside and he had begun to shiver. I stood up and took his hand. I imagined we looked ridiculous, two grown men holding hands like little kids, but appearing ridiculous has often seemed the world's way of telling me I was doing just the right thing.

Dias showed us a harsh, judgemental expression, and it was gratifying to discover I didn't care. 'I have just a few more questions,' I told her.

'Good, because I need to get back to packing,' she told me in a businesslike tone.

I gave Ernie's hand a final squeeze and let it drop. 'So do you think Sandi's mother realized what was happening to her?' I asked.

'I doubt it. Sandi hoped she'd picked up on her clues, but she didn't want to know.'

'You tried calling the girl over the weekend, but she wouldn't answer.'

'That's right.'

'Were you going to tell her you killed her father?'

'She must have figured that out already. She guessed what I was thinking of doing when I told her I understood what she was going through.'

I realized then that Sandi had been trying to protect Dias when she'd denied knowing anything about the painting that had been taken by the killer. Very likely, she'd also hidden – or destroyed – the photographs of the living room that her mother couldn't find.

'Did Sandi ask you not to do anything violent?' I questioned.

She eyed me angrily. 'You want to hear her death is my fault, don't you? Let me tell you something! Not even her looking like a skeleton put Coutinho off! If you could have heard her voice when she told me that . . . She was so desperate. She told me she didn't want me to hurt him. It's true. But she was telling me one thing with her words and another with everything else about her! Still, I agreed not to hurt him if she'd do something for me.'

'What?'

'I told her I'd give the police an anonymous tip about him. I assured her that no one would ever hold her responsible for his arrest. But I also told her that we had to try to find some photographs of him with other girls – as evidence. But

326

she couldn't find them anywhere. At least, that's what she said. I had the feeling she'd have preferred starving herself to death to getting Coutinho in trouble or participating in any way in my plan. So I sneaked over to her house once when her parents were away and made her search with me. We didn't find any pictures, but something in her manner, something reticent and anxious ... I began to suspect that she'd found the photos already and wasn't going to tell me where they were – which gave me no other choice but to take matters into my own hands.'

I sensed Gabriel standing by the door again. Somehow, I was certain that he wanted me to disregard my professional and personal codes and let Dias go free.

'I'm guessing you'll get rid of your cell phone at some point,' I said, needing to buy myself a little time. 'So how do I reach you? In case someone else in the police figures out it was you.'

'I suppose I could give you my mother's number in Bordeaux,' she said, as if it were being charitable.

I jotted it down.

Did she see something accusatory in Ernie's eyes while I was writing? She slashed her hand in the air between us. 'I don't regret what I did!' she shouted. 'You can both think I should, but I don't!'

Chapter 26

You step outside after a disagreeable interrogation and are surprised to find that it's still early morning, and you trace a streamer of sunlight across the pale yellow façade of the building across the street, and you marvel at how it folds, jagged, around the bevelled column of a black street lamp just ahead of you, and you count one, two, three, four, five motorcycles parked on the traffic island at the centre of Rafael Bordelo Pinheiro Square, and you watch a white cat with a pirate-like black eye-patch crouching under a silver Honda – maybe scenting its own mortality in the dry wind sweeping in from Spain – and finally, calmed by the give and take of friendly voices coming from an apartment above you, you look up and spot two pigeons on a rooftop and imagine – smiling to yourself – that they're having the conversation you're eavesdropping on. You see all these things as though they were necessary, because you believe – improbable though it may sound – that all of them are sure to become important at some point in the story. Which story? Your own and the world's, for at that moment there is no separation between the two.

I turned around to Ernie. He smiled his sideways smile, and it was reassuring precisely because it was his and always had been. He put his arm over my shoulder and told me something that made me laugh, and although I doubt it was about how I used to call him Wyatt Earp when he was a kid, that's the way I remember it.

When Ernie was nine, I started secretly teaching him how to load and fire the Colt cap and ball revolver that Dad had given me for my thirteenth birthday, and within a few months, he could hit a Dr Pepper can from thirty yards nearly every time.

Ernie doesn't recall what he said that amused me. We're pretty sure it wasn't about Dias, however. She left us both feeling as if we'd escaped a battlefield. I do remember the weight of his arm. It seemed to hold me in place, but in a good way.

Were presentiments not only possible but inevitable? Maybe that was why I looked from the street lamp to the five motorcycles to the cat and to the pigeons. They were like props to an actor; I needed to make sure they were there – each in its right place – before my life went off in the direction it had to.

When I think of that moment now, nearly a month later, I have a vague sensation of falling. And I recall an explosion so loud that I wasn't able to hear anything for a few seconds afterward. It seems to me the explosion came after my fall, but that can't be.

According to Ernie, we started walking down the street towards our car, and I told him I'd call for backup once we got there. When he asked if I was going to arrest Dias, I replied, 'She was largely responsible for Sandi's death, so what else can I do?' And he said, 'You could let her go.' And then a figure wearing a hoodie was standing in front of us.

Ernie would have sworn that the hoodie was grey, but it was green, according to the police report. As every cop knows, mistakes of that sort aren't unusual: eyewitness – even alert ones – often get a lot of details wrong.

The man in the hoodie pointed his gun at us. Sensing he was about to fire, I threw myself over Ernie and shouted 'No!'

The first shot hit me in the back of my left leg, three inches below the knee.

I didn't reach for my gun because I must have decided – having only a fraction of a second to evaluate my

329

alternatives – that I couldn't get off a shot in time and had only one chance to protect my brother. Gabriel took over then, according to Ernie, who said that I crumpled to the ground and shouted at our attacker, *You'll pay for that, you little fucker!* Bleeding all over the pavement, I still managed to kneel. I lifted my gun out of my pocket as a second shot hit me in my right shoulder.

Ernie must have picked up my pistol when it dropped from my hand but he doesn't remember. When he fired, the man fell backwards and hit with a thud on the pavement. His eyes were open but were staring at nothing. At so much nothing, in fact, that Ernie began to wonder at the expanse of death, at how infinitely bigger than each individual life it was, and how it had now seemed to surround the three of us.

Ernie called 112 and said his brother had been shot twice in a square in the Chiado. 'What square?' asked the woman on the other end of the line. Ernie looked up and found the plaque indicating its name and told her, and he added for good measure, 'My brother is a chief inspector for the Judicial Police. His name is Henrique Monroe. And I think he's going to die if an ambulance doesn't get here very fast.'

Amazing that he had the presence of mind to speak so coherently, but he told me that after an initial tremor inside him, a hypnotic clarity surged in him, and he knew exactly what he needed to say. While we waited for medical help, a crowd gathered. An elderly woman brought me a glass of water, he says. I like to think it was the same old lady who spoke to me about Lisbon's meteorites.

Ernie had shot the hooded man above his left eye. He'd been aiming for the centre of his forehead, which means he was only about an inch off his target. Pretty darn good. My brother later claimed that he hadn't fired a gun in twenty years, but Nati told me just a few days ago that he'd spotted his uncle shooting at Coke cans down by the stream that runs through his property just two years ago, while I was out buying groceries in Évora.

I don't remember any blood, but Ernie said that I looked like something from a horror movie. My face had turned so pale that he figured I wasn't going to make it. My hands were freezing. He said I was panting and that I told him I was having troubling getting enough air into my lungs. I don't remember anything like that.

At some point, I said to Ernie, 'Got any chocolate, kid?'

When he said he didn't, I told him not to worry about it, but he asked the onlookers around us if anyone had any. A young man handed Ernie a Mars bar, and my brother helped me hold it while I took bites. Picturing the two of us working so hard to eat that gooey little chunk of chocolate – or the three of us, if you include Gabriel – sometimes makes me laugh out loud.

Since I wasn't breathing well, chewing was a slow struggle, but I managed to finish the Mars bar. Ernie lifted the glass of water to my lips whenever I told him I was thirsty.

My eating that chocolate and then licking my fingers seems proof to me now that you never know what your last wish is going to be.

Ernie says that after the empty wrapper dropped out of my hand, I hugged him tightly. He scented my fear. My teeth started chattering but I smiled at him and said that he was a man now and that everything would be all right, and that he had to be very good to himself or I'd be angry with him.

I don't remember saying anything like that to him.

Ernie says that he could tell that Gabriel had given me back my body when I started grimacing from the pain. I have no memory of that either. Or of whispering that I was counting on him to help take care of King Kong and Godzilla. And finally, of asking him to apologize to Ana for me for all the lies I'd ever told her.

Chapter 27

Ana was asleep in a chair near the foot of my bed. Her head kept falling to the side in a tortuously slow descent, then jerking back up. She looked as though she were caught in a time loop. She was also snoring, and it seemed to me that she must have been having agitated dreams. I watched her without speaking because my love for her was now a physical presence between us – patient and absolutely certain of its own importance – and it seemed to require silence.

The next thing I remember is feeling cheated that Ana wasn't in bed with me and wondering why my pillow was lumpy and the air smelled like ammonia. I fought to sit up, but when I pushed off my right arm a slicing pain in my shoulder made me moan. Thick bandaging covered it, and the tenderness underneath flared into a burn at the probing of my fingertips. Looking to my side, I spotted an IV pole. A plastic bag full of clear liquid dangled from it, and I traced the long tubule carrying the liquid to a thick, mean-looking needle sticking into my forearm. I wanted to pull it out but I was sure that that would get me into trouble with Ana when she woke up.

My left leg began to throb, as though it had been badly singed. Had my car burst into flames? If Jorge and Nati had been with me, then . . .

When I called out to Ana, her eyes fluttered open.

'Where are Ernie and the kids?' I asked.

Without taking her astonished eyes from me, she jumped

up and peeled off her coat, tossing it behind her onto her chair. While holding my head in both her hands, she kissed me on the lips. 'You're in the hospital, baby, and everyone is fine. We're all okay.'

She smiled down at me as though I were a present she'd just received. Her lips were chapped and her hair was a bit shorter than I remembered it. 'So nothing bad has happened to Jorge and Nati?' I asked.

'They're worried about you, of course, but they're all right. They're with my parents.'

'And Ernie is okay?'

'Yeah, he just stepped out for a bite to eat. The poor man was starving.'

'So he wasn't killed in the accident?' I asked.

'There was no accident.'

'I didn't smash my car into a big tree – a walnut tree? Along the road to town.'

She shook her head and kissed my brow, then my eyes. The touch of her made me understand I was just where I was meant to be, even if I couldn't remember what had happened.

'And you're okay, too?' I asked.

'I'm fine. We're all fine.'

A tight knot of gratitude formed inside my throat but I didn't cry. My emotions seemed stuck to the confusion in my head. Ana read what I was thinking and said, 'You're in the Santa Marta hospital. You were in the Intensive Care Unit but they transferred you to a regular room today.'

She pressed her lips to mine, and she smelled now of all the worry I'd put her through, so I said I was sorry I'd given her a scare and made her come to the hospital.

'Better here than a few other places I can think of,' she replied.

One of the curtains around my bed had a big yellowish stain. I don't know why it interested me, but it did. 'What got spilled?' I asked, pointing.

'Beats me.'

'Are there other people in this room?'

Pointing to my right, she whispered, 'There's another patient over there. He had an emergency appendectomy yesterday.' She mouthed, *He's small and hairy – like an orang-utan.*

Ana laughed like people do who've been crying. I took her hand and held it tight and rubbed it against my cheek. We looked at each other in silence for a long time, so that the place where I ended and she began seemed to merge.

'So how did I get here?' I asked.

Ana recounted what had happened, starting with my interrogation of Maria Dias. I didn't remember anything about that. She said I'd been shot twice on the street, but that neither bullet had hit any arteries or vital organs; my left anklebone had been broken badly, however, and had had to be set in place with a metal rod. Today was Wednesday. I'd been operated on two days before, to extract the bullets and repair my anklebone. She had my bullets at home if I ever wanted to see them. There had been no complications. The surgeon had told her that if everything went according to plan, I'd be leaving the hospital in about ten days. He also told her I'd been extremely lucky, all things considered.

'Getting hit by two bullets isn't exactly lucky,' I pointed out.

I hadn't intended to be funny, but Ana laughed until tears began sliding down her cheeks. As I fought to sit up, she embraced me as if we'd been apart for an entire winter, and the warmth of her must have reminded me of other things because I got hard in spite of thinking it wasn't such a good idea, given that I probably needed all my available blood circulating around my bullet wounds. But just to make sure I was all right down there I reached for myself.

Ana took a look under the covers and grinned.

We kissed for a long time, easily, as if there would never be any need to rush again. When we finally separated, Ana fetched Debbie from her shoulder bag and hung her around my neck. On my request, she then held a glass of water to my lips. By the time I'd finished my drink, a wave of exhaustion had passed over me. Going back to sleep seemed like my best option.

'I need to call the kids first,' Ana told me.

I gave her the thumbs-up sign, then let my head fall back onto my pillow.

Ana's conversation with Nati and Jorge was like soft scratching on the edge of my hearing – like an LP that has ended but is still going round and round on the turntable.

Jorge insisted on speaking to me so she shook me awake enough to take the phone. He asked me four times if I was all right and four times I tried different variations of *I couldn't be better*, in both English and Portuguese. Finally, Nati grabbed the phone from him and told me, 'I want you to quit the police!'

'Right.'

'I'm not joking!'

'And I'm not entirely sure I'm fully conscious. Maybe we could start this conversation over.'

'I'm sorry, but I'm not happy about this!' he said. 'Not happy at all, Dad.'

The knot of unfallen tears was back in my throat. I couldn't even whisper a reply, so Ana took the phone. After finishing up with Nati, she told me that her mother and father would bring the kids over right away.

When I next awoke, a tall, wiry man with stubble on his cheeks, long, unruly hair and a bandage on his forehead was standing beside me, peeling off his surgical gloves.

'Hello, doctor,' I said, raising my hand in what I intended was a friendly way.

'Hi, Rico,' he said. 'How are you feeling?'

He had rugged, work-toughened hands and loose-looking arms, and his crooked smile was all the way up there by the ceiling. When he opened his eyes wide, as though to ask me why I was looking at him with such shock, their deep green colour and long lashes gave him away, though he seemed older than I remembered.

I waved him down to me because I needed to make sure

he was who I thought he was. His scratchy kiss and oatmeal scent confirmed it was him, which was a big relief.

'Things seem a bit weird at the moment,' I told him.

'You've been through a lot.'

'My leg feels as if it's been burnt. And I'm not too happy about the needle in my arm. Where did Ana go?'

'She wanted me to have a few minutes with you alone. She went to see if she could buy you some chicken soup at the Bela Ipanema.'

I wasn't hungry, but I'd do my best to eat the soup if she went to all that trouble.

Ernie said something but I missed it. It might have been about his surgical gloves, because he set them down neatly on my bed. Dropping down next to me, he pressed the back of his hand to my forehead.

How had I become the only person he could touch without risking illness?

'No fever,' he said, giving me a satisfied nod.

'What'd you eat?' I asked.

'Two lemon muffins. I brought you back two bran ones. You'll probably need a lot of fibre because of the painkillers they've got you on. You want them?' He pointed to a brown bag on a shabby white chair by the door.

'Hasn't anyone in the administration figured out that white vinyl shows every stain and scuff?' I asked.

'Rico, concentrate! I'm asking if you want a muffin.'

'Are you sure they have muffins in Lisbon?' I asked.

'I just ate two.'

'I guess that means you're either sure or hallucinating.'

'I'm sure. I never hallucinate anything worth eating!'

That seemed genuinely witty, but I still didn't laugh.

A nurse darted in. She was in her thirties, I'd have guessed, with a pixie nose, Cupid's bow lips and unruly black hair. She looked a bit like Debbie Harry circa 1980. When she heard my accent, she said she'd worked in Manchester for a year, in a Persian restaurant. All the customers thought she was Iranian and fleeing the ayatollahs and were disappointed when they learned she was Portuguese. Ernie and I looked at each other and decided not to spoil her fun, so we confirmed that we were from England – from the town of Woodford, I said. That name just popped out of me. Later, I remembered that Dad's favourite saxophonist, Johnny Dankworth, came from there.

The nurse, whose name was Rita, explained to me that the IV was giving me antibiotics and added that the doctor making his rounds would check on me later. She showed me where the bell was at the side of my bed and told me to ring for her if I needed anything. I took it in my hand, and when I looked back up, she was already rushing out of the room.

'Folks sure move quick round these here parts,' I said in my best Colorado accent.

Ernie laughed, then sat beside me, and we talked in conspiratorial voices about our favourite childhood meals. While he was going on and on about some *posole* stew he swore we'd eaten in Denver when we'd gone to the zoo, I remembered a statue of the Buddha wrapped with bath towels. And big, metal suitcases.

'How many days have I been gone?' I finally cut in.

'You were shot two days ago and operated on right away.'

I tried to think back to the operation. All I remembered was a very strong light burning my face. 'What time is it now?' I asked.

He checked his watch. 'Ten to nine in the evening.'

'Were we going somewhere with metal suitcases?'

'No, it was Maria Dias who was leaving – the woman you questioned.'

'Who is she?'

'Coutinho's daughter by his first wife.'

I nodded as though I understood, but I had only the vaguest recollection of the Coutinho family. When I asked where this Dias woman was headed, Ernie patted my chest, as though he were making sure I was more solid than I sounded, and told me about her trip through Spain to France. None of it sounded familiar.

337

In reply to my next questions, Ernie told me that the man who'd shot me was named Alberto Trigueiro. He had been only about fifteen feet away from us when he fired. That distance stuck in my memory like a splinter, but I didn't know why. He told me that killing Trigueiro made him feel sick at first, and as though he'd tumbled off a high cliff. He gave me a look that meant he needed me to say something meaningful, but I didn't know what that could be, so I said instead, 'What was the cliff made of?'

He thought about that a while. 'Maybe it was made of every good thing I've ever tried to do,' he said. 'The thing is, Rico, after the ambulance took you away, and while I was standing alone on the street, looking down at your blood all over my hands and trying to keep from screaming, I realized that defending the two of us meant that we had the right to be alive. And that I hadn't fallen off anything at all.'

Since he looked so relieved, I said, 'That's a very good thing.'

'You know, sometimes it seems as if I've spent my whole life apologizing for being alive,' he continued. 'But all that blood you lost . . . It ended all that. Or maybe killing someone did. I never in a million years thought that would happen.'

We looked at each other, and I could have been eight and he could have been four, and we could have just started to learn about the cramped, combative, irrational dimensions of the life we'd been born into.

'I feel really terrible about lying to you all those years ago,' he said.

'What are you talking about?' I asked.

'I told you I was afraid that Dad would come back and take me away – after he disappeared, I mean. But that wasn't true. I'm really sorry, Rico, but I was afraid that the police would come for you and accuse you of making him disappear. And take you off to prison. That was why I made you swear you'd never talk about how he vanished to anyone.' Choking up, he added, 'That's why I made you lie to Ana and the kids. I shouldn't have done it, but I did.'

338

'It's okay, Ernie, don't worry about it. You didn't make me do anything I didn't want to do.'

He pressed his thumbs into his temples and closed his eyes. Noticing that the sleeves of his shirt were too short, and wanting to divert his attention, I asked, 'So whose clothes did you steal?'

'Yours,' he said, grinning.

'Who gave you permission for that?'

'No one, but I had no other choice.'

'Why's that?'

'You refused to stop bleeding all over mine, even when I asked you really nicely not to!'

Ernie's provoking me back felt like just the right move and we had a good laugh. His laughter seemed an amazing sound, as if it were the best thing about him and what I'd fought all my life to save, and what made even getting shot worthwhile.

For years, I tried to find the roof above all I felt for my brother, but listening to his happiness I realized there was none. In Ernie's presence, I was open to the sky.

He said that Luci had introduced herself to him after the ambulance took me away. She'd ushered him into the back of a police car and asked him to tell her what had happened. 'She didn't seem to mind that I couldn't tell things in much of an order, and that I had to keep stopping to get my breath,' he told me. 'You lucked out with her.'

'True.'

Ernie told me that Luci knew Trigueiro's name and that he'd been twenty-seven years old because he'd had his wallet in his front pocket. Later, she learned that he had served two years in the state prison in Paços de Ferreira for a series of burglaries in Porto, which gave us the idea that he'd probably been responsible for trashing Coutinho's house.

Manuel Marques, another of the chief inspectors, had questioned Ernie at headquarters.

'Was he tough on you?' I asked, fearing the worst.

'No, not at all. I expected the good-cop, bad-cop routine, but he was the only one who talked with me, and after I told him how you'd been shot, and how I'd ended up firing at Trigueiro, we talked mostly about the Alentejo, because he'd learned by then I lived near Redondo. Did you know he was born a few miles from Elvas?'

'No.'

'His sister still lives in the family farmhouse. She has a fifteen-foot-high Canary Islands Dragon Tree in her front yard. Imagine that, Rico! He invited me to visit sometime.'

It was one of Ernie's talents that he could get almost anyone conversing about plants. While I was considering how he did it, he asked, 'So why do you think Trigueiro tried to kill you?'

'He didn't,' I said, because hearing that question voiced aloud made it clear why his distance from us – at the moment he shot me – had lodged in my mind. 'He fired from close range,' I continued. 'He could have put a bullet in my heart if he'd wanted to. He just wanted to put me out of action for a while. At least, at first.'

'Why did he need you out of action?'

'Because I must have been getting too close to whoever told him to shoot me.'

'And who was that?'

'That's the big question, Ernie.'

My brother stood up and gazed off, and it seemed to me he was weighing this new information against the finality of having ended another person's life.

'You did the right thing,' I told him.

He faced me doubtfully.

'He'd have killed both of us if you'd missed on the first shot,' I continued. 'Whoever organized this isn't playing around. The stakes are too high. His second shot was meant to put me in my grave.'

Ernie nodded as if he agreed, but I could see I'd need to reinforce my message over the coming months. A few seconds later, we heard Jorge approaching from down the

340

hallway. He was jabbering away about a cartoon, and my mother-in-law was trying to get him to speak in a quieter voice. Stepping into the room, his mouth fell open and Francisco dropped out of his hand, which made me realize I must have looked pretty scary.

When I opened my arms, he hesitated, as though he were testing what it would feel like to hold himself back for just a second from all he needed, then shouted *Dad!*, and rushed to me like I was his promised land.

Ana got his shoes and trousers off while I was kissing him, and Nati helped manoeuvre him into bed beside me without him banging into my bad leg or shoulder. '*Cem por cento fruta!*' the little monster shouted once he was settled with my arm around him. *A hundred per cent fruit!*

'The new ad campaign for Bongo juice,' Ana explained with a comic groan.

Jorge nestled his face into my neck. His breathing was warm, and his weight against me seemed a talisman against everything bad that could still happen to me. After a minute, he was sound asleep.

Nati sniffed at the air around me – clearly a member of the Rabbit Clan – and said, 'Dad, I hate to break this news to you, but this room of yours stinks like fifty years of farts.'

I laughed with Ana and Ernie, but mostly because seeing Nati – those serious eyes of his, and the expressive way he gestured with his hands – reminded me of so many happy surprises that he'd given me over the years that only laughter could contain them all. He asked me if I wanted a back rub, but turning over would have required painful contortions. 'Just sit with me,' I told him.

He was too young to know that the most useful thing he could do for me was just to let me hold him, so he showed me a disappointed face, and for a moment he looked so much like my mother that apprehension made me turn away.

Once he was seated, Nati lay his head to my chest, ear down, as though listening to my heartbeat. I loved the astonishing rightness of that.

Chapter 28

I awoke at dawn the next morning with a message written in my hand: *Coutinho may be six feet under but that bastard goes right on saying cheese!*

I took that to mean two things: that the tragic consequences of what he did were still very much present in the world; and that – like Dias – G was sure that Coutinho had kept pictures of himself with teenaged girls.

G had dug so hard into my flesh with the tip of my pen – on the word *bastard* – that I had to blot the blood from my hand with my hospital smock. Reaching behind me to my night table, I grabbed the new cell phone that Ana had bought me.

After I assured Luci I was fine and apologized for waking her, she stunned me – and maybe herself, too – by giving way to tears. 'I'm really sorry, sir,' she said, sniffling into the phone. 'I know I'm being silly, but seeing you unconscious in the hospital and all bandaged up ... I tried to prepare myself for the worst. And now, the relief of hearing your voice, it's just too much.'

After I answered all her questions about my medical condition, I was able to steer her onto the subject of work. I explained that my old phone had been bugged and asked her to bring me Coutinho's flash drive from its hiding place in my office; I wanted Joaquim to search it thoroughly before I made any other move. Luci agreed, but she also said that

I ought to probably tell Romão I'd found it; he was now running the case.

I made no reply; having to take on my workload meant that Romão wouldn't have either the time or the resources to fully investigate the case. Turning over the flash drive to him would be pointless.

'I'm sorry if I've offended you, sir,' Luci said in a cringing tone.

'No, you're absolutely right,' I replied. 'I'll speak to Romão later today. Tell me, Luci, have you been reassigned to him?'

'Yes, sir.'

Romão was a brilliant investigator but he was also a bully who believed that women were too emotional to make good cops. He'd never let Luci direct her own investigation into how the burglary at Coutinho's might be connected to my shooting, which made this switch in assignment perfect for whoever had had me shot.

I tried to sit up – craving greater perspective over this downturn in our fortunes – but as I slid my left leg over the sheet, the pain made me howl. It felt as though a nail had been hammered through my wound into the bone.

'You all right, sir?' Luci asked.

'Just a little discomfort. Listen, I've got to go – the doctor is here. We'll talk later.'

Ana answered our home phone as though my voice had rescued her instead of the other way around. I didn't like being so needy. I wasn't sure she ought to trust a person with holes in him as deep as the ones I had.

When I told Ana that there might be a powerful politician or businessman who had hired Trigueiro to stop me from connecting all the dots around Coutinho's murder, she asked how we could confirm that.

'Given that Ernie put a bullet into our one link to whoever is afraid of me,' I told her, 'we're not ever going to know.'

'Maybe your colleagues can follow the payment that Trigueiro must have received.'

'He'd have received cash. There's not going to be any trail.'

Before Being Shot and After Being Shot. Two distinct continents, each with its own mountain ranges, river valleys and cities. And here, on the rugged, rocky coast of After Being Shot, would my wife believe I was telling the truth when we sat together on the isolated dock and I explained about my childhood?

Ana asked me about how I was feeling, and I told her about the crippling pain as if it were a joke. A test? She passed it by not laughing.

'What if it takes me longer to get out of the hospital than the doctors think?' I asked, wishing to tell her something about my fears by naming one of the least important of them.

'You're going to heal quickly. You're strong. And we'll all help. You'll be home before you know it.'

Ana told me that Ernie had proved an easy guest. 'And this morning,' she said, 'he and Jorge got out of bed early and made us all Colorado French toast.' Happy to talk about trifles, she said, 'They left a mess, too. I really wish you were here to yell at them!'

My wife passed the phone to our eldest son, who spoke to me about *Moby Dick* as a way of sharing something meaningful with me, and for the first time I realized there was a danger he'd live too fully in books. Why did it take me getting shot to see Nati's resemblance to my mother so clearly? It seemed now that my job might become encouraging him to close the covers of his novels now and again and join me outside in the world.

'Why do you think the novel starts with the narrator saying, "Call me Ishmael"?' Nati asked. 'Instead of something like "My name is Ishmael," I mean.'

'I've always thought it's because Ishmael isn't his real name,' I said.

'But why would he lie?'

'Because he doesn't trust his readers enough to give them any intimate details about himself – to know his real name. It's only the first chapter, after all. How can Ishmael be sure that the reader is on his side? He needs to tell his story first.

There are a lot of people who grow up without a single person they can trust, Nati.'

'So I've been led to understand,' he said knowingly.

When Jorge got on the phone, he raced headlong into his need for me to hear about his adventures with his neighbourhood friends, and it was a blessing to listen to his wayward stories. When Ana took the phone back, she said – as though speaking an incantation – 'As you can see, our kids miss you a lot.'

I didn't reply because I wanted to hold on to this moment.

'Are you there?' she asked.

'Ana, I'm sorry for withholding so much from you. I'll understand if you don't want to—'

'Hank, Ernie explained what happened to you as kids,' she cut in. 'He showed me his scars, too. So I understand why you made up so much about your childhood. I'll tell you this – seeing Ernie's scars made me want to kill that father of yours!'

A sense of climactic arrival made me look down at my watch. It was four minutes to eight on Thursday 12 July 2012. It was suddenly clear that I'd waited all my life for a woman to tell me she'd defend me and Ernie to the death.

'You'd have stood up for us?' I asked.

'Listen, Hank, I can't know exactly what I'd have done, but I sure as hell hope I would have had the courage to A) report your father to the police, and B) testify against him. And if that didn't work, to C) put him in his grave!'

That Ana spoke like an outline written with rage made me want to throw my arms around her.

'You know, I was up half the night figuring out how I'd do it,' she continued eagerly. 'It was that suicide you had the other day – with cyanide – that made me figure it out. When I remembered that, I knew how I'd get rid of your father.'

Hearing the unshakable determination in her voice, I felt the pleasant, dizzy disorientation you get when you hike above the tree line, up there with the unpredictable, feathery, high-flying thoughts you can't normally reach.

345

'Well, what do you think?' she asked.

'Cyanide tastes like bitter almonds. He'd have spit it out.'

'No way, I'd have put it in his rum!'

The back-and-forth intimacy between us was like a game of hide-and-seek, which was how I began to understand what I'd never put into words before: that my love for Ana was also a form of child's play.

'Maybe that would work,' I told her. 'But we'd have to get rid of the body, too – and without anyone seeing.'

'I'd let you and Ernie take care of that.'

'I guess we could haul it off to Black Canyon and toss it over the rim.'

I wasn't sure why I said that, but it seemed our best option.

'Listen, Hank,' she said, shifting tone, 'lots of things make sense now that never did before. But what I can't understand is why you'd think I wouldn't believe you?'

'The emergency room doctor who treated Ernie the first time Dad hurt him badly was certain that I was the one who'd cut off half of his ear.'

I'd waited more than thirty years to protest that unfairness. And yet I didn't scream or holler, as I always thought I would.

'How could any doctor think that?' she asked. 'You were only a kid yourself.'

'Because that's what my father told him. The doctor swore he'd put me in a juvenile prison if I hurt Ernie again. And you should have seen the way he looked at me – like I was dirt. So I could never risk telling anyone.'

'I don't see why one thing follows from another.'

'Because if I was in a juvenile prison or home, I wouldn't be able to protect my brother. Sooner or later, Dad would have killed him. Ernie and I both knew that. We wanted to tell people what was happening to us, but at the same time, we were terrified that someone would find out. Because we knew Dad would end up charming whoever we told. Waiting for bad things to happen is a killer, Ana – maybe

346

even more destructive than the bad things themselves. And keeping quiet was the hardest thing I ever did – that *we* ever did. And we got nothing for it. Nothing!'

I started hiccupping, but that didn't stop the rush of words spilling out of me: 'And then later, when Dad vanished, we didn't say anything about what he'd done to us, because the local police thought Ernie and I might have killed him. They separated us. That was really bad. They questioned me for seven straight hours. They probably still think I did it, for all I know. Ernie has worried about that every day for twenty-eight years. He still thinks I might get extradited and put in a Colorado jail.'

Ana told me then that she hated talking about such serious matters with me over the phone. 'I'll be right there. Don't go anywhere!'

As soon as she arrived, she emptied her backpack on my cot, and four sunset-coloured mangoes spilled out; I'd begged her the day before for tropical fruit. While I was turning one of the mangoes over in my hand, she sat next to me and said, 'What more do you need me to know about what happened to you as a kid?'

I was stunned that she'd asked such a perfect question, but I was also having second thoughts about telling her too much. 'Ana, I don't know where to begin.'

'You've dropped hints about how going to church was awful. Start there.'

'All the folks in town thought Dad was the ideal Christian father,' I told her. 'And in a way, he was. He led the congregation sometimes in hymns.'

'Was that important?' she asked in disbelief.

'It counted for a lot where we grew up. He had a great singing voice.'

I sang the opening lines of 'Soldiers of Christ Arise'. Without irony. As I'd sung it as a kid, when I'd done my best to believe in the invisible being everybody I knew seemed to worship.

'You're the one with the wonderful voice!' Ana said, laying her hand on top of my head as though to bless me.

Had Ernie told her there'd been a competition between me and my father over him?

'My voice is my father's,' I confessed.

'Is that why you never sing to me any more? I used to like that – being serenaded while you were scrubbing me in the tub.'

As though I'd landed in a place I'd never even imagined before, I realized that it was neither my fear of my father nor my contempt for him that kept me from singing to Ana.

'Love is more persistent than hate,' I told her. That seemed an amazing discovery to make.

'Does Gabriel . . . Does he love your father, too?' she asked hesitantly.

'No, I kept all the love,' I said. I didn't know how I knew that, but I did.

'Tell me about him,' Ana said, as if we'd finally reached our destination.

'You won't like what you hear.'

'Let me be the judge of that.'

Seeing the resolve in her eyes, I realized I'd under-estimated Ana for a very long time – maybe since we'd met.

I told her what I knew, mostly from back to front, building up speed in a kind of lunatic rush, like an LP that got switched to 78 RPM. But she didn't interrupt, even when I made no sense. I ended by telling her about the first time he'd come to me.

'I want to speak with him,' she told me when I'd finished.

I flinched as though she'd slapped me. And then backed far into a corner of myself.

She stood up and began tying her hair in a ponytail, as though readying for battle. She stared down at me urgently. 'I need to tell Gabriel something.'

'Bad idea,' I replied.

'Hank, I have to talk to him!' she repeated.

'No,' I said, because any encounter with him would make her think differently of me – as though I'd never been the man she thought I was.

'I went to the library and got a book about this,' she said. 'It seems that you might be able to bring G to you whenever you want. And Ernie told me that G always takes you over when you picture a lot of blood.'

'I can't permit you to meet him. Jesus, Ana, I hate the idea of it!'

'We've already met – and in our bedroom.'

I decided to win this argument by not responding.

'Hank, you have to do this for us. It's the only way forward.'

I counted the seconds passing. At seven, she said, 'If not for us, then for the sake of the kids.'

'It's not fair to bring the kids into this!' I snarled.

'You think I'm going to play fair when it comes to you!' She laughed caustically. 'If you think that, then you *are* crazy!'

'He'll be rude to you. He'll make fun of you.'

'Who cares? Hank, I can take care of myself – you know that. This is the way it has to be.'

We argued a bit longer, but I knew I'd already lost.

I pictured Jorge falling off his bicycle. Just a small accident, but he cut his knee and the gash bled all over my hands.

When I returned to myself, my eyes were awash with tears. I was out of breath, too, which made me realize that Gabriel had been talking to Ana, from our ranch, or somewhere else high up in the mountains.

Chapter 29

Ana told me that my body went limp. And that when I sat up, the dismissive, irritated look in my eyes wasn't one she recognized.

'You have any cigarettes?' Gabriel asked her.

To Ana, my Colorado accent seemed more pronounced than usual. And my voice was deeper. 'You're ... you're not Hank,' she said, and though she intended her words as a statement, it came out more like a question. She was seated in the white vinyl chair, trying to look casual. She felt distant from herself, as though she'd wandered into someone else's life.

'No, Hank's not home right now, honey,' G replied. 'Come back later. So do you have any cigarettes?'

'No, I'm sorry, I don't,' she replied.

'What good are you?' G asked, frowning.

'Not much, I guess.'

With her quick admission of uselessness, Ana was hoping for a smile from G, but he glared at her instead. 'You want me to be sorry about hurting you, but I'm not!'

'That no longer matters.'

'So what does?'

Ana sat forward and put her hands together. 'Hank matters.'

Gabriel looked her up and down and grinned. 'You've got nice-looking breasts.'

'Very thoughtful of you to let me know,' Ana replied.

'And your Argentinian accent is *muy hermoso*.' G winked.
'I bet Hank likes you talking dirty to him in bed.'

'Who wouldn't?' she shot back, pretending his talk of sex
didn't discomfort her. 'Though just for the record, what I do
in bed with Hank isn't any of your business,' she added.

G pounced on that. 'Everything that concerns Hank is my
business!'

Ana looked away, unable to find a reply. She began to
understand more about why I'd never told her about G. At
length, she said, 'Maybe we should start over.'

'Do us all a favour and don't try to be Aunt Olivia.'

'Look, I asked Hank to let you come to me because I
wanted to thank you. That's all.'

'Thank me, why?'

'For one thing, for defending Ernie all those years ago.'

'And now you want me to be all friendly and nice –
because you've thanked me. Look, honey, I'm not friendly.
That's Hank's department. And, by the way, what's the story
with the purple streak in your hair? Your fortieth birthday
hit you hard, didn't it?'

Ana turned away, intimidated by G's condescending stare.
Tears were rising inside her chest.

'Getting old isn't easy, is it?' Gabriel continued.

Ana felt that she had to win G to her side or she wouldn't
be able to say the other thing she needed to tell him. 'I wish
I'd been with you in Colorado,' she said, 'because I'd have
had Hank's father arrested.'

'On what charges?'

'Child abuse.'

'That seems unlikely. He'd have fooled you like he fooled
everyone. You'd have thought he was a charming guy. You'd
have sucked his cock any time he asked.'

'I don't think so.'

'You'd have hated Hank's mother, too – for not protecting
him and Ernie.'

'I don't want to judge her.'

351

'Oh, go ahead! What's life for, if not for judging people you don't understand!'

'Hank hardly ever talks about her. And Ernie never does.'

Gabriel took a gulp of breath and rubbed his hand over his cheek, suddenly seeming unsure of himself. 'The thing I regret most is not being able . . . to save her,' he whispered. 'I wish I'd known how to do that.' He made an ugly frown. 'I don't know why I'm telling you this. I must be crazy!'

Ana hoped he'd spoken to her of his failure because he, too, wanted them to be fighting on the same side. 'You saved Hank long enough for him to meet me and create Nati and Jorge in me,' she told him. 'Even if you never end up trusting me, I want you to know I'm more grateful to you than I think you could ever understand.'

When G reached his hand to his lips, she noticed it was shaking. He leaned his head on his hand and gazed away. He looked like Ernie to her – scanning a faraway horizon for signs of danger. His dejected, crooked posture gave her the impression that his strength was giving out.

When G finally faced Ana, he said, 'Bring me some dark chocolate. Leysieffer chocolate-covered coffee beans are my favourite.'

'I'll try to find them.'

He licked his lips like a cat. 'Smoking a cigarette after eating chocolate-covered coffee beans is the best thing I know.'

Ana sensed in his look of delight that something between them had shifted.

'You can't smoke in the hospital,' she told him. 'But you'll be out of here pretty soon.'

'Still, if you really want to thank me, smuggle me in a pack of Marlboros!'

'Don't take this the wrong way, but I think that's a bad idea – for Hank, I mean. It might . . . compromise his recovery.'

'His mistake was stopping smoking in the first place.'

That remark struck Ana as so heartfelt but politically incorrect that she laughed.

'I'm glad you find me entertaining,' G said in an amused tone.

Ana felt encouraged. 'Listen, I'll want Hank to start . . . talking with a therapist when he leaves the hospital,' she said.

'I'm afraid there ain't no cure for what he's got.'

'What's he got?'

'He loves a man he hates, and he hates a woman he loves.'

Ana thought that sounded just about right.

'He's irreversibly fucked,' G added. 'I mean, if you want my opinion.'

'I just want him to accept himself and . . . me. I want him to be the person he wants to be. Is that too much to ask?'

'Yeah, I think it probably is. Besides, I'm not going to go away.'

'I don't want you to.'

'Of course you do!'

'You've been a part of him since he was eight. I just want you to be kind to him right now. And me. We've been through a lot of late.'

'Who hasn't? And in any case, I don't know what *kind* means.'

'You'll figure it out. You're smart.'

It was Gabriel's turn to laugh.

'I'm glad you find me entertaining,' Ana told him.

When G grinned, his eyes took on a handsome depth that seemed to be mine as well. 'I can see why Hank picked you,' he said. 'Go ahead and give therapy a try. Tell Hank he has my blessing – as long as he doesn't try to get rid of me, that is.' He winked. 'I wouldn't like that one damn bit!'

Chapter 30

When Ana first recounted her conversation with G to me, she left out the part where she told him I'd need to see a therapist. After pressing a gentle kiss into my brow, she now said, 'I want you to start talking with someone professional.'

'Like a carpenter?' I asked, stalling.

She rolled her eyes. 'No, like a psychologist. You'll have a few months before you get back to work, so you might as well use them usefully. And seeing a therapist will get you out of the house at least once a week.'

'I'm not sure it's a good idea.'

'Hank, this isn't a request,' she said – but gently. 'I'll go with you at first, if it will help.'

'I don't want to jeopardize Gabriel's wellbeing. That wouldn't be fair.'

'I thought of that. But Gabriel says he doesn't mind you going.'

'You asked him?'

'Well, I figured it concerned him, too. Hank, I think he understands you can't live under the protection of lies any longer. It's way too much work. And you'll end up pushing me and the kids away for good. I'm guessing that sooner or later you'll figure that out, too.'

After Ana left for home to pick up the kids, and while I was thinking about how therapy might change me, Ernie showed up. He stayed in my doorway, however, his cowboy hat in his right hand, his left hand behind his back. He had a wily glint in his eyes.

'I hope you didn't bring me a reptile,' I said, because he'd once made Mom shriek by presenting her with a baby whip snake that he'd invited to lunch.

'No, no reptiles this time,' he said. 'But I got you these!' He took out a spindly bouquet of blue and red wildflowers.

His fingers were badly soiled, and I was reminded of how Ernie needed to spend part of every day in a kingdom ungoverned by men and women.

'Wow – beautiful!' I exclaimed 'Where'd you find them?'

'An abandoned lot just down the street from the hospital. Two old men were living there, in a makeshift hut, but they gave me permission to pick them.'

When he held them under my nose, I took a luxurious sniff.

'Ana just called me to say that things are good again between you,' he said in a pleased voice.

'Yeah, thanks for helping.'

After he'd hunted down a vase – blue glass – and put the flowers on my night table, and while he was washing his hands in the sink in my room, I gave him a rundown of all my misgivings about seeing a therapist. Saving the worst for last, I said, 'I'll never solve another case without Gabriel.'

'Who said he's got to disappear?'

'Ernie, any therapist I have is going to want to make me normal.'

He laughed. 'Hank, I hate to break this to you,' he said, still giggling, 'but you shouldn't hold out much hope of reaching the planet Normal. It's in a distant galaxy, and no one in our family has actually ever caught a glimpse of it.' He sat on the end of my bed and looked at me purposefully. 'My guess is that your therapist is going to want you to integrate G.'

'Jesus, Ernie, what the hell is that supposed to mean?' I asked.

355

He picked up one of my mangoes and gave it a squeeze. 'I'm not entirely sure, but Darth Vader used to talk about *integração* all the time. I think it's a way of accepting even the strangest things about yourself.'

When Ernie was in high school, we nicknamed his psychiatrist Darth Vader because he had a bass voice and absolutely no sense of humour.

'Look,' he said, as though I was being unnecessarily difficult, 'you just have to tell your therapist what you want and what you don't want.'

'Could I do that?'

'You're *supposed* to do that, you moron!'

While I was trying to figure out if he was telling me the truth, Luci called.

'Sorry, sir,' she told me, 'Coutinho's flash drive isn't where you said it would be.'

'It's not in my file of the robbery in Estoril?'

'No. I took everything out to check. I also looked through the other pending cases.'

'Shit!' I threw off my covers.

'Who could have taken it?' Luci asked.

'One of our dear colleagues!' I said angrily. 'Who else has access to my files?'

'Stealing evidence would get an officer fired, wouldn't it?' she asked.

'I'd have thought so – at least, until recently,' I said.

'This case has changed your mind?'

'If the cop were well connected, or important to someone in the government . . .' I let the rest of my implication go unspoken.

'Still, it has to be a cop willing to risk an internal investigation – maybe someone who wanted to hush up a bribe he took from Coutinho. Or that a good friend of his took. Or is my way of thinking crazy, sir?'

'No, it's not crazy. But the thing is, a cop could probably go on leading a pretty good life after a bribery charge, but it would ruin him forever if he were accused of statutory rape.'

356

'I don't understand, sir.'

'I think there might have been incriminating photos on the flash drive. Or, more to the point, whoever took it out of my files has been worried that that's what it contained.'

'What kind of incriminating photos?'

'Of Coutinho with young girls. And with friends of his. Maria Dias led me to believe he got off on looking at himself in a mirror while having sex. And when he was still married to her mother, she found an incriminating photo of him. I get the feeling he used his camera a lot.'

'So a colleague of ours is protecting Coutinho's reputation?'

'More likely he's protecting the reputation of someone who's still alive – someone who'd have to get out of the country in a hurry if the pictures were made public.'

'But you found only vacation photos on the flash drive, and a list of possible bribes.'

'I must have missed a hidden file. Damn it! I should have had Joaquim go through it. Though, like I said, it may be that whoever had it stolen isn't sure what's on it and wanted to play it safe.'

'So what do we do now, sir?'

I didn't reply. I was thinking about how Sottomayor had mentioned to me that Coutinho had made bank transfers from his wife's account. So it seemed possible that he might have also sent emails about his sexual escapades from her computer, as well – and just possibly with some damaging photos as attachments. Whoever received them might even have been in the photos – and been warned by Coutinho where to find his flash drive in an emergency.

I told Luci that I needed to speak to Susana Coutinho and would call her back. On the ninth ring, Morel picked up. He asked right away about my health, which touched me, but underneath everything I said to him about myself sat the heavy dread of knowing that I couldn't put off any longer telling him about Sandi being molested by her father. 'Have any of my colleagues called to tell you about the evidence we turned up on Sandi and her father?' I began.

'No, all we are told is that you are shot.'

When I gave him the news, he said in an incensed voice that Coutinho could never have hurt his daughter – and that it was unethical for me to denigrate such a good and caring father after his death.

'Our techs did the test twice to make sure the blood under Sandi's fingernails was her father's,' I replied. 'Sandi tried to fight him off at your house and failed. Coutinho raped his daughter at your house. And what happened there explains everything she did after Easter, too – why she chopped her hair off, why she started starving herself . . . It even explains why Coutinho was so keen on not separating from Susana.'

'If what you say is true, then she—'

'It is true!' I interrupted. 'And Sandi couldn't live with what had happened.'

I decided not to tell him that Sandi had been pregnant. The shock of that might set him against me, I thought. Or maybe I just hadn't the will to destroy the little that was left of the life he and Susana had tried to make together. When I asked him if he'd tell her about Sandi being molested, he said, 'I'll have to. Though I don't know if she'll understand what I'm saying.' He explained that Susana was still being tranquillized by her doctor.

'Do you think she might be able to talk with me for a minute?' I asked. 'I have a less disturbing subject I need to discuss with her.'

'She wouldn't make any sense at all,' he said morosely.

'Okay, just tell me if she owns a computer.'

'No, she hates them.'

'Does she have some kind of other device from which she sends emails? Or on which another person might have stored some files without her knowing it? An iPad, for instance.'

'No, she owns nothing like that.'

'I find it hard to believe she never uses a computer.'

'She uses Sandi's portable when she needs a computer.'

'Her laptop?'

'That's right.'

After hanging up, I asked Ernie to help me sit up, but as he guided my leg over the sheet, the pain made me shudder.

'I think you ought to just lie back,' my brother said.

'For fuck's sake, Ernie, just help me do what I need to do!'

Once I was seated on the edge of the bed, I called Luci back and told her to rush over to the evidence room used by our computer techs.

'Good news!' she told me on calling me back. 'Joaquim has Sandi's computer.'

She passed the phone to him. 'Listen, Monroe, I'm sorry I haven't had a chance to look through the girl's files yet, but with you out it didn't seem like a rush. The good news is I'm done with her dad's computer. But there was nothing I could find on it about bribes.'

'Do you have the girl's laptop with you now?'

'It's right in front of me.'

'Turn it on. I first want you to look for a file of photos. It's probably deeply hidden. To open it, you might even need a password.'

'What kind of photos am I looking for?' he asked.

'Old men with teenaged girls.'

'What are they doing in these photos?' he asked suspiciously.

'Everything you wouldn't want them to be doing.'

'You can't really think that a fourteen-year-old kept porn photos on her computer.'

'I think her father hid them there. Safest place in the world. No one would *ever* look on her laptop. No one would even suspect – not even Sandi.'

'It might take a while to locate them.'

'Joaquim, you need to find them right now. With me out of action, this case is going to get so fucking lost it will never be found again.'

'I'll do my best, though . . . oh, shit!'

'What's wrong?'

'Just a second . . .' After maybe a minute, Joaquim came

back on the line. 'We have a problem, Monroe. I need you to hang on a little while longer.'

As I counted the seconds passing, Joaquim let go with a string of curses. 'We're screwed!' he told me when he got back on the line. 'The hard disk must have crashed!'

'Just now?'

'No. Somebody must have crashed it on purpose sometime after it was brought here.'

'Are you sure it wasn't already blank when it reached you?'

'I'm positive. I opened it to take a quick look. And now everything is gone.'

'Is crashing a disk easy to do?'

'Monroe, everything on a computer is easy to do if you know how to do it!'

'Are you absolutely sure all the files are gone?'

'That's what I was checking. There's nothing left. Whoever did this fucked us good, Monroe.'

'Where did you keep the computer?'

'In my office.'

'Under lock and key?'

'No, in that cabinet I have – you've seen it.'

'Joaquim, have the laptop dusted for fingerprints – every last key – and then call me back with the results.'

Ana arrived with the kids a few minutes later. Jorge skipped over to me and showed me the drawing he'd made of a loose-limbed stick figure with blue scratches for eyes (me) inside a giant yellow square (the hospital), with pink pterodactyls guarding the roof (seagulls). I gave him kisses of praise and tried in vain to stop thinking about Sandi's laptop. He and Nati then set up the fold-up table covered with green felt that my in-laws had lent them. Ernie fetched more chairs. Once seated, my boys started on their jigsaw puzzle of the island of Manhattan as seen from space.

Watching them, I thought, *This is why I survived; this is what my life is about; this is what I will remember when I'm old.* And yet hopelessness pursued me all morning. Near noon, Joaquim called to tell me that the only fingerprints he'd discovered belonged to Sandi and her parents. From the position of her father's prints, it appeared that he had carried her laptop with him on more than one occasion.

'I'm really sorry, Monroe,' he said. 'I screwed up, didn't I?'

'It's not your fault. Whoever wanted to keep us from discovering the photos would have had his police accomplice smash any lock you'd used.'

Fonseca, Sudoku and Quintela visited late that afternoon. Ernie and Ana took the kids for a walk to give them a chance to talk with me. To divert us from my debilitated state, we ended up making fun of the politicians in our government.

My colleagues concentrated the full force of their ridicule on the deputy prime minister; the news had just come out that he'd earned his bachelor's degree in Political Science and International Relations at Lisbon's Lusófona University in only one year instead of the usual three. He'd taken only four courses instead of the usual thirty-six. University administrators – some of them friends and colleagues in his political party – gave him credit for 'life experience' in thirty-two classes.

We ended up making a list of life experiences and courses for which he'd been given equivalencies:

For eating Chinese food on two occasions at the Mandarim Restaurant in the Estoril Casino, he had received credit for Asian history and culture.

For seeing the DVD of Avatar *with his nephews, he'd passed both Game Theory and Computer Science.*

For driving to work at the National Assembly in his Mercedes CLS . . .

Stepping back from our banter for a moment, I realized I'd have preferred a minute of silence – from everyone in Portugal – as a form of protest against the kind of corruption and influence-peddling that had brought him to power. Or a candlelit march down the Avenida da Liberdade – a funeral ceremony for the small but hopeful democracy we'd thought that Portugal would one day become.

And I realized, too, that our filtering system was badly broken: instead of weeding out the most unscrupulous people, our political system allowed them to rise to the top.

Just before my colleagues left, I asked them to keep watch over Luci for me and let me know if she was having trouble with Romão. Once I was alone again, I began to wonder if the person who had had me shot was another of the provincial go-getters in fancy suits who now ran our country. And if he lived so high up that I'd never be able to bring him down.

That evening, after my family went home, a surprising guest appeared in my doorway. It was after visiting hours, almost nine p.m., but he told me that he'd been able to get past the 'guard dogs' at reception because he was good friends with the Director of Surgery, who often played golf with him and the head of the Bank of Portugal at the . . .

Sottomayor proved himself a terrible namedropper that evening, but I didn't mind. It seemed just one more of his aristocratic flourishes – the verbal equivalent of the red and yellow paisley cravat tied so elegantly around his neck.

He'd brought along an assortment of Godiva truffles the size of a Monopoly box. 'We should make sure to eat extra sugar and fat when we are feeling vulnerable,' he said, which was so opposite the advice I'd received from Ana and Ernie that I had a good laugh.

After opening the box, he tilted it to show me the impressive selection.

'Take one,' I encouraged.

'Dare I?' he asked, raising his eyebrows like a rogue.

When I nodded, he popped a dark one in his mouth. He chewed with a side-to-side motion, like a sheep. Feigning a swoon, he said, 'I lucked out, it's whisky-flavoured!'

He put the rest of the box on my night table and sat down

362

in the chair by my bed. He scratched his chin and shrugged as though lost for a purpose, so I told him that hospitals were a bore and that he was under no obligation to stay. To my surprise, he wagged a finger at me and said in a concerned tone, 'I absolutely insist that you be more careful with yourself! You gave us all quite a scare.'

It was comforting to hear his worry on my behalf, though I didn't entirely believe it. It was as though we both agreed to participate in a harmless little farce intended to make us feel that the world still valued consideration and good manners. A man who lived in the tower was being kind to one of the little people. No one could blame him for such an act of generosity, not even me.

'I'll do my best to stay away from bullets from now on,' I told him.

'And I don't want you going to the Cayman Islands or anywhere else that's far from home. I retract my offer to pay your airfare.'

'Duly noted.'

'How long are you going to be out of commission?'

'A few months. I'll need physical therapy after I leave – I'm told I may have a limp for quite some time, maybe forever. I've got muscle damage, and my anklebone may never be quite as reliable as it used to be.'

He grimaced. 'I find that there's an atmosphere of predatory violence on the streets of Lisbon these days,' he said. 'Have you been to the Rossio at night of late? The young men walking around there look as if they'd slit your throat for fifty cents.'

I told him that our most recent statistics indicated that our murder rate had fallen over the past year, and that he was probably reacting to the obsession of television news reporters with violent crime, but he waved off my recitation of the figures and told me, 'I have something more important to tell you. In fact, that's why I've come.'

Leaning back and crossing his legs, he told me about an operation he'd had for skin cancer in Zurich seven years earlier. On regaining consciousness after the procedure, he'd taken one look around at the sixteen vases of roses and chrysanthemums in his room – 'My rather-too-easily impressed eldest son had counted them for me!' – and realized he was stuck in a life he hated. 'The day I was discharged from the hospital,' he continued, 'I told my wife I wanted a divorce and I moved into my office. We'd been married twenty-eight years, Chief Inspector. And though these past seven years without her have been the happiest of my life, I know now that I needn't have bothered separating from her.'

He eyed me in a way that made it clear he wanted me to ask why, which – ever eager to please my visitors – I did. To my surprise, I found it pleasant and comforting to do what he wanted – like having a good role in an entertaining play.

'I needn't have bothered, because my darling wife had fallen out of love with me years earlier,' he said, 'and she didn't give a damn if I slept around. But people can be perverse animals, so when I asked for a divorce, she swore to me that she'd make my life a misery. She ended up taking me for quite a bit more than the half of everything she might have been entitled do. And she told all our friends that I'd abused her *emotionally*. I wasn't sure what that even meant, but our friends were. Many of them have never spoken to me again, and, additionally, I had to listen to the insufferable lectures of my two lamentably moralistic children. Still, her lies cost her badly,' he added, smiling mischievously, as though he were a little boy who'd got away with murder. 'I kept her in the courts for nearly four years. She ended up going through hell!'

My expression must have given away what I was thinking. Pointing his cane at me, he said, 'You'd have thought I was Colonel Gaddafi from the way she described me to the judge. It was shameful!' Lowering his cane, he took a calming breath and said in a contrite voice, 'Though you're quite right, I should have behaved more nobly. In any case, what I mean to say is, don't make any big decisions until you've been out of the hospital for at least a couple of months. Give yourself time. Relax. Forget about the important issues in life. Don't concern yourself with who's winning and who's losing in this sad little country of ours. There are obviously some very dangerous and violent men out there who don't mind hurting good police officers like you. So enjoy your kids. Fly to Madeira and work on your tan. Let your colleagues deal with the bad guys.'

'I'll try.'

'Good man!'

Before leaving, he patted my good shoulder, as though we were fighting in the same platoon and said, 'As long as your ding-dong still works, you'll be fine.'

For ding-dong, he used the word *pirilau*. It seemed a fatherly sort of comment. Or maybe that was only how I wanted to hear it.

'My ding-dong is just fine,' I told him, permitting myself a smile, 'but it may be the only part of me that is.'

He raised his arm and made a fist in that way the Portuguese do to indicate an erection and said, 'If you can make you and your wife happy two or three times a week, the rest is just icing on the cake.'

Chapter 31

The next morning, Friday, I woke up out of the covers, with my blanket on the floor, and my mouth tasting of chocolate. It was just after six a.m. While I struggled to find a position that would relieve the howling in my leg, I discovered that Ernie had already arrived. He was sitting in one of the two chairs in my room, a paperback open on his lap.

'When the hell did you get here?' I asked.

'A little while ago. I couldn't sleep.' He stood up and came to me, resting his hand on the top of my head. 'How's the pain today?'

'Maybe a little better.'

He frowned. 'I thought you weren't going to lie any longer.'

'To Ana. To you, I can say whatever comes easiest.'

He covered me with my blanket and dropped down next to me. 'If it helps, you can be as mean as you want,' he said, grinning like he does when he's sure he's being cute. 'You can yell and call me names. I won't mind.'

'That's a generous offer, Ernie, and maybe I'll take you up on it sometime. But don't you have to get back to your garden one of these days? The roses and azaleas must be worried about you.'

I wanted him to leave so that I could finally lose myself in tears; the steady and slow accumulation of physical pain – and my frustration at having key evidence vanish – had just become too much for me.

366

'Luisa is watering everything,' he said. 'I thought I told you that?'

Luisa was a neighbour – a retired schoolteacher.

'Ernie, don't tell Ana, but the pain is worse. And being stuck in here is killing me.'

'Wait here, I'll be right back!' he declared, and he rushed away.

Twenty minutes later, he led the physician in charge of my recovery into my room. Dr Amorim had failed to shave this morning and pouches of skin sagged under his eyes.

'A long night?' I asked.

'Dinner at my niece's house. She's about to get married. Seven courses, and the flan is still in my stomach. So what seems to be the trouble, Chief Inspector?'

After I told him, he said that my pains were normal under the circumstances but prescribed something stronger. A nurse brought the pills to me a few minutes later, and forty minutes after that, I lifted effortlessly out of my body and floated out through an imaginary window behind me. The warm wind swirling around me helped me rise high enough to have a breathtaking view over a city of red tile roofs and hidden gardens that seemed far more real and beautiful than the one I normally lived in.

Somewhere inside ourselves, we are always floating. That's what I concluded while sailing over the Belém Tower. *And if we were floating all the time, then maybe other things even less likely were also possible.*

That evening, when I told my wife and kids about what I'd learned, they laughed; I kept it a secret that I was absolutely serious, though I decided to share the truth with them after I was safe at home – as part of our celebration.

Ernie arrived the next morning at sunrise once again, this time with Jorge – in his Tweety Bird pyjamas – cradled in his arms. He woke me up when he stepped in.

367

'Sweet Pea made me promise to bring him along,' he whispered.

He eased my son into my chair, took the boy's favourite blue blanket out of the duffel bag he'd brought along and covered him tightly, making him look like an Egyptian mummy.

When Rosie poked her head out of the duffel bag, I jumped. She was preparing to bark so I pointed a threatening finger at her. 'Don't even think about it!' I told her.

'You can't bring a dog in here!' I whisper-screamed at my brother, though I was charmed to be part of a conspiracy involving a small dog, a seven-year-old kid and a cowboy. Ernie's orchestrated chaos was like being home again.

'Of course you can,' my brother told me, lifting Rosie out. 'Portugal,' he said, opening his arms as if to embrace the entire country, 'is where all rules are just suggestions!'

The dog wriggled and whined, so excited that her tail was slapping against Ernie's arm.

'What's going on over there?' the new man sharing my room called out from behind the curtain that separated us. He had introduced himself to me the evening before. His name was Duarte, and he was a plumber.

'Sorry,' I called back. 'My youngest son and my brother have arrived.'

'One of them sounds like a dog,' he noted.

'That would be my son. He's part poodle.'

The Portuguese generally didn't understand my humour but Duarte laughed hard, which energized me. And I was suddenly in the mood for comedy. Sensing that, Ernie held Rosie's forepaws and stood her on my bed like a circus dog. She danced around, straining to kiss me. I fended her off while imitating Frank Sinatra crooning 'I've Got You Under My Skin'.

Jorge squirmed out of his blanket, stood up, and zombie-walked over to me, leaning in for a kiss. He smelled of sleep and old leather. 'Have you been going to bed with your soccer ball again?' I asked.

He nodded and threw his arms around me.

Ernie let Rosie go, and she started licking us as if we'd been away for years, which made Jorge giggle and clamp his hands over his eyes, since he didn't like the dog kissing him there.

Later that day, while Ernie, Jorge and Nati were taking Rosie for a walk in the Estrela Garden, Luci arrived. Ana was sitting with me. After the introductions, Luci smiled at the two of us timidly and handed me a small white box. 'I made you some . . . some almond biscuits,' she stuttered, perhaps fearing that my wife might react badly to a friendly gesture from a pretty young colleague, which was why I munched down a biscuit right away and told her it was delicious.

'And they don't have any cholesterol,' Luci observed proudly.

'Do I look that fat?' I joked.

Instead of easing her discomfort, as I'd hoped, Luci flinched. 'Oh, no, that's not what I meant at all. I was just saying—'

'Luci, it's okay,' Ana cut in. 'I'm afraid you're going to have to learn not to pay too much attention to my husband's so-called humour.' She blew a kiss in my direction and added, 'Hank can sometimes be *too* adorable, if you know what I mean.'

Through such tender-hearted criticisms of me that day, my wife was able to start a friendship with Luci. After she went out for some decent coffee, my young colleague pulled up a chair close to my bed. When I asked her about the Coutinho case, she confirmed that Romão hadn't done anything about it since I'd been shot.

The despair that shook me seemed connected to my ongoing doubts about ever fully recovering the use of my leg and shoulder. I hadn't realized how much hope had still been in me until it was gone.

Sensing our conversation was dependent on her now, Luci pointed to the book on my night table, *Deaf People in Hitler's*

Europe. 'Maybe you should be reading something less depressing,' she said.

'I don't find it the least bit depressing,' I assured her.

'No?'

'Luci, did you know the Nazis started sterilizing deaf people in 1933, as soon as Hitler was elected? It was even forbidden for deaf Christians to use sign language in public with their deaf Jewish friends.'

'No, I didn't know. And you like reading books that make you upset and angry, sir?'

'Rage is an undervalued emotion, Luci. It has proved very useful to me on many occasions.' I might have added but didn't, *And I get the feeling that if I'm going to be able to keep this case from closing forever, I'm going to need all of it that I can muster.*

'Whenever I've needed rage, I'm afraid I didn't have enough,' Luci confided, and I was reminded of the depth hiding inside her. And of her willingness to be seen by me.

An hour later, while I was napping off my preoccupations about the case, a heavyset man in an oversized grey suit and rumpled, midnight blue tie – perfect for the small-town funeral director in an American sitcom – knocked on my door. Ana had returned a little while earlier. He introduced himself as Lourenço Brito and told us he was from the Personnel office at the Judiciary Police. He had the wheezing respiration and sweating brow of a man grinding his way towards a heart attack.

He sat with me and began a wordy explanation of official police policy with regard to officers injured in the line of duty. He tapped a pen against his knee the whole time. Given my pay cuts over the past two years, I interpreted that as a menacing sign.

'Have I been fired?' I interrupted.

'No, of course, not.'

'So I'll continue to get my salary for as long as I'm out?' I asked.

370

'The limit is ten years. And even after that, if you have a relapse of your health problems, you can get further benefits.'

'So what's the bad news you have for me?'

'There's no bad news,' he assured me. 'You'll be taken care of.'

He continued his explanations, and they sounded reasonable, but the moment he was gone, Ana said she'd bet me fifty euros that a notice would arrive in the mail – limiting my benefits – within a month.

I took the bet and we shook hands on it. '*Cop Shot Twice on Duty, Loses Benefits* would make a really bad headline,' I told her. 'They won't take the risk.'

'Hank, where have you been? Nobody in the government cares about bad publicity any more. That's all they get! They just add up figures, and if the sum is too high, they start erasing things – including people like you and me.' She showed me a hard look. 'I'll want the fifty euros in cash, if you don't mind!'

My final visitor that day was Chief Inspector Romão. He arrived in the late afternoon with a present for me of eucalyptus honey. He handed the jar to me stiffly, his head erect, wearing that invisible crown he struts around in. When we got down to serious talk, I told him why I thought whoever had had me shot wanted to keep me from investigating the Coutinho case. I made certain to purge emotion from my voice, since the way he leaned away from me in his chair was his way of reminding me he was uncomfortable around any displays of weakness. No more than five minutes into my explanation, he started looking at his watch, which rattled me badly. God only knows if I even once used the subjunctive correctly. He told me – as I'd expected – that Trigueiro's bank records didn't show any payments he might have received for the hit on me. Also, his phone log had turned up nothing suspicious. And he had no leads for whoever had broken into Coutinho's house. 'Things don't look good for us,' he concluded.

Us? His body language and manner told me my injuries had nothing to do with him. Realizing that Romão was already certain that we'd never find out more about who had ordered me shot, I moved on to Coutinho's illegal housing development on the Sado Estuary and asked him to follow up with Maria Teresa Sanderson. Before leaving, he shook my hand hard, as though to instil confidence in me. To keep our pretence alive, I assured him I'd send him a summary of my notes over the next few days.

At two in the morning, I awoke to the sound of footsteps crunching across ice. My heartbeat raced off, as though towards the exclamation point always waiting for me at the edge of my fears. I turned on the lights, but no one was there.

Lying back, a still, quiet, perfect sense of safety – of being safer than I'd ever been before – seeped through me like a warm liquid. I was alive. My life was real. And the soft voices of two women conversing in the hallway were the night's way of telling me that all was well.

I experienced feelings of quiet ecstasy on and off for the next two days, most often in the middle of the night, inhabiting the soft islands of noise in the warm reef around me.

On those two wondrous nights, I realized clearly that *loss* was the voice that the past had always used to get my attention. But I saw now that I might be able to change the way it spoke to me.

On the third afternoon, Ana sat on my bed and told me about a transsexual dancer in Berlin whom she'd interviewed on the phone that morning. Listening to her speak of the history of ballet – and other things I knew nothing about – was like being saved from a shipwreck. In such ways throughout my life I have learned that I prefer listening to talking.

When she finally grew silent, I said, 'Meeting you was the single most exciting thing that ever happened to me' – because I couldn't let any more time pass before telling her one of the things that unexpected joy had taught me.

She embraced me and kissed my hands, breathing in their scent with her eyes closed, as if they reminded her of moments long gone, which proved once again that she could be counted on to make the right moves even when I didn't have any idea what they were.

The next day – Wednesday 18 July, nine days after my operation, I was transferred to a private room with a window. The view was modest – of some down-on-their-luck apartment buildings and a grizzled café. But what a thrill to see the sky! I was eager to look in on all those strangers' lives, too, like Jimmy Stewart in *Rear Window*, but the tenants kept their blinds tightly closed.

'The selfish bastards never open them!' I complained to Ana that evening.

'Three hundred years of Peeping Toms in the service of the Inquisition and dictatorship have made the Portuguese just ever so slightly wary,' she reminded me.

She'd been peeling me a mango and put a first piece in my mouth. 'Where do you think we'll be in twenty years?' she asked me.

'If the kids are still here, we'll be in Portugal.'

'What if they've emigrated by then?' She showed me a sorrowful look. 'I don't like not being able to predict what's going to happen.' She snuggled close to me and leaned back. 'Uncertainty doesn't work for me.'

I realized then that it had cost her a lot to be so strong since I'd been shot. I rubbed her shoulders just like she liked, and after a while she closed her eyes, and I told her she could drift off if she wanted to, and she did.

To celebrate being able to see the outside world, I decided not to take any painkillers that day. It was while I was fighting the murderous throbbing in my leg that I had my first useful thought about the case in days – that Maria Dias's

373

mother might not have burned the compromising photograph of her husband with young girls. She might even have threatened him with it in order to make sure he never abused their daughter or anyone else ever again. That was, at least, what I would have done.

I reasoned that one of the men pictured in the photo might have remained friends with Coutinho after all these years – and could have been the person who'd had me shot. But even if that wasn't the case, obtaining the incriminating snapshot might enable me to identify some men who ought to have been locked away somewhere where they couldn't get at teenaged girls.

Senhora Dias was surprised to hear someone speaking Portuguese on the line, but after I identified myself, she told me that she already knew that her ex-husband had been murdered; Monsieur Morel had discovered her phone number and called her a few days before. When I told her that I'd questioned her daughter about a week earlier, she stuttered, 'But I . . . I thought you said you were in Lisbon?'

'That's right.'

'My daughter hasn't been in Lisbon all summer. She's been in Paris.'

'I understand that she might have told you that,' I replied. 'Maybe she even made you promise to say that to anyone who called. But I can assure you I was with her in her flat in Lisbon this summer.'

'Please don't argue with me, Inspector. Nothing you say or do will be able to convince me that I'm wrong about this.'

Her definitive tone led me to believe that insisting would indeed prove pointless. And it seemed a clever strategy; by sticking to this particular lie, she could effectively block most lines of questioning the police might try.

'Don't worry, senhora,' I told her. 'I don't want to arrest Maria. In any case, now that she's in France, she's safe. None of my colleagues has any idea of where she is or what she's done.'

'So why did you call? What do you want from me?'

374

'There's something important I need to know. Do you still have the photograph that Maria found of your former husband with two young girls and some other men? She found it in—'

'Look, I'm not going to talk to you about that or say another word to you about my daughter!' she cut in, and with such sudden, incontestable fury that I knew I had no chance of changing her mind.

That evening, I typed up my notes on my laptop and transferred them – along with all of Coutinho's vacation files – to a flash drive. Ana agreed to drop it off at headquarters.

The next morning, when I called the French High School, the assistant director retrieved his file on Maria Dias. He surprised me by informing me that she'd started teaching four years ago, not eight, as she'd told me, which probably meant that she'd come to Lisbon in pursuit of Coutinho, since he had moved to Lisbon at close to the same time. He also mentioned that she'd been a world-class archer and was training two senior girls for the national championships. Dias had told him that it was her father who'd taught her to use a bow and arrow.

It was then that I realized why Coutinho had called her Diana when she was a girl. She hadn't wanted me to know, but he must have chosen a pet name for her that was equal to her talent: Diana was the name of the Greek goddess of the hunt.

Chapter 32

I was allowed home on 22 July, twenty-one days ago, after nearly two weeks in the hospital. A walking cast had been put on my left ankle. I couldn't put any pressure on my foot, so I was completely dependent on crutches to get around.

Once I was back inside our flat, Ana helped me take off my right shoe and sock, and as I hobbled around, my bare foot began to read the familiar grain of our old parquet, translating what it discovered into a relief so deep that it might have been all the love I'd ever felt.

Ana put her hand in mine and led me from room to room like a girl showing a long-lost friend her secret hideaway.

After I'd gone to the bathroom to dry my eyes and wash my face, Nati helped me into my favourite nightshirt, and Jorge let me hold Francisco, and I hobbled back downstairs, leaning on my wife harder than I needed to because I needed her to know I trusted her to help me remake my life. I napped on and off all day on the floral-patterned couch in the laundry room, because across the street is a big old apartment house with a façade of blue tiles that reflect so much sunlight that we call it the Super-Nova. A house made of light is hard to come by, even in Lisbon, and it reminded me of all the nearly forgotten beauty that was waiting for me at home – patiently, never asking anything in return – all the time I was in the hospital: Ana's yellow pencils with their tooth marks, Jorge's and Nati's wicker hamper, my own down pillow . . .

On my second afternoon at home, Ernie decided to collect seeds at the Botanical Garden, and he took the kids with him because – out of the blue – Morel had called to ask if he and Susana Coutinho could join us for tea. When they rang our bell, Ana was still upstairs, changing out of her sweatpants and T-shirt. Susana stepped in first, as though she feared a false step might make the floor give way, her right hand ready to grab for a wall. She wore faded jeans and sandals, and a white peasant blouse that must have been a loan from her hippyish sister-in-law. She wore neither lipstick nor make-up. Her voice was raw and hesitant, her eyes washed-out and grey. From the way she fought to smile just before we kissed cheeks, I saw that she had not yet left her daughter's graveside. Did any of us have any right to ask her to be anywhere else?

She handed me a big pink box – a fruitcake from the bakery of the Versailles café. After thanking her, I searched for something to say that would be of some small help, but the best I could come up with was, 'While I was in the hospital, I thought about you and Sandi nearly all the time.'

She smiled at me again, but from the urgent appeal for help she showed Morel, who rushed up behind her to take her arm, I saw that I'd spoken a name aloud that she'd have preferred to hear only in her own head.

I'd seen no point in handing over the earrings that she'd given me to Inspector Romão, and I had them ready for her in a small envelope. Handing it to her, I said, 'You left these with me for safekeeping.'

On peering inside, Susana exclaimed, Oh, my goodness – I'd completely forgotten.' She poured the earrings onto her palm, then looked up at me worriedly, as if she just realized that she might have inadvertently offended me. 'I intended them as a gift,' she said.

'I know, and they're very beautiful, but you were under a lot of stress when you asked me to have them.'

She handed the earrings to Morel and took both my hands in hers, which seemed to change everything about the way I looked at her that day. And even the way I would soon see her in my dreams.

'I want you to have them more than ever,' she told me. Her eyes held mine, and it was as though she were telling me that we were not nearly as different as I might think. 'I owe you a gift for being so kind,' she added. 'And for risking your life.'

Thankfully, Ana came down the stairs and saved me from having to make a reply. After I introduced everyone, Susana held up the earrings. 'I intended your husband to give you these a few weeks ago, but he apparently believed I might change my mind.' She gave them to Ana. 'I really do want you to have them.'

My wife dangled them in the air. 'They're gorgeous!' she exclaimed. 'But they must cost a fortune. I'm sorry, I just can't accept them.'

She tried to hand them back but Susana waved away her effort. 'They were a gift to me and now I'm giving them to you.'

From her definitive tone, I realized her husband had given them to her.

'I think it would be rude not to accept them,' I told Ana, to avoid more heartache.

My wife leaned forward and kissed both of Susana's cheeks. On separating, Ana's eyes shone with admiration for our guest, which pleased me because it meant that we shared the same opinion.

While Ana showed Susana the view of the Tagus from the second floor of our duplex, I confirmed that Morel had told her that Coutinho had molested Sandi.

'I have no choice,' he said. 'The mystery of why Sandi kills herself becomes too much to bear. At least now she has an answer.' He reached out for my arm. 'Is there a place where we can talk in private?'

I led him to the encampment I'd made for myself in the laundry room.

'So Susana believes what I learned about her husband?' I asked.

'She knows it is true but she still denies it. It is a compromise she makes to continue living.' From the Gallic puffing sound he made with his lips, I believed he intended for me to understand that he, too, had chosen to make a compromise, and I had the feeling it was this: to live as though he could never have figured out that his god-daughter was being repeatedly molested.

'Now tell me what you learn,' he said urgently.

I explained about Maria Dias – and about my conversations with her and her mother.

'Where is Maria now?' he asked.

'Back in France,' I said, and then I told a lie: 'Before I could arrest her, she fled the city.'

Morel stood up and went to the window. His eyes looked sad and defeated. Lighting a cigarette with anxious hands, he drew in the smoke as if his will to go on depended on it. It was then that I should have told him that Sandi had been pregnant, but I feared now that Susana might take her own life if she knew.

'Do you mind telling me what you know about Pierre, Maria's brother?' I asked instead.

'Pierre? After the divorce, he quits school. He starts taking drugs, loses contact with his mother and sister . . . He has trouble with the police. Maybe he is still in prison. Or perhaps he is dead. I must say I do not understand it at the time – this self-destructive behaviour of his.'

'But you understand it now?'

Morel smoked thoughtfully. 'If he finds out what is happening to his sister . . . If she needs him to defend her and he is not there . . . Yes, Monroe, I understand it *very* well.'

'What will you and Susana do now?' I asked.

'We go to France. When her doctor is happy with her progress. There is only death for us here.'

The next morning, Ernie announced that he and Rosie were heading back to the Villa Ernesto. He hadn't wanted to tell me the day before because it might have kept me up all night. Ana prevailed upon Jorge to help her dry the breakfast dishes so I could say goodbye to my brother alone. Panic was squeezing hard on my gut, and I ended up accompanying him outside to give us a few more minutes together. I put on the black cowboy hat he'd found for me at a shop on the Rua da Rosa and grabbed my crutches. We walked to his car as though to a graveside, which I hated, but the short time left to us gave us no other option. Rosie trotted behind us, her tail drumming, sniffing at the world of wonders hiding in our Lisbon sidewalks.

After Ernie was buckled up in his seat, he removed his surgical gloves and took my shoulder. Rosie had flopped down in the passenger seat. 'You'll be okay, Rico,' he said.

I grabbed his hand and kneaded it, imagining him as the little boy he'd been. After a few seconds, he tried to take it back but I didn't let him; I'd decided that if I never let him go, nothing bad could ever happen to either of us.

'You sure are a handsome critter in that hat, Rico!' he told me, giving a low whistle. 'Who bought it for you?'

'You did,' I said.

He smiled with exaggerated pride, doing his best to lighten our mood. He seemed the older brother at that moment, leading us both away from despair, but the best I could give him to repay his effort was a glum little nod.

'You might even have ended up as a star of big-budget Westerns if you'd gone to Hollywood,' he said.

My breaths were hesitant and shallow, because I wanted so badly to say the right thing – the incantation that would make him feel free of me, unburdened by my love. 'We could still go,' I told him.

'The hat is black – you'd have to be the villain,' he pointed out.

'No problem, they get all the best lines anyway.'

Even the silliest of conversations must sometimes be able to reveal what is hidden from your conscious mind, because I knew then what I had to tell him. 'I want to see Mom's grave again. I need your nephews to see it too.' I pressed Ernie's hand over my chest so he could feel all the urgency in me. 'Maybe I'll want to bring her body back to Portugal. We can decide that later. But I have to stand by Mom one more time now that I know what I know. I have to, Ernie.'

'What do you know?'

'She didn't leave us alone with Dad on purpose. She couldn't help herself – she was too depressed to do anything else. She'd have stayed with us if she could have. You see, I have to tell her I forgive her.'

He looked down. To keep from making him feel pressured, I looked up. Somewhere in the middle – conspiring together to understand how forgiving Mom might change us – were our speculations about the future.

He was unable to reply, so I leaned in through the window and kissed him on the lips. Would I ever fully understand how we'd become men? Would he? Maybe there were mysteries you didn't really ever want to solve because solving them would make the past seem so much less unique. And we all have the right to regard our own life as singular and special, if nothing else.

Have any two boys ever journeyed further beyond the landscape that destiny originally planned for them? That's what I was thinking as I released his hand.

When he took off the parking brake, I tapped the door to get his attention and told him to wipe his eyes so he could see any wild animals that might try to cross the road, and he said: *What kind of wild animals?*, and I said: *I don't know, but it would be nice to have some coyotes in Lisbon*, and he did what I said and wiped away his tears with his thumbs, because he was my younger brother even if he behaved more maturely

381

than I did, and then his big, rusty Chevrolet started away, and pretty soon it was grinding down the street towards the river, and Rosie had jumped into the back seat and was staring at me longingly through the window, and I wanted to tell my brother that his silencer needed fixing, and I almost shouted it, but I didn't want to cause him to crash, so instead I just kept watching him and Rosie leaving me behind until long after they were out of sight, because what other choice did I have?

The next day, my fourth at home, at three in the afternoon, Nati woke me from one of my floating dreams. I reached out for his hand because gravity had no power over me when I took a full dose of painkillers.

'I've got something serious to tell you, Dad,' he said.

I yawned and started kissing each of his fingers, since I was too far away to care that I was embarrassing him.

'Dad, listen to me!' he interrupted, tugging back his hand. 'This is really important.'

'I'm listening,' I said, but I closed my eyes again because weightlessness was too beautiful an experience to give up so easily.

'Remember that CD by Florence + the Machine?' he asked. 'The one that belonged to the girl who committed suicide?'

'Of course, I remember,' I said, but I wasn't following his words; I was lifting high above our apartment, and my son was just a voice.

'Dad! Dad, wake up!' He glared at me.

'I'm here,' I said. Sitting up, I stretched my arms over my head in an attempt to return to him. 'Stop making faces and get me some water.'

Nati fetched me a big glass. I gulped down half. 'Okay, now I'm back in the world,' I told him. And I nearly was.

'I thought you said you listened to the CD by Florence + the Machine,' he said.

'I did. I wanted to study the lyrics, so I looked them up on the Internet and then watched the videos. I watched the one for "Dog Days" three times, I think.'

'So you never actually listened to the CD itself?'

'No.'

'That's what I thought. Come with me into the living room. You need to know what's on it.'

I held out my arms to him. Pulling hard, he managed to get me to my feet. While fighting the dizziness, I bent over. On standing back up, I realized what should have been obvious; I'd failed to turn over Sandi's CD as evidence. And somehow, Nati had got hold of it.

'Where did you get the CD?' I asked as a wave of guilt washed over me.

'Uncle Ernie gave it to me.'

I picked up my crutches. 'And where did he get it?'

'He said that after you were shot, when you passed out on the street, he found it in your pocket. He took it for safekeeping.'

'And he gave it to you?'

'Yeah, he asked me where he should put it, and I told him I'd keep it safe for you till you got home. Only I . . .' He grimaced, as if he might be in big trouble. 'I put it on my bookshelf and I meant to give it to you, but I forgot about it till just a little while ago. I'm really sorry.'

'It's all right. What with everything that's happened, I—'

'Dad, it's not *Lungs*,' Nati interrupted.

'What's not *Lungs*?'

'What the girl left you – the CD.'

'What are you saying?'

'It's not *Lungs*! It's something else. Dad, you need to see what she wanted you to find.'

Once we were in the living room, Nati picked up the remote for the DVD, opened the drawer and placed the disc inside.

'No, you'll damage it!' I hollered.

'It's all right. I've already checked.'

He handed me the controls, then stepped into the kitchen.

'Don't you want to see it?' I asked.

'I watched a minute or so by accident. That was more than enough.'

The DVD is forty-seven minutes in length, but I've watched only about twenty-five minutes of it. I don't want any more of it in my head.

Four men are filmed with two girls. One of the girls is Sandi. She's lithe and slender, with a fawn-like, hesitant grace. She hasn't yet chopped off her hair.

The other girl is flat-chested and slim. She looks younger than Sandi. I'd guess she is twelve or thirteen – at the final edge of childhood. She has long black hair and a bronze complexion, a touch of the Brazilian rainforest in her eyes. I called her Girl Number Two at first, but Ana told me angrily that she deserved a name. We call her Mariana now.

One of the men is Pedro Coutinho. Another is Sottomayor. The other two have been identified by Morel as Coutinho's Parisian notary, Gilles Laplage, and a Venezuelan sugar exporter now living in Rio de Janeiro named Sebastian Forester. Morel told me he is an old friend of Pedro's.

When Morel came over to watch the DVD, he told me it was filmed at the flat Forester keeps in Lisbon. He had been there once for dinner and recognized the gilded furniture and Louis XVI wall mirror. The flat is a penthouse suite in one of the big monolithic eyesores that line the Avenida Estados Unidos da América. I discovered a week ago that Sottomayor lives one floor below him.

Susana Coutinho doesn't know of the existence of the DVD. 'You can be sure she will take an overdose of pills, like Sandi, five minutes after seeing it,' Morel told me in the resigned voice of a man who has learned way too many lessons about grief over the last few months. He came to our apartment two weeks ago and watched the film, his head in his hands, chain-smoking, until he jumped up at minute thirteen and told us he refused to see any more.

It's up to the viewer to guess how many times Coutinho has molested his daughter before making this film, but you can be sure it happened often enough to convince her that there was no point in resisting. Apparently, taking her virginity did not prove to be enough for him, as he must have first led her to believe. Or maybe Sandi told her best friends that because it was her last hope.

At seventeen minutes and forty-three seconds into the DVD, shortly after Coutinho has finished violating Sandi, and while he is kissing the back of her neck, she turns to the camera. Her eyes are vacant – all but dead.

Sandi looks at you and me and anyone else who is watching. Does she realize that some of the men who will end up watching her on this DVD will find her absent and anaesthetized submission to her father exciting?

The first time I saw 17:43, with shame slicing through me, I hopped across the room without my crutches and smacked the off button on the DVD player. I took out the disc and gripped it in my hand. I wanted to snap it in two – to crush it until my hand bled.

I might have really done that, but I needed to get to a bathroom quick. Ana sat on the rim of the bathtub while I got everything out of me and then helped clean me up.

Sandi looking at the camera makes everything so much more cruel. Being filmed at the worst moment of your life shouldn't happen to anyone, least of all to a young girl.

17:43 is the worst thing I've ever seen.

After Sandi looks at whoever will one day view this DVD, the camera changes angles, and for the next twenty-one minutes and four seconds, according to Ana, who has timed the filming, Forester and Laplage force themselves on Mariana.

The last eleven minutes and seven seconds show Sottomayor having his way with Sandi. Holding his duck-headed cane, bracing it behind the girl's head, he pulls her toward him and smiles at the camera. It is the mischievous smile of a boy who knows he is getting away with murder.

Or, in this case, who thinks he has.

It was that smile that told me the truth.

'Forget about the important issues in life. Don't concern yourself with who's winning and who's losing in this sad little country of ours. There are obviously some very dangerous and violent men out there who don't mind hurting good police officers like you. So enjoy your kids. Fly to Madeira and work on your tan. Let your colleagues deal with the bad guys.'

He'd been hoping I'd let the case drop, and warning me for later recall – in the event that I learned about his preference for young girls – that he was at the very top of the list of violent men who considered me expendable. And before this last warning, he'd been trying to get me sidetracked on the bribes Coutinho paid.

He'd pretended to be gay to win my trust – and because it must have amused him to fool me so completely.

When I explained what I'd figured out to Ana, she said she was only astonished that he hadn't poisoned the Godiva chocolates he'd given me. But he hadn't needed to do that, of course; he'd achieved exactly what he'd wanted with the two bullets he'd paid for.

Chapter 33

After locking the DVD in the drawer where I kept my handguns, I realized I was not nearly as brave a man as I thought. Or perhaps I'd lost the last of my innocence and credulity; I no longer had any doubts that the men who ran Portugal – and their well-placed friends in other parts of the world – would kill me in order to avoid having to answer for their crimes. Having to hobble around my house – and maybe limp through the rest of my life – was proof of that. Falling a thousand feet to the cobblestones of Lisbon or Porto – or Shanghai or London – was the last thing any of them would permit to happen. They would much rather that I took that fall for them.

Or you. Remember that, even if you remember nothing else.

Ana told me that she realized as well as I did that Sottomayor was a dangerous man, but that I had to bring the DVD to the State Prosecutor's Office. 'We have to try to protect other girls like Sandi and Mariana,' she insisted.

She didn't realize that we no longer had that option. 'They might put two bullets in you next – or in one of the kids,' I told her.

Just voicing such a possibility made my legs go weak and the world start spinning around me. I sat down on our sofa and bent my head between my legs.

'Look, Hank,' Ana said, 'we can't live in fear. Once you start to do that, then you—'

387

'Why did your parents flee the dictatorship in Argentina?' I interrupted.

She bit her lip and turned away from my challenging gaze. She didn't reply to my question because we both knew they'd emigrated because her uncle Javier – her mother's older brother – had been arrested by the police for leading a student protest and murdered. His skull was found twelve years later in a mass grave in the garden of a shoe factory outside Buenos Aires. He was identified using dental records.

When I started hiccupping, Ana fetched me a glass of orange juice. After I'd gulped it down, I told her, 'This goes way to the top.'

'What are you saying?'

'The DVDs stolen from Coutinho's house must show some high-flyers with girls like Sandi – ministers, ambassadors, corporation presidents ... They won't let anything about what they're really like become public. They had to have the house robbed – before Susana Coutinho or someone else found the filmed evidence of what they've been doing.'

'All right, so what are we going to do?' she asked.

'Ana, I think we're going to have to forget what we've seen.'

I took enough painkillers that evening to set me soaring up the coast of Portugal all the way to Santiago de Compostela, but at dawn I found myself sprawled like a drunk on a bench in Santa Marinha Square. My crutches had been tossed in the children's playground. On my left hand, G had written: H – *While dying with you on a Lisbon sidewalk, I watched the city vanish. It took less time than you'd think for all those crumbling old buildings to disappear. The last thing to go was the river.* On my right hand, he'd added, *The river had embraced the shoreline for thousands of centuries, and it just wouldn't let go! H – I don't know what to do now. Am I real? Are you?*

388

After hobbling home, I scrubbed the ink off my hands and hid my police notebook in the set of silverware that Ana had inherited from her grandmother. Tiptoeing into Nati's room, I woke him up and told him never to tell any of his friends about the DVD.

'I wouldn't do that,' he assured me.

I stood up and went to the window to make sure no one was watching us. Returning to my son, I pressed my hand to his chest. 'You can't even mention it.'

'I won't.'

I was too jittery to eat breakfast. After the kids had wolfed down their cereal, I locked myself in the laundry room so I could think things out. To keep from panicking further, I told myself: *Don't do anything more for now. You have time.* I ended up getting out my laptop and listening to the YouTube video of 'Dog Days Are Over'. I sang the song to myself until I had the melody and lyrics memorized. I needed it to be a part of me.

When our doorbell rang, I discovered Luci on our landing. She'd brought along a fold-up bicycle – silver, with a basket in front. The relief of seeing her made me want to kiss her, but I didn't want to embarrass her.

Jorge ran in from the kitchen and cornered Luci before I could stop him. 'Hey, is that for me?' he asked.

'No, sorry, it's for your father,' Luci told him.

I tugged Jorge a few steps back from our visitor, then asked her to come in. Once we'd entered the living room, I held my son's shoulders to keep him from getting out of control and asked her if it was really for me.

'Yeah, I was told it would be good for helping you get back the muscle tone in your leg.'

'I want a bicycle, too!' Jorge whined, looking up at me with enough hope in his big dark eyes to immediately defeat all my arguments against the purchase.

'If you leave me and Luci alone for half an hour,' I told him, 'then I'll buy you one on my first trip out of the house.'

He jumped up and down, then punched me in the belly to reinforce his point. 'You promise?'

'I promise.'

Once Nati had managed to lure Jorge out of the room, I told Luci she shouldn't have purchased me an expensive gift.

'It's okay, I got a good discount,' she replied. She smiled with the pleasure of being able to help a friend, but a shadow seemed to fall over her face when I asked her to come into the kitchen and talk with me about the Coutinho case. I'd decided by then to ask her not to discuss our investigation with anyone.

Once I had her seated at our kitchen table, I asked her what was wrong.

She reached into the pocket of her jeans and pulled out a slender black chip – only a little bigger than a SIM card. She handed it to me.

'What is it?'

'A bugging device. It was found taped to your desk – under the rim. We've already checked for fingerprints but there's nothing on it.'

I knew right away who'd put it there. 'Sottomayor wore leather driving gloves the day he came to see me,' I said. 'And I – stupidly – figured it was just another of his affectations.'

'So what do we do, sir?'

'Is it in working order? Can it still send out a signal?' I figured that Romão might be able to trace it back to the people who'd been listening in on my conversations.

'It stopped working a while ago,' Luci said. 'The techs told us it was only meant to last a few days.'

'Did they have any ideas about what we should do?'

'No, they said it's homemade, so there's not even a manufacturer we can contact.'

While working this new discovery into my list of grievances against Sottomayor and his buddies, Luci shocked me with a question I hadn't let myself ask: 'Sir, do you think it's possible that Chief Inspector Romão might not be interested in finding out who had you shot?'

'At this point, Luci, I think anything is possible.'

She looked as if I'd informed her of a death in her family, so I added, 'Listen, I don't want you to talk about me or Coutinho or this case with anyone. Not even with your husband.'

'Did you find out something I should know?'

'Just that Sottomayor isn't as innocent as he's made himself out to be,' I told her.

'Has he threatened you?'

'No, nothing like that,' I lied. 'In any case, it's better for you not to know too much about him.'

'He's the one who had you shot, isn't he?'

Had something in my tone of voice given away the truth? 'Luci, I'll be very angry with you if you ask any more questions!' I told her, trying to sound fatherly and gruff.

'What were we getting too close to, sir?' she asked.

'Luci!'

'I've a right to know.'

'We may never know for sure,' I said. 'The important thing is that you have to keep quiet about anything you suspect. We can't risk you ending up like me.'

'I don't like this at all. It's not why I joined the police.'

'Look, there'll be plenty more cases where you can try to be Dr Watson,' I told her, trying to make our current dilemma sound insignificant. 'For now, just do what Romão tells you, and if anyone asks you about me being shot, or about Coutinho, tell them that you've had way too much work lately to think about all that.'

Eyeing me as if this were life and death, she said, 'All right, but when you're back to work, I want to be reassigned to you. I won't work with anyone else!'

My sense of failure eased somewhat after I convinced Luci of the need to keep quiet – at least I'd succeeded in protecting her. I was able to eat some dinner with my family and even help Jorge draw houses in his sketchbook. When Ernie called, I gabbed with him about his heat-dazed pear and apple trees.

At about ten o'clock, I started to feel the skin sensitivity on my arms that usually indicates I'm about to get a cold. I took two aspirin right away and went to bed, but I awakened at three a.m. with my forehead burning and a fever of 101.4. My throat was sore and my nose was stuffed. I didn't want to bother Ana, and managed to fall back to sleep after a while, but she woke up when I started coughing. She put a cold compress on my forehead and made me take two more aspirin. I wanted to embrace her – I needed her affection to get me through this – but I also didn't want to give her what I had.

When I fell back to sleep, I dreamed that Gabriel came to me at Black Canyon. His long unruly hair had greyed. And his slender, timeworn face was deeply creased with wrinkles. He looked to be in his late sixties. I could see him and hear him as well as I could see and hear Ana and my kids.

Was it a dream, or had the fever taken me to a twilight state where I was able to speak with my other half for the first time?

I know most of what G and I said to each other because – as soon as I came to myself – I wrote down what I remembered of our conversation on the inside front cover of *Deaf People in Hitler's Europe.*

'You've aged,' I told him. It seemed unfair and sad.

'So have you, partner!' he shot back, laughing.

We sat together on the canyon's rim. Above us were cottony white clouds floating in formation towards the eastern horizon. Two thousand feet below us was a jagged, dun-coloured snake: the Gunnison River. We talked for a time about the landscape. It seemed to be his way of making me comfortable being around him. And then he said, 'I didn't like nearly dying.'

'No, neither did I,' I told him.

He apologized for not protecting me, and I told him it wasn't his fault. His frown indicated that he didn't agree. 'Anyway, the thing is, nearly being dead taught me something,' he told me in a confessional tone.

'What was that?'

'That all this might vanish.'

When I asked him if he meant Colorado, he unfurled his hand to indicate the land and the sky and even the river far below. 'Colorado and Portugal and everything else,' he said. 'I wrote you about it. I saw Lisbon vanish – building by building. Every street faded to nothing, and there wasn't a damn thing I could do about it. It was crazy. And upsetting. It took me a while to figure out what it meant.'

'What did it mean?'

He patted my leg. 'It's like this, kid – I'm not built like you. I can't just do nothing and let everything I've worked for disappear.'

'Is that really what's at stake?' I asked sceptically; I thought he was exaggerating.

'Either we win or they do – like Cowboys and Indians all over again. And you and me and Ernie . . . we're the Indians!'

'It's not that simple,' I observed.

'Doing the right thing seems pretty simple to me.'

'Look, I can't risk losing my kids or Ana. You're going to have to forget about bringing Sottomayor and his friends to justice.'

He looked east, towards the rising sun. Mountain sunlight was pouring over us, golden and warm.

'I thought I lost my shadow when we were shot,' he said. 'It's scared me badly.'

'Yeah, you told me, but it's right behind you now,' I said, pointing.

He turned around. The shadow cast by him was long and slender, and edged with a faint reddish glow. It seemed less stark and sure than it would have been in real life.

'Oh, that little thing,' he said. 'That's not what I mean, at all.'

'Then what do you mean?'

'If you think you can live without me, then you figure it out!'

'Why can't you talk more clearly?'

'Because I don't want to!' he shouted.

The enraged, defiant way he looked at me terrified me – but also made me understand what he meant.

'You thought I was already dead, didn't you?' I said.

'Yeah, and I panicked.'

'All the more reason why both of us have to be a lot more careful now,' I told him.

'All right, then which way do I walk, east or west?'

'I don't know.'

'You have to choose for me. You're the one who sets the rules around here, kiddo, even if you don't think so.'

East is where Portugal is, I thought. But I didn't want him to join me there, because he might put my family in danger. 'West,' I told him.

'You were always the sensible one,' he replied.

The disappointed smile he showed me seemed to mean that this might be the last time we'd ever see each other.

'Give my best to Ana,' he said.

And then I woke up.

My fever grew worse over the course of that morning. By lunchtime, I was too weak to leave my bed, and I discovered that I couldn't keep down any solid food. My father-in-law, Esteban, was a radiologist, and he came over to examine me later that afternoon. He assured me that my wounds were healing fine and hadn't become infected. '*Parece que apanhaste uma gripe, filho,*' he said, shrugging. *Looks like you caught the flu, son.*

I was worried my kids would get it next and didn't let them into my bedroom over the rest of that day. Jorge sat with his toy giraffe on the floor just outside my doorway reading his Dr Seuss books. When he grew bored, I had him fetch his sketchbook and suggested he do my portrait. I ended up looking like a frazzled blue bird in a nest made of tissues and newspapers.

I got no word from Gabriel that day. Maybe he would walk west forever.

In bed that evening, while wondering if I could make a life without him, I remembered Sandi as she'd been on the day I'd questioned her. It occurred to me then that she might have reacted so badly to menstruating for the first time because she had already sensed that her father had a special fondness for pubescent girls. And maybe she herself had been the figure in her nightmares who entered her house and hurt her parents. Her dreams were a warning for her to keep quiet. Like me and Ernie, Sandi had figured out that if she ever told the truth, and managed to convince anyone of how she was being abused, she'd put her father in prison and destroy her family.

By the next morning, I was feeling well enough to sit up in bed and eat some toast with jam. It was Saturday 28 July. Ana needed to work that afternoon. She left the apartment around 11.30 a.m., after having made me alphabet soup for lunch. I still wouldn't let my kids get too close to me, which started Jorge crying, so I had to pick him up in the end to calm him down. We sat together on our sofa for a good part of the day, watching the Olympics on television. We saw mostly the swimming and cycling, but towards evening we also caught the synchronized diving competition. The mirror-image oddity of the two divers twisting and rolling through the air seemed silly at first, and a bit pointless, but the more we watched, the more it seemed like a true art – like the human need for kinship and solidarity given form.

I slept nearly ten hours that night and woke at just after nine a.m. – alone in bed – with a message in my left hand:

H – Forgive me for walking east. I had no choice. In my right hand, he'd written a name: *Jean Morel.*

I knew immediately what G was proposing. I threw off my covers and got to my feet.

I called Joaquim at home because it was Sunday. He agreed right away to help me. I still had a low fever and Ana was in favour of me staying home, but when I told her I'd take a taxi if I had to, she agreed to drive me there. Joaquim made me a copy of the DVD that Sandi had left me and agreed not to ever tell anyone.

I next called Morel and asked him to come over and see it.

That was the day Morel identified the two men who'd participated in the filming – along with Coutinho and Sottomayor – as Gilles Laplage and Sebastian Forester. After he'd watched the first twelve minutes of the film, he refused to see more, but I insisted he take a look at minute seventeen.

Morel agreed to my plan after seeing 17:43, but made me promise never to tell Susana about the existence of the film. Since he spoke almost no Portuguese, I dictated a note for him to hand to the prosecutors, explaining how he'd found the DVD in Coutinho's library and a summary of what was on it. Knowing that Coutinho must have kept his pornography hidden inside classical music CDs in his locked cabinet, I also had him write that we'd found the DVD in question in Pascal Rogé's recording of Debussy's preludes, since Ana owned that CD and had agreed to donate the cover and liner notes to our cause. Morel drove Susana's car to the Prosecutor's Office.

I was sure that anyone who read the text I dictated would believe Morel's story; no one would suspect I'd found the DVD and given it to him. My family and I would be safe from reprisals.

Morel and I spoke that evening. He'd given the film and our note to Bruno Cerveira, the government prosecutor assigned to the case.

Two days passed without word from Cerveira, but I was mostly over the flu and feeling confident, as though G and I had struck an important blow in a war that most people didn't even know was being fought. And as though I'd returned from a trip that took me so away from myself that I'd needed Gabriel's help to return.

On my third day of waiting for a reply from Cerveira, a physical therapist assigned to me by the Judicial Police came to my apartment for our first session. His name was Pavlo and he looked to be about thirty. He was from Kiev and had lived in Portugal since 2004. His thick black hair, parted in the middle, formed wings over his ears, giving him the slightly comic but highly romantic look of a Hollywood heartthrob in a silent movie. From the way Jorge stared at him, open-mouthed, squirming as though he needed to pee, I became convinced that my son had been pierced by Cupid's arrow for the first time. He dashed off awkwardly to his bedroom, tripping over himself, which gave me the idea that he might even have sprouted an erection.

I surprised myself by not being the least bit upset. Instead, I was filled with amused admiration for the little demon.

Under Pavlo's guidance, I was soon able to get around on my crutches much better. He became more concerned about my shoulder than my leg because the muscles had stiffened badly, and I could no longer lift my arm over my head. He went over a series of stretching exercises with me that I was to do twice a day.

It cheered me up to be given orders by a young man who seemed to regard me as a worthy human being simply because I was older and more experienced than him.

That night in bed, when Ana and I got to talking about Pavlo, I found myself telling her that I thought that Jorge might be gay. The dramatic tone I blundered into – fearing that she might be disappointed in our son or upset – made her snort. 'You can't really think that what Jorge might do in bed would bother me,' she said.

'I thought that his being our son might make it different.'

She kissed my brow as if I were her third child – and the one most needing her guidance at the moment. 'You love him so much that you worry too much. He's going to be okay.'

'He might not have it easy,' I insisted. 'There's still a lot of prejudice.'

'He's stronger than people think. He's a tough little guy.'

'How long have you suspected?'

'For a couple of years.' She gave a little laugh. 'Who'd have thought he'd go for Rudolph Valentino?'

'So you noticed, too?'

She pointed her index finger straight up and gave me a cagey look. 'I'd appreciate it if you told him what a hard-on is for, when you have a chance.'

'Why me? You know what it's for at least as well as I do,' I shot back, which made her wrestle me onto my back.

'There's one other thing,' I said, looking up at her, pleased to have a wife who liked to take charge now and again.

'What?'

'Ernie told me that he's slept with men. So I guess that makes him gay.' I left out that he'd gone to bed with prostitutes.

'Big news,' she said, pretending to yawn.

After the lights were off, the pressure to tell her even more made me put her hand over my eyes like a blindfold.

'What's wrong now?' she asked.

'There's something I never told you about me.'

'You enjoy your close-ups of my pussy far too much to be gay, so don't try any bullshit on me!'

'No, but I had sex with boys when I was in my teens. In Colorado. And then in Évora.'

She turned around. Her breathing was warm against my face. 'Very enterprising of you to have sex on two continents, Chief Inspector.'

'I never told anyone till I told Ernie a couple of weeks ago. Aunt Olivia never knew.'

'Oh, please,' she said. 'She loved you to the end of the earth. She could never have been disappointed in you.'

'My father would say I was an embarrassment.'

She sat up. 'Oh, Hank, you can't really care what he'd think!'

'I might.'

'Well, don't!' she ordered, and she bit the Thunderbird tattoo on my arm to make her point.

Easing back onto her side of the bed, she turned on her side with her icy feet nudging my good leg, which meant that she wanted me to spoon up behind her, so I did.

'What about when Jorge figures out he's gay – if that's what he is?' I asked.

'What about it?' she whispered.

'Maybe he'll get upset.'

She pulled my arm around her and said, 'If he needs any pointers, he can ask Ernie.'

'He may not be very knowledgeable on the subject.'

'Well, then he can ask his father.'

'I'm serious, Ana.'

'Hank, you have an uncanny ability to worry about everything! Stop! Besides, if Jorge is already getting erections at the age of seven, he's going to be very popular!'

The next afternoon – 2 August, nine days ago – Morel phoned. Cerveira had just called to tell him there was nothing on the DVD that he could use to prosecute any of the men involved.

'How is that possible?' I asked.

'Because Sandi is dead. So she cannot testify against Sottomayor, of course.'

'The DVD testifies against him!' I hollered.

'He says it's not enough. He must be sure she does not agree to what happens to her.'

399

The rage inside my chest was a form of explosive madness.

'Does it look like she's happy about what's happening?' I demanded. 'She was only fourteen years old, for Christ's sake!'

'Cerveira confirms that fourteen is the age of consent in Portugal.'

'That's only true if there's no coercion involved! Did you hear a word I said the other day?'

'Do not yell at me, Monroe! You cannot imagine what I am feeling at this moment.'

'I'm sorry. But listen closely. If a man forces a girl to do something she doesn't want to do, he can be charged with statutory rape. She can be fourteen or fifteen or any other age.'

'Still, he tells me the DVD is not enough to get a conviction.'

'Did he watch the entire film?' I asked. 'Did he see minute seventeen?'

'Yes, he tells me he watches it all.'

'Did you remind him that the blood Sandi got under her fingernails proves she fought her father?'

'He says Sandi is dead and her father is dead and there is no case.'

'If he saw the DVD, he knows that Sottomayor forced himself on her, too. And that son-of-a-bitch is very much alive! We need to show the DVD to another prosecutor. I know others who—'

'Cerveira tells me he speaks to two other prosecutors,' Morel interrupted. 'They all agree we have nothing.'

He excused himself to fetch his cigarettes. When he got back on the line, he said, 'I need to explain something else, Monroe.'

He sounded glum. 'What else has happened?' I asked. 'Is it Susana?'

'Yes and no. Once, you and I speak of the mountains where you live when you are a boy. Do you remember?'

'Vaguely.'

'These last days . . . It is as if I am at the bottom of a high mountain – a mountain where I once live. I look up and I see the top, and I know I can never climb back up. I am too old and tired. I cannot fight any longer. When you are my age, you realize that life is always about fighting – fighting for what you want, fighting to be heard . . . It is a struggle from the first day to the last. But I cannot do this any longer. I am sixty-two. And the top of the mountain is very far . . . very high. And Susana – she is no longer there, in any case. She is down here with me.'

'Which means exactly what?' I asked.

'Susana and I will stay where we are. We know we cannot win. And the worst has already happened, no?'

'But what about Mariana? She may still be suffering somewhere.'

'Cerveira says that maybe she is fourteen, too.'

'No, no, no! She's younger than Sandi – it's obvious!'

'*Mon Dieu*, you are impossible! The point is, we have no proof!'

'You know what Cerveira is *really* telling us, don't you? That nobody in the Prosecutor's Office is going to pursue this case – *no matter what!*'

'Yes, Monroe, I understand,' he said wearily. 'I think I understand it before you, in fact. I grow up in a country where this also happens. *Egalité, fraternité* . . . It looks very good on old coins, but I do business in France for forty years and I know that how things work in the real world is different.'

'How do things work?'

'Either Cerveira already knows he will not win, because the odds are too big against him, or he is on the side of those we wish to fight. It makes no difference which.'

'It does – morally.'

'Morally?' he repeated, as if it were an absurd notion. And he had himself a brief laugh, though I also sensed he was near tears. 'What do you think morals have to do with this?' he demanded.

'Everything.'

'No, they have nothing to do with it, Monroe! This is a negotiation – a business deal. And the outcome is already decided.'

I wanted to shriek something at him that would shame him for giving up. More even than that, I wanted to shout that I would kill Sottomayor or frame him for Coutinho's murder. But the silence I let go on too long made me understand that I'd never permit myself to take such a risk – not as a husband and father. The only option left to me was to locate Mariana, but that could take years. And even if I did find her, Sottomayor and his friends would undoubtedly keep her from testifying – with money or threats.

As my last hope, I suggested to Morel that we go to the press with the DVD.

'No!' he hollered. 'Susana does not want the world to see what happens to her daughter! Do not forget your promise to me! And what about Sandi? You think she would like the world to see her with her father?'

We both knew that her suicide was proof that the answer was *no*. 'But if we don't give the DVD to the press, nothing will happen to the men who killed her,' I said.

'It was her father who killed her!' Morel hollered at me.

'We could at least ruin their reputations,' I told him.

In a slow, beseeching voice, Morel replied, 'We can ruin their reputations only by letting everyone see what happens to Sandi. Her face at minute seventeen will end up on the Internet. Millions will see it. And Susana will not survive such a thing. And neither will I. So the question becomes, Monroe, do you want to kill the two of us?'

On hanging up, I walked to my room and eased the door closed behind me because I didn't want to draw attention to my decision to leave behind the kind of world where

Sottomayor and his friends would never pay for their crimes. Shouldn't we refuse to play the game if the rules always favoured the other side? Wasn't it our moral duty to go on strike?

Once I was alone, I removed the bandages from my shoulder and stood naked in front of our wall mirror. Studying my railroad-track scars, which were deeper and uglier than I'd feared, I apologized to my mother, because she'd brought me into the world without a blemish and had nursed me at her breast, and I should've taken better care of everything that she had given me.

After closing the curtains, I sat in the dark, trying to understand how I had reached this impasse. Where would I be now if I'd died? A question that makes no sense at all, but I asked it anyway, over and over, as though calling into the darkness after someone who might soon vanish without a trace.

That evening, Ana made Leonardo da Vinci's recipe for polenta with prunes to improve my mood, but I refused to leave my bed. Nati carried supper to me on a tray. Looking at the apprehension in his eyes, I remembered – with a violent shudder, as though a rocket were taking off through my head – that he'd been frantic over his project on bossa nova music. I asked him to forgive me for not helping him.

'It's okay – ancient history,' he said.

'Not so ancient,' I told him. 'Just a couple of weeks ago.'

'It was before you were shot.' He fought back tears.

So it was that I learned that my son's short life already had a before-time and an after-time, just like mine. Silly of me not to have understood his depth of feeling. When I hugged him, his slender chest trembling against mine made me realize for the first time that there was a great deal of my own past already in him, transmitted in ways that had been under my radar. That realization was enough to make me return – briefly, hoping to feel as little as possible – to my own small version of hell: I told him – in fitful stops and starts – about the first time my father had tested me and Ernie.

I gripped Nati's hand while I spoke, and he didn't resist me. He must have sensed I could not do this alone. Maybe, too, he already understood that touching was a great comfort to me at my worst times. When I was done, he asked, 'Did your father ever test you again?'

'He sure did. And sometimes I didn't find Ernie in time, so Dad would hurt him. He hurt your uncle very badly on a few occasions.'

'So there was no rototiller?'

'We had a rototiller, but that wasn't how Ernie got his half-an-ear.

'You should have run away!' my son exclaimed, as though my brother and I still had a chance to make an escape; the unforgiving border between the past and present had proved impossible for me to accept at his age as well.

I explained that Ernie and I realized while on our way to Crawford that Dad might teach Mom a final lesson if we ran away, and we'd be responsible. He nodded as if he understood exactly what had been at stake for us, but I could see he hadn't a clue what I was really talking about. Which was probably a good thing.

'You and your brother – you aren't . . . aren't like other people,' he said, shrugging with frustration, because he'd been unable to find the words he wanted.

'Maybe kids who grow up the way we did can overcome the borders that keep them separate from each other. Their identities aren't so protected. Under certain circumstances, they might even merge into each other a bit. I think your uncle and I were almost like the same person for a while.'

Nati nodded to acknowledge that he understood my meaning. 'Listen, Dad,' he said, as though he were about to say something I wouldn't like, 'I don't want you going back to work. Not ever.'

Before I could reply, he burst into tears. Ana came running. After we'd calmed the boy down and they returned to the living room, I realized I'd do what my son had asked me. I didn't see I had any other choice, in fact.

At bedtime, on slipping under the covers with me, Ana asked if I was still on strike.

'I think so.'

'So having sex with me is out of the question?'

'I might make an exception just this once. At least, if we can figure out a way I don't have to use my bad shoulder.'

'I'll be creative.'

'I need to say something first.'

'What?'

'Would you be upset if I didn't go back to work?'

'Hank, is this because of Nati?'

From her tone, I guessed she was going to tell me that our son would soon get used to my work again. And everything would get back to normal. But I didn't want things to return to normal. That would be an affront to what I'd seen at 17:43.

'No, it's because of me,' I said. I told her about the men in the tower and said I'd no longer work for them – that I hadn't figured out yet how I was going to fight them, but I would.

'Maybe I'll find out where Sottomayor likes to eat dinner and pay someone in the kitchen to slip cyanide into his food,' I said. 'Maybe his end will come when he's least expecting it.'

Ana gave a little laugh. She thought I was joking.

While embracing her, it seemed possible that I'd gone on strike not so much as a protest against the unfairness of the world but really to keep myself from taking violent revenge on Sottomayor.

I imagine now that a lot of what I said to Ana that day seemed like lunacy or paranoia. Maybe she thought I'd taken too many painkillers over the past weeks. And probably, I had. Still, she listened to me without interrupting, and she kissed me on my eyes and nose and lips when I was done. A few minutes later, she climbed on top and drew me into her, but I turned the tables on her nearly right away and got her under me, needing, I think, to know again what it felt like to be in control, even if it was just for a few minutes.

I had my first therapy session five days ago. My psychologist, Lena Carvalho, has thick, shoulder-length brown hair and ever-curious green eyes that – happily for me – often seem to sense when they are asking too insistently for my thoughts and turn away to give me back my right not to tell her too much about myself. She must be about forty years old.

There is a lot I'll never understand about this woman, was what I thought over the entire first hour of talking to her, because her no-nonsense temperament seemed so different from mine and because she seemed to have such an easy confidence in herself.

Lena and I talked for two straight hours, double the usual length of a session. When she asked me what I most wanted to tell her, I said, *I've got a lot of things I should probably talk about*, and she said *Pick one*, and I got onto the subject of my father having vanished when I was fourteen, and how I was always waiting for him to show up, which was when she came to the same conclusion I had and said, 'Maybe there are some mysteries we'd prefer not to solve.'

I said that I thought she was right, but that I believed I was ready now to know what happened to him.

'Then we'll find out together,' she told me invitingly.

Her smile made me go all tense, as if she were trying to trick me, and I couldn't stop myself from replying in a harsh tone, 'I can't see how, unless you plan on flying to Colorado with me and following a trail that went cold nearly thirty years ago. Or unless you are in touch with Nathan.'

'Nathan?'

I explained who Nathan was and about the possibility that he might have murdered Dad or somehow forced him to go

406

away, though I didn't mention anything about what his connection to Ernie might be. That would have to wait.

'Maybe,' she said. 'But I'm betting there are things you might have overlooked – clues in your memory that you've never looked at for very long. I can help you with that.'

She sounded as though she wanted to persuade me it would be an adventure – like Huck Finn's raft trip down the Mississippi – which made me have a good laugh, because going back to America with me wasn't going to be scenic at all.

About halfway through our session, she brought up Gabriel and asked me if there was anything that I wanted to tell her about him, but her being so direct about him made me want to rush out of the room.

'Maybe you could write to me about him,' she suggested.

'Write to you how?'

'Start writing letters about him to me. I've done that before with patients. Lots of people can write down what they can't say.'

'I'm not sure,' I said, meaning *no*.

'Just think about it. There's no rush. We'll take it one step at a time.'

Very near the end of our session, when Lena asked me if there was anything more that I needed her to know before we separated, I told her about the day Mom died. I admitted that when I was feeling most angry at her and lonely, I hoped that she had been in crushing pain for two or three seconds after her crash and before her death. 'It's the thought I'm most ashamed of,' I said, 'and I don't want to have it any more.'

'Because?'

'Because it makes me feel that I'm a very bad person.'

'Being bad is appropriate at times. At the very least, it's human. Don't you have a right to be human?'

'I suppose, but I don't want to be human in that way.'

'These bad thoughts about your mother . . . What would happen to you if Ana and your kids knew about them?'

407

'They might think a lot less of me.'

'And then what would happen?'

'I might lose them.'

'You think that Ana would leave you and take the kids with her because you occasionally have bad thoughts about a mother who abandoned you?'

'She didn't abandon us!' I said with an anger that shocked me.

'If I understood what you told me, she took her own life when you and your brother were kids. Isn't that right?'

'You don't understand. She had no choice.'

'Maybe so, but she still left you and your brother at a time when you couldn't possibly take care of yourselves. But let's get back to your wife for now. It sounds as if you think she might abandon you, too.'

'She got very angry at me the other day. I was terrified I'd never see her again.'

'But she made up with you. She didn't leave you.'

'True.'

'Might your terror be connected to what your mother did?'

Lena was trying to imply that I'd missed the obvious. And maybe I had. My sense of shame made me squirm.

'What are you thinking?' she asked.

'That I was a big disappointment to my mom,' I replied.

'If you take the guilt all on yourself, your mother is free to be a wonderful person. Are you aware of that?'

After our session, I stepped into the sunshine outside her office building, so grateful for the warmth and light that I closed my eyes and held my arms open as if I were unfolding my wings. I came to myself nearly two hours later on a bench in the Praça de Alegria. In my coat pocket was a pack of Marlboros with two cigarettes missing and a small blue lighter.

G had tossed my crutches into the bushes behind my bench. After I retrieved them, I made my way down to the

Avenida da Liberdade and took the Metro to the Baixa, where I caught the number twenty-eight tram back home.

The next day, just after lunch, Gabriel brought me to the same scruffy little park. I watched an old woman crocheting a yellow baby outfit, and a bearded man in a blue tracksuit jogging up the hill, and a young woman walking her bouncy, overweight collie, and scores of others rushing around. They seemed as though they were participating in a grand exhibition passing before my eyes. I sat very still so I could appreciate the freedom of not having to be in their show.

Later, while riding up through the Alfama on the tram, I realized that I seemed to have landed outside the flow of time, on a very small planet of my own. Being on strike seemed a very good thing.

The next day, however, at just past noon, I came to myself on the Avenida Estados Unidos da América. I made my way past the gigantic, hideous residential blocks to the Roma Metro station. It was only after I boarded my train that I realized I'd been standing in front of the building where Forester and Sottomayor had their apartments.

Forty-five minutes later, while waiting for my usual tram, a young man asked me for a light; as I reached in my pocket for G's lighter, I found Sandi's ring. Surrounding it in my fist, I knew what G was telling me, but I wasn't ready to leave the quiet of my own little planet. I wrote on my hand, *Give me time to think things out.*

The next morning, G wrote back, *If you give me some time, too.*

I thought of calling Luci to have her take the ring as evidence, but it seemed entirely possible now that she'd been chosen by people high up as the perfect person to win my confidence and report back to them about me. Maybe she'd been ordered to steal Coutinho's flash drive and crash Sandi's disk.

I liked Luci a lot, and it was nearly impossible to believe she could have betrayed me, but it seemed clear to me at that moment that I ought not to trust anyone outside my family. And in any case, I couldn't risk turning her thoughts towards this case again. When I was ready to move on to the next stage of my life, I'd invite her and her husband over for dinner and we'd have a long talk.

Two days ago, I found out exactly what Gabriel meant by 'if you give me some time, too'; I disappeared from two in the afternoon until five-thirty and came to myself at home in my kitchen, with a cup of hot tea waiting for me on the counter and two express mail receipts stuffed in my pocket. One package had been sent to Tom Bagnatori at the Minestério Público on the Avenida Marechal Câmara in Rio de Janeiro; the other had gone off to Denis Gershon at the Prosecutor's Office on the Quai des Orfèvres in Paris. Each package had weighed 148 grams.

On checking my cell phone registry, I discovered that G had made three calls to Rio de Janeiro over the past three days, and two to Paris. On calling the Brazilian number, I discovered it was the Prosecutor's Office. The same was true for the French number.

Gabriel obviously hadn't felt as morally obligated to Susana and Morel as I did.

The return address he had used on the express mail receipts were inventions. The name he'd written – Santorini – was Ana's maiden name.

To check my reasoning about what he'd sent off to Brazil and France, I called Joaquim.

'Hey, Henrique, I'm really glad you called,' he said in a relieved voice.

'Why's that?' I asked.

'You didn't seem yourself when you came over.'

'I've been a bit disoriented of late,' I told him. 'But listen, I called because I think I forgot to ask you what I owe you for the copies of the DVD you made for me.'

410

'You must be joking, Henrique. If you get any of those bastards, I'll pay *you!*'

Bagnatori called yesterday evening at just after seven o'clock, Lisbon time. He asked for Gabriel Santorini and told me that he'd just watched the DVD I'd sent him. *'Uma gente inacreditavelmente ruim,'* he said in his singsong Brazlian accent. *Unbelievably bad people.*

'Yes, I'd very much like to see them prosecuted.'

'Who wouldn't!' Bagnatori went on to say that he'd been accumulating evidence on Forester for years.

'So why haven't you arrested him yet?' I asked.

'He's well connected and smart. And the girls won't testify against him. You have to understand a lot of them are so poor they've never been in a hotel before. He takes them to the shops in Ipanema to pick out dresses from New York and the Palace Hotel in Copacabana to drink French champagne. They've never seen a crystal chandelier before. Or waiters in dinner jackets. They're from the favelas. And they discover that it's nice to sleep in a bed with satin sheets. It makes no difference that a sixty-year-old slob pants on top of them for a few minutes. They figure that's his right for buying them so many presents.'

'Is there anything you can do about the other men in the movie?'

'When we spoke, you told me one lived in Portugal and the other in France.'

'Sottomayor – the guy with the cane – lives here in Lisbon. The fat guy – Gilles Laplage – lives in Paris.'

'Unless they come to Rio, there's nothing I can do. I told you that already.'

'If they are friends with Forester, maybe you could somehow lure one or both of them to Brazil. Maybe you could arrest foreigners more easily than Brazilians.'

He laughed in a burst. 'You ever been to Rio de Janeiro, Monroe?'

'No.'

'Sex tourism is the main industry here. Tens of thousands of American and European men fly to Rio every month, eager to drink caipirinhas and fuck Brazilian pussy until their dicks fall off.'

I replied with silence.

'Look, I know you're disappointed,' he said, 'but that's the way it is. You wouldn't want me lying to you. It's economics. If we started arresting men like Sottomayor for getting some young tail while on vacation, then our fancy hotels would all go broke and my boss would have my ass!'

Denis Gershon hasn't phoned yet. I don't expect him to. I no longer have any hope of convincing anyone in a position of authority to take over this fight for me.

When we fail at something, we are reminded what is possible and what is not, and I think that maybe I've known all along that this wasn't going to end in any sort of satisfying way. I thought that I couldn't hear the messages the world was trying to tell me of late, but it's possible that I'd already heard them and simply couldn't accept what they had to say.

And yet it's also true that the idea of embarking on a slow and solitary campaign for justice – entirely in secret – appeals to me. After all, in a year or two, or maybe only in a few months, Sottomayor is sure to miss the sly pleasure of telling a thirteen-year-old girl to get on her knees for him. Given his personality, I think it's very unlikely that he's going to give up such extracurricular enjoyments just because one of his partners in crime met a violent end. Or because he had a bit of trouble with a Colorado-born cop who can't even speak Portuguese correctly.

I'll have to study his routines closely, of course. And learn all I can about him. The tricky part will be coming up with a plan for trapping him that won't put me or anyone I love at risk. Of course, it's possible that I'll end up having to admit that it just can't be done – that he's simply too high up in the tower for me to reach. But my childhood has made me resourceful and patient. And quietly devious, as well. I think it would be silly to bet against anyone who has survived what I've survived. Gabriel and me both.

Private detective work? It's probably what I've been preparing to do nearly all my life.

Chapter 34

Today is Saturday 11 August 2012. I woke at dawn this morning and watched the pink and gold sunrise while sitting at my bedroom window. I considered floating up and away towards all that colour, but I preferred to stay with Ana and my kids.

When I stood up to go downstairs, my wife turned over and told me in a half-asleep voice that she almost forgot that she owed me fifty euros in cash since my police benefits hadn't yet been cancelled. I told her I'd take her and the kids out to lunch at Nood with my windfall, and she puckered out her lips so that I'd give her a kiss, and after I did, she rolled on her belly and went back to sleep.

I'd decided the night before to return Sandi's ring to her mother, but after eating my oatmeal and blueberries I discovered that it wasn't in the spice cabinet where I'd left it, which meant that Gabriel wasn't ready yet to part with it. Hunting for it gave me other ideas, and while my second cup of tea was steeping, I took out the box of my mother's treasures from its hiding place and ripped open the yellowing tape I'd sealed it with twenty-eight years earlier. Mom's copy of Pablo Neruda's *Twenty Love Poems* was at the bottom, under the charcoal drawings she'd done of me when I was little and the old amethyst brooch she wore every Sunday to church, and my half of the deck of her cards with Lisbon monuments on the back that I'd divided with Ernie. I didn't know that her book was what I was after, but when

I saw the cover – a white kite flying against a pale blue sky – my heartbeat began to race.

When I opened the book to the title page, a flower fell out – a golden columbine.

I put the papery, faded-yellow flower back where it had been and paged forward. The book smelled sour, like dust and vinegar. On opening the first page, I discovered it had been published in 1942 by Collección Cometa. How did I remember after all these years that the quote I wanted was in the fourteenth poem?

> *I want to do with you*
> *what spring does with the cherry trees.*

You could tell a lot about Mom just by seeing how perfectly straight she'd underlined those beautiful words.

The tip of her pencil had been right here, I thought, pressing hard below the first line, so that a fraction of her graphite would come off on my fingertip and become part of me. *She'd looked at this page, right where I'm looking now.*

Over breakfast, I called Ernie because I'd finally figured out that our mother had understood what she most wanted for us after reading Pablo Neruda. While I was having trouble putting the closeness to Mom I felt into words, I realized that what she wanted so badly had, in fact, come to pass, which meant that I didn't need to explain much of anything. 'We've had really good adventures, haven't we?' I said instead.

'Yeah, it's been amazing!' he replied in his little brother voice.

'And we're not finished yet.'

'No, lots of good things are sure to happen over the coming years.'

His enthusiasm prompted me to tell him about my therapy. When I was finished, he told me that I'd done really well. He also said he'd help pay for my sessions.

'My benefits cover them,' I told him.

'Then I'll start paying you and Ana back for what you've given me over the years.'

'Ernie, did you rob a bank or something?'

'No, I sold two paintings.'

'I don't understand.'

'Two of my flower paintings . . . I sold them. About two weeks ago.'

'Why didn't you say anything?'

'You'd just gotten home from the hospital and it didn't seem the right time, and then we got to talking about other things – and anyway, I'm telling you now.'

Across the sixty miles between us, I could see the smile of a man racing so far ahead of our expectations for him that he could no longer even spot them behind him any more. 'Who bought them?' I asked.

'The owner of a restaurant in England – it's called the Jardine Bistro. It's in a town called Wivenhoe. His name is Chris. He's originally Swiss but he's lived in England a long time.'

'How did he find out about your work?'

'One of his friends found it on my Facebook page. She's interested in flowers. Her name is Jo. She told him about me. I'm in touch with them both.'

'You have a Facebook page?'

'Yeah, I made one a few months ago.'

'And this Swiss guy bought two of your paintings?'

'That's right.'

'Without seeing them in person?'

'I have high-definition images of them on my Facebook page. I also took close-ups of the most important details and mailed them to him.'

'Ernie, how much did he pay you?' I asked in a suspicious voice; I was expecting that the restaurateur had taken advantage of him.

'A thousand euros.'

'For the two?'

'No, each.'

416

That was far more than I'd expected, but something didn't add up. 'You asked for a thousand euros each?' I questioned.

'It's way too high a price, I know, but—'

'It's not too high!' I exclaimed. 'I'm just amazed you asked for a decent price.'

'I asked so much so he wouldn't buy them.'

'I don't get it.'

'The ones he wanted I really liked, and I wasn't sure I wanted to sell them, so I asked for a ridiculous price and he agreed. My plan backfired!' He laughed merrily. It sounded as if he'd climbed up to a sunlit hillside inside himself.

Ernie told me he'd sold a large landscape of Black Canyon and a portrait of Rosie sleeping on her rug.

'Have you got the money yet?' I was still looking for the burnt underside of this miracle.

'Yeah, Chris did a bank transfer the other day. And he's planning a show of my work at his restaurant. He has art on the walls. He changes the shows every three or four months. Mine will go up in late November. He says people still spend money at Christmas in England – the economic crisis isn't as deep there as it is here.'

I didn't want to cry in front of him, but I also didn't want to hang up. So I chose the middle route and said nothing.

'You there?'

'More or less,' I whispered.

'Yeah, it kind of stunned me, too,' he said. 'Anyway, I figure I can pay you half of what I've received so far and still have enough money to keep me and the garden going for a while.'

I still can't get over Ernie's success. I want to meet Chris and Jo – to meet two people who understand how talented my brother is. He agreed that we would go to Wivenhoe for the opening. He said he'll drink a lot of valerian tea before the flight to steady his nerves. I'll keep some Valium ready in case that doesn't work.

417

I've looked up the Jardine Bistro on the Internet. It looks like a big brick house. According to Wikipedia, Wivenhoe has about ten thousand people and is on the banks of the River Colne. At the website for British National Rail, I discovered that you can get there from London's Liverpool Street Station. The journey only takes an hour and five minutes. The flights from Lisbon to London take just two hours.

I figure we'll stay in London for a couple of nights, then catch the train to Wivenhoe. And from there, riding high on Ernie's success, we'll head up to Scotland, since he and I have always wanted to see Loch Ness. Maybe Ana can find some transsexuals to interview in Glasgow or Edinburgh.

Strange that it never occurred to me that I could reach an English-speaking country so easily. Thinking about being there makes me giddy – as if I'll be going beyond everything I could ever have hoped for me and Ernie, the moment we pass through passport control. Maybe seeing his paintings hanging up in an exhibition will mean that I can stop comparing him and me to the men we might have been. I really hope so, but I think I'll only find out when it happens.

Over the last three nights, after Ana is asleep, I've sat at her desk in the living room and written to Lena about Gabriel, starting with when I was eight and he scribbled a first message on my hand, though what I told her was a lot more than just how and why he comes to me. Trying to convey feelings I don't entirely understand made me stutter a lot inside my head and do a lot of rewriting. And made me see that it would be impossible to tell her about G without also explaining a lot about my parents and Ernie. And about why I had to finally stop lying.

Just this morning, I discovered that I like making the kids' beds and cleaning up their rooms. To see their blankets smoothed down neatly and ready for them to climb into . . .

418

What more could I want to accomplish? Ana understood. While watching me cleaning Nati's windows, she told me things she'd never told me before: about bicycling to the port of Buenos Aires when she was a girl so she could watch the big ships being offloaded; and the red velvet curtains in the fancy hotel where her uncle Javier got a summer job playing piano, just a few months before he disappeared; and how her father used to show her the constellations in the night sky. I think she told me all these things because she knew I'd listen closely to what she was saying and go right on cleaning.

And this is what I realized: the sound of her voice – ambling through memories of her childhood – was the same sound as my own longing for a love that would never end.

Ernie told me he's coming over tomorrow. He's going to bring our baseball mitts, too. We're going to have our first catch in thirty years, in Santa Marinha Square, and he isn't going to take it easy on me; he's going to throw real hard and make me run all over the place, because he said I need to strengthen my bad shoulder and leg. He told me that if he was satisfied with my effort, and didn't start what he called my 'usual whining!', he was going to take me to the Gulbenkian cafeteria after lunch for a double helping of avocado mousse.

After that, Ernie is going to drive us over to Coutinho's neighbourhood. I want to snoop around the abandoned house with the shattered skylight that's just behind his home. I've already got the stepladder, crowbar and flash-lights in my car. I doubt I'll find any evidence worth collecting, but that house and my shooting are connected, and I need to see it for myself.

Almost dying of gunshot wounds changes lots of things, of course. If you have a little brother who is thirty-eight years old but who still isn't entirely convinced that he has a right to be alive, then you do pretty much anything he asks of you, and you call him every night before bed, and you order seeds for his garden from nurseries in France and Italy, and occasionally you remind him that you used to picture what he'd look like when your mother's belly first started growing with him, and once, when you are feeling particularly tender, you even say that months before he came into the world you knew exactly what the colour of his eyes would be, and the texture of his hair, and the way he'd tug on his ear when he was reading, and how his neck would smell when he was sleepy and lots of other things, which was how you came to understand – without being able to put it into words – that wanting something enough could make it come true.

If you have a teenaged son, then you probably ask if you can comb his hair after his shower or help him put on his favourite T-shirt for the simple pleasure of touching what time is stealing from you, and you know you are irritating him with every glance that goes on too long, and by insisting that you lead while teaching him to jitterbug, but you also realize that his annoyance is the price you must pay for never forgetting that his life and yours are not nearly as separate as you've been led to believe.

If you have a seven-year-old son, then you are in luck, because on those nights when you cannot sleep, and they are many, you can slip softly into his bed, and he will fold himself around you like a loose-limbed rubbery creature made of trust and slumber, and he will breathe warm against your cheek, and maybe just once, the in-and-out movement of his back against your chest will erase every border between you, and you will realize that it's this unbearable love you feel for him that might, one day, finally make you stop fearing your own death. You also buy him a bicycle, of course, and in silver – 'Just like yours, Dad!' – and teach him how to ride, and take him out for adventures in the countryside by Ernie's house, and even though there's little danger of him

420

having an accident there, you make him wear his helmet, because there are things worth risking and things not worth risking, and it's important that he learn the difference.

And if you have a wife who has agreed to overlook your bad moods and rudeness, at least most of the time, then you hold her in bed tighter than you ever have, and you promise to keep going to therapy sessions every week and, during a quiet moment, maybe you even admit that you aren't nearly done hunting for justice even if you have told everyone you are, but that your search will have to take another form if you are to remain the person you want to be, and you even risk sounding like an idiot and tell her that we are always floating across the cities and countryside inside ourselves, riding on the most subtle inner winds over rooftops and staircases and parks and canyons, in Portugal and America and Argentina and everywhere else, even when we're certain we haven't the strength to get out of a hospital bed.

If you think enough about having nearly died, as I do, then you have also probably figured out that you don't understand very much about the way life works – about its additions and subtractions, about those who vanish and those who don't – but that's okay, at least for the moment, because whatever else happens, you will crawl into bed every night next to a person who enjoys putting her cold feet against your legs, and who lets you kiss her anywhere you want, and just maybe she'll give you permission one of these days to start another life inside her, and perhaps this time, if all goes according to plan (as it almost never does, of course), the baby will be a girl.

And if you are anything like me, then you sometimes pause while making love to your wife or husband, and listen to the swallows swooping outside your window, chattering endlessly about the most fragrant summer winds they have known and the biggest mosquitoes they've ever swallowed and all the difficulties of living in Portugal, and just about any other subject – no matter how silly-sounding

– that you are willing to propose to them. And maybe, if you are in a philosophical mood, you realize that even if you had died a few weeks before, bled to death on a Lisbon street corner, those crazy-hearted birds would still be diving across Santa Marinha Square – or whatever the name of the street outside your window happens to be – and speaking to one another about the same surprises and joys and disappointments and miseries that they do all over the world.

[The End]